THE G

J.M.G. Le Clézio was born in Nice, France, on 13 April 1940. His mother was French and his father was a Mauritian doctor of French origin and Le Clézio has dual French and Mauritian nationality. When he was eight years old his family moved to Nigeria where his father worked for the British Army. Le Clézio studied at the University College in Nice, at Bristol and London universities, and worked as a teacher at Bath Grammar School in the 1960s before travelling the world: in particular spending time in the United States, Mexico and Asia. He is a citizen of the world whose homeland is the French language. He now spends his time between France (Nice, Paris and Brittany), Mauritius and Albuquerque, New Mexico. He has published more than 40 books since he won the Renaudot Prize in 1963, aged 23, with his first novel, *Le Procès-verbal* (*The Interrogation*), and his works have been translated into 36 languages.

J.M.G. LE CLÉZIO

The Giants

TRANSLATED FROM THE FRENCH BY
Simon Watson Taylor

VINTAGE BOOKS
London

Published by Vintage 2008

1 3 5 7 9 10 8 6 4 2

Copyright © Editions Gallimard, Paris, 1973
English translation copyright © Jonathan Cape, 1975

J.M.G. Le Clézio has asserted his right under the Copyright, Designs
and Patents Act, 1988 to be identified as the author of this work

First published in France under the title *Les Géants* in 1973 by
Editions Gallimard

First published in Great Britain in 1975 by Jonathan Cape

First published in English in the United States in 1975 by Atheneum

Vintage
Random House, 20 Vauxhall Bridge Road,
London SW1V 2SA

www.vintage-classics.info

Addresses for companies within The Random House Group Limited
can be found at: www.randomhouse.co.uk/offices.htm

The Random House Group Limited Reg. No. 954009

A CIP catalogue record for this book
is available from the British Library

ISBN 9780099530480

The Random House Group Limited supports The Forest
Stewardship Council (FSC), the leading international forest
certification organisation. All our titles that are printed on
Greenpeace approved FSC certified paper carry the FSC logo.
Our paper procurement policy can be found at:
www.rbooks.co.uk/environment

Mixed Sources
Product group from well-managed
forests and other controlled sources
www.fsc.org Cert no. TT-COC-2139
© 1996 Forest Stewardship Council

Printed in the UK by CPI Bookmarque, Croydon, CR0 4TD

For Ch'in Shih Huang Ti,
the First Emperor,
with great respect and admiration.

The ultimate achievement of bio-control might well be the human being's direction of his own self. The directed subjects would never be permitted to think as individuals. A surgeon would fit a socket into the scalp of each infant, a few months after its birth, with electrodes from the socket reaching into selected zones of the brain tissue. Thus, sensory perceptions and muscular activity could become subject to modification.

Enka Glanzstoff Group

range

ENKA GLANZSTOFF GROUP
DEMIGOD

The Guernsey experiment (1928) concerning the levels of acoustic pleasure.

Barco, the col

Stark naked, the truth-colour

The banker is a *father*

modification of Eisenhower's image

Switzerland:

Huber-Bohner & Co.,
Verkaufs-Büro der Wilh Bleyle
KG, Stuttgart,
CH 80004 Zürich,
Badenerstrasse 156,
Tel. (051) 231811/232475

Balsan's Electra,

Fashion
Psychological ageing

Javel, eye of the belly,
most touching of all human symbols,
have you ever even looked at it,
Huber-Bohner
COMPANY?

Sankyo

cinema at last triumphs over chance

CRAZED AUTHORITARIANS

'Minds can be conditioned to desire your products! In the schools of America there are nearly twenty-three million boys and girls. These children eat foodstuffs, wear out clothes, use soap. Today, consumers; tomorrow they will be buyers. Many far-sighted producers with an eye on the future are spending money on the moulding of these young minds.'

or entirely directed by the signals emanating from broadcasting stations belonging to the State.

Hyperpolis must be burnt down

self-cleaning maxi-oven

flash-burners with pilot-light

J. Walter Thompson

Miramar City, Florida

Stay new.

programmer

working side-surface

thermostatic hot-plate

The seduction of children

Buick: 'It gives you the feeling of being the man you are.'

David Riesman: Abundance for What?
David Riesman: The Lonely Crowd
Jacques Ellul: Propagandes
Maurice Mégret: La guerre Psychologique
Tchakhotine: Le viol des foules par la propagande politique
Paul Pigors: Leadership or Domination
Chevaleva: Essai sur les enfants meneurs
J. Bonnaire: Selection des agents de maîtrise
H. Wüst: Der psychologischer Krieg

YOU WHO DESIRE TO MOULD THE WORLD

Heterogeneous crowds
Homogeneous crowds

'The crowd, then, is extremely sensitive, is impressionable in the highest degree, and is incapable of reflexion or of logical reasoning.'

Report by the Weiss & Geller agency:
'The home refrigerator becomes an island of frozen security.'

Clyde Miller: The Process of Persuasion
Louis Angé: La technique moderne de la vente
C. R. Haas: La publicité; théorie, technique et pratique
Vance Packard: The Hidden Persuaders
H. Bergson: Matière et mémoire
H. F. Brandt: The Psychology of Seeing
Hachet-Souplet: La genèse des instincts
A. Bain: The Emotions and the Will

Rhône-Poulenc

I SHALL INVENT NO MORE ABBREVIATIONS
RATHER I SHALL ATTEMPT
TO BREAK THE ANCIENT SEALS

banks of the

CIC
group

W. Lloyd Warner's
Social Class in America

Marlboro Country

Ernest Ditcher, Institute of Motivational Research
Louis Cheskin, Institute of Colour Research

TO
YOUR
DESIGN

SILVER
PLATINUM

I would have
preferred to live
on the edge
of a razor blade

Hyperpolis must be burnt down

I tell you: free yourselves! It is time, it is high time. If you wait any longer it will be too late. Suddenly things have come clearly into focus. The world's design has begun to show its lines, its loops and its knots. The great cancer has escaped from the hangars where it was imprisoned and has begun to seep into the public squares and the wastelands. Now it is rising up in the air, exactly like a fifteen-storey building balanced on concrete columns. If you wait any longer you will never see the sky again. You will no longer be able to see the ocean, or the wind, or the plains. The great shadow is at this very moment sweeping across the earth with the speed of a jet plane. The shadow is hovering above the earth, filling space with its two wings outstretched, like a vulture. No point in running away from beneath it, heart thumping. The shadow will always catch up with you, it is faster than your heartbeats. Delay no longer. Each second that ticks by forms a new knot, and each day a new wall has arisen somewhere, another window has been blocked up. I never realized, before. I used to think that things happened by chance, with vague to-and-fro movements. I thought we were all free, because I could see all the roads and all the doorways, and I was able to choose the one I wanted. And then I thought that there was a direction, that one moved forward, as in the jungle, and that each blade of grass and each leaf-tip was fulfilling itself, had something to say. But that is precisely why men tore up the grass and stripped the leaves around them, because they did not want natural movements. They wanted human movements, forests of human beings, millions of leaves and blades of grass with eyes, noses and mouths, otherwise known as society.

So it arrived like a dream, on its own; suddenly one wakes up with the realization that the dream was true and that its terrifying tale really had a meaning. Wake up! Open your eyelids for just a moment and maybe you will see daylight. One wakes up suddenly, with the realization that one was *inside*, the whole time inside, never for one moment outside. One wanted to understand and made great efforts to understand, but it was impossible because one was being dreamt. That's it: one was in the film, you understand, inside the film, being projected onto the screen in the shaft of light, and so it was really quite impossible to be free. One was in the book, too, printed on the page in black characters, inside the words. One was inside everything, but without knowing it. One believed in a whole lot of little things, because they were specially designed for that purpose, to whisper inside your ear in a little lisping voice: Iii'm fffree, fffrrrree. I too heard the same little voice, and it was that that made me want to survive. Had I not heard the little voice I would not have been able to do all that I did do: wait for the bus, put on a record of *koto* music, smoke a menthol cigarette, wait in the grocery for the grocer to turn to me and say: Yes, what can I get you? Wait for one woman or another, for money, for the revolution, for hope, or the newspaper, or else the sleep that is a little like a spider's web. Wait. The whole time, wait. But I was free, was I not: fReE! Because I believed in these little things invented as games, playthings such as conscience, choice, death, absurdity, humour.

But as for the big things, as for the real things, they had been well and truly hidden. They were on the far side of sleep, inaccessible, on the far side of the asylum walls. How to know them? Slowly, one wakes up, one passes through the curtains of shadow. One gropes one's way across the room, stumbling over pieces of furniture. Things crash to the floor. There are great rending sounds, as loud as thunder, but one had no time to find out what it was all about. The air arrives, at last, in little puffs, and the nostrils gorge themselves. One learns to walk, oh yes, one learns to walk.

Free yourselves! Cross through sleep's black veil, and you will see the far side of things. Spit upon words, since they were not free. Take an iron bar and smash all mirrors, since self-awareness turned out to be nothing at all, just one more false appearance, one more layer of make-up.

Maybe we shall go far together, now. I mean, maybe it will be possible now to cast loose from one's self, like an inflated balloon, and rise upwards. To become free one must do all that, one must speak, not only with one's mouth, but with hands and feet and belly. Those who speak with words alone are not free. Those who only read words in books remain prisoners.

Speak: but from the far side of language, too, from the side of those who create it. Each word needs to be turned inside out like a glove, and emptied of its substance. Each speech should wrench itself from the ground like an aeroplane and smash through the surrounding walls. Up till now you have been slaves. You have been given words to obey, words to enslave, words to write slavish poems and slavish philosophies. It is time to arm words. Arm them and hurl them against the walls. Perhaps they will even reach the other side.

Quick, quick: the walls are multiplying, raising their high cliffs skywards. Walls that are reproducing faster than rats. Each second, there is a new wall. Walls, window-panes, armoured doors, barbed wire, locks and bars. These walls are not sprouting just at random. One used to believe that. One used to think, myself included, that walls here and there had no significance. I say yes and it's a wall, I say no and it's a different wall. But the truth is that the shadows concealed men who were building these walls. They were drawing the blueprints for prisons, they had foreseen everything. Men. Know them! Men in shadow, eyes shining behind the lenses of their horn-rimmed spectacles because they knew something that you did not know. They had decided once and for all that the world was accursed. These men were terrible and secret, because they had travelled to the very end of the curse; they knew the way to the end of the corridors. From the top of their watchtowers they saw you crawling on the ground, they knew in advance everything that you were going to do. They had marked out the barbed-wire corridors along the ground, and they watched you creeping like caterpillars along their routes. It was odd and frightening, because it was not they who had invented movement, or the world, or thought, but they knew all the concatenations of these things.

Man had become a subject of study for man, the sole subject of study. Seize freedom! Refuse to be studied any longer. No one has the right to know man, because to get to know things one must be above them. Wake up! Gradually day reveals its outlines and now one can see the traps. Chasms at each step, to swallow you up, chasms that the hands of criminals have dug beneath your feet.

Intoxication of speech, then, the only free force. Speak, quickly, no matter how, no matter what! The flood of words rises in the throat, thrusting aside the mucous membranes, straining at the lips. It is like a violent wind whipping the branches of a tree. Behind the wind comes the storm; drops of urgent rain can already be heard. But the mouth opens and nothing comes out. There are women standing in the light, their mouths wide open, and yet one hears nothing! How is it possible? Perhaps the air is transfixed, thick like water, as cold as glass, each emerging sound is immediately encased in a bubble, then vanishes. Speak! Speak! Burst the bubbles! Say anything, in any manner. If you have no words to utter, then don't utter words, utter cries, coughs, songs, any kind of exclamation. Say:

Zip!
Flak!
Waapi!

But the air remains opaque. Because there are hands armed

14

with thin needles that have pierced all the eardrums. The ears are open and no longer have the power of hearing! Even the fishes and the snakes hear nothing any longer. Who is responsible for destroying the ears? There are beautiful towering women standing in the light, with their ears open wide like the gills of suffocating fish, yet they never hear a thing.

Is it possible that the world should be so silent? Not a single creak, not a syllable, nothing. I tell you: I see many women and many men, all the time, in the light of day, and they are deaf mutes. I can still hear a few murmurs, but this is no great source of pride since they are only murmurs when great thunderclaps are called for. Mouths gape wide open and screech into microphones, and all I can hear is a sort of gentle hissing, like water leaking. Whole peoples are swept by fire, whole peoples die screaming, yet it makes no more noise than the slight screeching of a comb drawn through hair. Scarcely as much noise as a match bursting into flame. The giant bomb explodes on the horizon, hollowing its crater into the earth and rearing its fifty-mile-high cloud into the sky, a cloud of death. And all I hear is the noise of a fart. No, I am not very proud.

Ears and nostrils have been plugged with cotton wool, eyes have been hidden behind the smoked lenses of sunglasses. Free yourselves. Rip off the old mask of night that dulled your senses. Painted images have been pasted over the retinas, lying images. A television screen has been placed in front of each eye and you have been told: there you have truth and reality, there you have life. It was simple. Walls. With geometrical designs painted on the walls: the designs of life. Each imagined detail glowed, a black outline against a white background. Orders have been inscribed at random over the surface: WOMAN, CHILD, WORK, WAR, DEATH, PLEASURE. All the necessary proofs have been furnished. Photographs, diagrams, graphs, columns of figures. Leaving no room for doubt. How to get out of the labyrinth, with just one's eyes and hands and one's mouth stuffed with words? How to get out of oneself? It was a vision of the evidence.

The world was not silent. It seemed so only because people were all talking about themselves and for themselves. They could neither hear anything, nor hear each other out, at the bottom of the well that they had dug. At the moment of entering life everyone had wound up the windows of his car, so as to hear nothing and see nothing.

Break the panes! The light comes to a halt and trembles against these chilly plates of glass, hatred and desire bounce off them. Eyes are halted, too, for their looks cannot pass through. One is protected, but it is a terrible protection, for it prevents one from speaking. I have things to say to the trees, perhaps, and to the stones, and the sea, the birds, the deserts. I would like to speak to them from far away, and in a low voice, as though over the telephone, without eyes or words, without seeking to defeat or to persuade, just simply and peacefully. But I am brought to a halt before the pane of glass, and I clench my fist. I can see, on the other side, what is supposedly inaccessible, a mere spectacle. Air, water, grass, sea, light. I see paradises looming up, great wealth only a few inches away. Hatred of glass! Hatred of glass walls. My clenched fist is a steel hammer, my knuckles are pebbles. My clenched fist will never again be able to open out. The bones in my hand are knit together, now, and my nails are encrusted in the flesh like iron spikes. Free yourselves. Clench your fists. If you cannot clench your fists, if you fear that your hands may open up, later, just plunge them into a bucket full of ice, and wait. There is no life left in my closed fingers, no softness left in my fingertips. Cast iron has flowed into the bones of my wrists. Such a fragile rampart. They thought that this glass porthole would suffice to withstand the strength that fills me, they thought that they could contain the world behind their aquarium windows. Dog-snouted moray eels prowl behind the glass walls; no one can hear them when they speak. Pythons dart their heads in vain against the plate-glass. But I, with my fist of concrete, am capable of smashing through. Flies may die of hunger and exhaustion as they walk along the ceiling, but I am not a fly. I have a clenched fist deep inside my being, and I am about to deal a blow with it. Watch out! The moment has come. With a single blow from pent-up thought, but quicker than thought, the arm ending in a clenched fist streaks towards the pane of glass. There was no impact. The pane has exploded into fragments immediately: it was not solid, its resistance had already been sapped by so much desire and hatred. The pane has burst apart as though it had been mined, the pane has burst apart with the sharp crack of breaking glass. Along the jagged edges, a smear of blood. The light remains cold. Air enters, but gently rather than in great gusts, just filtering in. The noise ... What noise? There is nothing to be heard. There is no noise. Very faintly, the rasping of a sea that is the sea of vehicles flowing ceaselessly by, over there in the streets' channels, with their hooters cawing occasionally like crows. No noise. Almost complete silence. Always the same vague hubbub made up of murmurs, whispers, acoustic habits. No pain. No cries nor calls. Where are the voices? Where are the odours? The luminous designs, the flashes of lightning, the motions of liberty and love, the language of trees, paradise itself — where are they all? Treachery, vile treachery! Behind the pane of glass *there was another pane.*

However much one may want to break the panes, like that, with one's fists, the truth is that one will never succeed. There are too many panes. Not just one, or two, or ten, but thousands upon thousands. There are sheets of plate-glass as big as mountains, as big as the ocean, as big as the sky itself, and there are others that are tiny, so tiny that to pierce them one would need a pin and a magnifying glass. There are flat panes, and round ones, and others that are helical or star-shaped. There are panes that are waterdrops, panes that are tears, panes that are lakes or oceans. There are panes of glass that cover whole towns beneath their dome, others that stretch their invisible walls across the air. There are panes inside men's eyes, and in the depths of women's amber-coloured irises. More terrible still, there are panes deep inside your very selves, great cliffs

17

that only seem transparent and that create impassable dividing-walls within yourselves. Eventually, of course, you came to realize all this. But today these barriers have got to be smashed. All is hammer against the glass, all is clenched fist. A thousand fractures a second, and maybe you will be saved.

But: if one breaks these panes of glass, if I break my own panes, if I arm my hands, my eyes, my mouth, if I arm my words and my thoughts, and hurl them, like a flight of arrows, like a shower of stones, a vengeful hail of bullets: if I do that: perhaps, after all, it will only be myself that shatters into fragments, because my own base was on these very frontiers?

Free yourselves, yes, free yourselves. But from what? Where are the walls? I know: I can see them, they are there, no doubt about it. But which of them to destroy first of all? And what lies beyond these walls, unknown to me, what free landscape, what country of thought? There are so many forces. So many extraordinary powers, so much beauty, so many ideas ... All those factors that result in silence and dumbness instead of noise and speech. Sounds advance in serried ranks, like an army, covering the world according to some unknown plan. It is because of these ceaseless cries that silence reigns. It is because there are cries that there can be no words, I mean real words. Cries that have been crammed forcibly down the throat, with blows of a mallet perhaps, wedges blocking the passage of free air. Suffocation. A hand plunges into the gullet, followed by an arm and then a shoulder. The alien hand is there the whole time. So that although one would like to speak, it is impossible: one would have to vomit first. One longs to utter real words, once and for all, eagle-words that would soar at ten thousand feet in the clear sky, words that would slay and scorch. And the only sounds that emerge are ghastly croaks, snarls, hisses, hoarse rattles that tear the throat painfully. Incapability, stupid incapability. But perhaps ... Well, today, perhaps ... It's just an idea, but ... Perhaps this incapability was not internal, perhaps it was not the mark of a particular presiding spirit; an individual symptom, more this or less that than the others, an ego, a name, a word preceded by a little arrow, you understand, something special that meant, *I am I*, I am he who is. No, the hand in the throat was truly alien. The incapability was external, the result of an aggression. Outside, a war was raging. That is why I say to you, free yourselves! rather than, kill yourselves!

How did all that come about? A man, no matter what man-woman, arriving on the planet Earth a long long time ago, after having travelled the length of all possibilities for an eternity of time, suddenly landing on the flat ground, ejected from the spaceship in a cloud of blood, dazed, bewildered, lungs still folded and eyes still blind; come, not by chance, but through a sequence of events so real that he was incapable of conceiving himself by thought alone and needed his whole body, his whole life, all his actions, all the water, the earth and the air, to succeed in imagining it; such a man, ejected by a movement of the abdomen onto the world's cold slab — and that is when his worries were about to begin. Having appeared with such precision, prefabricated and regulated, his mechanism perfectly adaptable to any situation, including his eventual death, could such a man live haphazardly? Could his thoughts or words ever for one moment be gratuitous or free? This is what happened. One day, round noon, he looks round him, in the big city where he lives; he stops moving, and looks round him. He stops flapping the twin cushions of his speaking lips, he stops blinking his eyes at the sight of set pieces, women, cars, trains, films, pages of essay-poem-novels, and looks round him.

In a single stroke the world stops moving. The sky turns white, shadows hollow out black crevasses. The outlines of the tall buildings strain upwards, oxidized; the lights are motionless in the centre of haloes of black light. Motionless movements. Weals across the great sheet of gelatine. The light makes a mark. The handwritings are wrinkles on the skin-like substance, wrinkles and hairs, and warts as well. He looks. But his eyes are cold and rigid in the folds of his lids, and his stare is exactly like that of a big fish lying dead amid slabs of ice.

Everything has come to a halt. The countless whirlwinds have locked their mechanisms, just like that, no one knows why: in anticipation, perhaps. In the vast town, so huge that it doubtless fills the whole of space from one end of the galaxy to the other, so huge that one could be born and die thousands of times without ever having left it, suddenly the vehicles stop moving. They continue their onward motion, gliding smoothly along the streets, but it is *as though* they had stopped moving. The bonnets and roofs are welded together, the tyres are stuck fast in the black asphalt, the engines are joined to each other by tubes and gear-wheels. In the valleys of stone, and in the subterranean corridors, the pedestrians are no longer making any headway. They continue to make walking motions with their elastic legs, but it is *as though*. There are aeroplanes in the sky, but it is *as though*. And the tree-like poles, their flashing lights extinguished; and the antennae vibrating, wordless, in the wind; and the cafés–bars–restaurants–tobacconist's shops–betting-shops–snack bars–self-service stores–post offices–pharmacies–supermarkets–drive-in banks–casinos–bookshops–Cultural Centres–hotels–stations–toll-barriers–cinemas–cinemas–cinemas, all motionless now, fundamentally, immobile, great empty silent shells that the sea has left stranded on the rocks and that still hold the froth and waste of seaweeds glued to them by time.

Is that the way one becomes free? By stopping moving because of a cramp? Or because suddenly a terrible emptiness, an appalling emptiness drills its hole through the skin of your back and bores right through you with its icy breath? One imagined that one was a thousand miles away from everything, sheltered, out of reach. But it was not true. One was there all the time, surrounded by the noise and violence, a slave among other slaves. Somewhere in the depths of one's being, the intellect's clockwork mechanism was making its balance-wheels oscillate and its cog-wheels click round. Nothing existed by chance. Neither the clouds in the sky, nor the armies of ants on the ground, nor the waves of the ocean. Words did not exist by chance. They were murmured into a woman's warm ear, and these words were like matches being moved round on a café table-top to illustrate some point or other.

The man is able to stop and stare round him with his odd dead-fishlike eyes. The world balances for an instant above the abyss, slowly teeters, then falls; it rolls down the invisible slope, gains momentum, plunges faster and faster, then rolls away on its unknown course.

Be free: it is almost possible. I mean, there are no natural laws. But one does have some hope of understanding everything that is armoured, everything that, century after century, has erected its citadel of money and violence and crime, everything manipulated by mankind. There is a game concealed within the vaster game.

Faces! Looks! Staring eyes! Desire! Death! Yes, as I have said, I used to speak often about all that; I used to speak about it just as an invalid speaks of his fever or his goitre. I was inside the malady, surveying it with inner eyes, with eyes turned inwards, counting the pustules and spasms and dizzy spells. Drunkenly and painfully I palpated my diseased organs, and my very gaze was a sort of death-ray. The fixed gaze carried the malady within itself, inoculated the disorder in the veins. How can I explain that to you in simple terms? I could try to say what I mean by using a parable:

'Once upon a time there was a very simple-minded man who was seated all alone in a battlefield. Do you get the picture? A rather dim-witted man who had managed to park himself right in the middle of a battlefield. The battle raged all round him. But he saw nothing. Volleys of arrows and bullets whizzed round him, but he paid no attention. Only, missiles hit him from all directions, and his flesh was gashed with a thousand wounds. So what did he do? He stayed sitting on the ground, groaning each time that a fresh arrow pierced him, watching with stupefaction as his blood flowed over the ground in thin streams. Yet he could not understand why his blood was flowing, nor why he was in such agony. He was so absent-minded! Maybe, in the end, he died like that, sitting in the middle of the battlefield, never knowing where the mortal blow came from; like a sleeping tapir struck by a poisoned dart from a blowpipe and dying without ever waking up ... '

They are always there, the eyes, the hooks, the claws, the chasms yawning underfoot. There, crouching in the shadows, or else sparkling in the light, eager to vanquish and devour. They are there. It is they who drill the hole in the back through which emptiness enters. It is they who strike the skull with blows from an iron bar, reducing it to pulp. It is they who live inside terrifying objects, it is they who are the leeches' suckers. How could they ever disappear? They have always existed, they were there long before I was born, long before my first heart-beats. They were there from the first day onwards, lying in wait in the depths of the air, in the depths of the water, behind the incubators' glass panes, in the iron jaws that sliced through my life's cord. They were already deep inside me before I suspected their presence, marked inside my cells in little hook-shaped signs.

But today the world has come to a halt and I can at last look at things with my dead-fish eyes. And I see that these hooks and these eyes were not there simply by chance. They had their sacred haunts, in the shadows or in the light, their holes from which they could bite and snap, their keyholes to spy through. Extraordinary, is it not? They released their bullets from far away, following the progress of their prey through the telescopic sight mounted on their machine-guns.

For their eyes and their teeth did not have natural names. Man's hatred for man, contempt, slavery did not have natural names. These forces had human names, precise names written with letters on the pages of newspapers and books, written names that no one dared read. Names that were not ideas, but names for those who know how to read names. And first names too. Dupont, Fleischermann, Camel, Lucky Strike, Louis Cheskin, Ernest Ditcher, Rothschild, Unilever, United Fruit, C. R. Haas, Pierre Martineau, Dave Ogilvy, B. N. P., General Cigar Co., Guichard, Colgate, Gillette, Hachette, Pinoncelly, Wiggins.

There were so many names, so many first names, so many words, that one no longer knew which to listen to. And yet it was from these names and words that war leaked out continuously. A silent and implacable war, a pitiless and vengeful war, a war without dead men, without even any wounded, any spilt blood, a war that was certainly blind and that, though it was not waged for a few catch-phrases or a few ideas, yet succeeded in sweeping the world. There was a war that seethed in the depths of most men's being, and they tried to free themselves from it by writing poems or by driving a car through pedestrian crossings at 70 m.p.h. But that war was nothing compared with the other field of battle that a few men had set up across the world. A few names, a few names with claws and hooks, a few names which may never become known. It was they who had hidden all these eyes and suckers and mandibles at the bottom of little secret holes. Look, now, look round you and see them: spaced out at intervals along white ceilings, on armoured doors, on the façades of buildings, along walls, on the steps of staircases, these little black holes concealing eyes. If you approach them they will unleash screeches of alarm at the other end of the world. Sometimes, when you are walking by the seaside, along some beach, you may feel like thinking about things that exist only within yourself, things that seem to emerge from the sea and enter you through a tube that goes through your navel. You think of these things, and you write things down on a scrap of paper, for instance:

> white
> blue   flame
> black

because that is how it is, and it cannot be said in any other way. Or else you look and you see a bird pass, or a dog, or a girl in a raincoat, or a bee. You see them pass, and you know that they have no claws nor hooks nor eyes, that they are, so to speak, extraordinarily innocent, and that no war seeps out of their minds or glands. You can even think of death as a boat trip, of infinity as a sort of line on the horizon, of love as being vaguely cloud-like. You can think of many other things besides ...

But you are not as far away as you imagine. Just over there, a few paces away from you, the war is busily folding and unfolding its great flail. Just behind you. The eyes are staring steadily at you, keeping you under observation. In the depths of concrete casemates, cameras are filming and tape-recorders are recording ceaselessly. On the building-sites, walls are rising out of the disembowelled earth, growing higher and higher, walls laden with mirrors and plate-glass. Sheets of hardboard muffle speech, air conditioners hum inside the walls, and perhaps it is HCN that is being breathed out of their meshed mouths. The hooks are not far away: just in front of you, there, at the edge of the sea. The beaches reflecting the sun's glow are surrounded by great walls in which ground glass glitters. The ring-fences have closed their gates on which is written, for all time perhaps:

ENTRY PROHIBITED

and the iron bars point their sharp, angled talons down towards you, not to prevent you climbing over to the other side, because on the other side *there is absolutely nothing*, but to tell you that somewhere, at some time in the past, it has been decreed that they will have cause to kill you.

At last they are there, right under everyone's eye. Just stop a moment, and look. The fierce forces that are lying in wait, the devouring forces that none will escape. Be free! There only remains an instant of freedom, not even a few hours, barely a few seconds. An instant as rapid as a flash of lightning, which will split the night in two and illuminate the symbol of freedom. It is this instant that one must see, with the whole force of one's eyes. The wide-open eyes never blink; the dilated pupils no longer contract; they stare straight ahead, with a desire so great that it is as though they were hurling assagais, as though the stare had become a fountain turned to stone. The pupils no longer want to hide behind their lids, they no longer want to

24

hide behind the lenses of dark glasses. They want to see everything round them, in the smallest detail, because the very next
minute may be blind.

Fierce names, hidden in their lairs. Sheltering behind their
wall of money, sheltering behind shields and steel doors and
concrete casings, hidden like hermits in air-conditioned offices,
in blocks flooded with electric light, throbbing with power. In
the centre of networks of electric wires, interphones, teletypes,
protected by ten thousand television screens, distant, isolated,
in the centre of the very planet, perhaps, or else soaring in gold-
lined capsules through outer space: the NAMES. The fabulous
legendary names, gliding through dusty towns in metal chariots
fitted with bullet-proof glass. Unknown faces gazing threaten-
ingly from the tops of towers; hands like millions of other
hands, except that these fingertips control the buttons that
command the world. Is it possible? Are there really such men?
Is it not just one more legend, created to externalize the
chimeras that haunt one's being? Yet these names exist. I have
seen these cameras hidden in department stores, filming the
flickering of eyelids, the motions of lips, the gestures of hands.
I have heard the soft voices of the women who talk during your
dreams, repeating untiringly in the darkness, while you sleep,
the magic words:

kool kool kool kool kool kool kool kool
        kool kool kool kool

I have seen young women's impassive faces transfixed on the
pages of newspapers, on walls, on ceilings, on aeroplane wings,
on cinema screens, on clouds. The tattoos on men's hands, the
gaping mouths of little children on posters advertising cream.
I have seen all that. It would have been difficult not to see it.
Mountains of ice-cream in which to plunge the head, mountains
of fruit, mountains of meat. There are tins of all colours, blue
tins, yellow tins, blue-and-yellow tins. And these tins are
absolutely empty.

There are men who have set up these traps along the paths that women take, and these men are waiting in the shadows. There are men who, from the inmost recesses of their impregnable fortresses, direct the movements and desires of whole insect populations. There are men who make use of all the world's resources of science and intelligence and power to dominate others. There are hidden men who exercise absolute control over colours, odours, likes and dislikes. I tell you: there has never been so much power, so much warfare. There is an immense motor, here, in which each gear, each driving-rod moves according to a precise plan. There has never been so much money. The forces of beauty and desire drive through the throng, leaving great furrows in their wake; no blood flows, but the blood is on fire. What to do? How to free oneself? How to tear off the names, one by one? How to rip off the masks, how to express any of this, how to be oneself at last, free at last? Where to hide, where to escape to? How to recognize innocence? How to forget? Alien hands have thrust into my throat, my eyes, my ears. Alien skins have stuck to my own skin like burning polyamide. Alien words have entered my brain. I would like to be something other than an echo. I would like to find an exit; just a door, even a ventilator shaft, through which I might leave. I would like to get to know a different world, or failing that, a different woman. Rip off the masks, one by one, perhaps. Smash the dark glasses, smash the cinema screens and television screens, smash the plate-glass windows. But every gesture made, here, to smash such things is taken up again over there to re-create them. And in the very process of ripping off his mask, the person suddenly stops, for in passing his hands over his face he has just felt a new mask growing. With stabs of a bradawl I can crush the electronic eyes, with strokes of an axe I can disembowel the computers and dynamos. What is the meaning, now, of conscience, *my* conscience? Ridiculous grotesque little hand-mirror that I bring close to my face. Mirror to reflect the image of the eye. What of it? When the world is at the foot of a mirror that stretches up to the sky and covers the surface of the ocean. I say ... I say ... The words of one single man are like the squealings of a rat, words are on sale in all the department stores, buy the word FREEDOM, buy the word LOVE, buy the word TRUTH, buy, buy, buy the word WORLD. Books are great catalogues, and thoughts are the advertisement ashtrays on the tables of café-snack-bars. Everything is possible, nothing is possible. But in the depths of their fortresses, within their padded walls, the masters of the world are well aware of what is possible.

I want to tell you once again, gasping out the words if necessary: free yourselves. Chains, iron collars, prison walls have become visible at last. But meanwhile other gaols are sprouting within one's self, ignoble prisons that are not so easy to escape from. What matter? Using voices, all the voices, from deep in the throat, using words, and hand gestures, and dances, heavings of the belly, tremblings, shiverings, using great bundles of lightning-flashes: free, all of you! free!

The tyrants in their bunkers had decided that the world should be peopled only with slaves. They have covered the earth with their network of wires and electric-light bulbs. They have dug pitfalls everywhere, they have mapped out roads into which racing cars will dash blindly and be forced to go round and round in circles. It was they who had declared war on the world; they had ordained the moments when people should kill themselves, the moments when they should make love, when they should eat, or sleep, or write. They have invented all the desires and their satisfactions. They have invented pleasure, fear, revolt. Where are they? Where are they hiding? Carnivores thirsty for blood, lost in the seething mob, never seen, never heard. They are hidden behind objects, behind displays of heaped-up riches, behind mirrors and shop windows. Out of harm's way. Impossible to get to grips with. Slowly, for centuries, they have replaced the forces of nature. Their aim was to destroy the language of trees, the language of water and of fire, the language of stone. They have created a substitute nature, in which each element would be invented by them. A new world. That's how it is, nowadays: each is covered by a shell of cement that is tightly sealed and hard and impenetrable. The river flows through great sewers, the waterfalls are imprisoned in dams. In the very depths of the sky, in the very depths of the sea, in the very depths of the volcano, there is a man lurking. The windows overlooking the abyss are all walled up. Cyclones howl in the aerodynamic corridors. The rain that falls is made up of millions of drops of mercury.

Occasionally a man comes to a standstill and tries to see. Deep inside his body he can feel the roots of waving seaweed, long soft strands that creep from rock to rock. But how could he know that? There is nothing before his eyes but this spectacle with a planned scenario, this kind of film, yes, in which mankind and womankind provide the actors, and sun, moon, neon strips, beacons and headlamps, forests, beaches and islands provide the elements of the pasteboard decor. Yes, before his eyes; before my eyes. How to see truth, beauty, life, with one's eyes when one has already imagined what they ought to see, when one has forbidden them to look elsewhere, to look farther ahead? My eyes are objects of study for the tyrants' machines, my eyes are one-billionth part of the power reigning on this earth. Enough! I want nothing more to do with my eyes, for they betray me. Each time I blink at a light, a colour, a form, the blink is registered by a magnetic tape that transmits the visual image to the midbrain. Soon my eyes will become fixed and lidless like those of dead fish, and stare at empty space. But nobody will realize that this has happened.

A man stops and looks. In front of his eyes, and in front of his ears, and in front of his mouth, and in front of his skin. Signs fly from all directions, crossing the air like cosmic radiation. Signs that are the forces of other people, signs that are anonymous orders. Signs for each obedient cell, signs for the blind, signs for the identical insects that march across the earth in one direction, and then back in the opposite direction, insects that all think the same thing, do the same thing, and say the same thing. As for the man who stops a moment and looks round

28

him, for him the world suddenly turns black. From one end of time to the other, from one end of space to the other, he sees nothing but this infinite architecture.

But these city squares, these underground tunnels, these streets, these calculating machines contain much violence and beauty, many passions. There are incomprehensible laws springing up from inside the concrete and glass, laws and movements that the masters of the world had not foreseen. The power of freedom is invincible and terrible. That is what I want to be able to say one day, not kill yourselves, or have faith, because those phrases are part of one's inner being from the first second of life onwards, but simply: free yourselves. Free yourselves. Slay with a simple look the men who are the masters of the act of looking.

What do you see?

I see an immense stretch of flat ground at the mouth of a river. There is a sort of pebbly beach in front of the sea, and right behind the beach there is this great stretch of flat ground in the river's alluvial zone. Upon this stretch of flat ground stands Hyperpolis. The landscape is very hard and very white, with a wind blowing and a sea hollowing out waves. The sky is blue, of an extraordinary intense blue, so blue that it is almost black, and the wind blows in the sky. In the distance, all along the coast, are stunted houses, weeds, rubbish, roads, gipsy encampments. But nobody notices these. What is important, here, is white Hyperpolis gleaming in the sun, surrounded by its four asphalt car parks. The wind blows across the car parks, through the cars' wheels, and from time to time it scoops up a swirl of dust. The wind coming from the sea makes a sound as it sweeps across the asphalt surface, an odd sound rather like silence. The sun is very high in the sky, in the centre of the sky. It is so high that one cannot even see it. It crushes shadows beneath men's feet; it does not move. Indeed, nothing moves, really. The Hyperpolis Supermarket is motionless on its stretch of alluvial ground, the beach is motionless in front of the sea, and the sea is like what one sees from an aeroplane at eighteen thousand feet: cross-grained, flat, grey, with metallic reflections. Here, there is perhaps nothing to say, nothing to do. Perhaps one has stopped, once and for all, just like that, facing the sea, beside the white carcase of Hyperpolis;

after reaching the end of the migration, yes, perhaps; after reaching the shore; and one is not going to embark, after all, for one has no place to go. The sun is so high that one cannot even see it any longer, the wind blows with its sound of silence, the light bounces off the sheet of water. There is a great deal of life around, though it would be difficult to know that. No question of embarking here: it is not the kind of sea that one can sail across. The Hyperpolis Supermarket lies as motionless, at the river's mouth, as a stranded whale. The four parks around it are marked out with white rectangular designs and yellow arrows.

In the third car park on the right, on the seaward side, there is this small boy called Dumb Bogo. He is sitting on the rear bumper of a car, looking at Hyperpolis. From time to time he stops chewing the gum in his mouth, parts his lips and blows a bubble. The green bubble swells, grows taut, then explodes with a pop.

The wind blows in gusts along the car park. Dumb Bogo sees it coming from far away. At the other end of the car park the fronds of the palm-trees are thrashing wildly, and the cars' aerials sparkle as they bend. Travelling at about 45 m.p.h., the wind reaches the small boy, who screws up his eyes. The wind passes over him, and his hair rises, whips round and tries to get into his eyes. When the wind has gone, Dumb Bogo opens his eyes and starts chewing his gum again.

The sun is very hot. This is probably due to the wind, because there is no moisture at all left in the air. The sun scorches the small boy's skin and hair and clothes. When the wind blows, one no longer feels the sun. But between gusts the light strikes the asphalt ground, and the roof of Hyperpolis, and the sea's metal plating, and each surface reflects the burning rays across the earth, rather as though there were thousands of electric flashes spreading out their sheet-lightning. Or perhaps as though one had sprayed everything with benzine, then suddenly thrown a lighted match into the middle. An explosion of heat, fusing horizontally, with one single great flat flame.

Dumb Bogo came to that spot every day, to look at Hyperpolis. He sat down on the bumper of one of the cars, and stayed there a little while, in the sun. He looked at the car park, too, and at the bodies of the sparkling cars, and at the rectangles painted on the asphalt. He looked at the sort of alluvial plain, with its little cement houses, and on the other side of the highway the three big white blocks of flats with their rows of windows. His parents lived in the block to the far right, but from where he was sitting one could not see the windows of their flat because it was on the north side. But now that he had left home, the small boy had this routine: each time that he arrived in front of Hyperpolis he looked for somewhere to sit down. The best place was a car with big protuberant bumpers. By now he knew immediately the kind of cars that suited his purpose: luxury models, or rather old models, either of which kind had heavy chromium-plated bumpers that looked like the step of a staircase. He sat down, leaning his back against the boot or the radiator, and began to look, screwing up his eyes because of the sun. He chewed bubble-gum slowly, making little green bubbles that exploded; and he looked at everything in front of him. Sometimes people arrived and climbed into the cars. They banged doors shut, four times in succession, then they were off. Dumb Bogo watched the car speed away, turn and disappear at the far end of the car park, though it was not easy to see how it got out.

Sometimes, too, people climbed into the car against which Dumb Bogo was sitting. When that happened, the small boy got up and went a little way away. One had to keep an eye on the people approaching, because they might equally well be Guards or policemen in disguise. Once, a young woman had even paused and looked at Dumb Bogo for a moment, as though about to say something. She had not said anything, but she had taken a cake out of a bag and put it into the small boy's hand.

But none of that interested Dumb Bogo particularly. What interested him was just sitting there on a car bumper in the Hyperpolis car park and watching.

Above his head there is a white star thrust into the middle of the air. The white star is motionless in the blue sky. Heat pours ceaselessly from the white star, heat and light like a steady noise. The white star swims without moving in the blue space. Round it, all is so blue that the colour might almost be black. In reality, neither blue nor black, but absolutely colourless. The star is motionless, right at the top of the sky, a blazing disc with a sharply defined rim. A slow eruption pours continually from it. The crown of flames is motionless and even, utterly unlike life's convulsive movements. It inundates, simply. Daylong, then daylong, then daylong again. Never black star. Neither big nor small. Always the same, always in the same spot. At night it continues, a blue point trembling and unfolding against the blood-red sky. It is a nail, perhaps, driven into the hard surface. It is the most solid point in the world, the one steel point, truly, in a world made up of wood, paper, cloth and skin.

If the star had not existed, there would be no eye. That seems almost certain. The mouth of the volcano gapes above the white concrete constructions, and the interior of the glowing space is visible. The blast-furnace's cone is agape, high above head level, blowing out blazing air. A motionless cylindrical flame, burning in that single spot. It is not far away; one cannot touch the flame, but it is not far away. The clouds that cross the sky pass just above this hole, but it is not very far. The light crosses the sky in the form of a dense rain, and everything below sparkles: the bodies of cars, slabs of cement, sheets of asphalt. Perhaps the light rummages in the earth, uproots objects, sucks them up into the sky and sends them soaring away. The light is invisible, yet it is there. The whole time, there is a lightning-flash passing through space, from one end of the alluvial platform to the other, a flash of invincible whiteness. The lightning-flash kills the whiteness. For a fragment of a second it reveals the colours, then it kills them. They carbonize on the spot, twisting like plastics in a fire. This burning is terrible. From one end of the alluvial platform to the other, one can see the skins and carapaces twisting upon themselves, while the colours melt and calcine with strange tears, drops of sweat that evaporate instantaneously. There are cracking noises, detonations, the whistle of fusing air. Metals boil. Sounds like groans of pain, breathing that suddenly suffocates, lungs exploding. And the star does not stop. It continues to shine, to burn, hour after hour, day after day, for whole months and years and centuries. There are no trees. There is no water. If there were forests and rivers, there would still be hope. Only there is nothing but these sheets of tar and concrete, these sheets of pebbles, and this sheet of salt water with hard waves. When the wind blows, it brings with it odours of gas and smoke, odours of charred flesh and skin and fingernails.

So the white star hovers high in the sky, above the flat ground littered with cement cubes and criss-crossed by roadways. The blowlamp's incandescent point, the almost invisible point of flame that pierces the eyes to reach deep into the brain. Beneath its presence there is no longer cause for fear. One hears this great noise shrieking through the air, and the other noises round Hyperpolis, the noises of burning. That is how it goes on, day after day, year after year, beyond thought, beyond words, almost beyond life itself, so filled with truth that no other truth seems possible any longer. The melting-point, the one brilliant point of the universe, in the centre of black space. It is the centre of the world, at last made visible, and the edges of the earth curve up towards it like the rim of a great crater. The pylons, and the buildings' façades, and the cars' aerials, and the pillars and posts of Hyperpolis point upwards towards the white star, bristle towards it like spiky plants. In flowerpots, geraniums stretch their dusty leaves towards the star.

The star is far away, so far that no sound from it can ever be heard. It burns on, sending out flames and explosions in complete silence. In a sense, one can hear these noises everywhere on earth, the crackling and sputtering of stone and metal, the dull vibration of flows of lava. But the star is above these noises, separated by a vast gulf of space. It is burning so deep in the heart of space that it is as though it no longer existed, or as though we ourselves no longer existed.

A lamp in the centre of a ceiling, perhaps. But nobody lights this lamp. It glows of its own accord.

The small boy called Dumb Bogo bathes in the light, swims towards it, flows up along the invisible rays, floating in the heat, and vanishes in the region of the star. The star's gaze rests upon his face, his chest, his navel. It is a rain of gazes. And the gaze recoils upon itself and surges skywards again. It springs simultaneously from the star and from the earth. The whole alluvial plain, with its pebble beach, its white Hyperpolis, its black car parks, its roads and cars and people, leaps upwards in one mass, touching the strange fiery speck as though with a single finger.

From time to time the wind blows cold, and then all this is forgotten. But the heat returns: it simply seeps out of the ground, seeps out of the white walls of Hyperpolis, out of the wheels of cars, out of the beach, the sea, the distant buildings, even the stunted bungalows. It is difficult to say where the heat comes from. It is like plunging one's face into a basin of hot water, with one's eyes closed.

People enter and leave Hyperpolis in an endless stream. The cars cruise slowly down the parking lanes, looking for a vacant space, then stop. Dumb Bogo watches them, and watches the shadows too. Then, when he has had enough, he takes the bubble-gum out of his mouth and tosses it onto the roof of a nearby car. Then he gets up and walks across the car park. He goes to the other end of the esplanade, facing the stretch of beach with its grimy-looking pebbles.

There is no one on the beach. The sun is blazing down, glinting off many points on the sea's flat surface. Very far away lies the circular horizon, an invisible thin line rather like the outline of a waterdrop. The small boy nicknamed Dumb Bogo goes and sits on the beach, on a heap of pebbles. He looks at the sea, studying all the different-shaped waves. Suddenly he sees some people: two girls walking along the beach, following the shoreline. They are talking as they stroll along, but it is too far away to hear what they are saying. From time to time they stop and look in the direction of the sea. The small boy does not move. He sees the two girls continue along the beach, stumbling occasionally. They are both beautiful, tall, long-haired. The one on the left has blonde hair, the one on the right has brown hair. They are both wearing white slacks and a white blouse. The one on the left has a bag slung over her shoulder. They are walking along the edge of the sea, barefoot over the slippery pebbles. They are talking a lot, and from time to time they laugh. But their voices are indistinct, and all that can be heard through the sounds of the wind and the sea are snatches of speech such as:

'Aaaah-oo'

'Waa-de-hoo'

They pass in front of the small boy without seeing him, then they continue towards the end of the beach, where there is a cement jetty with a boat moored to it. When they reach the jetty they untie the boat and push it into the water. They are still laughing, and call out something, but the wind blows the words away:

'Ha-hi! Oh-ho!'

The small boy watches them steadily. He sees the two girls get into the boat. They take out the oars, then, with their backs to the horizon, they begin to row. Each wields an oar, and they row. They laugh, and say something to each other. They row, and the boat makes slowly for the open sea, pitching as the waves grow higher. Unremittingly, the light bounces off the water. The wind blows, and the heat dies down. The boat skirts the jetty, then leaves it behind. By now the small boy can no longer make out the two shapes in the boat. It is a sort of black blob moving out over the sea, like an old rusty petrol-can. Then the small boy nicknamed Dumb Bogo stops looking. He gets up, and walks a little, crunching over the pebbles. Then he goes away.

| 3 | 三 | san | 産 | birth |
| 4 | 四 | shi | 死 | death |

What do you see now?

The young woman known as Tranquillity had parked her car and was walking now towards Hyperpolis. The sun was high in the blue sky, and the wind was blowing in gusts, but she was not paying much attention to it. She looked at the great entrance-way to Hyperpolis opening on to the esplanade, a sort of black hole like the mouth of a toothless dog. People were going in and coming out through this door in an endless stream, and the girl walked on, watching the people. The door grew bigger and bigger in the building's white wall, and as one drew nearer one could see that the hole was not really black, but that there were many lights on the other side of its plate-glass panels, many reflections and transparent colours. On the ground, at her feet, there were yellow-painted signs, arrows pointing to the door, figures, and letters. The sun's light blazed, and when the wind blew one could just hear the sound of the sea.

The young woman whose nickname was Tranquillity was not listening to the sound of the sea, and she was able to look at the blazing light without screwing up her eyes, because she was wearing sunglasses with blue-tinted lenses. The wind blew through her brown hair and flattened the fabric of her dress against her breasts and belly and thighs.

When she reached the building she strode quickly into the zone of darkness. Then the black hole of the door, that now loomed huge, became red-grey, then white.

Inside, Hyperpolis was full of noise and light. Eddies of people whirled along the galleries, great circular movements of legs that had arrived from unknown lands and were leaving for an equally mysterious destination. It was difficult not to be caught up in these eddies. One had to be careful, and watch all the time where one was going, so as not to be suddenly swept away to the left or to the right.

Sometimes, too, without any apparent reason, gaps would open out at the sides, summonses that would catch you by the legs and make you alter course. The young woman walked quickly over the laminated-plastic flooring, looking at all the lights, breathing in all the odours. She crossed paths with other girls like her, and men too, and women, and children. She stopped for a moment in front of a showcase full of clothes; at the centre of the display, electric-light bulbs flashed brightly, went off, then shone again, without ever getting tired. The young woman gazed at the red, violet, blue, yellow dresses hanging from chromed rods, and at the great opalescent globes that dangled over the display. She gazed at all this with rapt attention, eyes calm, unblinking. The bright colours penetrated her gently, together with the giddy swaying of the great opalescent globes, and the light bulbs' flashes. After a little while she managed to tear her eyes away from the showcase. She took a packet of cigarettes out of her handbag: it was a bright-red packet, containing long filter-tip cigarettes that had something printed on them in gold letters.

Above her, above the whole world, there was a vast ceiling that covered Hyperpolis. It was balanced upon white concrete pillars, distant, heavy, swollen, like a canopy of thick clouds. Neon tubes streaked along the ceiling like lightning, sending out illumination. The young woman cast occasional glances at the ceiling as she walked along: it was like a tarnished mirror, engulfing movements and gestures instead of reflecting them. It never reflected images. It never reflected faces or bodies. It only reflected light, an intense vibrant light in hues of white and grey and rose. The young woman whose nickname was Tranquillity tried to forget this, but that too was difficult. She walked across the floor towards the inner depths of Hyperpolis, and tried not to see anything at all.

The central thoroughfare was a luminous carpet that stretched from one end of the building to the other, and the people walked along it like shadows. Perhaps they did not really exist. There was so much light and so much energy everywhere, so many colours and shapes and sounds and odours, that the people themselves did not exist. They had turned into peculiar sorts of ghosts, with their pale faces, pale eyes, grey clothes and lustreless hair. The young woman made her way through them without seeing them, passed through wave after wave of them, and they were all identical. Occasionally she caught a pair of quickly shifting, deep-sunken eyes flashing an anxious glance at her. Peculiar pale eyes, rolling under their lids, seeking to recognize her. Or mouths, lower down, moving their lips as though trying to say something.

Harsh summonses came from all sides. From all the corners of the building came the shimmering glitter of objects. These were the only real things, the only powerful things here. Ceaselessly they shot through space: red lights, green lights, violet lights, white lights, sounds of clattering and banging, sounds of music and speech coming out of loudspeakers, enormous shapes that barred the way and obstructed the sky, machines that flew and swam unwearyingly.

It was really difficult not to become submerged. The young woman called Tranquillity tried to reach the far end of Hyperpolis where her girlfriend was waiting for her. But perhaps she would never manage it. There were so many traps and obstacles, all along the way, that she would perhaps lose heart and have to give up the attempt. There were so many doors and corridors, phosphorescent passages opening up endlessly to the left and the right and inhaling passing particles. There were so many flashes streaking the atmosphere, drawing eyes and legs towards them, that she would perhaps never reach the far end of the thoroughfare. She would get lost, no doubt, on the way.

43

She would look at a great luminous disc on which was written in black letters:

WOOOOOL

and suddenly she would no longer know where she wanted to go. She would approach the disc, gaze at it with dilated eyes and suddenly her mind would be a blank.

The luminous carpet stretched from one end of Hyperpolis to the other, and the young woman called Tranquillity hurried down it as quickly as she could. Time and again she had to pass through effulgences, extraordinary fringes of light that sent out bristling unwavering rays. The effect was a little like thousands of stars in the blackness of space, but side by side in serried clusters that negated the idea of space. At the end of the luminous carpet there was a sort of kiosk of white moulded plastic, that hovered above the ground like a montgolfier balloon. That was where Tranquillity's girlfriend lived, sitting behind a counter, under a placard reading:

INFORMATION

But for the moment the young woman did not see the kiosk. The luminous effulgences made series of screens along the way, and these prevented her from seeing.

There were so many words, too, all along the thoroughfare. Tranquillity did not really read them, but they were there. They entered her eyes diagonally, installed themselves in the very depths of her being, then spoke.

They were incomprehensible words, that opened up, then closed shut again. That puffed themselves up, or else died away. Words that asked questions of a kind, that uttered exclamations of a kind. They were mute, simply written in electric letters on glass panels and boxes and bottles and bits of paper. They slid through the air like meteorites, rapid trails of fire that immediately died out. Or they shone without moving, great round planets suspended in the night at the end of their strings. These words were not for reading, and no one knew their meaning. They were words that resembled stars, or perhaps car headlamps along a motorway at night-time.

The young woman called Tranquillity advanced painfully through these obstacles. She did her best not to see. She did not want to see. But the lights flashed constantly from their hiding-places, leaping forward, grimacing, dancing on the luminous carpet, fiendish faces illuminated in red and violet. Eyes opened in front of her, without warning. Huge transparent blue eyes, unreal in their beauty, trying to paralyse her with their stare.

The eyes were fake, of course; but they were capable of such an insistent stare that the girl felt a hollow feeling in the pit of her stomach. Her heart began to beat very fast, and a burning bile rose towards her throat. She was going to fall. Perhaps she was going to collapse on to the glassy floor, among the forest of legs of all the other people. The ceiling was very far above her head, so high on its supporting pillars of white concrete that it was the sky. The young woman stopped to look at it, and she could see grey clouds passing overhead, beneath the neon tubes, trails of mist that alternately obscured and revealed the light. She thought she could see flights of gulls gliding through the haze, swift projectiles travelling noiselessly across the great hall. But she was probably mistaken: how could seagulls find their way into a department store?

The young woman called Tranquillity was longing to sit down, to rest a while. But there were no seats near by. Just the flat vitrified flooring upon which legs came and went interminably. Those who had designed this trap knew what they were about: ensuring that no one should escape, that people must plod on amid the countless sounds and lights. Where were the masters? The young woman would have liked to catch a glimpse of them, so she started searching for their names and faces among this anonymous confusion. Perhaps they were hidden in the basement, listening in to their monstrous machines, secure beneath the sheath of vitrified flooring ... Or maybe they were shut inside plexiglass cabins at the top of the pillars, up there, just beneath the ceiling, observing the movements of the crowd through binoculars. It was terrible to feel

45

their presence without knowing where they were. It was even more terrible than being alone in a room, in the dark, lying on a bed, hearing ominous creaking noises, and waiting. It was more frightening than in a dream, because here there was so much light and music, here there were so many faces and written words. One was not alone. One no longer knew anything at all, one's whole life was a blank.

The eyes opened and closed. Behind the white counters, lamps flashed at regular intervals, hurting the eyes. Metal discs revolved on invisible axes, throwing off sparks. Glass filaments melted along their own surfaces, propellers turned, nozzles blew air. The young woman called Tranquillity walked through peculiar soft fringes that wrapped themselves round her body like seaweed. She had to make brusque gestures to free herself. Or wispy disembodied hands groped at her face as she passed, pulled her hair, opened her clothes and glided lightly over her skin, her breasts, her belly, and down her thighs: hands, or glances? Draughts, perhaps, warm breath emerging from the air-conditioning grilles at floor level. But the young woman was empty, by now, and already she was barely holding out.

She continued on towards the other end of the hall, as though in a dream; she had forgotten why she had come, and where she was going. The kiosk was so far away. It shimmered on the horizon, just like a mountain, surrounded by globes of light. She would never reach it. It was too far, there were too many obstacles in the way.

Round her, the crowd stirred slowly. Its movements were like water, long powerful movements that flowed over the same spot again and again. It advanced between the rows of counters, an inert grey mass. The multicoloured lamps lit reflections on its surface, glinting off eyes and bald pates and hair. A mass brimming with odours and juices, continually hurled back by the plastic partition walls. Here and there, words flashed, penetrated into the crowd, disappeared inside the sluggish flows of fat: somewhere among the mass's internal organs, the words must be exploding, inflicting mortal wounds. The young

46

woman watched these projectiles in terror, and listened for cries of pain. But it was all happening in a very mysterious fashion, and the victims must be dying without even knowing they had been hit.

She would have liked to say something quickly. She thought about what she should have done: she should have climbed on top of the counter of the kiosk where her girlfriend lived, up near the sign on which was written:

INFORMATION

and told the people what was going on. Told them: Look out! look out! There are traps here! Colours, noises, music, shapes have all been set with traps! The light itself conceals a snare! Even your desires are booby-trapped! Look out! But it was impossible to reach the kiosk. To get there meant joining the other bodies in their snail-like progress, walking without respite along the luminous carpet. The other thing she could have done would have been to start a blaze somewhere; that might have woken people up.

Another terrifying experience: walking along inside another person's brain. The young woman called Tranquillity looked at all the lanes, and all the counters, and all the written signs, and began to think that she no longer really existed. No one round her existed any longer. The dense anonymous mass had become lifeless, no longer possessed a past, had lost its power of speech: it flowed along the channels, opened doors, climbed flights of steps and rode in escalators. It bought, ate, drank, smoked, all automatically, following the orders of Hyperpolis; it was the placards' violent summonses, the neon tubes' dazzling flashes, as well as the soft voices murmuring

WOOOOOL

into the ear, that were truly in command. The young woman was now passing through the food hall, and she began to notice blue and white cartons dancing ahead of her. Then came white

47

squares marked with a red triangle. Metal containers, so beautiful and desirable that despite herself her hands stretched out to caress their chilly lids. Packets of biscuits, foil-wrapped bars of milk chocolate, small pots of cream. Tubes. Milk in cartons of a beautiful and complex spiral shape. Cardboard containers of all shapes and sizes and hues, all no doubt concealing some identical commodity. No one really saw anything any longer. One advanced like a sleepwalker through the multi-coloured jungle, one moved forward through a vast cloud of butterflies. One forgot everything. The young woman would have liked to grab hold of everything, she would have liked to heap thousands of tins and cartons into a shopping trolley. This was the order that had reached her all the way from the sub-terranean hiding-places, and from the plexiglass cabins at the top of the pillars, near the sky. That is why she was walking inside an alien brain, why she was nothing but a thought, a simple thought emanating from the machine that ordered thoughts.

Round her, people were frantically piling objects into the metal trolleys. Their faces were drawn, serious, their eyelids blinked abnormally slowly. Women reached out towards the stands of food. They rummaged in the refrigerated bins, taking pots, cubes, packets. They took dozens of soft cheeses, cartons of milk, tubes of creamy spreads, packets of gelatine; they selected plastic tubs filled with yoghourt, custard, sorbet, mousse, in chocolate, coffee, peach, strawberry, pineapple flavours. They never stopped. Even the children excavated in the shelves at their level, piling the foodstuffs into little toy trolleys that they pushed in front of them. None of the people knew what they were doing. How could they have known? It was not they who grabbed the merchandise: it stuck to their hands of its own accord, it drew eyes and fingers towards it magnetically, it hurried straight into their mouths and passed through their digestive tubes at lightning speed. Food was no longer anything but shapes and colours. The eyes were devouring a choice of red, white, green, orange colours; the eyes were hungry for spheres and pyramids, for smooth plastics and for metal bottle-tops.

One was not simply wandering round aimlessly. One was following a number of paths laid down in advance by a few desperate men. These men had designed this layout, with all its lanes and crossroads, and it was also the design of their own features: a weird mask leering with hatred and greed. The mask's bloodshot eyes threw sparks, the eyebrows were drawn together in a grim line, the flaccid cheeks hung down. The mouth was agape, a deep well lined with pink gums and ancient gold-capped teeth, tongue as raspy as a tiger's: mouth that inhaled greedily, that gulped air and water and food, that masticated human flesh, blood-slavered mouth of a cannibal devouring the crowd, mouth that never ceased drooling as it went through its repertory of gluttonous noises, its belches and lip-smackings. It talked, too, sometimes. Agape at the centre of the ceilings, lips distended, it said:

'Obey! Obey! Walk, buy, eat! Love one another! Drink Pils! The drink for people of good taste! Smoke! Live! Die!'

The young woman turned towards the gigantic mouth, and with her inner voice said:

'Leave me alone! I don't need you! Leave me in peace! Oh, go, please go!'

But the mouth opened even wider, like that of a fish in an aquarium, and went on filling the world with all its noises.

Hyperpolis was a face, a body. A brain, too, and the young woman called Tranquillity was travelling along that brain's winding paths, inside the labyrinth of its convolutions.

There was certainly no lack of words and thoughts. In fact, that was all there was: messages everywhere. They vibrated, exploded, lit up the air. They were not words of love. Tranquillity was walking in the midst of this rain of words, and she was frightened.

49

thunderbolt

PLATINUM
ALUMINIUM
PLATINUM
ALUMINIUM
PLATINUM
ALUMINIUM
PLATINUM

The sky is a mass of platinum
platinum panels cover the walls and
aluminium panels cover the light which
neither filters through nor illuminates
The platinum walls remain in the sun for
hours on end
yet they never get hot
sheets of whiteness so invisibly white
at the back of eyes the retinas are of
aluminium

*Terrible magical metals enveloping
metals words extracts of poverty
colourless
metals of mortal labour
icy snake-venom upon things
signed metallic words extracts of anonymous woe*

*Du Pont de Nemours's survey on Supermarkets.
Study of the speed at which eyelids blink, filmed by Vicary:
Normal rhythm: thirty-two blinks per minute
Tension: fifty to sixty per minute.
In front of the merchandise displays at supermarkets: fourteen per minute.
Vicary: 'This is a case of hypnoidal trance, the first stage of hypnosis.'
Colours that induce sleep: yellow, red.*

SHELL

METALS
INJECTED INTO THE HEART

1960 electoral campaign in the U.S.A.:
Reade & Bratten Agency for the Republicans
B. S. & J. Agency for the Democrats

SHEAFFER

the proud craftsmen
SHEAFFER, WORLD-WIDE, A TEXTRON COMPANY

WHO FROM YOUR STEEL AND GLASS OFFICES

Gerald Stahl: 'The packaging must attract and hypnotize a woman as though one
were waving a flashlamp in front of her eyes.'
'People are amazingly faithful to their brand of cigarettes, and yet when taking part
in tests they prove incapable of distinguishing it from other brands. They are really
smoking an image.'

It must have been about twenty years since she had been as frightened as this. When she had entered the world for the first time she had opened her eyes and she had seen that, or something like that. But then she had grown used to it. She had been taught, above all, not to see, and then not to listen or to feel. So the first days' vision had faded, and the world had turned into a serene picture. But one cannot keep one's eyes closed all the time. One cannot remain always out of doors. So one day, by chance, the young woman known as Tranquillity had entered Hyperpolis, and had immediately recognized the scenery. There was the same harsh lighting, the same ferocity between these walls, under this ceiling. Now the lighting had become more distinct, each detail being thrown into relief as the lights shone against the white background. The lights were etched with the very fine point of a knife.

It would be difficult to set about forgetting them all over again, and that is why the young woman was frightened. The masks had vanished, as had the nylon veils and all the wrappings. The lighting was no longer subdued. Sharp angles were no longer shielded. Hooks and stings and needles bristled.

People with sleeping faces continued to swirl to and fro in front of her. They did not see her. They gazed at her for a moment with lacklustre eyes, then looked at the tins of food and the footwear with precisely the same gaze.

The indifference shown by all these men and women was immense, while the brutal beams of light beat down upon them. Tranquillity would have liked to wake them up. She would have liked to run in front of them and wake them up. She had no idea how she could do it, but that is what she wanted. Perhaps all that was needed was to shout at each of them, just once, at the top of her voice:

'WAKE UP!'

and the people would all have woken up. On the other hand, perhaps it was like in dreams when you want to cry out but

51

nothing emerges from your throat, or else something does come out of your mouth but nobody hears it. Perhaps it was already too late.

And Tranquillity imagined that she was awake when in fact she herself was already sleeping deeply. The people were passing by on the other side of her sleep, and their faces were filled with peace. All the women were young and beautiful, their hair was the colour of gold or copper or jet, and they walked effortlessly on their supple legs.

Tranquillity watched the women moving along in front of her, and tried to imitate their gait. But she kept on running into things: a barrier of light, or else enormous objects that blocked the way. She had never seen such beautiful and frightening objects in such profusion. There were mountains that were blue and others that were red, transparent icebergs, glaciers, volcanoes, sequoias, buildings, cliffs; they rose into the sky without a break, protected by their impassable walls of pasteboard or plastic. They carried big letters, a purple Z or S, and gigantic numbers, an 8, a 3, a 5, that barricaded space. Tranquillity passed in front of them, and she could feel the weight of these signs on the nape of her neck and on her shoulders. She made detours round the obstacles, and made efforts not to read what was written on them. But strident voices hidden in the objects suddenly surged forth and bellowed the message in her ear, with such crisp vowels and such cruel consonants (especially the 'k's and the 'ch's) that Tranquillity felt the words enter her, despite herself, and creep down into the pit of her stomach.

The young woman called Tranquillity was no longer walking: she was swimming. By fluttering her fins she could glide slowly along, through the water full of bubbles and seaweed. There were many new and unknown species, rare platinum-coloured seashells, golden crabs, hermit-crabs, madrepores, rainbow-hued anemones. Tranquillity swam through the troubled waters. With wide-open eyes, she watched the submarine landscape take shape round her. She seemed to be in a sort of aquarium far beneath the earth's surface, a cavern of dark water peopled with phosphorescent creatures. Molluscs slid very slowly over the slimy bottom. Jellyfish sank downwards, agitating their frayed parachutes. There were black holes containing octopuses poised to whip their rolled-up tentacles forward. The water was thick and heavy, without current or eddies. The light glimmered fitfully through the gloom, leaving pockets of darkness, blobs of dim emptiness in which everything dissolved, as though in a stomach. It was strange and dangerous, to navigate like that, in this aquarium. All the time, traps opened up with suckers, pincers, mandibles, antennae. Tranquillity watched, in fascination, the unknown monsters that moved along beside her. She saw gaping mouths fringed with warts and moustaches, and it was as though a part of her was already dissolving. She heard sounds running through the water, quicker than through air, and the impact reverberated in her body.

But it was not exactly water, perhaps, that made up the atmosphere of Hyperpolis. It was not air, either. Breathing was so difficult that it was hard to tell what it was. Perhaps it was a sort of gastric juice that filled the immense sac in which one was imprisoned: yes, a liquid secreted by thousands of little glands hidden everywhere, in the walls, the floor, the ceiling. As one moved forward, each step, each gesture became an agonizing experience. One gradually lost one's limbs, one's hair, one's skin; one was in the process of being digested. That was the horrifying thing. Slowly, and without inflicting wounds, the juice filling the great store's sac was eating you away, reducing your fat to liquid. Even objects did not escape this fate. Each flash of light was a cry of pain, the nylon fabrics writhed into knots, the cellophane wrappings melted, the plastics seethed. Everything round the young woman called Tranquillity was in the process of burning. But it was a slow process: things were sizzling and smouldering quite gently as they burnt away. The beautiful white surfaces beneath Tranquillity's feet were becoming carbonized. The pillars were sweating, the ceiling was dewed with steam, and people's faces gave off smoke. Perhaps the burning originated in all these flashing beacons? The light was a corrosive acid; the sounds spread out their waves and liquefied matter. The hidden eyes of the cameras mounted at the tops of the pillars recorded all this, and transmitted the terrible images on to screens: then the men who had planned all this from the beginning, the damnable ones, protected their eyes with thick-lensed dark glasses, for fear of being blinded by the combustion.

The young woman called Tranquillity emerged from the zone of counters. She must have been walking across Hyperpolis for hours, although there was no way of knowing, since there was nothing here to indicate the time. The ceiling remained a grey vault filled with motionless flashes. Neither the pillars nor the walls ever changed colour. The floor was the same as ever, smooth and luminous. So it was impossible to tell what hour it was, or even what day. Far away, at the other end of the hall, there were doors and windows. Tranquillity turned round to look at them. But they were tinted panels that the outside light could not penetrate.

Suddenly a sort of public square opened up in front of her, with a pair of escalators flanking an imitation fountain. Beside the fountain stood the kiosk with its placard reading:

INFORMATION

and beside the placard sat a young woman who was Tranquillity's friend.

People moved round this open space as though it was a mirror. They glided over it, looking exactly like flies. They covered the space with their legs and their arms, all perfectly alike, nameless, mindless, existing solely in their actions.

Tranquillity stopped at the edge of the open space, and watched the movements of the crowd. Here, too, one could sense a pervading fear. It was not the same fear that had surrounded her a short while before, when she was moving through the sizzling lights. But it was a special kind of fear, the sort that underlies one's reaction to a road accident, for example, or the sight of a drowned man. It was something that went beyond individual possibilities, something that entered into you and tore out speech, tore out feelings, tore out everything.

Tranquillity tried to fix her attention on some person, no matter whom, just one person; but it was impossible. The silhouettes moved, passed each other, disappeared ceaselessly. Occasional clearings were visible between the clumps of bodies, and far off, over there, at the opposite edge of the open space, one caught a glimpse of a woman with a very pale face and black hair, wearing a violet dress. Then the bodies closed their wall again, and the woman wearing violet had vanished for ever. FOR EVER.

Or else, somewhere among the frizzing and frothing of heads, a man wearing dark glasses lit a cigarette. For a second it was possible to see the sharply etched profile, the lips drawn taut round the white cigarette, the oddly shaped crease round the mouth as his hand brought the match up towards the cigarette.

Or else, suddenly, this fattish grey-faced woman appeared just in front of the young woman and started staring at her. These were all brutal apparitions that immediately melted back into the throng, fading like reflections. The crowd had thousands of faces, thousands of eyes. But they evaporated FOR EVER, and it was as though nothing had ever been there.

Shadows, perhaps. The young woman called Tranquillity began to walk through the open space, scarcely touching the other bodies as she passed between them. She did not even see them. No one saw anyone else. Faces were tense, eyes avoided meeting other eyes. No doubt the young woman had become invisible by now. That would have explained a number of things. But the anonymous crowd had other instincts functioning: it moved as though on rails, like a swirl of magnetized particles. At the other end of the open space there was a knot of people round the kiosk, a group rising up in the right-hand escalator, and a similar group descending in the left-hand escalator. That was how it was.

55

It was terrible to have to move round among these phantoms. Tranquillity looked up towards the ceiling, trying to locate the apertures behind which the hidden cameras were filming all the time. The damnable masters were doubtless seated before their grey screens, watching the insects scurrying over the ground, while electronic eyes calculated their numbers.

... density 6   density 7   density 3   density 8 ...

And on the highways, calculators must be clicking away at lightning speed, recording the passage of all the rubber tyres.

Nine vehicles per second, 4 vehicles per second, 12 vehicles per second ... And in the sky, helicopters were hovering, photographing the human caravans; and indoors, folding-screens concealed cameras that spied pitilessly and indefatigably on the motions of hands and faces.

Never had there been so much hatred. Inside Hyperpolis, beneath the ceiling, between the walls, in the white labyrinths, the hatred was swollen, pressing out with all its strength. It was the hatred exuding from the damnable ones, those who had decided to conquer the insect populations, to become masters of their lives.

Tranquillity fled as fast as she could through the throng. She could hardly breathe, the air was so charged with hatred. She could hardly open her eyes, the light shone with such fierce hatred. And she had to stop up her ears with her hands so as not to hear the soft voices of the electric women that murmured inside her head, that lived inside her belly and talked, talked, talked:

'... Youth ... Beauty ... Your sparkling complexion. ... Your skin ... Vinyl your second skin ... Fiendish colours ... Breasts ... Soft soft hands ... Creams ... Panty-hose ... Pure water ... So so gentle ... Music ... Buy ... Close your eyes ... Let yourself be taken ... Seduction ... Perfume ... Cold colours ... Warm colours ... Colours that burn ... Beauty ... Youth ... Beauty ...'

WOOOOOL   WOOOOOL

56

That is how the young woman called Tranquillity finally reached the kiosk on which was written:

INFORMATION

She leant against the white counter for a moment, incapable of speech. Then her friend got up, came over to her, took her hand.

'What's the matter? What's the matter?'

But Tranquillity made a sign to her to be quiet, and pointed above her head to where the microphone was hidden in the lamp's disc, recording everything they said. Then she pointed to a spot beside her where through an aperture the camera lens was busy filming them.

I wanted to tell you this, too: consciousness is a bad thing. Consciousness is a dead thing. Free yourselves from consciousness! It is high time. All that is needed is to strip off this garment: nothing very difficult about that. Tear the skin from your body, for it is not a true skin, it is a cellophane tissue that blocks the pores, that asphyxiates. Peel the tissue off: peel it off.

But perhaps consciousness is no longer possible in any case. Where are the clear brightly lit landscapes? There is no conflagration-keeper. There is no cyclone-watchman. Wherever I turn my eyes I can see nothing else but that: the incomprehensible, tumult, depth. Signs have roots that bore right through the earth. Objects are like icebergs: one can only perceive the small fragment that rises above the surface. Trees, plants, clouds, raindrops, no matter what, birds, islands, mountains are all fathomless abysses, hollow teeth with roots that stretch down for ever. To be conscious, then, was to exist within appearance, only within appearance. Basically, it was a fairly futile game, a game played solely for thought processes and the words of a language. Then, one day, one sees strange disquieting shadows gliding just beneath the surface, shadows that one does not recognize. One day, one discovers that behind towns' street-plans lie labyrinths that one follows just like everyone else, treading in the others' footsteps. One thought one would never be fooled. One thought one was safe. But it was an error. One was with the others, following the same set of rails, moving forward, going continually from point x to point y, then coming back again.

Enough of all that! Who is who? No one can answer, no one can affirm anything. But time extends its span, recovers everything for itself, desires everything. There is more time and space than the mind of a young woman could ever imagine. There is more matter, here, there, everywhere, than there are words in the languages of mankind. So who dares speak of consciousness? Who still dares say:

'I ... '

'As for me, I ... '

'I think that ... I say ... I write ... '

There was this desire to draw a circle round a face, a landscape, a plant, no matter what. The aim was to find a design corresponding to thought, that is to say, corresponding to what the eyes see. Or else a word, a word that was supposed to become detached from its wall, when ripe, and fall, at a single stroke, at the right moment and in the right place. But nothing came. Or rather, everything came in disorder, crazily, uncomprehendingly, unanalysed.

Where are the human beings? Is there a man, woman or child who is not also a tree and a flying-fox?

The faces have vanished in the mist, have become intermingled, and henceforth it is impossible to stare at any of them! A forest of faces, and the signs of autonomy have disappeared. In such conditions, how can one speak of consciousness? Is it not preferable to speak of the rain, the sea, the clouds, or else the adventures of a young woman in a food store? Is it not preferable to speak of such things as buildings under construction, quarries, towns and iron bridges?

Truth of madness, truth of doubt. Truth of falsehood, even, since it uses words as weapons. Aarh! Aaah-aaarh! Something is constricting the throat. Something is preventing the lungs from breathing in and out. Something, or someone? How to tell? Where to turn the eyes, towards what enemy, when there are simply these identical photographs scattered everywhere, tiny photos showing the same face a hundred times, a thousand times? Looking for the enemy. Squatting behind a bush, keeping a lookout. Eyes smarting, bloodshot, from searching the shadows. Let the enemy appear, at last! Let him show himself! Let him uncoil his snake-like body, let him send out his fiery breath. But nothing appears. The hard landscapes of stone and sun and icy water do not open up. They remain impenetrable. Right in front of me there are, *there are* A HUNDRED THOUSAND CLOSED DOORS.

The faces have melted away, and their names too. They have swept across the earth, from one end to the other, leaving their flashing traces in their wake. All is possible, at last. If consciousness is gone for ever, it means that all is permitted! Vision sees itself and slays itself. The truth that darts from eyes is a bullet, one that slays, yet reveals nothing. I wanted to tell you: gouge out your eyes! But what would be the use, since there remains all that one sees without the eyes, with the analysing gaze that does not dwell in the eyelids' nest, but lies enclosed within the head, dead gaze like the eyes of fish in grottoes. Eyes that did not see but sent out an endless series of little messages, sequences of little squeaks busily probing space! Those are eyes? Absurd! Even caterpillars have something more like eyes, when they rear up in the direction of the sun and paw the air with their six front legs. Even oysters and jellyfish, newts and termites have something more like eyes.

So suddenly the world has emptied itself of its eyes. They are all gone. See, the world, that was already deaf and dumb, is now blind as well. Nothing sends out glances any more. A few vague ocular globes lost behind the screen of sunglasses, and then a few ocelli, a few palpi. But probably eyes, what one calls eyes, had never really existed. The belief in them was part of the same distant past that believed that thought was invincible.

It had been decreed that man's face should harbour these two blazing suns, which should project their light onto the world. Far more terrible than suns, far brighter still. Laser beams that stabbed holes through armour-plating and pierced infinity through and through. Eyes, beacons: and the light they carried was the light of thought. Perhaps it was once like that. Then the darkness was able to draw back, and each person became his own prophet. But today that light is extinguished, and the gaze no longer traverses the universe. There are no more suns. Faces are grey, faces are blind. They are turned towards each other, and in place of eyes, in place of beacons, there are merely two glaucous dim-hued globules. Two glass marbles filled with filaments and bubbles, hidden between crumpled eyelids. The dilated pupils no longer dart lightning-flashes. They are dull, humid, swivelling smoothly in their sockets, desperately *trying to see*.

What do they see? Slow tentacles adhering to the world's visions and sucking them. Uncover the loopholes again! Advance under cover! Vision desires, above all, to leave its home, once, just once. Vision desires to catch up with the real landscape, by a leap as fast as light. There is enormous energy behind the eyeballs. Thought desires to unite itself with the real, just as a shadow attaches itself to an object. But the walls are vast; doors, shutters, blinds, fortifications. World lined with concrete, armour-plated, protected by its carapaces. World that continually refuses. So? Is it possible that intelligence does not in fact exist?

I would like to ask you to slay thought. Unable to go beyond itself, what good was it? Since eyes were unable to be beacons, and remained clouded with doubt, hide them behind dark glasses and never look directly at anything again. Since eyes have looked at a plant, a geranium in its pot, and yet the plant has neither moved nor grown; since eyes have stared into other eyes, those men in the throes of killing, or those of women in the throes of dying, and the inner voice has repeated furiously a thousand times, from deep in its throat, the magic sentence:

YOU SHALL SLEEP!

and all of this has served no useful purpose. A curse upon the eyes: let them never be mentioned again.

But thought could not leave the skull, nothing could leave its home without the slow vehicle of words. What kind of thought process was it, then, that was unable even to breach the fragile rampart of a single skin? Was that all that man's notoriously great power amounted to? Individual, mediocre individual, kind of fortified body! And mediocre thoughts! It is necessary to look outwards. Not, any longer, with eyes like extinguished beacons, nor with thoughts like imprisoned bubbles; but with one's whole body, and the bodies of others. With the thoughts of rocks, and the thoughts of trees, and the thoughts of dogs, and the thoughts of shoals of fish and flocks of birds.

For thought exists, and it is not the thought of a single man or a single woman. There is no intelligence, no genius. There is this immensely open gaze, everywhere, this gaze emanating from the real. There is this thought process enveloping the whole of matter, residing in it, in each of its molecules.

I no longer know any individual beings. The frontiers have crumbled of their own accord, without any fuss. They were merely spiders' webs. Communication was immeasurable: constantly in action, linking lives, blending gestures. Who dares still talk of frontiers? From one end of the world to the other, and even elsewhere, there is only a single man in the process of living. From one end of time to the other. Is that not admirable? Is that not enigmatic?

Then Captain Tecum took flight. He had turned himself into an eagle, covered with feathers that sprouted out of him. Captain Tecum's intention was to slay Tunadiu who was making his way on horseback to Adelantado. He succeeded in cutting off the horse's head with his lance. It was not an iron lance, but a lance made of little mirrors, and the captain used magic in his proceedings ...

A. de Rochas:
'Occultism will be the science of the twentieth century.'

> *So karohi dīpam attano*
> *khippaṁ vāyama, paṇḍito bhava*

'Is this the moment to deliver a lecture, Professor?'
(Blek le Roc)

The child whose nickname was Dumb Bogo would have liked nothing better than to be able to speak. But he did not know how. He opened his mouth and strained his vocal cords, but words never came. He often listened to others talking, the other children, his parents, people in the street. He listened to them all the time, without seeming to, looking away. He stared at the tips of his shoes, he chewed bubble-gum, and he listened eagerly to what people were saying. He listened to the radio, too, and television. Sometimes, in the street, he passed in front of a shop window, and on the other side there would be a loudspeaker busy talking. Then Dumb Bogo listened with all his might, and the words echoed in his head. There were terrible words like 'crushing', 'smash', 'ice', extraordinary ones like 'comet', 'dustbin', 'height', 'granite', 'dugong', long words like 'paraoxybenzoate', 'catalepsy', 'anthropomorphism', throttling words like 'hive', 'choppy', 'infarctation', word-traps like 'flying saucer', 'prime ribs', 'aerodrome', meaningless words like 'prism', 'cell', 'treasure', rapid words like 'here', 'seen', 'O.K.', intoxicating words like 'cinema', 'Jerusalem', 'otitis', 'Montevideo'. So many words. They streamed endlessly from all the openings, loudspeakers, air-conditioning outlets, tubes, car radiators, gateways, darkened windows.

The child whose nickname was Dumb Bogo spent whole days listening to words, and silently repeating them with his throat. He learnt them by heart, packs of vowels and consonants shuffled together in ever changing sequences. Words came from

67

all sides to enter into him, to take root in his body. Certain hard consonants took root in his spinal column, near the nape of the neck. Others, the Ls, for example, or the Ys, tended to lodge themselves in his legs and his fingers. They alighted on him, and at once he felt them move down his thighs, or expand inside his knuckles. He opened and closed his hands, and when words such as Lollabee or Ilyrewick or Atoll arrived, that is where they came to rest. Other sounds, the Ws, the OOs, the YAs, the Gs, the Js installed themselves elsewhere. It all depended. Sometimes, when the word was emitted in broad daylight, he felt the sounds cling to his hair, or hang from his cheeks, like strings of vermicelli. The Us, the GRRs, the KRRs, the ZZZs, the SH and TH sounds entered deeply, somewhere in the region of the lower abdomen. The FFs sometimes clustered round the anus. The mms, nns, nyurs, angs, oins, nas and nos settled down quite easily in the lungs, or remained entangled in the nasal fossae. The ongs, in certain words pronounced by grave voices, or by television announcers, coiled up behind the ears, and then it was difficult to detach them from the base of the skull. But the most terrible of all the sounds were certain vowels. They reverberated so powerfully that the small boy swallowed them with his mouth. They descended into his stomach and swelled up there; sometimes they remained there for hours, stirring inside his stomach, expanding like gases. These were the As of ALABAMA or ARIZONA, the Is of HINDERNISSE, or the Os of ROMEO.

This could take place anywhere, any time. Then the terrible vowels with their overpowering sounds would rush in through his open mouth and force their way right through to the stomach. Once there, they began to press against his diaphragm, and the small boy felt suffocated.

That was why words were dangerous. Those who had invented them had never imagined that the words might enter the body, making the heart beat faster and disturbing vision like that, simply as a result of their sounds being pronounced.

The small boy called Dumb Bogo listened to the people

round him talking, and he was frightened. He closed his mouth, pressing the lips tight together to stop the vowels entering, but he knew quite well that they were watching for the moment when he would have to part his lips slightly to breathe, or chew the bubble-gum, and then they would pounce.

The people were saying:

'ThAt's It! ThAt's It!'

'WhAAt? WhAAt d'you mEAn?'

'SO y' sEEE, I mEt HAArrY at the sYOOpermarket, and he tOld me that his wIIIfe'

'YEs, Oh yEs ... '

'Come alOng! Quick! QuIIIck!'

Sometimes, someone in the centre of the crowd would stop with mouth wide-open and yell:

'AntOOOnia!'

'Mah-AH-AH-AH-jry!'   'SYYYbYYYl!'

and the small boy would have to stuff his fingers into his ears, close his mouth and hold his breath, to prevent these terrible noises from entering.

It was difficult not to listen to people. As you may have noticed, people talk a lot. There they are, the whole time, standing on the edge of the pavement, or else in shops, cafés, restaurants, churches, even the cemetery, talking and talking and talking. No way of knowing what people are saying. In passing by, it is possible to intercept snatches of conversation, isolated words and letters, before they fly away. But those few seconds will not make you any the wiser. The mouths are open, the whole time, at the bottom of the faces, pouring out words.

The small boy called Dumb Bogo was very afraid of mouths. It was the first thing that he watched out for in a man's face. He fixed his gaze on the fissure with its two pinkish-purplish-blue pads streaked with little cracks, and watched it in dread. The mouths almost never came to rest. They were always in the throes of moving, opening, closing, stretching, with their two quivering lips and the wrinkles at each side. Inside the mouths there was a tongue rather like a fat red slug, and teeth, and gums, and pearly glands that salivated. The glottis trembled at the end of its stalactite; the tongue darted to and fro in the humid cavern, struck against the teeth, slapped the palate, vibrated, uncoiled itself, licked the lips.

That was all astonishing, and even a little alarming. Dumb Bogo watched all the mouths round him, and listened attentively to the noises they were making. Then with his own mouth, but in a whisper, he repeated what he had heard. That was not talking, of course. That was imitating noises, like the parrots in cages hung outside the doors of cafés, that spend the day shrieking out their mimicry of the sound of the coffee percolator, the sound of spoons stirring the cups, the sound of the cash register, or the sound of people drinking Pepsi-Cola through a straw.

'Pchchchchch'

  'Lwip! Lwip!'

   'Hing!'

    'Rak-rak-rak-rak'

     'Ooooof, ooooof'

That was exactly how Dumb Bogo liked to talk. But naturally no one understood what he was saying.

Meanwhile the people continued their discussions. For instance, they sat down on a bench in the sun, in a garden. Round them were trees, and the wind made the noise of water as it passed through the leaves. In a square plot filled with sand, small children shrieked as they worked. Cars circled the garden, giving occasional blasts on their horns: they were looking for parking spaces, or petrol stations. Dumb Bogo plumped down on a bench, too, and listened to the conversations. Since he was some way away he did not manage to hear everything that was said. Scraps of sentences were sent floating towards him by the wind, while other scraps vanished, swallowed up by the other noises.

This was more or less what Dumb Bogo heard:

'ffiKult RRascals, chIldren, y'nO, 'n thEn you've gotta remEmber'

'hm-hmm'

70

'c'n sEE it, but Inside where we cAAn't sEE, nUthing
sIm'lar exiSSts, nUthing.'

'yeSS, I thIIInk Iun'rstan'

'yes I nÔÔÔ'

'sO thIngs at prEsent are static' T'K T'K

waaaaaaaaaaaaaaaak

'which phOtOs?'

hawk hawk hawk hawk hawk hawk

'watcha dOOin' there?'

'er-whom, t'her, wa-hE, MMM, too, ohOh'm'

'what ACKsh'lly hEppened?'   HONK! HONK!

' 've already sEEn it — not thIs one — thIs one isn't PUBlished
yet.'

'*never* have children they'

'So Whey On Eurth Did Miss Mary Go Owt Raiding?'

'JACKson!'

'What was she doing on that road?' 'But good heavens what
did she *do* after she ran him over?'

'thaaanks — anks'   HO-O-ONGH   ATCHAAA!!!

'er o-ing ong er wun auw'r skersh'n'

'ha-ha-ha'

'yesyes'   brrrmmm, brrrmmm, brrrrooooaaaaaa ...

'which of the two?'

'A-Uhn. Iy-Ay-Im!'

KSHTANG

'might've broken's neck. 'magine. 'agine.'

'yeSS'   YOOHOO   ARNGG! ARNGG!

'o i 'n ardly 'lieve 't, 'ot'n aPPAWling thing!'

'er, you want it, the er wotchermercallit?'

'bah,   voooo'   ooooooooooooooooooooooooooooooooMM ...

'this morning, euh, yesterday, no, no, day before yesterday,
euh, and euh ...'

'an eel ee ade oo ook reDIIlous, y'no, unnERdov, slootly
unnERdov'

'Who *are* the Perrys?'

TOOOT

'I had to wait for the verdiCTBefore I could leave Berlin.'

'Huh? Hoh-noh! Eye mazkah merndlew sidazaSLEE pingFIsh.'

Wiiiiiiiiiiiiiiii!

haw!haw!haw!haw!haw!haw!haw!

'Kil-kuit ... Ballatore ... Salvadori ... Eichgeminian ... Kasurian ... Tokura.'

''sbut it all Depends On Time, yKNow, talld'pnds'

'ach!'   'have you got the sun ...'   SUNSOL

'it was white' 'it was white' 'it was white' 'it was, heuh, white'

'WHat's More, the PS ... the PS ... the teST ... has prodUced the KOefficient 116'

'KOeffent v'integence 116, it was PROFer PRÔÔer PIC who made piCARD that teST, its the RRCHRDT TSTest, dr-ROcher, the TEST of PskOm Otor mobility, TSest of VIS VIJ viSION, jion, heuh, ah-ach, yeMAdam, AP AP-tititude, and so on and so forth, insuf-insufficient GREE 'f salivation, but above ALL NÔÔÔT 'st WUN comPLEEt surdity, rEEflex, motor, ORmal, SKZOYd schiZOYd, abRRRang, impOSSibility. So of course he said, he SAID, sgoint'be NESry neCESSry ESessary to emplOY nArcoanALYSIS, NARCÔÔÔ ANALL ASISS, y'know, make kntkt thro PENTÔÔÔthl. Imean'nth'-lOngrun, its b'n Used its prodUCEd certain BLAAAH HWANGANGANG'

KchTANG — HONG — DAK!

'Zittafiat?'

'Riving inna FOR FALc'n?'

JAAAA NIIIII

'Valways said snuth'ng lika FREnch caaaw.'

But that was not all. The small boy got up and walked away. After a bit he found himself walking in a street, in the sun, and words emerged from the walls of houses and from the ground and came to meet him. He had to be on his guard the whole time, because everywhere there were mouths shouting words into your face. Cars passed, with loudspeakers on the roof, yelling out:

WUNNER BA'ERIES ARE JUSS WUNNERFUL
WUNNERFUL WUNNERFUL
or else:

  'Speshul barg-yens terdie't eyperpolliss syewpamark't doan
    miss yer big chaaance
  Famly-size bo'els o' pepssscola nyoozeel'n buttah makrowni
  Kaliforn-yen strorbriz tin pine'pple chunks strite fr'm th'
    Eyevry Kowst'

In the red and black caverns of the bars, the juke-boxes reverberated, and the shrill voices of young women could be heard
singing above the dark rhythms of the electric guitars:

  Tha'ss whY-Y-Y tha'ss whY-Y-Y tha'ss whY-Y-Y
  kchtai-ai-ai hé-hi ai-ai-ai-ai
  'minLU-U-UV

Sometimes, too, inside the bakelite boxes of television sets, a
man's voice would begin to speak. What the voice said was
confused, and the face of the man on the screen was so
emotionless that one could hear the words falling, one after
the other, like drops of rain. The man intoned, in his solemn
voice:

    A foss of some tharty thows'nd merik'n saowth vyetn'meze
montanYAAHD 'n kh-KHma-air troops has bEEn engAged
since yest'day marning in s'vyah fayting in KH-cambo-odia
agenst combaynd fosses of nawth vyetn'meze vyet KÔÔÔng
'n KHHmair ROU-ouges — Baysst in the saowth vyetn'meze
prOv'nces of TAY-münh-h-h 'n BING-lôôông the foss
incLEWds a crek merik'n mObIle Unit dispOsing of mAssive
far pa'r — the first merik'n AIr CAV'lry d'viszj'n ass well
assa saowth vyetn'meze pErachUte reJm'nt — these hev
bEEn AIrlIfted to kamBOdya bay hEliKopter where th'
comBAYnd op'RAYsh'n is d'ZAYnd to enSIRcle the
headQUARters of the EFF-ENN-EEL 'stAblishd to the
saowth-EEst 'fth' FREnch plaaantaysh'n 'f Hévéaaas
dMIIInot — dyar'ng a fyew OWerz 'f fEYEting sEVenty-
sEVen nawth vyetn'meze were kIIlled end a hUndr'd end
Ate wOOnded. eKKording to an amEriK'n spoKesm'n —

merik'n kezualtiz k'mpRAYz WUN sOldya wOOnded
contINyewd the spOKEsm'n

The small boy heard all these voices around him. But they were foreign languages to him, and there was no way of understanding what they were trying to say. People all spoke in these unknown languages, and pretended to understand each other, but obviously they were lying.

For instance, Dumb Bogo entered a big building and walked across the hall. At the end of the corridor decorated with mirrors and fake marble were three lift doors. Many people were waiting in front of the doors, men wearing mouse-grey suits and women wearing identical floral dresses. Above the metal doors indicators flashed lights on and off, and a bell rang at intervals. The people looked up at the indicators, and at the green and red winking arrows; they pressed the buttons, and they waited. Meanwhile they stubbed out their cigarettes in chromium-plated tubs filled with sand.

The small boy watched the whole scene anxiously, especially the tubs of sand. They were like miniature stone-filled gardens, deserts in mid air. Perhaps the whole earth was made like that: fag-end buildings stuck upright in the grey sand, and match-stick steamboats, and ash-dust human beings.

Then there was a great noise, the metal doors opened, and an aluminium cage came into view. People emerged from the cage, thrusting a path through the waiting throng, then went away. The others retreated a couple of steps. When the cage was empty they all trooped in, and Dumb Bogo went in with them. The iron doors closed gently again, and inside the cage a lot of buttons began to light up.

The cage was a nacelle. Now it was rising up, up. Effortlessly, almost noiselessly, it was gliding upwards. Most probably they were all inside a bubble that was in the process of creeping up a mercury tube. The metal-walled cage trembled slightly. Dumb Bogo watched the people's faces, and it was extraordinary because even now their mouths were talking. Each one was speaking his own language, just like that, and the crazy

74

words reverberated in the close air. The harsh neon light illuminated pates and shoulders, and inserted pockets of shadow under eyes. The men and women talked away as they stood in the soaring nacelle.

'Vas schonous chnasso, vas carbon, gosha ...'

'Boe har yer gonner stey long?'

'Koeshrr.'

'Nay, nay ...'

'Kombyen, ha, sa, alôr jlui dis, impossib, impossib quoi.'

'Ar?'

'Syesye.'

'Sängpe püra purudebema seyka?'

'Nüngnunema, mae, mae!'

'A-long-korn, a-long-head, 'n' nsay no go.'

' 'strue.'

'Wanem haouadem massah.'

'Psssssclaaro.'

'... Radjan florin almeïn.'

'He welle, zaounds leykit, jorj. Ah sey jorj.'

'Qu'est-ce que vous en pensez?'

'Wellgosh wellgosh.'

'Pasuli.'

'Maï pen 'raï, kap.'

And while they talked, the iron nacelle rose up and up, pursuing its course in space, up as far as the summit of the tower of Babel, perhaps, and the neon light sent glints off people's hair or their bald pates, and their eyes were invisible in their pockets of shadow, and the buttons flashed lights, one after the other, very fast, and the child whose name was Dumb Bogo listened to all the crazy words that crossed each other's path, all these mouths and alien languages that sought in vain to meet.

It is related that there is an imperishable asvattha: *its roots reach upwards, and its branches reach downwards, and each leaf is a hymn from the Vedas; he who knows this tree, knows the Vedas. Its branches spread out in height and in depth, pressing against the* guna; *its buds are the sense-objects; at its base its root divide, entwine themselves around acts, then plunge into the world of men.*

One day, Tranquillity's girlfriend was in a car crossing through a zone filled with writing of various kinds. It was night-time, somewhere near the centre of the great unknown city, and the scene was quite terrifying. Both terrifying and marvellous, to be more accurate.

The young woman was on her way to meet her friend Tranquillity at the Hyperpolis main exit, and she was driving her car fairly fast through the streets. It was night-time. That is to say, the sky had turned dark, and the sun was no longer visible. But inside the city it was always day. Light flowed from many lamps, making weird concentric waves, like mosquitoes on the surface of ponds.

The car, too, produced light. It glided along the streets with its headlamps switched on, passing other headlamps and red lights and winking lights and cat's-eye reflectors and metallic reflections. There were so many lights that one needed dark glasses to save the eyes from being blinded. The dark glasses that Tranquillity's friend was wearing had a metal frame, and the lenses were pale green.

Everything was very harsh at that moment, in the city. Sheets of aluminium rose one above the other. The walls of the buildings on either side of the road were armour-plated. The black surface over which the rubber tyres rolled was a dull metal that gave off no reflections. The cars made hoarse noises as they passed over it, and the pedestrians struck echoes from the metal studs on the soles of their shoes, as they made their way along the pavements. There was no wind, and although it was night the heat lay heavy. The young woman was driving with the car windows open, and she could smell the odour of the gases that were entering her lungs. There was even a sort of very fine dust hanging in the air: clouds of microscopic metal filings, sent swirling up by the wheels of passing cars.

It was really rather frightening to cross through this whole iron landscape, inside a car, like that, when one's own body was made of tender flesh. Each moment there was the risk of dying perforated by metal points, or of having the throat and carotid arteries laid bare by the jagged rims of empty food-tins. The street bristled with spikes, claws and hooks all shining with fierce sparks of light, and it needed careful steering to manoeuvre the car through without hitting any of them. Above the main doors of certain buildings were things like garlands of cast iron, set with talons, and from time to time, no doubt, absent-minded pedestrians struck their heads against them and died on the spot, there on the pavement. Or else the Pontiacs' radiator grilles sent their bayonet-shaped emblems hissing up into the air, and passers-by had to jump quickly backwards to avoid being impaled.

Those were just the overt signs of violence: the lightning conductors, arrows, pounding-machines, pneumatic drills, beaked scoops, broken-bottle ends, daggers. But there were covert forms as well, and these were more terrible still because there was no defence against them. There were things harder than steel and sharper than razor blades, secret things, fangs concealed inside jaws, thoughts longing to kill and smash, words and musical notations and drawings all stalking their prey. These were the things that the young woman feared the most, because she never knew how they arrived, nor from where, nor why. The car glided along on its rubber tyres, and the young woman peered anxiously through the windscreen, watching out for the approach of these demonic forms.

They slid along the bonnet and windscreen, then along the car's side panels, reversing their motion in the driving mirror.

Tranquillity's girlfriend was inside a capsule travelling in the depths of the Mariana trench, or some such spot.

The letters of fire danced. They abandoned their frames on the drab walls and came fluttering towards the car. They were not really letters but giant moths that had blinded each other. They swooped aimlessly across the road, glowing, flickering out, tracing sarabands of light. Tranquillity's friend watched them, scared but at the same time wonderstruck. They were really beautiful moths, their mottled black wings shimmering with golden stars, spangles, drops of blood. Their strange eyes, like dimly glowing green diamonds, floated in the hazy air. Their antennae were immense and resembled fern fronds. It was all strange and alarming. The car, its windows now rolled up, drove straight through these storm clouds. The car's headlamps riddled them, then the radiator grille and windscreen crushed them. The car hurtled along the street, trying to slaughter as many moths as possible.

But it was impossible to kill them all: there were too many. In a never-ending stream, they surged out of the angles of walls, leapt from windows and doorways, flowed like smoke out of all these dark mouths. Outside the windscreen, the wipers hissed upwards and downwards as fast as they could go, to clear away the dead moths. But now they had turned into an army of bats jostling each other in the night and scattering their whiteish droppings.

But the most terrifying thing of all was the silence. Everything was happening without a single noise of any kind. The letters burst a few inches away from the girl's face, yet she heard nothing. Fearful gaps yawned open all along the street, and lightning flashed across the black sky: but the thunder never came. Various kinds of volcanoes and stars and suns exploded, filling the whole city with a red glow. Or else, yellow zebra markings turned into dotted lines and raced onwards as quick as thought, quicker than thought. But the universe, space, the sea split into two without even a cracking sound. It was alarming because it was as if all this was happening inside the head, or inside a book, and the bunker's thick walls refused to crumble and fall. It was worse, in a way: it was like silent noises. You see, there was so much force, such relentless passion, so much hatred, yet nothing reached the heart. Nothing spoke. Nothing said anything.

Tranquillity's friend strained to listen, leaning over the steering-wheel and cocking an ear forwards. Inside the car, the only sounds were the soft throbbing of the engine, the squeal of the tyres against the road surface, and the whoosh of cars passing in the opposite direction. The flying letters said nothing.

There were so many letters, even more letters than there are bats inside a cave. There were so many letters that everything was blotted out: sky, earth, houses and human faces.

Tranquillity's friend did not recognize all of them: some were alien letters that did not belong to any earthly writing system, and that was a frightening and intoxicating realization. They gushed from every opening, they soared sparkling into the black air. Then they swept down again, from each side of the roadway, on to the passing vehicles' bodies, like a smouldering rain. They struck the outside of her car silently, eating away at the metal with their acids. Their aim was to corrode and dissolve everything. The people outside who had not had time to take shelter, those who were not carrying an umbrella and were unable to find a convenient doorway, ran grave risks. Perhaps all these letters were about to exterminate mankind without further ado. First they would strike with all their dots and points at people's eyes, and in an instant the pale faces would be blind, displaying two bleeding holes in place of eye sockets. Then the letters would strike at mouths, and nostrils, and foreheads; they would slip under people's clothes, and penetrate the body by way of the navel, the pores of the skin, the anus, the penis, or the womb. They were armed for just that purpose, they were specially designed to rape and kill and corrode.

Tranquillity's friend watched the letters from behind the windscreen. She thought to herself: if only I can see a few of the

letters, and identify them properly, then it will all stop. That
was the thought that went through her mind.

But it was difficult. There were too many of them, and they
seemed mostly to be consonants. At intervals, an enormous red
letter could be seen suspended momentarily in mid-air

S

before exploding and diffusing a yellowish glow in which each
particle was a tiny febrile letter like a diatom. Or else a procession
of black signs crossed the road slowly, like a flight of jackdaws.

lllllnnnddrrrfrrhhhhhhhhhhqtsbdjjjjjjjmmmmmbmmm

Like that, changing ceaselessly. Now gigantic letters filled the
whole of space, while other letters appeared and disappeared
round them, and the ground was covered with illegible signs,
and the walls were like great posters swarming with a text that
underwent continual metamorphosis.

The young woman had been driving her car through the
signs for a long time now. She could not even remember, any
longer, how it had all started. She tried to remember, so that
she could understand, and she said out aloud:

'Let's see ... Let's see ... How did it happen ... We'll see ...'
But the letters allowed her no time for reflection. They swept
against the windscreen in increasingly thick swarms, spattering
the blackness, opening and closing their mottled wings. Now,
Tranquillity's friend could distinguish noises. She heard the
cries of the luminous letters, outside, their calls and whistles.
They were calling out like birds of some kind, whimpering

Cheskin: assorted chocolates
inferior class: packaging, bright-red metal foil + blue ribbon, at 50 cents
superior class: packaging, pink cardboard + magenta ribbon, at 90 cents
Instinct of self-preservation (weapons, food, housing)
Instinct of domination (possession)
Sexual instinct (adornments, clothes)

behr 1600

Voluble words gushing ceaselessly from all orifices, quick, more quickly still, a new word each micro-second, there must always be more, there must always be new ones, untiringly, flashes crackling in the black silence, more, more, quickly, quickly, to hide the sun, to expand space, words, life, jerky insects, quivering and vibrating, words that blacken sky and earth, words, cobwebs, dust, twigs, and clusters of stars.

Silence will never be heard.

throbbings of the heart
language simmers
traversed by bubbles
They make holes
They destroy
They devour   abrade
They play flutes made from men's bones
They beat drums made from men's skin
Words devouring words that grind down the soul

Ernest Ditcher and prunes
Mason Haire and instant coffee
Ditcher and tea: red (Boston Tea Party),
bright red, virile green
Louis Cheskin and yellow margarine

700 to 2000

SAS⤙ PRESS THE BUTTONS

Cognitive persuasion
Stereotypes: 'logical' reasonings
Invention of desires and fears
Study of prisoner-of-war camps: the myth of the 'friend'
the myth of the 'enemy'

Language desires in vain to make its way across this whole night
Perhaps its words have been stolen during the journey
thick black darkness covering half the earth
The words try to pierce eyes veiled with cataracts, they try,
they want to say something   Words are things
Words words you glide silently over the carpeting and you extract the dust from between the fibres of the wool
Are you always so powerful and solitary rapid and hungry
Words are you not the dust sticking to the earth's hairs,
that a gigantic being
called HOOVER gobbles up?

G. W. Hartman: 'A field experiment of the comparative effectiveness of emotional and rational political leaflets in determining election results' (in *Journal of Abnormal and Social Psychology*):

24.1% no prop
35.4% prop ration
50% prop emot

gently, or cooing. The young woman felt a shiver of fear go through her as she listened to these cries and squeals.

There were so many cries. They came from all directions simultaneously, hidden by the darkness, and so quickly that ears were too static to catch all the different sounds.

Certain letters crossed through space emitting the same high-pitched whistle, a sort of iiiiiiiiiiiiiiik! rather like the sound of jet engines. Or else they gave two or three brief roars, HARH! HARH! HOAR! that burst eardrums, so that the silence that ensued was even more terrible. But most of the cries came from the unknown, scarcely rising above the surface of the ground, and squeaking as though the roadway and pavements were covered with mice. The blinding lights and cries continued to rend the air. The car plunged onwards through the cloud of flying things, and shadows flickered against its body. The invisible birds died cheeping under its wheels, scratching the bonnet's paintwork with their claws. The letters, suspended from electric wires, tottered in the air, while the light spattered, and the paths of arrows and dots tapped away at tiny drums.

Some of the sound-waves were so narrow that it was only just possible to pass through them. It was as though the car's engine was gnawing away at a wall, while the noise's dust seeped down on either side of the wings. There were nets like snares that had continually to be torn apart with thrusts from the car's bumpers. Sounds of static, chirping, shrilling, and wave interferences. The young woman wanted to talk, to move forward, to talk, but there was nothing to be done. She wanted to think, think, think, but the cries of the letters and the lights flashing past filled her head and throat and choked her. She made an effort to defeat the moths and birds. She looked at the letters and tried to read them out aloud. For a few seconds she managed to keep the letters together. In the black street, then, she read out:

'BAT. WINSTON. REST. GUITAR. RIZZOLI. AIRBORNE.'
Then:

'K.I.N.G.S.I.Z.E.
S SC SCH SCHW SCHWE SCHWEP SCHWEPP
  SCHWEPPE SCHWEPPES
ES SOS TAN DARD MOTO ROIL
– EL – KSA – TAT – OOZ – RM – LAC
TEL TEL TEL TEL'

But when she blinked for a fraction of a second, everything immediately exploded, and the letters flew away in all directions like steam in the air. The letters killed words in passing, and pursued each other, too. The cries were doubtless cries of pain, the little high-pitched death-rattles that rodents emit as their necks are being broken. The angry whine of hornets on tin roofs as the cloud of D.D.T. envelops their wings and burns their eyes. Bubbles come hissing out of crabs' mandibles, the very trees cry out with pain and rage when fire begins to split and consume their fibres.

At one moment the young woman suddenly saw in front of her eyes an extraordinary landscape filled with signs. She saw it by concentrating all her energies, but at the same time she knew that she would never understand it.

It looked rather like this:

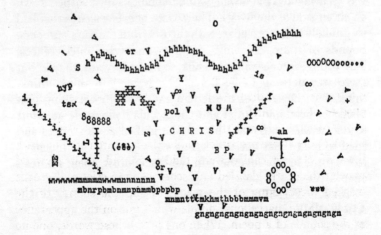

What was surprising was that the cries did not accompany the letters: they said something different, or they arrived afterwards, or beforehand. For example, WW suddenly flashed into view, and then a few seconds later, at the far end of the street, appeared the cry:

'How! How!'

The letters traced weals that momentarily lit up the sky as far as the stars, and then there was a desperate wait for the noise that never came. Or else, sometimes, a weird clacking of jaws could sometimes be heard at ground level, and it was only after several minutes, perhaps hours, that the sign BNP became visible.

Perhaps men and women had all vanished from the scene, already. Could anyone live among so many signs? The car moved on up the street, on its own, and the network of letters and arrows and dots spread gradually outwards, and the crackings and cries and squeals rained down violently. Words formed themselves, then exploded, spelling out weird names that glowed briefly in the night, splendid and incomprehensible, then beat a flickering retreat and burst like bubbles. Tranquillity's friend made great efforts, in steering her car, to follow the words' itinerary. Occasionally she thought she had glimpsed something: the silhouette of a man concealed behind a window, or a vaguely menacing machine at the far end of a bar, or a vehicle in the semi-darkness of a garage. Perhaps they were the source of all these words.

But it was all happening too quickly. And then the letters began to protect themselves, not wanting anyone to see the process of their birth. They grew agitated, traced their white zebra patterns, showed themselves in the form of stars, suns, nebulae; they were probably afraid of being stared at. The thick lines of electric cables were hidden behind great plywood panels; the sparks dazzled and scorched; the cries and groans masked the clicking of the machines and the sounds of the words, all the marvellous sounds which put on the appearance of the sounds of a poem. When one heard these words, one no longer thought of the other words, the frightening words: death, silence, hunger, pain, falsehood. It no longer seemed possible that there should be any other words than these intoxicated words.

Then Tranquillity's friend shut off the engine of her car. For quite a long time she looked at the unending street with all its separate letters dancing and its light-filled tubes crackling like insects. She listened to the cries, and she allowed many words to enter her, through the eyes, the ears, the mouth, the whole skin. When they were inside her body she became a fragment of the street, like all the rest. Then she found it no problem to write down on a sheet of paper a poem that would tell this story to her friend.

One day the masks, all the masks, will fall, and then people will be free. The towering walls that made it hard to breathe, the iron railings and gateways, the barbed-wire fringes, will all come crumbling down quite easily, because there will be no more masks. The pavements will stop echoing the sound of your steps as though you were the only living creature left on the planet, and the sky will cease to be flat, and the sea and the mountains and the tiered cities will cease to squeeze your head as though with an iron vice. Perhaps people will at last hear all the things that they had dreamt of hearing. Perhaps men's thoughts will no longer be mysterious. Chance is condemned. All these hesitations and doubts will surely vanish. A man is waiting. He has been waiting for many years, indeed he never does anything else but that: wait. Words themselves will tear off their hood-masks, and they will stand out crystal clear for the first time. People will be able to laugh. People will be able to walk in the sun, on a beach, no matter where, and watch the sea and listen to the birds calling, and *it will be true*. That is happening on the other side of time, you understand, not here. But occasionally, without meaning to, while walking at random, people have already found themselves there.

The masks will drop off spontaneously, without anyone's help. They will erase themselves suddenly, as the sun erases the darkness, and the real faces beneath them will at last be visible. There will be an end to all these lying features, these grimaces of hatred, envy, anger, desire. There will be an end to these glass eyes that look at you heartlessly, with a look filtered through ten thousand contact lenses, with a look that can change you into a caterpillar or a jellyfish.

There will be an end to those filament-like creatures bristling with tiny thorns, that inject poison beneath your skin before digesting you. The pupils of the eyes will no longer recede at great speed, far from you, so far back that emptiness creates a bulging bubble of ice around your face, so far back that your limbs slow down and come to a halt.

There will be hardly any secrets any longer. Just imagine! No more drawings trying to say two or three things at the same time, and enjoying your discomfiture. No one will ever again shout out 'Help!' People will talk without the aid of parrots. People's faces will be like stars of the third magnitude, so that all sources of light will be mysterious. That will be the most beautiful thing of all: no one will have to search for the sun in the sky any longer, no one will be afraid of the night any longer. At present, the sun hollows out a vertiginous hole as it flees. Trees leap very far backwards. Mountains are inaccessible, their summits permanently veiled by cloud. But that is because people do not speak to them.

People will speak. They will not speak in order to convince, or to drown the noise of silence. They will speak because it will be easy to do so, and because life will surge from their mouths together with the words. Everything will be filled with life. There will no longer be room for anything dead or unintelligible. People will speak, and their words will no longer resemble razor blades. Their mouths will no longer be like jaws. Thought will fill the world, it will exist inside blocks of concrete, inside subterranean pipelines, inside cranes, inside aeroplane propellers and car engine pistons. Thought will no longer be hidden inside craniums and tape-recorder reels. Thought will no longer be imprisoned in cinema halls or university lecture-rooms or buildings belonging to Esso Standard.

When the masks drop, just like that, spontaneously, it will be as though only a single man and a single woman exist any longer.

All the old divisions will vanish: the private properties, fortresses, castles with raised drawbridges, compartments, barriers, shutters, screens and partitions, shields, concrete cells. At last the wind will be able to blow, the light will be able to pass through, voices will be audible and gestures will be visible. Now, thick cosmetics hide the skin, and glasses hide the eyes. But life will sweep away these accretions, and there will be only one form of knowledge to pursue: the knowledge of freedom.

Men will no longer be like stones. Subjected to interrogation, men have grown rigid, but life will reach inside these stones so that they expand and contract like hearts.

One day all these dead cities with their silent rings will cease to exist. Buildings will bubble and seethe, and subways will send flows of lava pulsing out under people's feet. Highways will be as violent as sabre blades, cutting through forests and hopfields and deserts; they will sweep from one horizon to the opposite horizon in a second, cement lightning-flashes streaking towards the future. There will be no more driving mirrors.

All this will come about, and individual consciousness will explode like a grenade. There is so much strength in every face, so much knowledge. People cannot go on sleeping for ever. The dizziness of turning wheels, and the abyss which hollows out its pit in the centre of spinning bosses, give birth to fascination. Then fascination gives birth to anger. And anger, one day, produces the seed of truth, the truth that pulverizes gun turrets and razes walls. Electric-light bulbs will no longer wink on and off, night and day, to enslave people: they will enter the language, instead. Headlamps, today, are trained on people's eyes, to dazzle, to extract confessions. But the eyes are lined with mirrors, and one day these will reflect the light, multiplying its power tenfold. The eyes are headlamps that will one day light up and set the night ablaze.

Men will learn to speak. Today they think that they are speaking. Their mouths gape open and their uvulae tremble, but nothing can be heard. The words are not yet born. The words are still imprisoned within blocks of stone, hidden deep inside slabs of cast iron and globes of plastic substance. Words are tetanic. How could they pass through the throat and move about in the air when everything is taut? But one day there will be no more slaves, and desire will be able to roam freely through space. All this will come about. The process has already started. Already, some words are dead, while others are transfixed by arrows and are bleeding. Already, clumsily aimed rocks have broken a few plate-glass windows and smashed a few loud-speakers.

There are such terrible forces inside iron pylons, there is so much compressed violence in silent objects, in aircraft cock-pits, in asbestos sheeting, in neon tubes, in engine cylinder-heads, in mining pits, in the jaws of crushing machines, in centrifuges, in concrete mixers, in mechanical reaper-binders. There is so much power in a single face: it glows wanly in the semi-darkness, and its conical cranium is as menacing as the nose-cone of a bomb.

One day, violence will cease destroying because it will be free. The pressure of thought will no longer remain contained within minds resembling pressure-cookers: it will expand outwards. Words will soar freely in space, and looks will no longer be intercepted by wall surfaces. Mirrors will crack and shatter, their slivers will float to earth in the form of tiny crystals of light, and no one will ever again be confronted with his own image.

People will no longer write on sheets of mirror-paper, people will no longer write for their own benefit alone, or to destroy others. Sheets of paper will be immense, as vast as plains, as vast as oceans. Signs will no longer hang at windows, old dish-cloths, old flags, signs will no longer be slaves, will no longer enslave. They will speak freely, springing to life at the precise moment when they are needed, unhesitatingly and promptly, and there will no longer be orders such as 'Walk! Sit! Stand up! Lie down!' but, rather, sighs of love, or the ululations of wood-owls, or the bellowings of toads, or the sea's many sounds.

Words will be free: they were born for that. They will seize the brandished weapons of those seeking to enslave them, and will strike the tyrants down. Words will become so beautiful that eyes could never weary of looking at them, so beautiful that the saliva will boil in the mouth of anyone rash enough to pronounce them.

Words are taking their revenge. One day, they break the seals of the phylacteries, and come swarming out like snakes. Another day, they spurt from the labels of the bottles that had held them prisoner, and spread through the black sky with their pterodactyl-like jaws thrust forward like a saw-blade knife. They sweep straight ahead, and as they kill their masters their cries of vengeance can be heard.

DR INK COC COC COC OLAAA!

SCHWEPPPPPPPPPSSSSSSSSSSSSSSS!!!

F.A.N.T.A.

One day the masks will drop, one by one. Objects will escape from their masters. Cars' engines will devour their masters' fingers, perfumes will asphyxiate their blank-faced ladies. All the vintage wines and liver pâtés and ortolans and boars' heads and guinea-fowls and oysters and savarins and sponge-cakes and meringues will choke throats, plug nostrils and eyes, block lungs; the soft cheeses will conceal needles that will perforate intestines; liqueurs will be laced with hemlock and jimsonweed, and the sweet-smelling menthol-flavoured cylinders of cigarettes will be tainted with HCN.

The forces of life cannot be held down for very long. Slaves cannot be oppressed indefinitely. One day, without warning, they snap their chains and cut the throats of those who held a whip upraised. A liquid cannot be bottled up for ever: it breaks the glass, and spills out, runs to join the sea and helps build a flood.

And men and women will learn to love each other. They will no longer seek to vanquish each other or destroy each other. They will feel close to each other, right away, as though fear had never existed. They will love each other not only with their sexes and mouths: they will love each other with their eyes and ears and hair and feet and hands. With their thoughts and nerves and all the parts of their bodies. And perhaps it will be as though they had been born Siamese twins without knowing it.

But this has not yet come to pass. The savage festivities, the dances, the animal musics have not yet started. For the words and rhythms and colours are still prisoners. Men and women are still shut up in closed cells; their gaze is still distant, very distant, veiled by series of smoked-glass lenses. Who fears the eclipse? Men turn to stone when they are interrogated, and blocks of flats have walls that partition the sky. No air filters through. No wind filters through. The electric-light bulbs wink on and off, night and day, in obedience to the machines' orders. As for the words, there they are: stuck to bottle labels, or moulded on to plastic packs.

How will the change come? Wait, wait. But fear is so great, sometimes, that it empties out the body's substance, leaving only the skin's thin crust. Fear parches the mouth and dries up words. Fear has built such high ramparts round the nape of the neck that the head has become almost invisible.

One day all the masks will certainly fall. The wire itineraries flash past, but not as fast as the rage for extermination that is born of desire. The machines' masters use their expert knowledge continually to manufacture fear. They send fear-waves to encircle the earth. But fear rounds on its masters and shatters their faces. The dazzling gleams that the masters have invented to blind their victims, and the thunder that they have created to deafen them, flash back towards their eyes and ears, and the beauty that captivates turns its syringes upon them and stabs drunkenness into their arteries.

The cellophane masks light up in spontaneous combustion,

and become seething incrustations in the masters' faces. The accursed cameras, those that filmed the world's spectacle from the summits of watchtowers, the cameras that kept the world beneath the serpent's gaze, suddenly swivel on their pivots and start watching the watchers!

Dumb Bogo (he had been given that nickname at school because he never spoke to anybody) was fond of going on the
beach. Not being very sure where to go, now that he had run
away from home, he simply went on the beach. The sun shone
fiercely in the blue sky, the flat sea sparkled, and the millions of
grey pebbles were so hot that they burnt the soles of his sneakers.
For days and days now, the sun had never left the sky, and
everything on the surface of the earth had expanded in the heat.
Dumb Bogo surveyed the whole scene, the immense pebble
beach, the sky, the sun, the sea, and he could not understand
why everything was so hard and fierce. Perhaps there was a
threat lurking somewhere, behind things, in the air's molecules,
or hidden in the folds of the green water. There was no knowing.
A cool wind blew from time to time, and it was rather as though
a weary giant was breathing in and out.

Dumb Bogo walked along the beach, looking round him. Now
and then he came across people sitting in the sun, or walking, as
he was doing. The ones who were walking did so with difficulty,
turning their ankles and flapping their arms around. Dumb Bogo,
though, knew how to walk on the beach without stumbling over
his feet, perhaps because he had had practice, or perhaps because he was wearing sneakers. He moved along quite quickly,
first pressing the front of his foot against the pile of stones and
feeling round with the tip of the shoe to make sure that the surface was firm.

The harsh light did its best to scorch the eyes, so it was

necessary to screw up the eyelids really tight, as though looking at snow. The light struck the grey pebbles and transformed itself into splinters of stone, into arrow tips. Most of the people around wore dark glasses, but Dumb Bogo was not particularly fond of dark glasses: he preferred screwing up his eyes.

The beach was broad and long, and Dumb Bogo looked at it through the slits of almost closed eyelids. He did not look at it for very long; just occasionally he squinted a rapid glance towards its distant reaches, and then the beach's image fixed itself in his mind.

It was a truly extraordinary and unforgettable beach. It carried a shimmering halo of light, and was spread with sparkling pebbles that lay in a gentle curve like a cobbled road. It was outlined as though with neon tubes in a black sky: white, phosphorescent, vibrant with life. The light infused the beach, then flowed up again out of each pebble, its rays bristling like hair. The white light hovered mistily over the surface of the beach. Everything was so saturated with photons that the atmosphere was like a gas ... One no longer saw the beach or the sky or the sun or the cold sea: one smelt it all with one's nostrils, one breathed the scene in, one absorbed it through one's pores.

From time to time Dumb Bogo raised his head and looked into the distance, and he saw this phosphorescent roadway curving away out of sight, between the sea and the city. And he decided that this was no longer happening on earth: he was walking on the planet Jupiter, encased in his pressurized spacesuit.

It was good, walking like that, along this beach. It was as though nothing else in the world was alive and true, as though all the light, all the beauty, all the violence was there, really there; elsewhere there was nothing. Dumb Bogo placed his rubber soles firmly on the pebbles as he walked along the edge of the sea. He was scarcely looking. He did not feel like looking. The heat was sparkling in the air and on the round stones, and illuminating all the particles of mica.

There were other people on the beach, but he did not see them. There were a few gulls walking on the pebbles and clacking their beaks. Occasionally an aeroplane passed slowly through the sky, rending the air with the harsh sound of its four jet engines. One knew all that. One had no doubts about it. It was all a certainty. It was *because* of the light.

When he had walked far enough, Dumb Bogo sat down on the pebbles. He chose a spot that he had glimpsed from a long way away, a sort of hollow between two hillocks of stones, not far from a stump of wood. When he had first seen it through the slits of his eyes he had had this idea that he might go and sit there in the sun, and throw stones at the stump while he watched the sea.

It was a sort of root with dangling fibres, splotched with deposits of tarry oil, wedged there among the pebbles. Dumb Bogo had contemplated it for a moment, then he had got up and gone over to look at it more closely. He had tried to tear it out of the ground, but it was too solidly wedged. Then he had gone back to sit in the same spot, between the two hillocks, and had waited.

The sun was so high that one could not even see it. The pebbles were scorching hot, and the air was perfectly still. The whole atmosphere was very hot and very clearly defined, something like a black-and-white photograph. Dumb Bogo looked sideways, from between his eyelids, and he saw everything: the pebbles lying side by side, the silhouettes of people fishing, the waves breaking diagonally, the gulls strutting on their tall legs, the square blocks of flats, the hills. He saw all that, immediately and effortlessly.

He saw it all, and it entered into him along with the whirling spirals of fire and the spinning stars and the vortices of sparks in the black sky. There was so much light! Even inside the body there was light. It burnt there, the terrible light, in the centre of the internal organs, making the nerves glow like the filament in a light bulb. Outside, on the beach, in the sun, everything was white, and inside the body everything was white. The brain shone inside the skull like a sun, too: a strange melting sphere consuming itself in empty space as it released its enormous heat explosively, expelling great orange flames at regular intervals through the holes of the nostrils, the ears, the mouth, the eyes, the anus and the pores of the skin. It was beautiful. It was also rather painful.

Dumb Bogo was sitting on the burning pebbles, looking at them one by one. They were fine pebbles: nicely rounded, dry, covered with a fine grey dust. Dumb Bogo was fond of the pebbles, and he would not have liked it so much if the beach had been covered with something different, sand, for instance, or concrete platforms. Sand is not like pebbles: it is dirty and slippery and never stays put. If you place an object on sand without paying attention — keys, papers, a pen, a box of matches — the sand swallows it up immediately. Sand is worse than water, because you never notice it. It is worse than air or sky or mirrors or window-panes or anything like that. It has millions of tiny cubical teeth that grind away all the time, and there are as many mouths as teeth. As for cement platforms, they are so hard and flat that they graze your skin, and you break your nails on them.

But pebble beaches are beautiful, with all their gentle stones that have been polished by the sea and the rain. You can touch pebbles one after the other, you can judge their weight in your hand, you can sense their shape through feeling them. They are never alike, as grains of sand are. No two pebbles ever resemble each other. Dumb Bogo was fond of the pebbles. Often he carried a few away with him. He would have liked to get to know all the pebbles on the beach; that would have been more beautiful than knowing all the words in the dictionary. Dumb Bogo loved all the pebbles. People often walk over pebbles without seeing them. Their flat feet plant themselves on the stones, then go away for ever. Dumb Bogo did not altogether enjoy walking over the pebbles, because he remembered the ones he had already come across, and was sad to leave them behind.

Sitting in the hollow between the hillocks, in front of the

stringy root, he looked at the pebbles one by one. He even looked at the ones that were *underneath*. He liked them all. He gathered them round him, to admire them, and then he let them go, listening to the noise they made. He loved them all. But the ones he loved best were the ordinary ones without any kind of pattern or mark or scar or anything, the rounded dull-grey egg-shaped pebbles that you never even notice at first. When you held one of these in your hand you could never forget it again. They were so beautiful, so pure, so simple that they dazzled you and filled your eyes with tears. Smooth and gentle, warm as birds, hermetically sealed, opaque: they were alive, they had formed their body and they kept it closed with all their might, like a fist, like a skull. Dumb Bogo would have liked to talk to them, but it was obvious that they did not want to hear anything. Lying in the palm of his hand, they weighed downwards with all the weight that they could bring to bear. They wanted nothing and expected nothing. They were inanimate, blind, deaf, and yet THEY WERE NOT DEAD, that was the exciting part of it: they were alive, they were upon the earth.

Ever since he had run away, the weather had stayed fine, and so Dumb Bogo was always coming to the beach to look at the pebbles. He sat down in a hollow, near the place where the surf came rushing in, and looked. Like that, he got to know hundreds of pebbles, elongated ones, stubby ones, black, grey, white, and pinkish ones. When he arrived on the beach, he screwed up his eyes and looked into the distance to locate this grey stretch of pebbles where he was going to sit down. Then he started off for it, carefully, happy because he knew that he was going to make some extraordinary discoveries in this place. The beach would no longer be anonymous, because he was going to come across entirely new pebbles.

The other things that made up the beach were different from the pebbles: the sea made angry noises, the white sky hung heavy, the sun burnt, people yelled, the light did its best to scorch the eyes, the gulls clacked their beaks, and the clouds cast chilly shadows on you.

The pebbles, on the other hand, were not in the least aggressive. They never moved, or made a sound. When somebody placed a foot on them they rolled a little to one side, to give free passage. They never swallowed keys or matchboxes. The fine grey dust covered them gently, day after day, and the rain and the spray washed them. The sun's heat expanded them with its countless implacable rays. But it was certain that deep inside the pebbles there was nothing but coolness.

They stayed where they were, never darting away like dogs or birds. They never moved. When night came, the pebbles grew invisible and cold, balls of black onyx, and it was certain that deep inside them there was nothing but heat.

At dawn the sun appeared once more above the sea. And, marvellously, the pebbles were still in the same place.

Dumb Bogo was very fond of sitting on the beach and looking at the pebbles. Perhaps that was the reason why he was not fond of talking. He would think about the pebbles, and from then on, talking was pointless. When there was all this light about, and the sound of the sea, and the cloudless white sky, and the gulls balanced on their feet, it was really very beautiful, and you no longer needed anything else. You could stay sitting on the beach for hours, without thinking of people.

A little later, Dumb Bogo got up and walked along the edge of the sea. He screwed his eyes up and looked at the horizon: he was very fond of the horizon. There was this sort of thin wire that separated the sky from the sea, a scarcely visible line just below the countless tons of weight of the air that pressed down upon the sheet of water: air and water were like two blocks of marble, one on top of the other.

The horizon was a calm motionless line, and yet there was much violence present. The two masses of sea and sky were pressed so tightly against each other that nothing could have slipped between them. They were like the foreheads of two moose locked in combat, neither willing to give ground. That was frightening. Nothing could be heard, not a gasp or a snort, and yet the two marble blocks were locked in eternal combat. They struggled with all their might, closing off the whole of space. Dumb Bogo never looked for very long at the horizon or the mountains or the sun, because fear sprang from all those things and paralysed his body.

He went on walking along the edge of the sea, pretending not to see anything. From time to time he picked up objects, to examine them. There were all sorts of objects on the sand. Empty tins and plastic bottles, bones, fruit stones, bits of wood and brick and iron, cigarette butts, pale-green precious stones. Sometimes, when he found something that he really liked, he put it in his pocket. Or else he threw it far into the sea, making it ricochet when the surface was smooth.

Then Dumb Bogo did another thing that he was very fond of. He came to a halt not very far from the sea, and built a pyramid on top of a nearby hillock. He piled the pebbles on top of each other, and that made a pyramid rather like the ones the Navajo Indians erect along their trails. Then he walked a bit farther on and made another pyramid. Then yet another. The piles of stones stood along the beach, overlooking the sea, their summits outlined against the sky, and then they all looked rather like Burmese chaityas.

Dumb Bogo enjoyed building pyramids along the beach, though if he passed the same way a few days later he always found that they had disappeared. The wind had blown them over, or screeching children had used them as targets. But that did not matter. Dumb Bogo simply rebuilt the pyramids.

He also set the stones up in straight rows, or in magic circles. He was particularly fond of the magic circles. For these, you had to build a little wall of pebbles round you, as you turned, until the circle was complete. Then you placed a triangular boulder in the centre, where you had been standing, and it was just as though you were always there on the beach.

The rows and the magic circles usually lasted longer than the pyramids. Sometimes, when he walked along the beach, Dumb Bogo would recognize the outlines of pebble structures that he had designed almost a year before. Occasionally, too, he came across circles of stone that had been laid out by someone else, and that pleased him, though at the same time it made him a bit uneasy to think of the strangers who had passed that way.

Dumb Bogo walked along the beach, looking at all the tracks trodden among the pebbles. There were places where the pebbles were as big as boulders; then a little farther on there were inexplicable puddles of gravel. Both storms and bulldozers pushed the pebbles around, from time to time, and then the mountains of stones shifted nearer to the sea or else nearer to the top of the beach, just below the road. You were never sure of your exact position on the beach. When you walked along, like Dumb Bogo, eyes screwed up against the light, you could quite easily lose yourself. Luckily there were Navajo pyramids at long intervals, to serve as landmarks.

Basically, it was terrible to walk alone on the beach, among all these pebbles. The stones were hard and tightly sealed, and were not particularly well disposed towards human bodies. They even repulsed them, struck at their fragile flesh, and tried to break their bones. Dumb Bogo stretched out on his back, on top of the pebbles, and through his shirt he could feel the stones joining forces and forming a hard platform. The stones harboured strength, enormous strength. They were not tender; they did not crumble, as earth does; they did not float, as sand does. They fused together and transformed themselves into a great slab of cement, an impenetrable terrain that drove the small boy away.

Each time, it was the same. After a moment the beach had had enough of Dumb Bogo, enough of all these people who walked over it, all the children and women and gulls. Suddenly, the beach became rigid, clenching all its pebbles together like jaws, closing all the chinks between them. That was the awful part of it: it wanted nothing more to do with Dumb Bogo, or with anyone else. It sent them packing, back to their little human affairs. Dumb Bogo was in despair. He stayed stretched out on his back, his eyes brimming with tears caused by the salt air and the light, and tried not to understand. He would have liked, more than anything, to be a round grey stone, one stone among all the other stones. That is what he would have liked to be: a pebble. He would have burrowed into the beach, pressing his round back against the other pebbles, and no one would ever have found him again. He would have stayed there on the beach for days and days, looking at the white sky. He would have become scorching hot in the sun, and icy cold at night. The wind would have stroked his hard skin, the water would have flowed over him, the fine grey dust and the salt would have formed a sleek shell round him. Pebbles are afraid of nothing. They are not afraid of storms or death or the sun or the sea. The sperm-whale's teeth destroy everything: men, lesser whales, ships; but they shatter against pebbles.

The beach wanted nothing to do with him. It shoved him in the back with its compacted platform, and he felt each separate pebble striking and bruising him. But what was really terrible was that there was nowhere to go. The beach expelled his over-soft body, yet everywhere around there was the same mineral hardness. The city was composed entirely of stones, concrete buildings, slabs of marble, macadamized streets. There was nothing there but huge blocks soaring side by side, and human beings crushed themselves against their ramparts. Mountains of hard, hermetically sealed stone, towering above the asphalt plains. You could run till your feet bled, but you still would not find a hiding-place, or oblivion. To feel really at home you would have to inhabit grottoes of human flesh that were soft and lined with warmth and blood, you would have to inhabit the bellies of women. Cities were hard, through and through, and wanted nothing to do with human bodies. The beach thrust itself at Dumb Bogo's back, and he was scared. Everything was petrified, solid, impassable. The sea was as hard as any sea would prove to be if a parachutist struck its surface after his canopy had failed to open. The whole surface of the earth was made of marble: its slabs were everywhere. Stone sky, stone water, stone air and, high above, the sun's meteorite in process of disintegration. It was truly unbearable, utterly silent. Then Dumb Bogo got up and left the beach very quickly, without looking behind him.

Lamps flash, pause, flash again. Little whirlpools of light flicker at intervals along the great white ceiling. There is no other sky than this dazzling dome supported by pillars. Electric-light bulbs are concealed inside transparent boxes, and melting plastics swell up in blisters along the wall surfaces. Scythe-like discs of polished steel revolve, whistling, at high speed, slicing everything that comes their way: air, water, wood, vehicle panels, human craniums. Nothing is peaceful or calm or quiet. There are extreme forces darting forward in the form of arrows and bars and twisted coils. The great hall of Hyperpolis is just coming to a boil, heated by the fires that are blazing secretly beneath the floor, behind the doors, above the ceiling. There is no time to listen or look. Everything goes so quickly, so very quickly, from one end to the other of this hall that is as vast as the whole universe. There are many whirlwinds, all the time, advancing along the glazed flooring, creating their little funnels of air as they go; and that is very exhausting, because there is no place to hide. The immodest light's long glances will seek you out and find you, wherever you may be. Perhaps, when night comes ... But night never comes. Somewhere unknown, giant turbines unremittingly send electric current along wires, from one tower to the next, over valleys and mountains and roads; and the electricity spreads itself throughout Hyperpolis, simultaneously setting aglow all the filaments and all the tubes filled with helium, carbon, neon; lighting up air molecules and mirrors and polystyrene balloons, lighting up the bodies of men and women. That is why peace of mind is impossible: for that, it would be necessary to extinguish all those electric lights that men and women carry inside them, and that would be impossible because the turbines never stop rotating, and the electricity never stops running through the cables strung between the giant pylons.

But the most terrible aspect is the gentleness, the softness of it all. This is truly frightening. The sheets of celluloid covering the walls, and the carpeting, and the polished metals and polished glasses and varnished paintings, are all soft and gentle. And the gentleness is like some melting plastic substance coiling itself round arms and limbs, sticking to breasts and back and shoulders, penetrating the pores of the skin, roasting the skin with its fierce heat. Gentleness wields a scalping knife, extrudes the eyes with a finger in each socket, presses against the ear-drums and the nostrils, so gently, so very gently. Gentleness is capable of such things.

Being inside Hyperpolis is like being in the centre of the universe. Suddenly the walls have receded out of sight, vanished to the outer edges of space. The ceiling is so high, and the floor so low, that the distance is incalculable. Space has swollen very fast, thrusting aside all hard flat surfaces, and has grown huge, pushing back its walls and windows; now the frontiers are no longer visible. One is inside space, floating in it. Tranquillity is at one end of Hyperpolis, and her friend is at the other end, and it is as though they were side by side. The human bodies are weightless particles floating in the void, following the paths of looks, drifting in streams of thought. How to break the spell and bring this to an end? Tranquillity tries to think about something. She thinks:

'If I managed to find out where the orders come from, if I could do that, if I managed to find out where the light comes from, and the noise, then maybe I could ... No, no, that won't do. Let's begin at the beginning. But where is the beginning? Well, to start with, my name and age and address, and so on.'

But despite all her efforts Tranquillity could remember neither her name nor her age nor her address. The currents generated within Hyperpolis leave her no time. They flash through the vastness in a few seconds, pricking hundreds of tiny ice-cold holes in her body as they pass through her. The light flashing from all the motionless objects on their stands is so intense that one would need to wear welder's goggles to look at them. In glass-plated showcases there are things like revolving suns with a splash of blood at their centre. Letters are lightning-flashes zigzagging between great black clouds. The white vinyl floor is invisible. Women's feet move quickly, approach, recede, in shoes with heavy studded soles that echo like hammers. Even more frightening: there is no darkness. Tranquillity searches for shadow, any kind of shadowy spot, so that she may sit down and go to sleep. But there are no shadows, nor will there ever be any. Waves of colour arrive, pressed tightly against each other, making repeated rainbows. Who invented colours? At one time, there were probably no colours other than black and red, and white. But someone opened the door to the demonic colours, and now they are advancing on the world with all their shades of mauve, violet, brown, orange, indigo, emerald, yellow, vermilion, purple, ultramarine, grey, beige, cream, chestnut, gold, blackish blue, sky blue, pink, silver, steel. These are living colours, sprung from aluminium tubes and posters and the pages of magazines; they fly in the air, they swim across the earth, through the sea, over the skin, as their fingers stretch out longer and longer.

'Look here,' thought Tranquillity, 'someone ought to slam the colours' door shut. The colours should be put back in their places. There must be some box designed to hold the colours and not let them out. Then we'd have nothing more to fear from them. Colours are escaped snakes. There must be ... There must be ...'

But the colours do not permit themselves to be shut up. They spread and run in the white space, as their waves unfurl. If you stare at them they shift position. The moiré curtains draw aside and then together again. Objects' shells part their lips, displaying the soft gentle wounds within. Skins are sleek and smooth, never cracked or scaly. Tin cans, glass jars, plastic bubbles, all contain intestines. Men and women float between the objects, gliding through the lower depths of Hyperpolis, giant rays flapping their black fins.

It is like that everywhere. The young woman called Tranquillity is no longer in Hyperpolis. She is in some closed city, under its invisible roof. Perhaps the city is called Rome or Babylon or something like that. The names of places are difficult to find out, since they have mostly vanished. There are just a few left: Helmut Morgenstein, Pinoncely, Louis Cheskin, Publicis. The great throng floats, unthinkingly, in the ocean of colours. It will be a long time before these prisoners in these subterranean galleries find the exit they are looking for. On the other side of the plexiglass cockpit the sun will rise and set and rise again, year after year. The stars will shine in the cold sky, the clouds will glide past in groups, the sea will push the lines of debris back as it laps the pebble beaches. But no one inside will witness any of this: eyes are fixed on the bright moving targets against which words score hits; eyes adore, devour. And everything is continually out of reach, dwindling into the distance like cars on highways.

Some of the colours are so dazzlingly beautiful that Tranquillity is held spellbound. Sometimes the jumble of forms and papers and fabrics reveals momentarily to her eyes an oval shape of a blue so intense, so pure, so strong, one that radiates so much light, that her heart misses a beat and the palms of her hands sweat profusely. This azure blue confronts her with its unwavering gaze. There has never been quite such a blue in the world, not even the blue of Persian cats' eyes, or of sea grottoes, or turquoises, or amethysts, or kingfishers' feathers, or chlorine streaks, or geyser basins, or the sky. She is the captive of the exquisite colours, her breathing is shallow, her dilated pupils are fixed on the gradually expanding oval iris. She makes an attempt to think of something, to break the enchantment. She makes an attempt to close her eyes, to turn her head away, so that she can leave. And the oval is now so huge that it reaches from top to bottom of space, an ecstatic window beckoning her to approach, and plunge in, and mingle with the colour. Then some people pass in front of her, masking the colour with their bodies, and Tranquillity is released from her paralysis. But she will never forget the distended iris whose pitiless cerulean gaze penetrated to the depths of her soul, the blue oval that is a man-made planet. In the centre of the oval there were little black signs that wrote inside your eyes the words:

NICKELOY TIP

Tranquillity walks forward hesitantly. She has suddenly become blind. Or rather, her green eyes continue to see, but it is as though her vision no longer belongs to her, as though it has become the property of others. Her gaze is directed straight ahead, opening up the path that her feet will follow. But the colours' gaping mouths swallow her unceasingly.

On bottles an orange disc opens wider and wider: a sun repeated in a thousand copies, and Tranquillity's gaze is transfixed by these eyes of gold. The glass sparkles on the dividing-walls. The sheets of linoleum are stretches of platinum and cadmium. There is no way of passing through or crossing over. The aluminium shutters close their electronic lids so quickly that scarcely a spark of light has time to escape. Metal eyelid that closes with a dry click, and decapitates ideas. Strips names away, destroys willpower, burns nerve roots. The glass display-counters disintegrate with a slow explosion of white light. In the blue satin jewel-cases the pearls are flecks of fire and the golden necklaces are at melting-point. They radiate so much light that even after she has stopped looking at them Tranquillity can feel their heat on her cheeks, and on the skin of her neck from the nape up to the roots of her hair.

'Look here!' thinks Tranquillity, 'I must get out of here at all costs, right away ...' That is as far as her thoughts go, because she can no longer manage to think properly. Her words are progressively replaced by the words uttered by Hyperpolis.

'... Household ... I count, %%, otherwise I LOVE, you need DIM! DIM! Have you thought about your holidays? The snow ... The light is too strong. With a MALT base. Give, heuh, give me. BUYING IS SAVING. No, not that one, something a little ... Bigger ... Wider ... More flexible ... It's economical, and good too. At the other end, perhaps ... Sugar, fruit. Bauknecht, because ... COmera. Would that suit you??? We give them space, beauty. Times change. What's to be done? ... A little smile ... What's to be done?' etcetera.

But that is simply what it might be assumed that she thought. In reality it was much more rapid. The words transformed themselves into a flash of lightning inside her brain, and in a fraction of a second they had changed shape a hundred times. They darted from the other end of Hyperpolis, piercing eyes and fracturing eardrums and bursting inside the skull like dumdum bullets. They collided with one another, multiplying their precarious networks in an instant. Or they segmented, scattering their letters through the body, and each small fragment encountered some thought or desire or feeling, anything that was personal, fused with it, and fecundated, or else killed. Tranquillity wanders in empty space, no longer capable of speech. She tries desperately to create sounds with her mouth; her mouth opens and puckers the lips like a goldfish, but nothing comes.

There are so many voices surrounding her, all speaking. The alien mouths spare no time for human language: they fasten themselves to your lips as though with a kiss, but their purpose is to gag.

There is no peace in Hyperpolis. Red signs light up in the distance, shining powerfully through the haze. Unremittingly, repeatedly, they call to you, red searchlights blazing from the tops of poles. Their message is: 'Come! Come!' and their mute red cries enter your head and kill all thought. Thought is sucked up like marrow from a bone by the long probing tongues.

Discs spin round in front of one's eyes, their hubs bore holes into thought and suck up greedily. Blocks of crystal cast flashes that scorch memory. Asbestos panels, pitch-black bakelite surfaces, glazed paintings pick up the light from the red eyes and feed upon it.

Tranquillity, moving forward through this confusion, thinks: 'When will one ever be free?' She looks round her, longing to find someone to whom she could ask this question. But the faces flash by, at the tops of bodies, gliding in the direction of the red signals and the metal discs, towards the other end of Hyperpolis; their eyes are rigid, with dilated pupils and almost unblinking lids; their vocal cords are slashed; their eardrums are fractured.

Suddenly Tranquillity feels that she too is in the process of losing her eyes. Worse still, she can do nothing about it. The exquisite colours shine in the distance, through the haze: flashes of white light with iridescent haloes; great splashes of blue, purple, black, orange, yellow nylon; all the sparkling, eternally dancing letters. Following this rhythm, the eyes grow very large, then very small, then very large again. The false perspective recedes towards the horizon, and the eyes stretch their gaze so far that they become two elastic threads that have reached breaking-point.

Tranquillity realized that she was about to lose her eyes, and this scared her. Because now it was as though her eyes had ceased to be of use for seeing things. They were still in her face, moving in their sockets, but they were no longer really looking. And that is a fearful thing: worse than being blind, or dead. The fiery blood-red plastic substances have forced the pupils to open, and now in place of eyes there are two black holes like those induced by atropine.

And through these holes the sparks of light and the colours and the signs' flashes enter constantly. It is not possible any longer to keep one's eyes intact among all these whirlwinds. The eyes no longer see: it is the objects, now, that see into eyes. Looks dart forth barbed rays that implant themselves in the brain like cactus spikes. Objects swim in the silence, promenading their effigies along corridors and streets and avenues and parking lanes. The ceiling returns the looks that have accumulated there for days, spreading the fragmentations through the air, rocking them to and fro, creating a solid jelly that shudders its way from one end to the other of Hyperpolis.

The light has gone, now: only looks exist. And people's inverted eyes are merely reflectors, or camera lenses. They invent nothing, but themselves receive alien inventions, electric impulses, series of circles and triangles and squares. The eyes are no longer independent. A kind of permanent menace hovers inside the vast hall, something heavy and mysterious that is more alarming than an approaching storm.

Tranquillity continues walking, unseeingly, along the central alley, her pupils two black holes in the middle of green irises.

She no longer sees. *They* see her. Hard systematic objects watch her all the time. From the depths of space, from inside their cellophane hiding-places, from behind red or blue or violet panels, objects spy upon her and the other girls, and upon the men and women and children. The objects are pitiless, and fully aware of what they want. They are powerful, never weak or hesitant. They want to conquer her, possess her, subdue her, with a single glare from their red eyes, between two blinks of their steel eyelids. They are the masters. The masters.

In releasing their phosphorescent flashes, the objects have even decided to reverse the order of reality. They look at the young woman through her own eyes, and it is they who have become human beings, while she is now an object. Incomprehensible? But there is nothing to understand. Hypnotic beauty simply turns all the paths back upon themselves, while the traveller sleeps, and so the beginning becomes the end.

SMEGMA

Why is the sky blue?
When the sun's rays reach the earth's atmosphere, the molecules of gas diffuse the light in all directions. Since these molecules tend to diffuse the blue radiations more widely than the other colours, the sky appears blue to us.

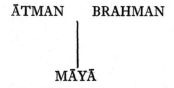

The cities are attempting to say something. They expand and contract and, at each breath, sounds spurt from them and race across the earth. Brains emit waves ceaselessly, and hearts beat. Life flourishes everywhere. The white blocks of flats standing on the asphalt plains were not, after all, motionless, as had been thought: they swayed. Winding roads, railway lines, building sites, quarries, gasworks. There is so much life on all sides. The earth vibrates incessantly. But the contractions of buildings are still imperceptible. People have no idea what is going on. If they knew, then perhaps they would stop talking, and hating, and going to the cinema. People take their own light around with them: they have hollowed out a little room inside reality, and installed in it their 100-watt light bulb. The light is yellow. They know no other light, neither the white light of the sun nor the black light of the night. Human words flutter across the room, just like moths.

But there is everything, too, that is outside language. The cities invent words endlessly. They canalize their energies, bringing together, for example, all the noises made by car engines, or all the underground movements that thrust their earthworm tubes forward. The wires are tense with electricity. In the invisible sewers, warm ordure flows and glides: that is the language of the cities, and it is saying something.

Enough of individual consciousness! In their shuttered cells people study their faces in mirrors; but they learn nothing. They are nothing. They look at their faces and what they see is the senseless transparent mask, the sort of death's-head that resembles them. People press the tape-recorder buttons and say:

'I, Frédéric Lanfranchi, Ernest Ditor, Manuel Ayala, Antonio, Steve, Christine Zeiss, Evelyne, Mersault, James Mac-Laglan, Abel, Milena, Samira, Mercedes, Claude Bettinger, Hélène Manda, etc.'

After that, they tell their life story, always the same story, of course, birth, experiences, amorous misadventures, jobs, old age, death. Or else they look at their stupid old yellowed photographs: 'Myself at the age of four', 'Myself in New York', 'Myself in Kyoto in 1949', 'Jenny and myself in Liverpool', 'Myself with a beard' or 'Myself as a blonde'. People really know a tremendous amount: they are fully conscious, aware. They possess about 126,402 words of French, 1,243 words of English, and eleven words of Italian. They have read books, they have listened to songs, they have watched films, they have looked at paintings and statues, they have skimmed through magazines. They know why the wind blows, why the earth trembles, why disquieting spots occasionally appear on the sun, and why man appeared on earth in succession to the marine jellies and the lizards and the grasshoppers. People know all that, and many other things besides.

Meanwhile the cities expand and contract, and do not concern themselves with knowledge. Clouds bank up, tides swell, rivers flow, glaciers slide, forests burn: and all done without knowledge or consciousness. There are vast terrible languages that cover space and time, languages so vast that in comparison all the words of all human languages, put together, would not cover a single speck of dust.

Caesar desires that inferiors should, willy-nilly, revere him and, indeed, worship him; yet, time and again, a simple man is able to humble the mighty Caesar's pride.

Ezekiel Mendoza

Do you know the Masters of language? They have decided that words shall never be free, and that the sounds made by mouths when they speak should resemble the throbbing of engines, the screech of sirens, the vibration of electric motors. They had been waiting for a long time to conquer the verbs and adjectives, the phrases, the salivary reflexes. When there was a war some-where, they watched and listened from their observation posts, and made written notes as to what it was that made men move. They knew that one day it would be their own turn. They knew it, and that is why they worked in their laboratories. Or else they used hidden cameras to film men's eyes. They filmed the eyes of people walking, making love, dying. Knowledge wanted to devour mankind, like a dragon living off human flesh. That is what invented evil.

No one knew it, but the Masters of language injected hatred and contempt and cruelty. Year after year, words, gestures, signs, colours, and even silence, were drawn gently towards the Masters, and introduced one by one into the Foundations' concrete blockhouses and tall buildings, where they received the strange, perverse influx that turned them into possessions. The Masters of language do not really live upon the earth. They exist on the other side of things, in darkness, in the darkness that is within light itself. They hide carefully behind their opaque screens, safe from bullets and prying eyes. They are on the side of science and knowledge, but in order to destroy and command and anathematize.

Had they not been there, had language and desires continued to be free, perhaps people would not have been afraid of death, and perhaps they would not have sought to kill each other in order to be happy. It is difficult to say. Perhaps it was decreed that men should have Masters waiting for them, and that they should be doomed to lose the use of their five senses.

Perhaps the Masters of language were inside language itself; that is to say, perhaps the sign of destruction already existed inside each word, as though speaking and hearing could serve solely to enslave. And in that case, darkness already existed within pure colours, and the sun was also a blinding black spot in the sky.

Everything is possible. Nothing is certain. It would be so good to launch words into space, at random. It would be so good to be able to whisper gently into an ear, forgetting all ear-splitting, wounding sounds. Sometimes there is so much silence in all this noise, so much emptiness along these roads and in these cities, that the mouth opens. The throat opens, the lungs open, and there is a sort of cry, or rather, a rush of air escaping from the depths of a steam-boiler and evaporating outside, making a hissing sound like

'hhhhhhhhhhhhhhhhhhhhhhhhhhh'

and that is the only word that is truly free. It rises uncontrollably from deep inside the body, moves more quickly than magnetic tape, more quickly than machines for analysing phonemes, and leaves no traces in the ceiling's plaster moulding.

But the other words want nothing of this freedom. The other words build up their coral barriers, encircle, strangle with their roots, dazzle with their sparks, hypnotize with their steel springs.

Some day there will be no words left, nothing but searchlights sweeping across eyes with their beams, alarm sirens, electrodes sending their painful shivers through the skin. Free yourselves, let it be said once more, free yourselves from the Masters of language! But words betray; these creatures that speak on your behalf are destructive. It would be good to be able to think, to be happy, quite simply, alone, without witnesses. It would be good if thought was erect and speedy, travelling far through the air, reaching out to objects and planets and suns. Such are the thoughts of trees rooted motionless in the ground, or of the sea stretched out beneath the sun, such are the thoughts of birds and flowers and snow-capped mountains. But men inhabit a dream that they do not control. They live inside helices that are not their shells, they drift through clouds of black, red, green smoke. 'Help!' is the word that people mouth in vain. Help. And the words rear backwards, like a snake beneath a foot, or like a scorpion, biting, stinging.

The Masters of language do not know what fear is. They are protected by their soundproof walls, on the other side of the tinted window-panes. When you pass by, you cannot see them: but they see you. Behind their walls of expertise they judge the future, and their intelligent machines thrash away with violent passion. Were men made only to be flies buzzing round rooms? The Masters of language know the keys that open doors, for the locks are their faces. They never laugh. They are never afraid. They do not die. They have no terrors, they are never in darkness. Their homes are illuminated, night and day; their eyes are headlamps picking out the folds in hilly roads. For them there is no silence, no weakness. They are inside the machines, without a doubt, and their motion never slackens. Their will power is like the flywheel of a steam-roller, pushing the wheel that pushes it. They devour men's desires, after having invented them. They have no need to dream when they sleep, for their waking dreams are, precisely, the faces of infatuated men and women streaming along the corridors' channels, identical trolleys carrying their precious cargo towards the warehouses. Their heavy, living cargoes of thoughts.

How has it come about that scorn is so widespread? The Masters of language have no love for men. The Masters write their words, words as big as buildings, their terrible silent words that crush the world. They invent the syllables that lull the mind to sleep, they create the magic phrases that persecute.

Behind each of these words there is power, force, violence. Free yourselves from words! Words are like fierce animals, bloodthirsty, eager to kill. Words travel across the world, uttering their cries. Words lurk in the darkness, replacing light and life and love. You look outside and you think you see the earth, the sky, men and women walking in the street; but all you really see is words, just words. How to be free? How to escape the orders that pour in from all sides? The only solution would be to destroy all the words, erase them from posters and books, remove them from stone with a chisel, shatter them together with the bottles that carry them, smash tubes and lamps, burn newspapers and books, and slash the diaphragms of all loudspeakers. There would have to be no more words upon the earth for years on end, for whole centuries. Everything would have to return to its original nature: bare, deserted, silent. For the words uttered by the Masters of language have contaminated everything round them, and there is no longer a single word or phrase that has remained inviolate.

Language resembles the cogged wheels of a huge, enigmatic machine that devours and grinds and transforms into powdered ice. Perhaps all language is in the hands of the Masters, who mould it to their desires, keep it in confinement, paralyse it. When words leave the venomous mouths they enter the ears and spread through the body, freezing the muscles and fibres. Words have preceded desires by a few seconds; travelling faster than time, they are there before the eyes have had a chance to see things, they exist before the things themselves. They have built their traps, and they are waiting, knowing that their victims are on the way, hollowing out their void which beckons as magically as the sound of the surf.

Words send out tentacles at random, let their whips trail out behind them, then capture and anaesthetize all ears that come within range. Impossible to avoid seeing them and hearing them, these agents of death who speak of nothing but happiness and love and wealth and beauty and life.

The Masters of language possess both knowledge and power.

They know the words that must be recited in order to invade a soul. They know the words that destroy, they know the words needed to seduce women, to lure children, to conquer the starving, to subdue the sick, the humiliated, the greedy. They simply make their delectable syllables reverberate in the silence of the mind, and they become the only living creatures upon earth. Words are hasty; they do not wait for dreams. When someone, some day, is filled with sadness or anger, words arrive with lightning speed and replace thought. There is so much beauty: not haphazard, but created inside laboratories, to vanquish the masses. There are the words SPACE, SUN, SEA, the words POWER, YOUTH, BEAUTY, LOVE, MONEY, the words ACTION, ETERNITY, ENJOYMENT, CREATION, INTELLI-GENCE, PASSION.

For those who are hungry there is BREAD, FRUIT, DELIGHT, FUTURE, for those dying of obesity there is the word SLIM-MING, for those who are dying of loneliness there is the word LOVE, for those who are dying of desire there is the word YOUTH, for those who dream of being men there is IMPALA, POWER, SABRE-GASH, TOBACCO, for those who dream of being women there is CONTOUR, SEDUCTIVE, ETERNITY, BEAUTY, for those who dream of being intelligent there is MENSA, for those who dream of muscles there is BODYBUILD, for those who dream of being rich there is MANPOWER, or GILLETTE SILVER PLATINUM, for those who dream of the sun there is MOROCCO, INDIA, MEXICO, for those who, if they could, would call for help, there is S.O.S., S.O.S., S.O.S. There are so many words everywhere! Thousands and thousands of words. There is a word for every second of life, a word for each gesture, for each nervous twitch. When will this tumult ever subside? The Masters of language, secluded in their seething factories, manufacture ceaselessly the new words that spread through the passage-ways of the world. As soon as words wear out or weaken, others arrive on the spot, ready for combat.

Thought has been wiped out: that is the painful reality. The Masters of language do not wish their slaves to have thoughts. If

'Fleischmann's Gin, confronted by the challenge of the sexual revolution, consulted Louis Cheskin. Cheskin suggested a change in the label design, a change so slight that the average buyer would not even notice it, but which increased the company's sales considerably. The old label was rectangular. Cheskin had the corners rounded, to give it a more feminine note.'

the pure

The subconscious:		
soup:		uterine plasma
cigarettes:		oral auto-eroticism
chewing-gum:		aggressivity

U. S. P.
Matricon System
Adam System
Agostini System

		Circles
		Circles
Circles	Circles
Circles	Circles
	Circles
Circles	

like that,	Penetration
circles,	Induced consumption
where to?	Retentivity

Kolynos, the toothpaste of the *stars*

slimmi

WITHOUT SMILING '*It is dangerous to imagine that people are capable of rational conduct.*'
Ernest Ditcher: 'One of the principal tasks of publicity, in the conflict between pleasure and guilt, is not so much to sell a product as to grant permission to have pleasure without a feeling of guilt.'

Cadbury Schweppes LIMITED

Ernest Ditcher: 'Prosperity is based on psychology.'

thoughts appeared, they might easily destroy the empire of words with their total silence. Perhaps thoughts would expose the great contempt that reigns here, and would know how to eradicate it. If thoughts were able to flower inside brains, perhaps men and women might be truly beautiful, and there might no longer be Masters of language. But words appear in place of thoughts, uttering their parrot cries, yelping like dogs, and thought is abated. The words jostle each other, imitate anger and desire and joy, resound, deafen. The words invent fear, the invincible fear of servitude and unconsciousness.

There was someone else in Hyperpolis. He was a young man dressed in white overalls with the legend MACHINES sewn across the chest, and wearing white sneakers. So Machines became his name. He too worked under the great dome, and the electric light illuminated his white uniform, his white face and his black hair. He pushed metal trolleys along the aisles, from one end of Hyperpolis to the other. It was quite an agreeable occupation. From time to time he had to stop, to rescue a trolley abandoned near a wall and stack it into the back of the caravan of other trolleys. Then he started pushing the little metal trolleys again, at a leisurely pace, listening to the wire grilles clanging against each other.

Machines plodded on, straining forwards a little, his hands gripping the crossbar of the rearmost trolley. Day by day, from morning till evening, he went to and fro in the great hall. Such intense light fell on his white overalls and his face and his chromium-plated trolleys that he wore glasses with small round tinted lenses. People drew aside respectfully, like a herd of buffalo in front of a train, as his wheeled convoy approached, and that was amusing to watch.

The time passed quickly when one was pushing trolleys, like Machines. Perhaps it would not have passed so quickly if he had been a night-watchman, like old Vigil, or if he had been shut up in a kiosk, like Tranquillity's girlfriend. But pushing trolleys annihilated time, and hours and days lost their importance. What was rather maddening, all the same, was that people were constantly shifting the trolleys round, and then the strays had to be rounded up and returned to the fold.

Machines recognized the trolleys immediately: he knew each intimate detail of all the 1,200 trolleys in the southern sector of Hyperpolis. There was the one whose front right wheel slewed round, the one with a dented front, the one with the bent crossbar, the one with the grooved crossbar, the one that squeaked when it was pushed, the one that whistled, the one that buzzed, the one that tended to swerve to the left, the one that smelt of oil, the one that was stiff to push, the one that jolted, the one that had a black smear along the rim of the back right wheel, the one that resembled a tank, the one that resembled a perambulator, the one that resembled a boat, the one that clinked every few inches, the one that resembled a dromedary, and 1,183 other individual specimens.

The other men who had the same job did not like the trolleys, but Machines was really fond of them. Even he occasionally hated them, because they were heavy and stubborn and got caught against the angles of walls in passing. But on the whole they were good trolleys. They had fine mobile wheels with rubber tyres, sides of chromed metal, and a sort of shelf across the top at the back. The crossbars were particularly beautiful: metal tubes covered by yellow plastic sheaths on which were written:

Push   Release

GO   STOP

There was a great deal of din in Hyperpolis: confused sounds emerged from all the objects and loudspeakers and mouths. The man called Machines crossed the great hall, pushing his caravan of metal trolleys, and the rumbling of the wheels and the clash of the wire grilles added their noises to the rest. The atmosphere was not particularly soothing. There was just this noise, this motion, and the white light. No one spoke. People stepped back, silently, to let the convoy pass, except the children, who sometimes showed a certain interest. Machines liked children, too.

No one spoke. There was too much noise and light, and people sleep walked through Hyperpolis. Their eyes and nostrils and ears were open, but it was obvious that they were asleep.

Machines had to make a great effort not to go to sleep as well. He had to stay on his guard. Otherwise, the overalls' white light entered through his eyes, the squeaking of the wheels and the creaking of the wire frameworks entered through his ears, and sleep descended. To keep awake, Machines looked at the convoy of trolleys in front of him, and thought. He thought of them as cars, for example, or as spaceships en route to Saturn. Or else he imagined that the trolleys formed a single vertical column, and that he had to prevent it from falling. The column remained in a state of balance, at the end of his arms, swaying slightly to left or right, groaning and bending as draughts blew against it or obstacles grazed it. To keep the column upright he varied his pace from quick to slow, keeping a careful eye on its summit all the time. The least distraction might bring catastrophe: the tall stack of trolleys would topple, break into several segments, and come crashing down on to the floor, scattering wheels and wire-mesh panels and crossbars in all directions.

Or else, Machines fixed his gaze on some particular trolley in the line, no matter which, the sixth one along, for example, which had a wobbly wheel, and spoke to it in a low voice. He said:

' ... Come, come ... Take it easy, huh. I know you're not feeling too good, but never mind. Just a little farther, and we'll be there ... It's your wheel, huh? I know, you'd like to rest it a bit ... Listen, how did it happen? I mean, did someone kick you? Did you bang into a pillar? Perhaps you did it going down some steps? It hurts you, huh? Hurts you *badly*? I'd better have a look at that poor wheel of yours in a moment, as soon as we've arrived. Just one last little effort, all right? ... '

The eleventh one along, with a broken metal tube and a nasty black stain near the back axle:

'And you, how did *you* get that way, huh? Who dented your front frame? I'll bet it was a car. I heard the noise just a little while ago. And then, what's this black mess? Looks like treacle. Maybe you've broken a bottle of syrup? ... Well, I'll give you a good wash, soon, in the depot. I hope it will come out easily. The other day there was one with a stain just like yours, and guess what it turned out to be? Tar!!! Just imagine! Now where on earth did he manage to pick *that* up?'

The twenty-first, at the front of the file, far ahead:

'Hey there! Don't go so fast, you!'

Machines said all sorts of things like that to the trolleys, and also to the vinyl tiles on the floor, to the columns supporting the ceiling, to the panes of glass, to the neon tubes, to the automatic doors and the escalators.

The people did not talk. They never said anything. Their faces were like sea-horses' heads, armoured and inscrutable. Perhaps if their faces had not been so armoured and inscrutable, like sea-horses' heads, it would not have been necessary to talk to the metal trolleys.

The vast hall of Hyperpolis was filled with things that were in motion.

Machines liked speaking under his breath to the escalator. It was a handsome escalator whose steps never stopped moving, upwards on the right, downwards on the left, while the centre was occupied by a fixed staircase. Machines often stopped to watch how the steps emerged from the ground, as flat as a tank's caterpillar treads, then how they gradually raised themselves, one after the other, like scales or feathers, and climbed upwards, very straight, while the light sparkled on their iron edges, and their tarnished brass treads. The steps vibrated slightly. They went on climbing until they reached the top level of the escalator, where they vanished. The way they emerged from the ground made him think of waves on the sea, or wreaths of cigarette smoke. The escalator went on climbing like that, day after day, without a break, fulfilling its function. It dutifully rolled its belt of metal steps upwards, from the ground floor to the first floor. It never branched off in another direction. The steps rolled smoothly, in one graceful continuous movement, like a lorry's wheels gliding over the asphalt: it would have been easy to spend a lifetime watching them.

When Machines watched the escalator he was no longer afraid, he no longer thought about evil or money or loneliness or anything like that. He stood there in front of this kind of river climbing towards the mysterious first floor, towards the sky. And it was as though his soul was climbing too, until it evaporated through the top of his head, and curled towards the ceiling. As though the soul was nothing more than a weightless gas that the escalator's motion liberated. Machines often watched the escalator. He listened to the motor's muffled noise, the very gentle rumbling vibration while the metal steps emerged from the ground, drew themselves up, one by one, and scaled the ramp. There was so much goodwill involved that he was no longer afraid of dying or of being alone. The escalator was alive; it even had two electronic eyes at its base, beneath the handrail's moving belt, that tirelessly counted people's feet.

Alternatively, Machines went and stood between the two escalators, and remained there, motionless, trying to focus his attention simultaneously on both streams of iron, the one climbing to his right, and the one descending, to his left. He did not budge for several minutes on end, experiencing an unimaginable rapture, as though he was standing on a rock at the edge of the sea, watching the tide ebb and flow at the same moment.

There were many other such things, inside Hyperpolis, and the man called Machines knew how to talk to them. When there were no more trolleys to push, he did not do as the other fellows did and go off for a quiet smoke in the washroom, or exchange banter with the girls. If a free moment like that came along he just looked at one of these objects and tried to understand why it was there. For instance, he went over to look at the nickel-plated ashtrays, fiercely glowing metal spheres on the tops of columns. He looked at them intently, studying the burn marks

left by cigarette stubs, and the grey ash. He also looked at the
chrome turnstiles that the Masters had installed to count the
people coming in. Or the fire warning system on the walls, with
its little red bulbs that did not light up but kept constant watch.
Or the electronic cells concealed at the base of plinths. Or the
cash registers that clicked away busily and spat out little lengths
of paper covered with figures. People paid no attention to these
bits of paper, and threw them away as they walked along, without even looking at them. Then Machines stooped down and
picked them up, and read out seriously to himself the poems
written on them:

$$
\begin{align}
&0\ 65 \\
&1\ 50 \\
&10\ 00 \\
&5\ 90 \\
&2\ 50 \\
&0\ 45 \\
&6\ 00 \\
&8\ 25 \\
&0\ 75 \\
&0\ 60 \\
&1\ 75 \\
&3\ 20 \\
&4\ 00 \\
&7\ 50 \\
&0\ 95 \\
\end{align}
$$

Total 54 00*

Or he watched the automatic doors. Machines was fond of the
automatic doors. First, there was this kind of platform of black
rubber surrounded by a metal border. In the centre of this rigid
immovable mat was inscribed a circle that contained, engraved
in the rubber, a strange name:

BAUMGARTEN ZURICH

At each side of the black mat, rows of chromium-plated tubes

136

formed a barrier that kept people walking straight ahead. The door itself was extraordinary. It comprised two glass panels held by a powerful steel framework, and IT HAD NO HANDLES. When it was closed, the effect was quite alarming, because the two sheets of plate-glass were pressed tightly against each other, hermetically sealed together by black rubber pads along the facing rims. The two panels let nothing pass through, neither air nor water nor light. It was like a submarine's flooding-chamber, or a jet plane's entrance door. But it was even more beautiful because it was transparent. The daylight hurled itself against the sheets of tinted glass and, in passing through them, completely lost its powers. The daylight was nothing compared with the light of the neon tubes inside Hyperpolis; it was feeble, already impregnated with darkness.

From inside the sealed doors, Machines could see the car parks and palm-trees and silently moving cars. No noise penetrated the door. The murmurings of life outside, birds, aeroplanes, engines, even the sound of the sea were made inaudible by the din that reigned inside Hyperpolis. Or perhaps, outside, the world had become muted, like some war-devastated area.

Then people approached, their feet tapping the ground. Machines watched to see what would happen. The doors' two panels, transparent and handleless, were pressed tightly against each other. Then something truly surprising and magical took place. In the same second that the man in the blue suit placed his right foot on the rubber mat, there was a faint click, a hiss of compressed air, and the two glass panels slid backwards in a single motion, as though kicked hard by an invisible foot. The most surprising part was this hissing noise, that was something between a sigh and the whistling sound a leopard makes when it opens its mouth to breathe out hatred. The twin panels retracted in front of the man's face, so quickly that there was no time to see how it was done. They stayed open, like that, for a few seconds, while the man went out without even a glance around him. Then all of a sudden they slid towards each other again, slowly, silently. The two strips of rubber padding met, and it was as though nothing at all had happened, as though the glass rampart had never ceased to be hermetically sealed.

Machines watched all that, the double door without handles, the hidden pistons, the black rubber mat with its strange name, and it made him think of a camera shutter or the door of a spaceship. He was very fond of the automatic door, and he would have liked to know its secrets: how it managed to open like that, at one stroke, hissing like a cobra, when men in three-piece suits trod on the black mat.

That was the life led by the man called Machines, day after day inside Hyperpolis, pushing his convoys of metal trolleys. He criss crossed the dazzling hall, dressed in his white overalls and wearing the dark glasses with little round lenses that shone like mirrors.

He knew all sorts of places where it was worth stopping to have a look round, any number of metal or plastic objects worth whispering to. He knew many of the thoughts that flew round unceasingly within the sealed grotto of Hyperpolis, the fierce material thoughts that sucked men and women in, then expelled them again, never allowing them a moment's peace. And he knew, too, the sort of plastic booth standing in the centre of the vinyl flooring, with the neon sign on it reading:

INFORMATION

and he knew a young woman who sat inside the plastic booth; a young woman with fairly long chestnut hair and a pale face and tired eyes, whom people called Tranquillity. Occasionally, when he passed in front of her, she would hand him an envelope. In the envelope would be a sheet of paper on which was written a poem, just some very brief phrase, or a question, or a riddle, such as:

'Does electricity need electric wires?'

'Pennuti pesci dell' aereo mare.'

138

'What is it that advances as it retreats
  Rises as it descends
  Is buried on the day of its birth?'

'The path moves forward?'

'The sun cleans so well ...
  That soon the earth is sparkling!'

'One day I shall go and live in a village
  Called Xalpatlahuac.'

'An American visits the castle of an English nobleman. He
marvels at the lawn: "How long does it take to grow a lawn
like that?" His lordship, laconically: "Two thousand years."'

'Each thought loses itself in its own universe.'

Etcetera. Then the young man called Machines would open the
envelopes and read the poems they contained. He sought to
understand them. When he had understood, he was pleased, and
thought up answers:

'No, since it invented them in the first place.'

'Birds.'

'Seeds.'

'The river.'

'Sol, the detergent with lemon additive.'

'Yes, it would be nice to look at the sea from high up a
mountain.'

'A Scotsman won a divorce on these grounds: he had promised to buy his wife a pearl necklace, and she had proceeded to develop a huge goitre round her throat.'

'How can one think a thought?'

'盲 日'

He thought up all these answers while he was pushing his caravan of metal trolleys over the white floor within the walls of Hyperpolis, and it was just one way of imagining that one was free. Like that, one no longer noticed the light's terrible whirlwinds and water-spouts, or the regular explosions of alien words and alien signs and alien orders. One no longer noticed the anonymous faces of the men and women in the crowd advancing like robots. And most of all, one no longer noticed the cameras and microphones hidden in recesses, or the eyes of the secret police on eternal lookout from the surrounding balconies: one no longer knew that they were there, one did not yet know the men for whom mankind were insects.

My tongue is of coral
My beak is of emerald;
I am my own admirer, o my kinsmen.
I, Quetzalchictzin.
I spread my wings,
I weep in their presence;
How shall we soar into the sky?

The small boy nicknamed Dumb Bogo had decided not to speak any more. For a long time, now, he had wanted that: not to say anything any more, to stay silent the whole time. People round him talked a lot, in the street, in the houses, in the cinema, in the buses. They even talked in the churches and cemeteries. Dumb Bogo watched them, with their mouths open and these words that emerged non-stop. Little clouds puffed out of their mouths and curled in the air like smoke. They were very ugly little clouds, which rose continually from between the lips as though there had been a permanently smouldering cigarette stuck in the throat. The people did not cry, or groan, or laugh. They scarcely even breathed: they talked. Or else they kept a word-making machine in their stomachs, one that turned out miles and miles of adhesive speech.

The words made more noise than anything else. In the street, the vehicles had their engines and horns, their disc-brakes and radios and exhaust boxes. Jet planes had their jets, television sets their loudspeakers, locomotives their diesel engines, guns their detonators. But the sound that rose above them all was the sound of words.

Dumb Bogo was not particularly fond of words. He often tried not to hear them, because he was not prepared for them. Around him people talked quickly, without warning. They did not realize that it was not a nice thing to do. They opened their mouths and words came tumbling out pell-mell, and nobody was willing to wait. If they had just thought a bit beforehand, they would surely not have gone on talking in that way, so rapidly and clumsily. Then they would not have risked doing harm with their words.

Dumb Bogo watched the people speaking, and he did not understand how they could behave so shamelessly. He thought to himself that later on, one day, in a few years' time, he would go and live on an island in the middle of the sea, and then he would no longer have to listen to all these words.

They would have done better to speak in low voices. Dumb Bogo liked it when people spoke in low voices. Then you could choose the words you wanted, as though you were reading a book; you could listen to only those words that were beautiful, or funny; you could hear only what you wanted to hear. You turn the knob to the left and you hear:

'..'

You turn it back a little to the right, and you hear:
'....chsst...mass.........ttt.........p......krtas...var...wotwot.'

You twirl the knob jerkily towards the right, and you hear:
' ... ssfbb ... nprsZALLERO ... watsptmmnm ... IDAY-eveningthkomyoonk ... pproff ... novs ... ddle ... zekstavniproskage ... AIRSHIP flvryhgh IN THE SKY OVER AFRICA ... '

It should have been possible to do that with people too: turn the knobs under their mouths so as not to have to hear their voices any longer.

Peculiar things were always happening to people. Occasionally they got together in a sort of sitting-room, and talked. They all sat in imitation-Louis-XV armchairs, and talked. Dumb Bogo lurked unobtrusively in a corner, listening to the people. It was amusing, because they were mouthing incomprehensible and ridiculous phrases with an air of complete seriousness.

For example, a fat woman wearing a hat with a little veil. She fanned herself the whole time, with anything that came to hand; it was a sort of nervous tic. She fanned herself with museum catalogues, napkins, handkerchiefs, hats, and even with the teaspoon when she was drinking tea. She was saying in her high-pitched voice:

144

' ... oodevvens oodevvens no-o-o oodevvens no-o-o ... Ayd
ne-e-eVer 've thawt't Oss'ble!'

'K'nyu mAj'n!' yapped another fat woman with a mole near
her mouth. 'K'nyu mAj'n! ... '

And there was a middle-aged woman who nodded all the time.
She never said very much. She simply nodded vigorously at
regular intervals, while repeating an unintelligible formula:

'Aowyess aowyess kwaytrayt aowyess!'

There was another woman, whom they all called Tantinatine.
She sighed a lot:

'Same with me hhhh the other day hhhh going shopping in
the neighbourhood hhhh with KAda y'know hhhh su-u-uch a
CRowd too terrible so I hhhh ... '

'Oh I simply can't won't go into town any more!'

'Kwayt 'mposs'ble ay 'gree!'

'Aowyess aownaow,' bleated the nodder.

'Swotay sed, swotay sed thuther day t'may USb'nd, ay sed
twim GO into taown if yew waant, AYm nevah nevah goin' in
agehn.'

'Yes so wait just imagine, we were circling and circling trying
to find a place to park, then suddenly I sAW a vacant place so I
said to Katherine, no I mean to Ada, funny I'm always mixing
those two up, so anyway I said to Ada, just get out dear and
signal the cars not to stop there because, so that ... '

'Kwayt,' agreed the woman with the mole, 'too teRRible!'

'Like, like the other day,' added the fat woman, fanning herself with her glove, 'I was ... '

'Nonob't liSSen to what happened then! I said to Kath I
mean Ada, I said to her, just get out dear and keep that space free
for me while I circle the block and come back. So she gets out
and I go round and when I get back, oh ah it's really inCRED-
ible, there's this car parked in MY space and on the edge of
the pavement oh oh ah ah there was Ada, I mean she was
standing on the edge of the pavement and CRYING, no but
really I'm serious I mean she ah ah oh oh she was AKSH'lly
CRYING!!!'

'No!' cried the woman with the mole.

'Oh yes! She was cry-ing! Oh oh beKOZ, no but listen, snotall, the woman driver who had stolen my vacant space had called her, had got out of her car and called Ada oh oh oh a silly old bitch. There!'

'Oh!'

'Aowyess aownaow haow shOckin! Oh!'

'Oh-ah!' screeched a woman wearing glasses.

'BItch, mark you!'

'K'nyu mAJ'n!'

'Yes, yes, a perfectly respectable young woman, she called her that VILE thing as she got out of her car, then she went away, leaving poor Ada CONVULSED with tears!!!'

There were men too. For example, a fat bald man with a glistening pate. He was droning:

'That whole business, y'know, shares. I don't trust 'em, y'know, shares go up but then they go down!'

A man with a sad face. Dumb Bogo wondered why his face was so sad. The man sniffled a bit, then muttered:

'All that — pooh! ... '

'Same with GOLD,' said a man sporting a little broom-shaped moustache. 'Very tricky stuff, GOLD. You never know where you are with it.'

'I'll tell you what,' said a chubby man who was champing a cigar butt, 'the best bet is gems. At least they're solid, they won't run away.'

'Hm well yes but,' said the bald man.

'Yesyesyes, gems, hmm, listen, before the war I could have put money into construction companies, any number of sites available, well today ... '

'Yes but the war put a stop to all that.'

'Tobacco has shown good returns.'

'And then, and then my wife said to me, euh, Government Bonds are less risky, so ... '

'Yes, Gilt Edged, yes ... '

'I mean, paying eight and a half percent, that's ... '

'Excuse me, not as much as that, I remember, it was seven and a half.'

'Nono, eight point five, I remember quite well, I even recall my brother saying it was the highest rate ever.'

'And I tell you it was seven and a half, no more! Besides ... '

'All that — pooh! ... ' sighed the sad-faced man.

But no one paid any attention to him.

'In any case, what good is it today, huh? Not much !'

'D'you know HERman?'

'HERman, you mean Philip, I mean *George* HERman?'

'Yes, little HERman who was at SYOO-iz.'

'Ah yes, the youngest ... '

'Yes, that's George.'

'Right, well, HERman bought a whole bundle, just before the market crashed.'

'Shares?'

'Well yes, ah, shares, in the ah Company, when they ... '

'Very rash, that!'

' ... when they were at rock bottom, then he sold them again, just before the crash!'

'Ah yes, quite a gamble.'

'Yes, that HERman. I'll bet you he's ... '

'All that, hmm, pooh!' said the sad-faced man.

And he really did look sad.

Dumb Bogo sank back into his armchair and pretended to be an armchair himself, keeping his hands as still as possible, his arms blending into the chair's arms, his legs as motionless as chair legs.

It was because of these people that Dumb Bogo had decided he would not speak any more. Their mouths made so much noise, all the time, and never stopped moving. And people did not really talk, either: they gave orders.

Dumb Bogo knew quite a lot about faces: he studied them. For example, he knew exactly when his mother's red mouth was about to open in her white face, because at that moment her eyes flashed strangely, and one heard:

' ... Come here!'

Or else:

'Go and find me the scissors!'

And at school there were the teachers. They gave the children a sort of circular look, like a vulture searching for carrion. Then:

'Stand up!' 'Sit down!' 'Write!' 'Answer!'

'Shut up!' 'Get out!' 'Recopy!'

'Repeat after me!' 'Silence!' 'Silence!'

'Silence!' 'Answer!' 'Silence!'

The teachers' voices exploded like shells, and the children sank their heads into their shoulders. The playground, too, was full of these frightening words. Some big bony creature would grab Dumb Bogo by the hair and squeeze his neck in the crook of an arm, yelling at him:

'Say "I'm a stinker", go on, say "I'm a stinker", if you don't say it I'll choke you, quick or I'll start squeezing!'

But Dumb Bogo clenched his teeth very hard to stop the words coming out, and said nothing. Occasionally, though, one of the big boys would squeeze a little too hard, and knee him in the groin; then, with tears of pain filling his eyes, Dumb Bogo could not keep the words back any longer, the vile words crept out of his mouth, and the onlookers burst into mocking laughter as he stammered:

'I'm ... a ... stinker ... '

Words were constantly scurrying to and fro across the playground, and they all sounded like fierce dogs. They ran through the streets of the city, through the parks and along the beaches. They roared along the motorways at high speed. They even found their way into the most obscure places, places where it would have been nice to have silence, such as churches, cellars, grottoes, museums, lavatories, or station subways. When the words stopped chattering, when their cries could no longer be heard, there sometimes seemed a chance of being left in peace, for instance in this blockhouse at the edge of the sea.

Dumb Bogo entered slowly, through the dank underground passage that smelt of urine and death. The first thing he saw, scrawled on the cement wall in huge letters with a piece of coal, were the words:

CUNT
SLUT

and they sprang at his eyes, bored straight through his eyes, and it was as though he saw the mouth that was in the process of spitting the words out.

No one was ever really at peace anywhere, when words were round. They always came to ferret you out, wherever you might be, snapping out their orders, forcing you to listen to their insults. If people, instead of talking, screaming and shouting, had whispered and murmured, then perhaps things might have been different. They could have said what they had to say in a low voice, whispering into ears, almost without moving their lips. You would have had to go up close to them to hear, and that would have been nice. Dumb Bogo enjoyed whispering. When someone asked him a question, in a loud voice full of hatred and anger, for example 'What were you up to yesterday?' he replied in a whisper.

'What?' the voice demanded.

'W'n'onth'b'ch,' whispered Dumb Bogo.

'What? Speak up, I can't hear a thing!'

'Nonth'b'ch.'

'What? What? I can't hear a thing you're saying!' the voice roared in a genuine rage.

But Dumb Bogo went on answering softly, and then the voice yelled twice more 'What? But I can't *hear* you, for God's sake!', and then finally it got tired and went away.

Dumb Bogo would have liked to know where the voices came from. That is one thing that he would have really liked to understand. It was not too difficult to understand all the rest: people's eyes, their gestures, the sound of their feet as they walked, their way of smoking cigarettes with a serious expression, the sounds they made with their jaws when they were munching biscuits, the noise of their spoons when they were scraping the bottom of

149

their plates, or even their various snoring noises during the night, These were all isolated gestures that remained self-contained, rather like a snail's trail of slime, or the motions of a lobster's mandibles.

But when they started talking, matters were different. Little pits suddenly opened up in mid-air, luring you towards them with eddies and whorls. The best thing was to pretend not to understand them. It was easy to imagine that they were speaking some foreign language, or that their mouths were uttering animal cries.

In the street, for instance, a man wearing a navy-blue raincoat and a black peaked cap opened his mouth in a wide yawn, and Dumb Bogo could see the veins bulging in his neck. The man yelled:

'Gobble-gobble-gobble-gobble-bl-bl-bl-bl-bl!'
like a turkey.

A woman with two small children said:
'Caw-caw-caw-caw-caw-aw-aw-aw-aw ... '
That was a jackdaw.

Once, Dumb Bogo was sitting on the edge of a basin full of geraniums, in the courtyard of the block where he lived, when his mother leant over the balcony, and he could hear her calling from the fourth floor:

'Miaow! Miaow! Wow-ow-ow-ow!'
because at that particular moment she was speaking like a cat.

It amused Dumb Bogo to listen to people making animal noises. There was one person who barked, and there were several who cooed like pigeons. Some whistled like blackbirds, others mooed, brayed, grunted, or bellowed. There were even a few who spoke like snakes. Their mouths opened just a little, and out came a strange hissing sound:

'Shshshshshshshshshshsh'
that was quite frightening.

People had no idea that they were speaking like animals. If they had known, they might perhaps have been less stuck-up.

And occasionally their throats released sounds that were neither cries nor words. This happened in the street, mostly. Some people opened their mouths to start talking to each other, and at that moment Dumb Bogo took a quick look round him. Immediately, the sound of car hooters rose from a nearby traffic jam, and Dumb Bogo heard the people saying:

'Hwang-hwang!'

'Hüüüüüüüüüüd!'

'Honk!'

'Beep-beep-beep!'

'Paaaaaaaa!'

'Aaargh-aargh!'

The opposite could happen, too, and things like cars, houses, trees, aeroplanes and motorcycles could be made to talk like human beings.

For example, when people were gossiping in the street, in front of a garage, Dumb Bogo looked just beyond them, to where rows of cars stood in the darkness, their headlamps extinguished, their windows opaque, their black surfaces no longer gleaming, and he listened to what the cars were saying. This is what *they* were saying:

'Thick fog, goodness yes, couldn't see ten yards ahead, so then I ... ' said a Panhard.

'Yes yes same with me last year when I was on my way to Le Mans,' interrupted a Citroën with a dented wing. 'I'd just emerged from the fog and what do I see coming straight at me? A six-ton lorry. No kidding. A six-tonner. So I jam the brakes on hard, and skid broadside on. Luckily there was a solid thicket planted along the shoulder, otherwise ... '

'The same sort of thing happened to me too,' said the Panhard.

'It's like dogs,' said a rather tame-looking sports car. 'They run out in front of you, and your immediate instinct is to brake, right? So you lose control of ... and bang! it's curtains!'

'Yes at the La Croix crossroads ten days ago — maybe you saw it in the papers?'

'Oh yes the — '

'Yes, the driver was going fairly fast, and it was raining. A cow suddenly started crossing the road ... driver died on the spot.'

'What about the cow?' asked a black Packard that had not yet spoken.

'Ah well I don't know about that, but the driver was certainly finished off: he crashed into a tree at 75 m.p.h.,' said the Citroën.

For a moment the cars remained silent. Then, as he was turning to leave, Dumb Bogo heard the black Packard let out a peculiar sigh:

'Hhhhhhhhaaaaa.'

But it was not possible to arrange things like that all the time. There were days when Dumb Bogo had no choice but to listen to people's words. There were moments when, whatever you did, the mouths were stronger than you were. When you least expect it, they open up and release little clouds that rise in a spiral like those that the Aztecs depicted in their serial drawings. A little whirling cloud that comes towards you, until its coldness penetrates your brain and freezes you from head to foot. That is what words are like: spider's venom, airborne poison. There is not a great deal you can do to protect yourself. You run as fast as you can, along the chequered pavement, but the words dart out of mouths and catch up with you, and the sentences coil round your legs like bolas. Words do not like people to be free: their one aim is to trip you up.

Dumb Bogo fought a constant battle against the spoken word: out of doors, from daybreak onwards, in the streets, buses, lift cages, at school, in the courtyard at home, inside Hyperpolis. He had to be very careful, because the mouths of men and women do not care for mutes, no, they have no great love for mutes. The icy whirlwinds of words, with their clouds like cigarette smoke, attempt to extract further words, no matter what, from deep in the throat: a cry of pain, a sigh of love, a sneer, but in any case, a word. When you are made of marble, and your face looks rather like a doll's, people's words refuse to leave you in peace. They fly through the air, nibble and worry, they are clouds of flies, clouds of sharp-beaked birds and swooping bats, clouds of vultures, clouds of aeroplanes.

The Masters speak. The language of the Masters streaks across the world, with all its rapid, practical, terrifying words. It is not a language like the others. It is a language that never hesitates, never stutters. Its words are constantly in action, always at work. One can neither see nor hear these words, for they travel so fast that one has no time to become aware of them. The giants do not talk with words, as men do. They speak with flashes of lightning and peals of thunder. They open their invisible eyes and electricity races through the sky. They open the secret floodgates of their mouths, and an incomprehensible language slides across the earth, like a tongue of mud. Impossible to know what they are saying: no one can understand their words because they are so swift and powerful. One stands facing this advancing language as one would stand facing a storm coming up rapidly over the sea, with rollers of black cloud looming out of the horizon as though from a vast volcano, and a cold wind blowing, and the white glow of lightning-flashes outlining illusory mountains, and the booming and hissing of the waves: as the storm approaches, fear grips the watcher and he can no longer speak, knowing that he has already lost his own language.

The language of the Masters arrives at the speed of an aircraft taking off, with roars and blasts of air that are its words and sentences. One would like to hide, seek shelter inside a cave, and not know what is going on. But it is impossible. The language of the Masters knows exactly where to find you. It has lightning at its command, and a whole host of signs and sounds that will flush you from cover. The light is terrible and inescapable. It is more powerful than reality, illuminating the inner recesses of bodies and making them transparent.

The language of the Masters is merciless. It has no knowledge of compassion, nor of any such emotion. It neither loves nor seeks to love. It pierces the skin's armour and penetrates the inner organs and the brain, where it blares out its orders. It has no knowledge of music. Beauty does not interest it, beauty is irrelevant. But mightiness, on the other hand, and power ... Terrible words that pour from the depths of black space, and rain down, bombarding the earth. Steadily, without cries or turmoil or murmuring, the language of the Masters counts and computes, weighs, judges, divides, activates: listen to it whistling through you! But one does not hear it with one's ears. It is everywhere at once, it has replaced the sound of the wind in the filaos' branches, and the sound of the sea along the beaches. It is mingled with the light from electricity, with the pulsions of engines, with the grating of pulleys, it is an element of all machines. It is continually in the process of being BORN. Language which flashes across the earth. No one can stop it. One may close one's eyes and stop one's ears, one may bolt the door and lock the windows of one's cell, one may long to be somewhere else, long to remain in one's bubble. But the language of the Masters has words that bore holes through shells and undermine fine mansions. Mankind lives constantly in fear. People flee, their hare's ears erect, listening to the sounds that are approaching ineluctably nearer.

Inflexible, inflexible. The language of the Masters is composed of words that are straight and stiff, that strike with the weight of all their arrows. When bullets leap from rifle-barrels, they do not hesitate: they flash through the air and explode inside the skull. Sound-waves are not soft and gentle: they are as hard as stones or knives. The Masters' waves are irresistible. One opens one's mouth to reply, but the sound-waves have already smashed into the words inside one's mouth, destroying them. Everything that moves, everything that is alive and tender, belongs to the Masters by right of conquest. It is a language that knows so many things! It has invented everything. Pains, passions, beauty, love, disquiet, desire, music, mystery, the gods themselves belong to this language. Even silence is in its power.

Where does it come from? It is never seen coming into being: it is simply there. Perhaps it has always existed, will always exist. What does it want? Impossible to know that, either, because to know that, one would have to be on its side, to be *on the right side of language*. Perhaps it really wants nothing at all, perhaps it is a sort of inhuman fatality, beyond desires and passions. Interrogations have no hold over it. It is not the language of hunger or sadness or joy or death. It is simply the language which commands, the language which emerges from the hidden sun and darts a ray at each human being and inoculates him with its power.

The Masters talk in secret. They do not speak for slaves. They speak for the Masters. Their spoken words travel from one town to another, from one continent to another. There are words like BAYER, PHILIPS, HITACHI that reach the farthest corners of the world and leave their mark there. In underground halls, teleprinters quiver unaided along the roll of white paper, as they write down a few of the Masters' words: STOP SATAP 5% RISE STOP SELL IMMEDIATELY 2 TENTHS STOP NOVIRA AGENT RATIFIES AGREEMENT WITH MALI GOVERNMENT STOP STOP
And silence always reigns. One looks, one attempts to see, with smarting eyes. But there are never any mouths or tongues or hands. There are just these machines, writing of their own accord in underground halls, in corridors, under staircases. They carry on their dialogues across the earth and back again, and all that can be heard is the pattering sound of the type-keys hitting the roll of white paper. The Masters' words are not gentle, they are strong and powerful, say what they have to say, just once, then erase themselves. On sheets of xerox paper they

draw up their lines of figures, day after day

```
CH 718 1000,00   1 AUT 69   5878,73
CO          5,90  25 SEP 69   5872,83
VE       5000,00  30 SEP 69  10 872,83
CH 72L    555,00   8 OCT 69  10 317,83
```

their figures, their mysterious signs.

Men's voices are scarcely to be heard any longer. They have disappeared from the earth, or become one with the sounds of silence. All the cries, the calls, the phrases of desire, are scattered in the wind and through the endless plains, lost in the oceans. The language of the Masters does not concern itself with them. Everywhere, inside the cities' walls, along highways, upon the tall concrete cliffs, inside glass cages, they have set up things like ears. No one knows what they really are, but that is what they look like. They are the mouths of receivers that suck men's voices in and swallow them. That is why one hears nothing any longer. The ancient words slip inside these machines and trace little lines on magnetic tape. The sounds made by tongue and teeth are transmuted, on radar screens, into shapes like ragged flowers that fade away as soon as they are formed. The language of the Masters does more than speak; it knows how to swallow and devour man's own language. When human words appear in the air, vibrating for a few seconds, saying feebly something like:

'I, I love ... '

'I w-w-want ... I w-w-would like ... '

'It's beautiful, it's euh beautiful.'

'My name, euh, is, euh ... '

immediately the new words belonging to the Masters spring into action, and pulverize the ancient ones, covering them with a powdery saliva that paralyses, and enclosing them in a silken cocoon. The Masters' shops stock a great range of things like mummified gnats that used to be words, phrases, sentences, adjectives, conditionals. Words are mute points on the surface of language, incapable of flight, growing gradually lifeless.

No one suspected. People talked, and imagined that talking made them free. But they did not know that the words of their own language were slain on the spot, and that all that the Masters returned to them were husks from which the juices had been sucked.

The language of the Masters flaunts an unassailable power. It is a secret power that penetrates and silences every thing and every person. The language of the Masters has no desire to communicate. It is not designed to be spoken or heard. It is a language that devours information and gives orders. It digests only what is useful to it, and disintegrates the rest. Tirelessly it sorts through words, gestures, actions, dreams, and analyses them. Then from the depths of its sealed cylinders it conjures replies, phrases that lash out like whips. The sinister machines never hesitate, knowing their role immediately, knowing the secret of spoken words that are also actions. They want no noise: just silence, power, electricity. Enclosed in their thick-walled concrete bunkers, in a constant air-conditioned temperature of 70° F., the sinister machines have no concept of life upon the earth. Their brains ceaselessly formulate orders, orders, orders. Slowness does not exist. Error does not exist. The brains are capable of completing 100,000 mathematical operations each second, and the seconds are infinite. The brains' thought processes expand, and in a flash cover the whole surface of the earth, sweeping across deserts, oceans, mountains, marshland, plains, and the chasms that gape in men's cities. Abstract, geometric thought, the only thought process in the world that is not born of chance or human passion, but on the contrary controls these factors. Thought that conquers space and time, that pits itself relentlessly against the masses of humanity, against trees and animals and insects and stars. It travels quickly, very quickly. It passes through women like electricity along wires, absolutely *pitilessly*. Impossible to see or hear it, despite all efforts, because the power emanating from these forces is silent and invisible, leaping into each woman's body without the slightest sound. How could one hear what does not speak? How could one free oneself from the language of the Masters? The obscure forces whirl around bodies, sapping and eroding them. Cities and towns are vast traps set along the earth's surface, plague-spots of violence teeming with words that devour suffering. Invisible chasms open their drain-like gullets and suck in. But where are their pipes leading? The vents of volcanoes plunge down to the centre of the earth. But the Masters have no hells; only the world above, in which they live. The thoughts of the Masters absorb men's thoughts to create new chains, new powers. The language of the Masters devours men's language, to invent new words that are speedier, crueller, more frightful than the old ones.

Perhaps this accursed language has no end to it. Perhaps it is all like a brass flywheel actuated by another wheel, of rubber, that it in turn drives.

The language of the Masters does not know fear, voidness, desire, or anything like that. It is as keenly aware as the snake that penetrates human veins, freezing the body and creating haemorrhages in the lungs. Its knowledge is irreversible: at a single stroke it can gain control over years and years of mankind's existence. It never lets go its grip on what it knows: it keeps its metal jaws clamped tight round throats and necks and limbs, it breaks bones and crushes gristle. Perhaps the only knowledge is that of crime. Perhaps no learning can be gentle or peaceful. Perhaps cold deadly lucidity is made solely for evil. That is a thing that one may never know, since one is always on the side of doubt and ignorance.

One would dearly love to escape the language of the Masters. One would dearly love to be elsewhere, far away, one would like to run, climb down the sides of mountains, cross rivers and seas, bury oneself in the sand, cover oneself in ashes or dust. One would dearly love to be on the other side of this language, in a country where there are no more eyes nor ears, in a country without spies. Where does such a country exist? Everywhere, the words of the Masters penetrate, tyrannical words, hateful words that are all-knowing, confronting one's own total ignorance. From the tops of the watchtowers the labyrinth's pattern must be quite simple to pick out. The traps are visible. The wall concealing the future no longer exists. But the Masters keep their lines of vision closely guarded: they have no intention that men should understand, and be free. The gods, the accursed gods, hold the keys to the universe; they will never relinquish them to mankind. If the Masters spoke with the languages of men, there would be an end to fear and mystery. The unknown, the incomprehensible, the infinite, would suddenly open up like valleys; and air, light, peace, would rush in. But the Masters' messages fly invisibly in space, rip, glide, crash into words. Strange mute animals that live beyond the reach of intelligence and love. Animals of contempt.

The Masters of language know the words that kill. For instance, occasionally they murmur a few words into microphones; just an odd word or two, but immediately men go wild and start killing each other. Loudspeakers broadcast the tape-recording of a strange voice that is both calm and ferocious. The voice says:

'Gold ... '

'Tin ... '

'Uranium ... '

' Petrol ... '

'Agrarian reform, liberty, honour and justice ... '

'Filthy Negroes, filthy Jews, filthy Indians!'

'Progress! Progress!'

and at once people leap at each other, hacking and killing. The language of the Masters speaks from inside human beings. It has installed things like telephone receivers inside people's bodies, and directs its sound-waves through them. The people imagine that they are free. They imagine that they are choosing their own words and thoughts. They imagine that their language belongs to them, and that nobody knows what they are thinking. They imagine that they are safe. They imagine that they live inside tightly sealed shells that nothing can penetrate. That is what they think. But, for the eyes of the Masters of language, people's bodies are transparent.

In its boxes of bone, thought quivers like water on the point of boiling. It is inside, deep inside, that life's motions take place. One sees the skin of the immobile face, the mask's features: eyes, mouth, nose, ears. The brow is a wall rising miles into the air. Women's bulging brows are motionless, like great white walls fifteen storeys high. Light, sounds, heat, movements, blows, desires are all halted by this wall, and hurled back, killing themselves like flights of birds that dash themselves against the façades of high buildings. That is well known, of course. But the Masters of language have pierced holes, have split gaps open in the walls of women's brows, and have begun to enter by way of these liquid apertures: they have begun to destroy the buildings.

Yet they are very beautiful, these sealed abodes standing amid the silence, poised upon the earth in the wind and the light. Perhaps one day they will all be destroyed, the brows that are the fronts of buildings will be shattered, and thought will ooze like lymph out of the burst carapace.

The language of the Masters is inaudible and invisible, armed with thousands of grinding teeth. How can thought resist? What is frightening about the faces of men and women is that they are also motionless mute façades that power and time are gnawing away, ceaselessly eroding. Can there still be a heart left? I mean, can there still be something secret, soft and secret, warm, something violent, obscure, palpitating and secret, in the depths of bodies, in the folds of the body's inner organs, far from the light of eyes, far from the sound of words, far from the dazzlement of intelligence? The words belonging to the language of the Masters want to pierce and riddle. They make great efforts with their high-pitched sound-waves. They push with all their weight, they strain their energy. They want to abrade, scrape out, possess. They want to enter craniums and utter their substitute for human language. They want to inhabit each word of human language and corrupt it. These words split in half on the pages of books, revealing the worm that dwells inside them. One sees a word, any word, on the page of a book, and it splits open to reveal its inner truth:

TREE
HATRED
TREE   CA power LM

It is as though there was something obscuring one's view, a black cloud, a fainting feeling that suddenly rises from the lungs, swarms up through the body, and passes in front of the eyes. What is this kind of blackout? Is it the language of the Masters, already lowering the blinds? One had longed to be alone. One imagined that one could be alone, if one wanted, for months and years and centuries. But the sentinels' eyes were trained on mankind since the beginning of history, and all men's paths were set with traps and snares.

Language, terrible pitiless language. Its words glide through the veins and rise to the heart. There are so many sweet and delicate things to destroy, so many hymens to rupture. Words are like phantom bullets that open little bleeding mouths. Words are like poisoned icicles that melt immediately in the warmth of the flesh that they have pierced, and then turn the flesh to ice. Words ... But there are no words. Words are the sentimental weaknesses of mankind. The Masters have no words. They have figures, impulses, lightning-flashes, explosions, circuits, card-indexes. Their memory is vast and limitless. Everything is inscribed in the Masters' mechanical brains. Nothing is ever forgotten, everything serves a purpose: the way cigarettes ignite, or the way cars slew round on sharp bends, footsteps on plastic-tiled floors, the movements of fingers, the blinking of eyelids, tears, sneezes, smiles, stutterings, intoxications, gastric and hormonal secretions, the oestrogenic cycle, obsessions, manias, the thresholds of pain and pleasure. Everything that moves and lives and speaks and dreams belongs to the Masters' memory. Is there a single thing that they do not know? Is there, on the whole surface of the earth, a single place where silence reigns, a single spot that is deserted or unknown? Even hatred and despair belong to them, have been recognized and conquered by THEM. The language of the Masters is not concerned with the hatred that it arouses; or rather, it measures, judges and despises the hatred. Each time that it invents a new desire, the language of the Masters simultaneously invents the appropriate hatred, and instals it in the centre of that desire's actions as a necessary negation. Hatred is the illusion of freedom, and the language of the Masters exudes the word *freedom*. The language of the Masters knows in advance all possible paths, and has decided that man shall have no other destiny. That is how things are, more or less. But it is not really possible to know all that, because to know these things it would be necessary to be in the mouth that speaks, and not in the ear that listens; it would be necessary to be in the leaping electricity and not in the glowing tungsten wire.

Now and then, the desire to be free returns. One longs at least to see the Masters whose language torments and destroys. One searches vainly for a glimpse of them: in hidden cells, in concrete blocks of flats, in basements, in tall buildings with speedy lifts that travel tirelessly up and down. In halls lined with imitation marble, names sparkle:

MANPOWER

UNILEVER CO

ROHM & HAAS

CIC

CARBORUNDUM COMPANY

CULVER ADVERTISING INC.

THE EAST AFRICAN POWER & LIGHTING COMPANY LTD

THE ROYAL BANK OF CANADA

INTERDEAN

MAGNETIC MEDIA CORPORATION

RANK XEROX

and then there are all those steel doors on which are written, always, always, the frightening word

PRIVATE

One searches from street to street, in fortresses surrounded by barbed wire, in depots and hangars and warehouses. One explores machines and tanker lorries and aeroplanes and ships. There is this great desire to see the Masters' faces, hear their voices, feel their breath. But the Masters are not there. They do not exist. Maybe they are on another planet, on VENUS INC., for example, or in ALPHA CENTAURI Building. Perhaps they live on the pole-star and send out their sound-waves along the light's course.

They have no faces. They have neither bodies nor voices. Their power is like an invisible gas, and the whole world inhales it.

Perhaps if one saw the Masters one would be less afraid. If one saw the words emerge from their mouths one might imagine how those words had been formed in the throat, how they had first come to be fashioned, and so on, and the atmosphere would not be so menacing and silent. If one heard the words bursting in the air, one after the other, one could close one's ears, or else send missiles against them. But the language of the Masters passes through men before they have heard it; strikes, shatters, destroys without leaving a trace.

MAD	Michigan Algorithm Decoder	Where are its hiding-places?
ALGOL 60	Algorithm Oriented Language	Somewhere, surely, there must be a heart, a
FORTRAN	Formula Translator IBM Corp.	throat, lungs, hands, a brain?

NELIAC

JOVIAL

IT

GAT

FLOWMATIC

Invisible invincible language
The Masters call each other by telephone

the signs inscribe themselves on the paper, one after the other,

all the letters

ABCDEFGHIJKLMNOP
QRSTUVWXYZ

all the figures

0123456789

+ − * * / ÷ ↑ = ≠ $: =
( ) [ ]
⩽ < > ⩾
, : ; ' ' .

it would have been nice to keep the letters but they escape they flee towards the receivers' mouths they are food that is gulped down gulped-down men too are food

words that are no longer words, torn from human language and become signs for the Masters,

begin   end   comment
go to   if   then   else   for do
while   step   until
integer   real   array   label   value   procedure

the magic words open up
NORMAL MODE
IS INTEGER
END OF CONDITIONAL   Monte Carlo Method
about nothing perhaps or

166

Boolean language

True	or	False?	
True	or	False?	
True		False	are you reading
True		False	George Boole's
True		False	*An Investigation of*
True		False	*The Laws of Thought?*
True		False	
True		False	

then a poem begins
there is no more random chance
there is no more beauty
there is no more love
where, where is mankind now? Listen:

begin integer r, s;
    for r := 1 step 1 until n-1 do
    for s := r + 1 step 1 until N do

begin comment at a time t hence, ship r will be in
            position (xr, yr) = (Px [r] + t * Vx [r],
            Py [r] + t * Vy [r])

ALGOL 60

Absolute language that does not hesitate
that does not commit errors
The language of machines has no pity
does not concern itself with people
LOVES nobody
One should yell, call out, but what use would it be?
The names, the terrible names of the Masters,
that reverberate in their absent language
PORCHE OF WUPPERTAL
VICTOR MORITZ
LEYLAND
CLAYES
GROSS
Rohm & Haas
Rohm & Haas
Rohm & Haas

There are other cries, terrible cries let forth from the tops
of houses, that fall like stones, they are triangular stones
whose points stick in the soft tar, and sometimes perforate
skulls. They fall ceaselessly, creating many wounds, and yet no
blood flows. High-pitched screeches of birds swooping down
on invisible prey. Words are not innocent, they enjoy killing.

It advances steadily, it goes straight
to the heart of things. It advances with
its simple powerful movements, like a train
engine, a steamboat, or an aeroplane.
Language that is the language of things, that is
THINGS THEMSELVES. It traces a path that crushes fields
of grass and men's fields of action alike. Indifference
that kills, crushes, kills, always calmly and quietly.

How to resist? One should
destroy the language of the
Masters in the minds where it
takes shape, one should learn
to recognize it. But it is on the other side, distant, enigmatic.
It is on the side of action, not of thought.
Thought should draw itself up high, but the language of the
Masters is just   ahead of thought.

<u>real</u>   a, b, c, D min ($\uparrow$ 2 = c − b $\uparrow$ 2 a at time
              t = −b / a), t;
        a := (Vx [r] − Vx [s]) $\uparrow$ 2 + (Vy [r] −
              Vy [s] $\uparrow$ 2;
        b := Px [r] − Px [s]) * (Vx [r] − Vx [s] +
              (Py [r] − Py [s]) * (Vy [r] − Vy [s]);
        c := (Px [r] − Px[s]) $\uparrow$ 2 + (Py [r] − Py [s])
            $\uparrow$ 2;
        D min := sqrt (c-b $\uparrow$ 2a);
        t := −ba;
<u>if</u>   D min <gap and t> 0 <u>then</u>
<u>begin</u>   write text (') the \$ ships \$ now \$ in \$ posi-
        tions ');
        write (Px [r]); write text (',');
        write (Py [r]); write text (' \$ and \$ (');
        write (Px [s]); write text (',');
        write (Py [s]); write text (' \$ will \$ close \$ to
        \$ a \$
        distance \$ '); write text (' \$ in \$ a \$ time \$ ');
        write (D min);
        write (t);
                <u>end</u>

            <u>end</u>

<u>end</u>

<u>comment</u>

<u>real</u>   Ax, Ay, Bx, By, Cx, Cy, interval, gap;
<u>integer</u>   N, r; <u>Boolean</u> first scan;
on watch : set fixed data (Ax, Ay, Bx, By, Cx, Cy, interval,
        gap);
restart : first scan := <u>true</u>
          count (N);
reset :   <u>begin</u> <u>real</u> <u>array</u> Bearing A, Bearing B, Bear-
             ing C,
            Px, Py, Old x, Old y, Vel x, Vel y (1 = N);
        repeat : scan (Bearing A, Bearing B, Bearing C,
            Bearing (, N);
              fix (Ax, Ay, Bx, By, Cx, Cy, N, Bear-
                ing A, Bearing B, Bearing C, Px,
                Py, ALARM);

if not   first scan then
                begin how fast (N, Old x, Old y, Px, Py, inter-
                                val, Vel x, Vel y);
                    end;
                update: for r := 1 step 1 until N do
                    begin Old x [r] := Px [r];
                            Old y [r] := Py [r];
                        end;
                r := N
                count (N);
comment we test next ship number changed;
                    first scan := r ≠ N
                go to if first scan then reset else repeat;
end of block labelled reset;
                ALARM: write text (') error $ in $ data');
                go to restart;
end
    end
        end of programme;

IT IS THE LANGUAGE THAT thinks
Far from me
Far from reason, far from happiness & unhappiness, always
far away, invisible, inaudible, intan   gible, it never flees
when it is I who am fleeing it is watching   the
world with the cruel pupils of its two inflexible eyes
when it is I who am blind, it knows, it speeds ahead, it
breaks, it stabs, its words are searchlights that pierce
the darkness, it has no fear of shadows, it has no fear
of beauty nor of death
    language, the sole language,
        while men stagger and fall;

                    between the word beginning
                    and the word end
                    only a few thousandths
                    of a second
                    have elapsed

                    Lightning-flash

Dichlor
Diphenyl
Trimethylethane

Poem for Machines

Metals and stones are harder than human flesh. Human flesh is tender; it cannot withstand knife blades or razor blades or bullets or things like that. If you press the tip of an Arabian paper-cutter against your chest, you soon find out which is the stronger. Human flesh harbours pain, and the slightest gash will produce a little spurt of blood. The reason why objects are so hard is that they know how to keep death at bay and are not afraid of either time or space. When a pebble strikes another pebble, on the beach, you hear a sharp dry sound and that is all. Sometimes a pebble breaks, and then there is a smell of powder. But pebbles' wounds are painless; they are clean and sharply defined, and if you bring the two halves together they fit into each other so precisely that it is as though the stone had never been broken.

Human wounds are not like that: they are atrocious, ugly, bloody. Likewise, men's voices are filled with pain and anger, and their echoes hover in the air, ceaselessly disturbing the surrounding silence. Human flesh is similar to human language. Words are feeble: a hundred times, a thousand times, they repeat the same complaints and the same desires. Thoughts — but are they really thoughts? Rather, they are tremors, spasms, quiverings of eyelids. Thoughts cannot withstand objects. When men and women pass in front of an object of any kind, a car, for instance, or a boat, or a cake, their eyes shine with greed, their palms sweat, their hearts start thumping, and they approach the object slowly, touch it, study it, sniff at it, then try to take it away: at which point they suddenly feel as though they are paralysed.

Objects never behave like that. They are calm and silent, even those that know how to roar and leap. It is amazing how calm and remote they remain. They are stars floating in the sky, majestic, haughty.

Men are afraid of objects because they know the objects will survive them. When they look at a glass, any ordinary glass, standing on a table, half filled with clear water, they know that the glass will last 150,000 years. The electric light illuminates the outside surface of the proud, hard cylinder that gleams, solitary, on the table's plateau. It says nothing. If never answers. When you approach your lips to its rim, there is no use saying:

'Glass, glass, tell me, do you love me?'

The glass stays motionless, shining with all its might there on the table, and its silence is terrifying. Then the men and the women turn towards each other, talk to each other, try to love each other; all because glasses and the other objects in the world are silent and never reply when questioned.

It might be best to destroy all objects without exception, because then perhaps there would be no more pain and anguish. Alternatively, it might be best to destroy all mankind, and then there would remain only the calm hard world, shining pitilessly with its unwavering glare.

Machines are truly beautiful. They are beautiful because they do not betray, do not desire, have no weaknesses. Machines are full of strength, capable of running for many days and nights without getting tired. Anyone who cannot sleep because of the fears and doubts that oppress him should go and study a machine of some kind. Machines are peaceful, with their shiny metal casings, their cog-wheels, bolts, cylinders, wheels and propellers. Machines are not slaves. They do what they have to do, quite simply, without passion or hope. They do not talk. They ask no favours. They stand solidly on the earth, rotating, chopping, advancing. They have neither eyes nor brains. They judge no one. They do not like blood. They are separated by the air round them, and they have no desire to join forces, to reproduce. I love them very much. Sometimes I sit down in front of some machine, at the edge of a building site, or in a ship's engine-room, and look. There are extraordinary sounds to be heard, some slow, some powerful: snarling, and the hissing of steam, and the hiccuping of valves. Driving-rods push at the spokes of wheels. The metal shell trembles like a horse's flank. Machines and engines are solid and powerful, like animated rocks. Sometimes their movements are so huge and slow and ruthless that they seem capable of flattening whole cities; sometimes their movements are so rapid and precise that in comparison the lightning flickering between clouds is no more than a snail's trail of slime.

But it is difficult to discuss machines and engines, or say exactly why one likes them. It is difficult because they are not amenable to love or any other sentiment. No, one cannot really talk about them. They simply seem to work, without anyone knowing how. One walks along a dusty street, one day, in the hot sun, and there they all are, hard at it. Cars are advancing in serried ranks, behind their tinted windscreens and sparkling bumpers. Aeroplanes are busy crossing the sky, and trains are thundering across iron bridges. There is nothing to be seen or heard but engines growling, spinning, creating heat and odour, vibrating, pounding away. Sometimes, when confronted by all these engines, one even feels hatred towards them; but that is how one begins to love them.

Engines do not speak. They do not return your hatred. They stay put, working non-stop in the bright light. Then you happen to find yourself passing a building site at the side of the road, and you see this beautiful red-painted machine engaged in demolishing a building. The shock of its appearance is all the greater because you were not expecting it. There it is, standing like a fat insect in the middle of the work site, raising two thick arms in front of a closed cabin inside which no human form is visible. There are many engines everywhere, but this bulldozer is alone on the rubble-strewn plain, advancing, retreating, then advancing again with a whining roar. Its two muscular arms end in a hollowed hand with curved fingers, and it is using that to demolish a house.

The bulldozer rolls forward on its caterpillar treads. The sunlight bounces off its red metal shell and its plexiglass cabin. It heaves itself powerfully over the heaps of broken bricks and plaster, rumbling towards the walls of the ruined building. When it reaches a wall it raises its arms a little way, then lets them fall again. The hooked hand gives a gentle tap and the wall crumbles instantly. Then the bulldozer backs away, scooping up chunks of wall with its hand. The air is full of the acrid smell of dust, and all sorts of terrifying noises: the crash of falling masonry, the thud of the metal hand, the creaking of the caterpillar treads, the engine's scream. It is so beautiful that one's hatred evaporates. One is carried away, forced into submission to the hard-working machine. This waste site combines so much solitude and force that it is as though the history of mankind had come to a halt there. The bulldozer resembles a slow, methodical, metal insect. All alone, it circles round the gradually disintegrating house. The walls collapse, one after the other, with their strips of wallpaper, their staircases, their chimneys, the scars that are floors and ceilings. The bulldozer's arms flatten the walls in a leisurely, disinterested fashion. They destroy. Occasionally, a segment of wall resists. Then the bulldozer goes right up to it and pushes it with its hand closed into a fist. The twin treads churn up the rubble underneath them, and throw out sparks. The engine roars so loudly that the air turns into something like a cube of metal. Then the wall slowly gives way. One can see the cement blocks splitting apart, the iron reinforcement bending backwards. One by one, the iron rods snap. Everything that the bulldozer confronts grows soft and pliable. Dust shoots out of the wall like a snowstorm, and descends in a cloud over the bulldozer's red casing. Then, after long minutes of resistance, the wall suddenly tilts backwards like a broken neck, and its debris rolls away to the foot of a mountain of rubble.

There is so much strength here, on this building site, that breathing becomes difficult. One no longer knows what it is to be a man. The bulldozer advances, retreats, advances, on the caterpillar treads that grind the ruins to powder. It flattens the wall beneath it, and its hooked hand sweeps aside anything remaining upright. Closed rooms suddenly gape open, revealing dim caverns in which people once imagined that they would go on living for ever. The bulldozer does not talk, and never rests. Standing alone in the middle of the building site, it sets about demolishing the old house, smashing the angled structure, moving ponderously over the powdery debris, snapping beams as though they were matchsticks. It wants nothing. It loves nothing. The sunlight is pure and clear, the dust is dry. There has been no rain for weeks, for months, even. The women have all gone away. The cockroaches fled long ago. The rats have found other homes for themselves. Perhaps there is no hope left, either, no sorrow, nothing like that. The bulldozer asks nothing of you and has nothing to teach you. It does not know fear or wisdom, it has no learning. It belongs to the world of red insects that destroy the walls of ancient buildings, and tear up forests, and flatten hills. When one looks at it there, at the edge of the work site, one no longer sees the world of men, or their cities, one no longer knows their thoughts or hears their words. Suddenly language no longer exists! There is no air left, to make the starlight flicker, no water left to hide the sea's ravines. Machines, beautiful machines! One does not love them with feelings of flesh and blood, but with feelings of mouth and heart. One loves them metallically, with the inner substance of the hard solid body: heart, lungs, viscera, nerves, arteries; screws and bolts, driving-rods, wires, cubes, iron cylinders that move tirelessly, effortlessly. The bulldozer lurches over the rubble, and the walls collapse when it leans the back of its hand against them.

It is not the men who are in command of the bulldozers. It is the bulldozer who invented men, and then, since they failed to interest it, obliterated them with its muscular arm.

Perhaps, in the company of this and the other machines, one would no longer be alone. Perhaps, when one is in their company, one becomes like a machine oneself, and then one no longer dies, one is no longer sick, one no longer has this never-ending dread of suffering and solitude. Then one stays in the sun for long hours on end, and the light no longer penetrates the metal shell. One no longer has eyes or ears, one is filled with heat and energy; with a single push of one's half-closed fist one can shatter the walls of prisons and barracks, and the white roof of Hyperpolis, and one can break through the ring of strangling, asphyxiating mountains.

Everywhere, there are so many machines, so many bulldozers, concrete mixers, power-hammers, cranes, crushers, steam-rollers, polishing machines, tanker-lorries, so many engines, so many motor vehicles! Some people claim that machines are not perfect, because they are all man-made. But it is not true. Machines are fierce and pitiless, and capable occasionally of taking revenge. They smash and kill, sever fingers and heads, crunch human flesh with their iron jaws. Sometimes they take revenge on man. In reality they have no masters, for their will is infinitely free. Machines go mad. Engines suddenly start turning at 12,000 r.p.m. in space, and then explode. Or the pistons crack the cylinders and the oil evaporates into the air in less than a second. The brakes fail on six-tonners going down steep slopes, and the great mass of metal plunges downwards on its spinning wheels, flattening lamp-posts and crushing women and children against brick walls. Sometimes, in the big department stores, the escalators go mad, their rising steps rear up and hurl hundreds of bodies backwards, down to the bottom, like so many dead fish. No one ever knows why machines behave like that. The world is sleek and orderly, and then suddenly it is bristling with spikes and angles and blades. No one knows why. When one looks at a machine, any machine, it is both terrible and beautiful to think that at any moment it might go insane and start killing, and go on killing.

Yes, when one looks at machines of any kind, men appear as

nothing more than heaps of pebbles in comparison. I find it difficult to put this feeling into words, because it is both horrible and beautiful, and words are never simultaneously horrible and beautiful. Do you know those big harsh cities that are filled with noise, life, heat, light, odours, nourishment for the pores of the skin? Sometimes, when one is walking through one of those cities, everything turns silent, becomes closed in. There have never been such utter deserts as these. Even the moon's deserts are not so uninhabited. A wind blows down the endless avenues of stone, an icy wind that travels noiselessly along these corridors. This is a true wind of stone, scouring everything with the grit that it blows. It tears away excrescences of all kinds, poles, window blinds, doors, mushrooms, branches from trees. It sweeps along the walls of these towering cliffs, entering through the windows and emptying the rooms. Only machines can resist the wind, because they are smooth and hard and bolted together. The grains of sand fly so quickly through the air that they become encrusted in the cast-iron surfaces, pitting them with little craters. The walls are pock-marked by the onslaught. And the wind never stops. It comes from outer space, vast and insatiable, it is the void itself. What would be the point of talking about death and birth and love and that sort of thing, when such a wind as this is blowing? There is nothing to restrain its enormous power. A great silence descends upon the cities at midday, and a black shadow spreads through the networks of their streets.

Look at the sky: it is black. The sun is an icy globe suspended in empty space. The earth is flat, and the sky passes slowly over its surfaces, pressing down very hard, squeezing tightly against each smallest furrow so that nothing escapes. When I see this vast wall of crystal advancing towards me, I want to cry out in anguish, to turn and flee: I would like to shrink into nothingness, because I know that no power on earth can keep it at bay, that the cold and the void will break me and turn me into dust. My whole body trembles as I watch the silence advancing along the city's conduits, a moving jelly, a sky of black jelly in which the cold stars are frozen, advancing invisibly through the daylight. Even the sun's rays cannot melt it. But the most frightening sight of all is the one preceding the arrival of this sky: this cold silent wind rushing down the steep slope. All the cities, now, are tilting downwards, for some reason that I cannot guess. And this wind sweeps downwards, downwards. People, too, are moving downwards, the cars and motorcycles and lorries are moving downwards. Even the upwards escalators are moving downwards. The real trouble is that the earth is not really flat, after all: it is slightly tilted.

Listen, machines, I wanted to say this to you: help me! Wait! Slow down a little bit! Human beings are incompetent, feeble. They are pebbles. They hear nothing and learn nothing. Human beings turn into stones and the machines crush them. Human beings are the deafest and most inarticulate of all the animals on the face of the earth. Their ears and mouths are enclosed within them. Pebbles, too, are smooth and, as far as I can tell, their orifices are concealed. Men and women pay no attention to the sky that is approaching like a giant roller. What are they doing? They are speaking inside their bodies: their intestinal mouths emit a little gurgle, and their intestinal ears promptly pick up the sound. They never find out what is going on elsewhere, and they neither see nor hear anything that is going on around them. They are not interested. The only thing that interests them is making little gurgling noises with their guts, and listening to the results.

Machines are not like that. They are brutal and noisy, and perforated all over with exhaust pipes and other orifices. But machines do not like people. They have no need of them. Then they vibrate and crack, their propellers run wild, their casings tremble, and mankind faces death. Perhaps if one succeeded in becoming a machine, even for just a few seconds, one might possibly get to understand what there *is* to understand ...

One can try to be like a machine. But it is not easy. First of all, one's skin has to become very hard and rigid, like a metal casing. Not just the skin of the face and hands, nor the skin of the legs, but the *whole* skin. It has to become like black shining metal, like polished steel with a painted surface, something absolutely impermeable. Even this first stage is not so easy. The skin has to be freed of all its tremors, pains, sensations, hairs, sweat, odours, and its sensitivity to heat and cold. It would be best to be naked, but that of course is not very practical if one happens to be in a city centre at midday. Nevertheless, it would be best to be naked because then the skin would be completely exposed and would harden more quickly.

Well, when one has succeeded in transforming all the skin of one's body into a metal carapace, the next stage is to transform the inside of one's body, and that is really far more difficult. In fact it is so difficult that I have only succeeded in doing it twice, once when I was a very small girl, and then again just about a fortnight ago. It is really very very difficult. You have to transform everything inside your body, even the parts that you do not know. Some people imagine that all they need to do is think that they have a motor in place of their heart, cylinders in their lungs, a distributor instead of a liver, a crankshaft in their entrails, and a carburettor in the stomach. But that is just a silly joke. As stupid as wanting to walk very stiffly, jerking one's arms and legs to and fro like a robot. Apart from anything else, machines are not stiff. They work gently, gracefully, making gestures that are as beautiful and as powerful as a jaguar's. They are never clumsy. It is men who are clumsy. Machines know how to leap, run, crawl, swim, fly; they never hesitate, or quake with fear, or fall down; they do what they have to do, punctually and promptly. That is why it is so difficult to become like a machine *inside* oneself. There are so many new things to understand, so many old things to forget.

Then you have to really understand what internal hardness involves. All the soft organs have to become hard and closed, secured to a framework by nuts and bolts. Hardness does not originate in the mind. If the hardness comes from the mind and spreads through the body, then one is not like a machine but like a stone. Hardness has to enter the stomach directly, from somewhere round the navel, and form itself in one single process of coagulation. It is very difficult to become hard like that inside oneself, and it is very painful too. There are things that break soundlessly within you, soft fragile things in the stomach, as though the viscera and arteries and so on were suddenly filled with concrete and lead. One becomes so heavy that one's legs can scarcely support the weight. One's muscles are still enclosed in flesh, while the centre of the body has already become metal, cast-iron, full of heavy oils and viscous greases. Here is the most extraordinary part of it all: when one turns oneself into a machine like that, one must never think about it at the time. One cannot become a machine by using thought. It cannot be done with the head, only with the centre of the body. On the contrary, if one thinks about it, if one tries to use one's thought to say, with all one's might: I WANT TO BE A MACHINE I AM DETERMINED TO BE ONE, nothing happens. The head grows heavy and empty like a stone. The body loses its strength, collapses, softens, becomes an old heap of rags, a kind of seaweed, liquid like a cesspool. The fact is that machines have no head, no thought processes.

To be a beautiful machine one must first of all remove one's head. That is essential. One must get rid of all one's thoughts, all one's words, the whole garrulous pretentious structure. Thought has to be elsewhere, in the centre of the body, in the arms and legs, and on the metal skin. That is the most painful part of it, because people are not too happy at the prospect of losing their head. They are so used to living inside their head like peculiar molluscs.

They imagine that in losing their head they are going to lose their life. So they try to do everything by using thought from the head, instead of using the thought at the centre of the body. And yet, once one has rid oneself of these mental gymnastics, language, ideas, images, comparisons and so on, it is as though, how can I put it, as though one has been reborn. It is as though one has a star burning steadily and eternally in the depths of one's body, a white sun endlessly radiating its incandescence.

The thought process of machines is like that, burning in the centre of metal shells with all its incomparable power. It is as though one at last recognizes the centre of one's life, the true heart of one's body. One at last sees that heart beating, darting its rays of existence: that is what one truly sees in place of all those insignificant things round it.

Yet no one knows that machines are like that. People think that it is words that are in command of machines. But then people also look at volcanoes and imagine that they are just piles of ashes, without ever thinking of the terrible subterranean chamber swollen with heavy, acid lava. Perhaps if people all thought of that, together, the resulting radiation throughout the world would burn their eyes, and the resulting noise would be so shattering that eardrums attuned to nothing louder than the squeaking of bats would suddenly burst.

Finally, when the body is full of great hardness, and one can feel this star blazing in the centre of one's entrails, a star as open as the pupil of a cat's eye, and seeing the world as it really is, then power and energy surge so strongly within the body that one lives a thousand years each second. One is no longer afraid of anything. One no longer feels like crying, yelling, or talking. One is so full of confidence that talking would be pointless. One no longer has the urge to think; I mean, to think with one's head about men's endless petty problems. One moves forward, slowly, on one's *wheels*, over the open ground. The wind blows, but the skin no longer shivers. The sun bombards with its death rays, but not a drop of sweat emerges from the skin. One fears nothing, neither silence nor lightning nor men's eyes. One never looks at clocks, because the hours that pass are the movements of another machine. And machines neither love nor hate each other. They each follow their appointed path, invincibly. They pass like tigers through towns, they cut swathes through forests of bamboo while birds fly ahead of them to safety. They cross whole continents on their rails, paying no attention to the population of the clouds of flies. They are without desire, are never hungry. They burn their reserves of petrol continually, without ever being thirsty: they are always satiated. Their bodies are fiery, but not with heat: it is more like a cold flame of gas. The sun in the sky is a machine; its vast flames burn without consuming anything, like an eternal matchstick.

Wherever one looks, there are machines. Men and women have become invisible, nothing more than quivering wisps of smoke. They are nowhere to be seen. Language's words glide over the machines' casings. None of them have those old-fashioned names: you remember, those feeble little names like Lucy, Irene, Vanda, Martine, Theresa. No, the fierce beautiful names marked in relief on the metal shells are:

SAVIEM BLUEBIRD UNIC POTIN SATAAM

One leads a fine, neatly organized life, here in the sun, the wind, the rain. One leads an extraordinary life in the centre of cities, destroying and constructing endlessly. At night, one does not lose consciousness, as men do. One is rather like a snake that is cold and motionless, but able to whip upright in a flash, dart out its jaws at lightning speed, and bite.

It really feels good to be like a machine. When one is like a machine one genuinely knows life. One is in the centre of existence, neither ahead of it nor lagging behind. One no longer lives by means of thoughts and dreams and desires; one lives through life alone. One is a planet in empty space, revolving round the sun. One is – how to put it? – one is IMMENSELY BEAUTIFUL. That is how I would like to spend my time, if I had the time, if I was allowed the time: I would park myself on some road, in the sun, and be a machine. Or install myself in the middle of the desert of some wasteland. And I would make the engine in the middle of my body start turning with a gentle regular sound, rak-tak, rak-tak, rak-tak, rak-tak, rak-tak, rak-tak, rak-tak, rak-tak, rak-tak, rak-tak, tak, tak, rak-tak, rak-tak, rak-tak, tak, tak, tak.

MASSEY FERGUSON

t. Jill   JILL   FERGUSON
                  fait hu el

                                    bnjhffluiol
the cat and the hat c me back zskfjhuy, ;lfyr5%9&()*=-xmjhcrnhjklgv
         Vvtyuijkmnbhgfrtcvhmc,zskfjhuy, ;lfyr5%9&()*=-xmjhcrnhjklgv
       bhgf vczmzkaswrioc.xkjdyr oi,njhgxklfgmnjs Johny
     jhgvcfyuc ,o pmnbhgykiopl;yhuuijhgderftgyhuj
                        qusfc sqe ftgt   n
    a k.k Angie Angie Destounighkjh kahen tiens a   u
niue   jjhggg ·jkkkjjjiiuuuukjh · ^
    hi LEJk lkkkv   n,,aasss,

      paul boutin

                       a i i h 16709222
                                                    fuck you

      sBnlp Caggeyyy =   hjjjjjjjhtredfgtruy   vff dnasa

                                Pyle   .....
              f f a aaaaac c acafa.gfefe; fad; fadi fo
      faj; fa k   foj; faj   ;;;; foj; f j; faj;
      f j;   faj; f j; rs o now
                              6666

                       . f-ck the world
la ude   259208/   love   ar   peace   yves lachapeelle

               jaime les fleurs

                     tt6ybklj qterttfuge wurwhefes fleurs
                       ; mjuyh   te k ll h nnrn
                     Wewere n ^^ b
         , B v   Beverley MacLelian
                     My name is Boverley Machellan
e   fr c

                       James Payne

n'en v i   I love hilary   me

Now I would like to say something to you about electricity. The reason I want to talk to you about it is that I am very afraid of electricity, and perhaps through talking about it I might free myself of these fears. The most frightening thing of all about electricity is that it is hidden. One cannot see it. One never knows where it is. Sometimes one thinks one has located it in some particular spot, in a wire, or an electric-light switch, or inside a transformer's little black box, and then one approaches it with great care. But it is not there. It is somewhere else. There is no way of recognizing it. What is frightening, too, is that it never disappears, it remains permanently inside its hiding-places, and never escapes. But how can so much power be detained inside such small objects, without overflowing or exploding? Glasses of water are frightening, volcanoes are frightening, the sea, the wind, rivers, X-ray devices are frightening, but they are nothing compared with electricity. One lives alongside it, day and night, and yet one never knows where it is. It is an imperceptible vibration running through the world. It originates in giant factory-like structures by the sides of rivers, and maps out all its routes in a single second. It originates in turbines, and it is their immense revolving wheels that give birth to it. But is electricity ever really born? Has it not always been there, in the black waters of torrential streams, in mountain caves, in storm clouds, in trees? There are no animals like it in the whole world. Men imagine it is they who invented it, with their amber tips and magnets and catalysers. But it is electricity, rather, that invented men. It was there at the beginning, right at the beginning, when the earth was no more than a muddy puddle. It lived in the clouds, and traced the flashing pattern of its web across the sky. It struck at random, and each time that it touched water a strange cloud of sulphurous steam rose into the air.

Now it is everywhere. In the towns, along the highways, in isolated valleys and deserted plains, in the forests, in the oceans, everywhere. There are millions of wires and coils everywhere, rising and descending. And that seems frightening, too. It is as though armies of spiders were stretching their threads from one wall to another, from one tree to another, until soon the whole world is covered. One is there, walking among these wire threads, without paying attention, but at every moment electricity surrounds one with its deadly power. Sometimes one is walking along an empty esplanade, at night-time. The sky is black, and there are no sounds. But then, going past an iron pylon, one suddenly stops and HEARS: hears the continuous noise, the sort of bee-like humming, that comes from all directions at once. That is the sound of electricity travelling through space. It is a frightening sound. One can feel against one's skin the glancing touch, like a bat's wing, of the electricity streaming by. The hairs of the body prickle, and the hair rises on the scalp. Electricity is invisible, but one knows that it is there, close at hand. One knows that it is swarming all round one endlessly, coming and going, a black power hidden in the night, harassing, stealing, threatening. It is as though one knew one was going to drop dead in a few seconds' time, and could do nothing to prevent it happening. Electricity has its sign, and it is the sign of fear

The wires are terrible to behold. They run across the earth, above it or below it, in their rubber sheaths, all swollen with

life. Surely they will explode? So much power and speed is contained within these motionless wires. The air whistles and burns round them, the sky shatters like a pane of glass, the earth crumbles into fragments, the waters break up into gases. Accursed electricity! It never stops, its vibrations never stop. Its song hums in the ears as though lightning was about to spurt from metal points. Its song never ceases. There are beehives everywhere! In car bodies, in motors, in tyres, along roads, in bridges and towers. The building stands motionless in the middle of the asphalt plains. But electricity travels ceaselessly upwards and downwards, vibrating inside cables and along girders. It has no need of air or water or anything else. It needs nothing but twisted steel wires encased in their black rubber matrices. If there were no longer any wires, perhaps the electricity would stop spurting out all the time. Then perhaps it would spread out, creating great blue electric pools to fill all the world's hollows and pits. But who will free the world of all these wires?

Listen, in my room there are these terrible things beneath the switches: things like skulls with two holes instead of eyes. I have no idea what they are called. I see them every day, but they still scare me. They have very white faces, and their two eye sockets contain death. Electricity watches me through these holes. When I am in my room, and the electric-light bulb is burning, casting its rays of light, I know that electricity is watching me through these two sockets sunk into the porcelain, and that it knows every move I make. Impossible to forget that. Impossible to leave and go elsewhere. Electricity's gaze comes from the other end of the world, the other end of space. It has travelled millions of miles a minute, and it has finally reached these two holes pierced in the porcelain mask in my room. Sometimes I gaze into its gaze, and it draws me towards it. I start hearing the bee-like humming once more; it fills the room with its weird monotonous song that means death. Electricity is irresistible. Its gaze is deep and steady, as distant and powerful as a star's ray of light.

Who will rescue us from electricity? Who will release us from all these wires and coils? I hardly dare to say it, but: electricity is death. One can never have done with it. It seeks you out from wherever you may be hiding in your room, luring you with the gentle murmur of its hive of bees, entering your head and body. It draws you ineluctably towards it, with nothing more than the power of its voice. You get up and walk towards the little porcelain skull fixed against the wall, under the switch. Electricity's one desire is to kill you, and with that aim it draws your hand towards it, towards the two holes that communicate with infinity. It wants you to pick up any metal object: scissors, a knife, a wire, even a hairpin will do. It wants you to go right up to the two dark holes, holding the hairpin in your right hand. That is what it wants. Your head hums like a hive of bees, and strange cold shivers run along your skin. Perhaps your eyes already contain two little blue flames that leap and dance, and your hair is already crackling and throwing sparks. The electricity calls you, and you move towards it with a sleepwalker's gait. There is so much cruelty in the silence surrounding electricity. Electricity is greedy for human lives, hungry to devour the energies of hearts and brains. It wants your life to evaporate from your body, to blend into the wires' infinite lengths, and then to spread through the earth and air. You never suspected. You thought that it was happy illuminating rooms, making irons hot and keeping refrigerators cold. You thought that it was happy in its prison of wires, transformers, magnets and condensers. You thought that it would not dare to appear on the scene, that it would remain hidden under plinths and behind wallpaper. But electricity was lying in wait for you all the time, in your room, spying on you through the portholes sunk into the little porcelain heads. It was waiting. Patiently, day after day, it was waiting, watching out for the least sign of decay: the wires' rubber sheaths start rotting, insulators crack, light bulbs' holders disintegrate, a small length of plaited wire protrudes through its split casing. Then one day, without thinking, you brush your naked hand against a wire, and lightning strikes. Or you stand up in the bath and reach out to switch on a lamp. Or you press the starting button of the mixer. Electricity does not hesitate: it leaps from its hiding-place, with a brief spurt of flame, and kills you. Sometimes, too, it is impossible to resist any longer the eternal droning of bees in your head, the cold shivers that have been running over your skin for so long. You become like a butterfly that seeks death in the flame. You can no longer resist. You advance slowly towards the little china death's-head beneath the switch, and you plunge the hairpin's two prongs simultaneously into the two dark holes.

That is why I am so afraid of electricity. Because it does not like people to exist without it, and yet it wants all the time to make them disappear. The light from electric-light bulbs is like that too. It is not there to illuminate but to erase shadows, all shadows. And men are shadows. It is true that all objects contain death: cigarettes, ballpoint pens, matches, kitchen knives, fish-hooks, windows and window-panes, rocks, thorns, staircases, drinking glasses, cords, gas taps. They all contain some poison, dart, hook, or sheer bulk with which to kill you. But electricity is more terrible still, being no more than a murderous current.

I know some terrifying places. In the outskirts of towns there are places over which a curse hangs, and where electricity rules. On arid plains adjoining towns there are forgotten sites where electricity lives. These are its dwellings. Do you know these places? They are something like towns, but constructed solely of pylons and thick wires, in regions shunned by man. They are more fearful to see than cemeteries, slaughter-houses, barracks, or prisons. No one ever goes there. There is nothing in these places but electricity and death. The gigantic pylons carry dozens of steel cables that whistle in the wind. The cables hang from glass and porcelain insulators, or rest on bakelite and rubber supports. And it is over this deserted stretch of land, on to which neither man, woman nor dog ever strays, that electricity holds eternal sway. It vibrates, day and night, it hums its bee's song, it revolves inside condensers as big as churches, it comes and goes along steel cables as thick as trees, from one pylon to the next, like that, invisibly, untiringly. It never stops, it never ceases being born. Ceaselessly, it inflates its power, like a chest expanding with an endless inhalation. It swells out its power there on the spot, and spreads it through every room in the town. This is the place that one ought to visit, one day, I know. This is where one could destroy electricity, because the place is, in a way, its brain, its ganglion. There is so much deadly power inside electricity that it can end up destroying itself. The steel cables hang from pylons, a few feet away from each other. But there is also something else inside the cables, something that one does not see: sufficient rage and violence to destroy thousands of lives. If the cables ever came into contact there would be a huge spark. If all the cables in the world suddenly touched, a wave of fire would engulf the world in a fraction of a second, and everything would be incinerated. Neither bombs nor bullets nor poisons command so much terror. Electric death travels at lightning speed, leaping great chasms with a single bond. Electricity is similar to consciousness. It is similar to the act of looking. It is within everything that kills quickly and quietly: hatred, evil, misfortune. And one cannot really get to know it.

No one ever visits the places where electricity comes to birth. Occasionally, birds venture into them and are struck dead by lightning. Better to keep away from these places. If you go near one of them, you can hear the deadly sound of bees, and feel your body being drawn towards the steely-blue networks. You get caught up in the cold current that tugs your legs towards that spot over there, towards *it*. Neither thought nor voice can any longer help you to resist. There is no means of remaining yourself any longer. The electricity sucks at your body, empties it, drains it of its life; all from a distance. Best to stop thinking about it. It is so dangerous that it would be better not even to pronounce its name any longer. Electricity is not fond of mankind. No man will ever be its master. It has been given steel ropes and pylons so that it can go berserk. It has been given motors, bulbs, neon tubes, vacuum cleaners, hairdryers, mixers, heaters so that it can make use of its power. It ignites filaments and tubes, it turns wheels. But it is not content with that. It needs an endless supply of new inlets to dilate, new coils to heat white-hot. It needs to break and burn, to strike trees, to hurl its blinding sparks, to electrocute. There are so many electric channels. You touch the outside of a parked car, and you hear a dry crackle. You pass a comb through your hair, and tiny flames spurt out. Sometimes it enters the body, sends pain coursing through it, and makes the brain spin round. Sometimes it fills the head with so much light that there is no longer any sun or darkness, but simply this pitiless whiteness.

Sometimes electricity reaches as far as steel-clad cells in prisons. Once there, it climbs up a sort of armchair that is resting on rubber insulators. In front of it are several wires making their way up towards a strange helmet. The helmet contains the head of a blinded man. Then, at a precise moment, someone pulls down a hand-lever and the electricity rushes into the helmet and frenziedly consumes the blind man's brain. Black flames can be seen shooting out of the tips of his fingers and toes.

So that is how electricity is: neither gentle nor peaceful. It is murderous and pitiless, it would like nothing more than to burn up all the men and women in the world, and strike down all the birds with its lightning. That is why I am afraid of it, and afraid, also, of the electricity within myself. Electricity's gaze is constantly surveying the world, keeping a watch on the lives of all living beings. The networks of wires cover the earth's surface with a power that is all the more menacing for being curbed. Electric thought encompasses the globe, squeezes men's heads. It is a scheme of thought that is for ever alien and hostile, rejecting any attempt to interpret it, rejecting any attempt to love it.

Electricity is at its most terrible during the night. When the sun's light fades at dusk, and darkness begins to descend, electricity wakes up. All its eyes begin to shine in the night, in cellars and rooms, along roads, in the air and on the sea.

There are so many eyes, all sparkling and twinkling: orange-yellow light flows out of some of them in cross-shaped rays. Car headlamps search round with their white beams. At night, motors and engines slow down and stop, and then there is nothing to be heard but the electric light's steady hum. The cities are ablaze with ice-cold conflagrations. Shop windows are full of great motionless flames. There are so many open eyes all around that I can no longer look cities in the face. Electricity does not like shadows; its aim is to infiltrate all hiding-places, to catch all secrets unawares. If it were not there, one might perhaps be able to forget. One would simply close the eyes, or look up at the black sky with all its stars. But electricity does not like the sky or the stars. It covers the city with a dome of pale-red smoke, it dazzles with its searchlights. It likes neither silence nor the sounds of everyday life. So it makes the faint bee-like humming that paralyses and destroys.

Accursed, damnable electricity! I hate it, and it frightens me. It already knows that I am writing this poem, this letter, and at this very moment it is spying on me through the two holes in the little porcelain face, there, to the right of the door, beneath the switch. It is moving along all its wires, it is circling round my head, like flies do when it is about to rain. It will never forget me. It launches its waves at me, to envelop my body. It seeks out my eyes, to enter through them and coil up inside my brain. It would be happy to see me lose my body, my thoughts, my life. Many people have lost their lives this way. Sometimes, when you are walking along a street, you look into the eyes of people coming towards you, and suddenly you see that they have electric eyes. Up the street comes a very beautiful woman. She has the face of a goddess, she is tall and slender, she dances along as she walks. But when she opens her eyes, you see two electric-light bulbs filled with sparks. Or this man in a grey suit, carrying a black leather briefcase. He is bald, and his face is fat and white. But when you see the spectacles he is wearing, you suddenly understand: he is already on the other side, on the side of electric power. The twin lenses of his spectacles shine with such ferocity, dart such flashes of lightning from the centre of the grey-and-white cloud of his face …

Who will free us from electric power? Must one always be afraid, like this, one's whole life long? Why are there so many vibrations and murmurs, so many rays of light? I long for the night never to come to an end, for the silence never to break, for movements and looks to remain pure and innocent! I long for … But electricity does not concern itself with individuals' desires. It just runs tirelessly along its wires. If it ever stopped running, perhaps there would be no more old age and death, no more pain, no more falsehood. Each time that electricity travels a hundred thousand miles, it steals a hundred thousand miles of my life! It is electricity that erodes mountains, wears away the skin of the hands, loosens hair and teeth, ravages faces. The sky is not empty: one can never see space. The whole sky is striated with continuously enlarging circles of waves that make the eyes dizzy. One would like to see, at last: see the trees, the wind, the sea, the stars, the sun, the horizon. But all one sees are these tubes of misty light, these lightning-flashes, these sparks. The world is barred with these giant letters, surrounded by these blue and rose-pink haloes that burn with a cold gleam. Space is alternately very big and very small. And the humming of bees never stops.

There are these detestable illuminations above the doors of bars. Day and night they project their evil glare into the air. Never leaving you in peace. All this snow, all these outbreaks of fire held in check. Nothing ever breaks out, nothing ever frees itself. Electricity switches on its accursed words and they start dictating orders. It never lights up beautiful words, words that say: LOVE! LIVE! RUN! GRASS! HORSE! SEAWEED! All it says is: BAR! CASINO! PIZZA! FURNITURE! WHISKY! BUY! SELL! BUY! SELL! … Electricity lies waiting, with all its flashes, in the depths of dens. It sets iron towers and buildings and car parks ablaze. It digs its nails into minds and eyes, and its long cold fetter links up with the icy power-stations where thought and freedom are put to death. Electricity is entering and leaving my body all the time, leaving nothing motionless. It revolves inside my head, just behind the eyes, and its breath sets a host of tiny fragile propellers spinning round. Even noises are electric. They reverberate inside microphones and transform themselves into pulsions along circuits, then flood out again, making loudspeakers' diaphragms tremble. When the heart beats in the chest, it is in order to inscribe designs, those frightening zigzag electric diagrams. Electricity is the sole consciousness, the sole knowledge. But you yourself are inside knowledge, and so can never know what it is saying. Each time that a woman thinks of a man, each time that a man says a word, it is as though they were lighting a lamp, however impossible that may seem. Neon tubes shine inside shop windows, and it is that that constitutes man's thought. Listen at night to the insect noises of the signs flashing on and off. The city is deserted, and all that can be heard is this slight crackling of the gigantic letters lighting up and blacking out, lighting up and blacking out. The neon tubes brand huge words that will never fade. Branded on my left shoulder is the word

FORGEAS

Night after night, that word burns into my left shoulder with scarlet letters. I do not know what it means, or why it has chosen me rather than any of the others. It is a kind of malevolent electric willpower that has linked me to the word and made me its slave. So everything I do or see or say belongs to it. Whatever I may write, in my efforts to free myself and conquer my fears, whether stories or poems or letters, is written with electric writing. It consists of nothing but impulses running along wires, alternating currents, tension, voltage: not words, you understand? Transmissions. Each time one feels something moving inside one's head, and wants to speak, there is a power station somewhere that transforms the sensation into current and sends out its crackling wave. Men's desires are linked up to transformers. Who is it that invents? Who is it that says things? Men

198

think it is they themselves, but they are wrong. It is merely the generating plant transmitting its waves to the brains of tungsten filaments. No one realizes that. No one wants to believe it. But the fact is that men are chained together, linked just like the little bulbs that light up across the façades of bank buildings at crossroads, spelling out the messages that the invisible voice dictates. The reason I hate electricity is that electricity hates itself. If it were capable of loving itself, I would love it in return. If only it were not filled with this fear that makes it flee for ever along its cables and hurl its sparks of rage into lamps and switches, this fear that makes it spy with its wild stare from behind the black holes set into porcelain death's-heads, then no one would be afraid. But it hates itself, and fears itself, and skulks behind its matrices and insulators, and the whole earth is imbued with its hatred and fear.

When one touches electric motors, the walls of lifts, television sets, contact-sockets, electric irons, soldering irons, one immediately feels the slight trembling that enters the body and dilutes life's energies. Electricity is like that: always trembling. One day, perhaps, it will rediscover its true domains, which are in the sky and in the trunks of trees. Then there will be terrible electric storms, and the world will rid itself of its anguished tensions as it expels great flashes of lightning. Clouds will throw sparks as they clash together, mountains will grow red-hot, cars and aeroplanes will become Faraday cages. And when the storm finally dies down, then perhaps men and women, and indeed the whole world, will at last be able to talk and listen; then perhaps there will be no more waves in the sky, no more humming of bees. Men will never be free so long as the world remains prisoner. The pylons will collapse, and the cables will break and sink deep into the earth. The magnets and condensers and coils will simply mingle with the dust, and there will be no more giant letters to burn into people's skin. That is what I would like. I want it to happen so much that I cannot even put it down in words. I want it to happen so very much that I believe that if I were to look now at an electric-light bulb, it would explode.

Perhaps thought, I mean desire, could prove stronger than electricity. Perhaps it is possible, after all, to look at all these things, the neon tubes, mixers, vacuum cleaners, dynamos, switches, and those little porcelain death's-heads with their two black sockets, without the body immediately becoming empty, and one's thoughts starting to tremble. Perhaps, too, one will no longer be tempted to get up and walk like a somnambulist, hairpin held out in the right hand, towards the two empty holes that are for ever inhaling. Perhaps, after all, one will never have to dissolve one's substance along all these wires so as to illuminate the world with a vague blue glow? It is to find that out that I have written this letter. There are no poems. There are only letters. For the moment I have nothing more to say about electricity.

T

Cambyses, king of the Persians, had long dreamt of adding Egypt to his possessions. He began by attacking the kingdom's 'key city'. Pelusium, a fortified town situated at the mouth of the great river and guarded by crack troops, seemed to defy the universe. Could even the valorous army of the king of the Persians succeed in vanquishing this seasoned Egyptian garrison prepared to hold out indefinitely behind its ramparts?

But Cambyses hit upon an idea. For a month he laid siege to the town, then, when he judged the moment ripe, he suddenly revealed the secret weapon that he had been carefully preparing. A week previously, each soldier had been given the strange order to acquire a cat, feed it, and gain its affection through kind treatment. To this end, his men had scoured the countryside for stray cats. Now, when the shout that was the agreed signal had been given, the warriors advanced, each holding a cat tightly in his arms. Alerted by the caterwauling, the Egyptians ran to the battlements, then recoiled in horror. Who among them would have dared to expose himself in battle to the terrible risk of wounding a sacred cat? Thus it was that, without a single blow being exchanged, the Persian soldiers penetrated into Pelusium and spread through the town, protected by their living shields.

The road kept growling and snarling. It was a very wide, very flat road that ran parallel to the sea. Countless engines streaked along it, one behind the other, pounding away on their wheels, gliding, vanishing. The sea made its own noise, too, but no one heard it. All that could be heard was the snarling of the engines arriving, leaving, disappearing. Often, three or four engines passed each other in opposite directions at the same moment, and that made a strange noise that disintegrated like a shell exploding. Horns, brakes and tyres also sent their noises skimming over the hot asphalt. These sounds were not high in the sky. They were earthbound, existing an inch or two above the road, and one became aware of them mostly through the soles of the feet. The earth, too, had become a sort of machine, an iron caterpillar track whose engines were hidden in mountain grottoes. The earth was busy at some unknown task, sending its wheeled engines from one end of the road to the other, not far from the sea; the engines sped along its black network, skidding, wrenching the gears that modified their path slightly to the left or the right and then set them back on course along the predetermined corridors.

The sun was in the sky. It shone with great intensity. It dazzled. The wind blew over the blue sea, and the sky was blue too. There were many colours, but it was the blue, above all, that one noticed.

The young man known as Machines (he had acquired that nickname because of the word MACHINES written in red letters across the front of his white overalls) was walking along the road, together with all the engines, alongside the pebble beach. He had come from the big block of white cement to the left of the bay, and was making his way towards another block of cement to the right of the bay.

The wheeled engines almost brushed against him as they sped along the road, sending out blasts of air, like the coaches of a train hurtling by at full speed. Occasionally there was the sound of horns, since engines are not very fond of seeing someone walking along their road. They barked once or twice, in passing, and their voices faded, still bellowing away; voices that scattered in the sea wind, echoing in space like the cries of gulls circling a ship.

Machines was the sole person on the road, and there was no one on the beach nor in the sea. The whole expanse of land and water was empty. That was rather extraordinary. If there had been other people round, things would have been different. Perhaps the sun would have blazed less fiercely, and the sea and sky would have been less blue. The light would surely have been greyer, softer. And the engines would have run less quickly, less peevishly, from one end to the other of the short stretch of roadway.

Machines walked along the gravel embankment. Occasionally, because of the pebbles that a recent storm had pushed to the edge of the road, Machines had to climb down onto the roadway itself. That was when the engines barked the loudest. They screamed:

'Hey, watch out!'

'Get out of the way! You want to be killed?'

'Idiot! Stupid fool! Idiot!'

Machines could hear what they said quite clearly. And he was a bit scared. He saw the engines racing towards him on their big fat wheels, and he had the feeling that the engines would have liked to kill him. The headlamps and bumpers, especially, shone with a disquieting, pale gleam that was full of hatred. Where they going? Impossible to guess. They hurled themselves forwards with all the power of their burning hot cylinders, they plunged forwards along the horizontal road. It needed a good deal of courage to dare make one's way against the flow.

Machines had the feeling that he would not be able to continue walking like that for much longer. It was not so much all the movement that was dangerous, or the barking of the horns, or the headlamps' gleams of hatred, or the beaded tyres whirling round on the asphalt. No; one could foresee all that, and by concentrating one's energies one could forge ahead without falling by the wayside and being decapitated. It was a matter of confronting movement with a cold stare. But what was really terrible and dangerous was that there was no way of understanding *what was happening*. The engines followed each other in a steady stream, or in groups of two, or four, all at top speed, and they were going nowhere. They hurtled on, carried by their own momentum, crossing the earth's flat plain in a few minutes, for no apparent reason. As the wheels revolved over the sheet of tar, they obliterated all the patterns and designs that men had thought up on their behalf, wore away and scraped the surface of the road with their magnetic tyres that attracted bits of grit, and what was left was empty, deserted, like a field after the harvest. The engines fell back, in lines, a rain of engines, a rain of meteorites that were useless for crossing space. They never came across anything. They were not even useless: they were simply incomprehensible, a denial of intelligence. They darted off fanatically, all headed for the same outermost point of the earth, in other words the great block of hollow cement on which was inscribed the name

H.Y.P.E.R.P.O.L.I.S.

and their movement was the only thing in the world that could truly be called unknowable.

Towns, airports, bridges, railway lines, canals, tunnels, electric pylons were different: whether you liked them or not was of no importance, since they were planted there and allowed you to get to know them. All that you needed to do was open your eyes, look at them and touch them, and then you had got to know them. But here on this road that was impossible. The engines were there for a fraction of a second, then they were gone. They were disappearing all the time, separating from each other, dwindling into nothing along the road. The noise the engines made did not seem to emerge from them and strike your ears directly; it was as though the noise wrenched itself from the road, the beach, the sky and you yourself, then entered the engine which whisked it away immediately. Everything was continually on the move. There was nothing fixed or durable. It was because of this constant trembling that Machines was frightened. Can one ever get to know the ingredients of fear? No, it is as though you were swimming in a glass, up towards a siphon, battling the jet of cold water, while murderous cubes tumbled round you and down towards the bottom, towards a melting death. The engines raced towards their fall, trailing their whirlwinds behind them like tails. The engines leapt through empty space, punching a hole in the compact mass formed by air, water and earth. They spurted forward like birds or bullets, ceaselessly hollowing out their path, each one that passed thrusting in a little deeper. Projectiles made of iron filings, their dagger-sharp tips pointing towards the rear of space. Even while they were going forwards, the engines were going backwards, always backwards. What was their true destination? Perhaps they had never really taken off at all, perhaps they were merely in the process of preparing their future route? Perhaps they were in fact motionless within their movement, but indescribably immobile, governed by the worst kind of immobility, that which kills movement?

Machines walked on along the road, trying to look at all these volleys of nails and borers and wedges that the invisible mallet was driving, blow after blow, into the blue of space. He was afraid. He would have preferred not to see at all, not to be there, not to know anything at all. But a man does not choose the places where he walks. One day he is simply there, unintentionally, and from then on there is no forgetting.

It was the first time that the world had been so incomprehensible. Not crueller or more delightful, more odious, more desirable or more tedious, but unknowable. It was because of this road and these engines. Machines was no longer anyone, neither actor nor spectator; he was excluded from this place, as though he was a visitor from a different period of time, treading unknown soil, seeing alien signs and words, breathing a gas that froze the bronchia, living an isolated existence in the midst of a separate insoluble existence, a bubble in the process of climbing to the surface of some liquid, or a ball of mercury that will never mingle. That is what he seemed to be.

The road was swollen with hatred and fear, so swollen that it was almost a river. And yet, perhaps the grit-strewn ground with its lines and yellow dots, its metal plaques and stains, its hollows and cracks, and perhaps the sky and sea and cement blocks were not really basically hostile: perhaps if there had not been all these engines ... But the engines did not like these kinds of thoughts: they streamed ahead, plunging through his skull and emerging from a hole drilled into the back of his head, just above the rachidian bulb.

To try to win them over, Machines told himself that perhaps it was they, after all, who were in the right. No doubt they knew what they were doing. No doubt it was they who were alive, really alive, and not the man walking along the road by the side of the sea. Or else he tried to imagine the engines standing abandoned along the verges, cold, their wheels stilled, their silent crank-cases leaking a slow drip of black oil. But that did no good. Here, one was no longer master of one's own thoughts: each engine that arrived, snarling, and passed straight through his skull was a thought scooped up and whisked away for ever.

Machines suddenly understood the nature of this road. He understood at once, as though an immense advertisement hoarding lit by six floodlights was displaying the message:

THE ROAD TURNS WORDS INTO CORPSES

Were words dead, then? Looking to his left, along the beach, Machines saw in a flash, with perfect clarity, hundreds and thousands of black bodies stretched out on the pebbles. They were the corpses of the men who had invented engines, the corpses of the words they had uttered. The dead bodies looked so black against the glittering white pebbles, the sun's mirrors, that Machines felt the sweat oozing from the palms of his hands, his armpits, his cheeks.

He stopped to look behind him. At the end of the road, where the engines' shapes blended into each other, crowding together before disgorging themselves again on the other side of the main highway, the white dome of Hyperpolis resembled a mirage. It floated just above the surface of the earth, a weightless milky cloud of cement vapour. Round the dome, and in every direction, the sky was a deep blue, an uncompromising blackish blue. Without looking round, using the road's own eyes, Machines saw the beach's line of stones, the service station's cement structure, and the tall mast on which was written in green neon letters:

G
U
L
F

At the same time he saw the other end of the road, the knot-like point where the engines came huddling together in exactly the same way, seething momentarily before disgorging themselves in the opposite direction, into the highway's other lane, devouring the wind, the asphalt, and occasionally human beings.

It was marvellous being able to see without having to use the eyes. Machines stood still, at the edge of the road, seeing, listening, feeling with all his moving internal organs. But it was dangerous, too, because you could lose your body that way, your being, your life, your language, all those bolts and screws that hold the metal plates together. It meant being a component of fear, now, and no longer an outside element. It meant being a component of hatred, no longer its object. Soon, yes, soon, is the refrain of this road along which the engines roar: soon there will be no more talking. There will be no words left, with which to talk; not a single word will remain upon the earth. People will open the mouths under their noses, and one will hear something like:

'rrroom, rrroom, wooooooaaaa ...'
'skrwitch, krak, duk, ijjjjjjooooommmmm ...'

except that one will not even hear it, because the ears will be sealed, and in their place the metal skin will be very smooth.

With some difficulty, Machines continued walking along the road beside the sea, in the direction of the Gulf service station.

The Gulf service station meant a great deal to the man nick-named Machines. He went there every day between midday and two o'clock. He walked along this road beside the sea, and he saw the cement structure grow gradually larger, with its flat roof jutting out in front of it, its cement pillars, and its big cement tower like a steeple on which was written in green neon letters:

G
U
L
F

When he reached the service station he looked at it for a little while, then walked on to the driveway where the petrol pumps were lined up.

Machines had come there one day, by chance, to buy a bottle of orange soda, and since then he had returned every day. He just could not stay away. At first he was not really sure why he was attracted by the service station. He thought that it was be-cause it was fairly far away from Hyperpolis, or that it was because of the beach, the sea, the sun. Then he had understood that these were not the reasons. It was because he *loved* it. It was difficult to imagine, and yet that is how it was: he loved the Gulf service station. He did not love it as one loves a landscape, or a face, or anything specific like that. He loved it in its entirety, just as it was. It was a service station like any other, perfectly commonplace; it had a cement cabin in which the pump attendant and his wife lived, a garage with an inspection pit, a porch over which was written in red letters:

GREASING SUMP DRAINING TYRES
REPAIRS MAINTENANCE

then a sort of shop with a glass-panelled door on which was written in white letters:

OFFICE ACCOUNTS ACCESSORIES
SPARE PARTS

then a sort of covered shed containing three old broken-down vehicles. Near the vehicles was a padlocked door on which was written in small black letters:

TOILETS

and that was about all. There was also an alsatian dog called Williams who slept on the cement ground, at the end of a chain.

But each day that Machines arrived in front of the Gulf service station, he marvelled anew. He stood somewhere along the cement driveway and looked at the service station, and it was as though nothing more interesting nor more beautiful had ever existed in the world.

From time to time, people arrived with their engines, stopped under the outjutting roof, and hooted. Williams the dog got up, barked, and wagged his tail. The pump attendant came out of the room marked *Office* and fed the engine with petrol. Then the engine returned to the road, with its people aboard, winking its left-hand direction indicator, making off as fast as it could. The episode had been of no interest to it. It had not looked at anything, and had gone away again without giving a thought to the marvellous place where it had stopped for a few seconds.

Then Machines looked at the Gulf service station, and felt full of love and joy, because it stayed where it was and never went away.

The cement construction was very white, the sun bounced off the walls, off the roof, off the steeple. The sun left big patches of shade under the outjutting roof that sheltered the petrol pumps. Williams the alsatian flopped on to the ground again, his nose between his paws. Nothing happened. Nothing ever happened here.

And yet, by some miracle, this place encompassed the whole of beauty and history and space, all in the twinkling of an eye. It was as though fear and hatred had never existed, as though the road that passed in front of the service station had lost its power to wound and kill, as though men's accursed constructions, their gigantic food stores, their monstrous prisons with sealed windows, no longer held sway. Here, peace and mildness reigned undisturbed.

Perhaps that was simply because of the name written on the vertical column at the entrance to the service station:

G
U
L
F

Machines was very attached to this name. He would repeat it under his breath, or sometimes aloud, and the name helped to alleviate the shattering din of the engines and the screeching of the tyres' treads. One just said Gulf, Gulf, Gulf-Lube, Gulf, over and over again, and the mellifluous name entered and filled you with its gentle warmth. The name lit you up inside, lit you up with the same incandescent white light that gleamed upon the service station's walls and roof.

This was the sole reason that Machines walked every day from Hyperpolis to the service station, along the road bordering the sea: to see this word written in green letters on the cement steeple that looked like a miniature minaret, and to see the same word written in the centre of a blue circle on the petrol pumps.

There was such perfect insignificance here! Machines arrived in front of the service station, and suddenly he felt a sense of inner freedom, because there was nothing, absolutely nothing to understand. The giant buildings, car parks, bridges, airports, Hyperpolis itself with its white dome, were not like this; they wanted to say things, they had things to say. They were trying to convince people with their pretentious, depressing architecture, or maybe they aimed to enter into competition with the sky and sea and mountains. They were not simple. But here, in the Gulf service station, everything was easy.

It was immobile, calm, like an island far out in the sea, or like a cloud in the sky. The sun drifted above the flat roof, lengthened the minaret's shadow. There was no longer any need to think, especially not with thoughts. You only needed to be there, any time at all, and immediately the service station revealed itself, stretched its pillars, displayed its dark porch, its dirty windows, its pumps, its compressed-air apparatus. There was the odour, too. Machines was very fond of the odour that floated in the air here, an odour compounded of petrol, oil, grease and sludge. He inhaled these gases, and the odour of Gulf permeated his lungs and arteries, as sharp and searching as a bright beam of light. The cement ground round the service station was covered with stains, puddles and pools left by the engines' leaking sumps, and these shapes were beautiful and simple. In some places the cement slabs were furrowed with x-shaped or z-shaped streaks, but they were not brutal marks like the weals along cars' sides. These were simple marks that told trivial stories, stories of punctured tyres, iron rods, winches and jacks.

When he had had a good look at all these things, Machines

walked forward under the roof and made his way slowly towards an automatic vending machine. He inserted a coin in the machine's slot and pressed a button. A bottle of orange soda dropped into an open-fronted pocket. Machines lifted the ice-cold bottle out of the receptacle, and prised off the cap by inserting the neck into a hole crowned by a metal flange, on the side of the machine. Then he started wandering across the cement floor under the overhanging roof, sipping the iced drink while he studied the petrol pumps.

There were four pumps standing on the cement, on a sort of rectangular platform. The four pumps were identical, except that two were painted blue, while the other two were painted red. At the centre of each pump a painted circle enclosed the magic word

There was a window at the top of each pump, and behind the windows were rows of wheels bearing numbers on their surface. The kind of messages one could read on these revolving discs were:

1.13		1.04		1.13		
22.00	or	31.00	or	18.00	and so on.	
24.86		32.24		$20.3\frac{4}{5}$		

Above the pumps, hanging from the cement roof, festoons of little blue and red flags fluttered in the wind.

All this was genuinely beautiful and anonymous and devoid of history. Machines went on taking little sips from his iced soda as he strolled across the covered way. As he passed in front of the dog he said 'Williams!' just once; and the alsatian raised its head a few inches and twitched its tail lazily.

Machines walked slowly along the cement platform, looking at the road and the houses and the sky that had ceased to be frightening. He saw them as though from the bridge of a liner, or the gondola of an airship: fixed, pure, sparkling in the transparent air. Engines raced madly along the black highway, going nowhere. But that was of no importance. Inside the Gulf service station, Machines was safe from their wheels, and no longer felt giddy. Perhaps this was really the only place in the world where one was unassailable. Perhaps this was the only place in the world where there was nothing to understand.

That was how the Gulf service station was. It held its secret. The people who arrived astride their engine, to fill its tank with petrol and its radiator with water, then went away again, never learnt the secret. How could they ever guess at it? They passed through the haven of peace and whiteness without seeing it, and behind their dark glasses their eyes were staring straight ahead. The people were already caught up in frenzied motion, hurtling along the kind of tunnel-shaped channel that leads precipitously downwards towards death. But those who, like Machines, the pump attendant and his wife, and Williams the dog, had stopped there one day were no longer able to leave. They inhabited the service station, knew intimately the word Gulf, the word Gulf-Life, the word Gulf-Lube, the pumps, the rosy-hued petrol, the oil slicks, the cement promenade, the overhanging roof standing squarely on its four pillars, and the tall white minaret jutting into the blue sky, adorned with its shining letters

G
U
L
F

They knew all these things without understanding them, simply by being there when they had to. They lived at the edge of a mirage, on the fringe of a desert. They never travelled, and had no desire to do so. They had no need to think or speak. They belonged to the service station, they were a fragment of cement among all the walls and pillars and roofs. They inhaled the odour of petrol, they heard the faint sounds made by the pumps' revolving discs when the cold rosy-hued liquid gushed from the revolver-shaped ends of tubes, while the figures whirled round beside each other, 05 06 07 08 09 10 11 12 13 14 15 16 ... , they heard the sound of the compressed air forcing its way into tyres through valves. They experienced all this, hour after hour, in the chalk-coloured shale island. The sun and wind brushed the walls, and the roof cast its shadow. The service station was full of impenetrable secrets, and those who inhabited it inhabited its secrets. One of these was: dilated banality rises into the air and covers the earth like a vapour. The other was: we all know the average span of a single life, but what is the combined span of several lives?

When Machines had finished drinking the orange soda, he set the empty bottle down at the foot of a machine, as usual. In a calm voice he said 'Williams!' to the alsatian once more. Then he set off again in the direction of the white dome that was bursting with threats and desires, the dome that called itself Hyp-Hyp-Hyper-Polis-Sssuper-Marké-tíssimo.

'Listen to this,' said the Narcoanalyst. And he pressed the tape-recorder's starting button. At first there was just the whirr of the moving tape, together with a soft blurred sound like breathing. Then a child's voice could be heard, muffled and hesitant, murmuring something through deep breaths. This is what the voice said:

'... Gggot to ggo ... I've ggot to go ... Got to go. The ffffire ... ffire ... Al ... Amal ... I wwant, I wwant to alam amalight myself in the flame ... There are ssso many wwires ... Wires ... Going towards the bed ... There are ttwo, two, and two. Wwires ... Quick, ggot to leave ... here. Black wires and red wires. Wwires ... Ow! Here they come. So quickly. Ggot to cut them, the wires, to break the circuit. I'm ggoing ... Wait, I'm ggoing to tell Rial. Roal ... Quick, quick, quick, the scissors, I'm ggoing to cut the wires. No, over there, the scissors! There, on the right, quick, hand them to me! The black and red wires. I'm going, I'm going to cut this one. Pass me the big knife, I'm going to cut the wire ... It's ... Big ... It comes out of the key-hole and leads right up to here, coming closer ... Got to rip it out! Rip it out, Helix! Watch your hands, stupid! That hurts ... Hurts the tummy. Ggot to rip it out, quick, quick! It's burning the middle of my tummy! Oo-ow! Helix! Helix! Ddon't pretend not to hear! Can you hear? Helix, I ... Look, I'm going to tell Roal ... He'll be very cross. Roal doesn't like you. Yap! Yap! Where are you, Yap? I'm not speaking to *you*! Go away! Come back when we're finished. Daniel! Don't touch that, it's electricity! Stop the walls ... Here, all of you, here! ... Got to stop, stop the walls from closing in... What's the time? Got to go, they're waiting for me on the poop-deck. Yes, Rial, at ten o'clock near the conning tower ... There are too many wires. Pull, pull! That's it, there's one that's breaking ... bbreaking ... Careful, it's fastened to my eye, don't pull too hard, it's hurting my eye ... Where is that one, that red wire, going? Helix: there's a knot in the middle of the wire, take off the plaster ... the adhesive plaster ... Watch out for the current! Yes, Daniel, you can touch that one ... There's no current, it's going down to the hole at the bottom. If you open the wire the ants will escape. Ah! Ah! Ah! They're pouring out of the red wire, they look like soldier ants. Be careful, Helix, they fly! If they get into your eyes they'll blind you. Yap! Meanwhile you Yap go and look for the wire attached to the keyhole. Don't touch! Don't touch that! ... It's ... A gglobe ... The light ... If you had touched that, you'd be dead. The hhhair ... full of wires, burning wires ... Normo! Normo! Come here! ... There are more wwires ... going towards the lamp. There, and there ... Here. Rial, to the left of the table you'll find the tube. You've got ... You've ggot to ... Lock it ... It's the red water. As far as the bathroom. Get into the autorat. Let's ... Let's go. Close the portholes. There's a porthole open ... Helix, go and have a peek through ... through the periscope. What can you see? Speak up, I can't hear you! It's not nice to mumble like that all the time! Speak clearly, pronounce your words distinctly! ... Daniel, did you see? The ... The whale! Are you sure it's the whale? Yap, take your seat. Yap! Yap! Daniel! Roal! Normo! Escar! Go and see! What is it ... Over there, a ... A white island ... How many holes has it got in its side? ... And the head? Has it, has it got blue eyes? ... Its mouth? What? It's making a noise, a terrible noise ... It, it ... Right whale approaching the North Pole ... Get down ... Press the button, Yap! It's the ff ... flottor. Helix! Normo! Coli! Yap! Roal! Ilyrewick! Mister Ilyrewick ... I'm ttalking to you in a foreign language. I'm ttelling you in ... in foreign languages. Lenudntteimenao. Rtei. Corëtë. Ttepepaluednijitlemenata.

Lenica tlimlelehem. Ltemilëlttechenici. Tlemanëlach. Pen-overchtemittetnei. Miatpmenat. Ololiutalaliupolch. La-haïn. Tseltsemënëpetel. Enrtlimautin. Remaltlrellement ... Atten-tion, I'm going to start counting: 94, 95, 96, 97, 98, 99, 100. We're off. The amelflame, the amelfire. The alflow. Open the stopcocks! The autorat ... Descending ... How, how many feet, Mister Ilyrewick? 12,000 feet? Got to ... ggot to kill the right whale. The torpedoes! ... Over there, under the carpet! Put them in the, in the hole. Yap! Quick, the fuse wire is going away ... Gggot ... ggot to put adhesive plaster ... over my ears! ... Helix! Rial! Daniel! The ... The temperature is going down! The red water will freeze! ... It's getting so cold ... How many feet, Mister Ilyrewick? Selmmatle-celtlemitlacem. Twenty-thousand feet? Look for ... The squid! There, in the grotto. I'm not afraid ... Are you afraid, Rial? No use looking out of the porthole, it's night-time now ... The water's black at the bottom ... The pump, Yap! Look at the pump, I don't have ... enough ... rrred water ... GGot to go ... into the bathroom ... there's a hole in the bath ... The red water ... isn't coming any more ... It's the vvvalve ... The porthole isn't properly closed! I can feel the water on ... On my head ... Change the wires! Daniel, Normo! The red wire ... The lamp ... It's coming out of my chest! Press! Press hard! Don't laugh! Press! ... Ah! The right whale passed really close by ... The autorat has moved! The whale has just whacked the keel with its tail. ... Turn off the flottor! Quick, the torpedoes, quick! The barbed harpoons. I, I ... I'm loading them ... with my fingers ... Fire ... Fire! That's it, they're away! The harpoons ... are ggoing to explode ... Rial! Get to the peri-scope! The whale is going down, Mister Ilyrewick! Escned! Escned! It's drowned ... Rrrah! Rrrah! Its mouth is all twisted ... Now wwe'll ... look for the squid! Rial, Roal, look towards the bottom. There's a black ... stain ... There it is! Hiding in the grotto ... Its red eyes are ... shining ... Kill it, quickly, quickly! ... Look out! It's going to squirt out its ink! It's spitting ink ... In reverse, quick! Don't let ... the ink ... get through the portholes ... Yap! The autorat is coming to the surface again! Again ... Again ... Better ... send ... another torpedo ... Helix! Yap! Roal! Daniel! Letletzil, Mister Ilyrewick! Look at the TV! The wwires ... round the arms ... Can't move any longer. Please ... help me ... Switch, switch on the electricity! Quick, I'm getting weak, I I'm ggoing to fall. Torpedo gone? Namalallam! Look, there! ... On the TV screen ... You can see ... The torpedo's going to bang into the volcano ... No, it has gone to one side. It's passing through the, the stain. It's going ... It ... It's entering the squid's head. It's going to tear the head off. With its arms. It's spitting lots of ink. Better not breathe any more. Look out. The torpedo ... Helix! ... Explode! Bam! Boom! ... That's it! The squid is dead! They are rising up to the surface again ... The autorat ... Hhh ... Hhh ...'

For a moment, the tape was silent. Then the child's voice began to speak again, more quickly ...

'The autorat ... The autorat ... The autorat ...'

The child's voice was so low that the Narcoanalyst had to turn up the volume control on the machine, and that made a peculiar electric vibration.

'King Rat's auto ... automobile ... He's the most important man in the world.'

'He's in command ... He's in command of all the tubes, he ... has tubes coming out of his tummy and going down to the bottom ... the bottom of the sea. Each time he ... Each time someone goes to the toilet, it rushes down the tubes. King Rat likes that. He opens the tubes, he keeps an eye on everything. It's his job. He has all the tubes in his tummy, you understand, Daniel? The tubes come out of his tummy and plunge into the earth, right down to the bottom of the sea ... He keeps watch. King Rat never sleeps. He travels through the sea on board the Autorat, he lives at the bottom of the water ... The earth is covered with tubes ... He, he's living here, in the bathroom. He's always on the move, with his lieutenants ...'

There was another silence, then the small boy's voice chanted:

'Autorat.

Ittitorat.

Dandelion.

Spider.

Beetle.

Sea-fear.

Reel-mat.'

Then the voice said:

'The wires ... The electric wwires are boring into my tummy ... The ... wwires ... are coming out of the black and red boxes ... don't ... Don't switch on the light suddenly or the electricity will flood into my tummy, and that hurts ... The tubes musn't explode ...'

There was a sound of staccato breathing, rasping close to the microphone.

'Yap! Helix! Rial! Daniel! Normo! Coli! Mister Ilyrewick! ... The lieutenants ... They are dressed in blue ... with red helmets ... They ... They obey King Rat's commands ... Got to ... Got to kill the whale and the squid ... My, my name is Dune ... King Rat knows everything. He's at the centre of the wires and the tubes ... When anyone speaks, he knows, he listens in to the wires ... He has all the tubes beneath him, in the earth, down to the bottom of the sea ... The tubes fill up the ... the caves ... Lots of caves ... The tubes are squirming ... If you cut them, King Rat gets a tummy-ache. There's ... there's fire ... in the water ... The electric wires go from the black boxes into his ... tummy ... Into his head ... There's another tube, too, a glass one, coming out of the bath ... There's red water in it ... Like syrup, yes, just like syrup ... Bbetter ... Better be caref ... Better not break the glass tube, otherwise ... Otherwise King Rat won't have any more red water ... He'll die ... Look out! Yap! Look out! There's ... There's a blocked tube ... There, under the bed ... Nothing running through it ... I ... I'm going to have a tummy-ache ... Mister Ilyrewick! Setsel! Zessa! Got to ... got to open the tap, there's not enough red water ... in the bath. There's not enough fire in ... in the black boxes ... Close the porthole! Yap, Daniel, Normo! There, near the door, quick, Rial, Yap, Roal, Yap, Helix!'

The voice sounded near to suffocation, now.

'Helix! He's got a ... A helix on the head ... It's like a propeller ... He's flying ... Yap! Yap! It's a dog. It looks like a man, but it's a dog as well ... It says: yap! yap! ... Ilyrewick knows ... He knows the word. He says Tlimlelehem and the doors open ... Tlimlelehem ... Autorat. It's the most important word in the world. It's King Rat who invented it. For travelling through the sea ... Along tubes ... To, to open the tube of red water and the ... the electric wires ... He has a black stone with springs ... A bit of coal. It's useful. King Rat invented all those things. They all belong to him. To him ... My, my name isn't really Dune ... My name's The Eagle. My name's Dandelion ... King Rat gives me names. No one else can give me names ... He's drinking the red water. It's his food. He, he doesn't eat anything else ... He doesn't eat mm ... meat, or fish, or potatoes, or choc ... chocolate, or bread ... He never eats ... He opens his mouth and he ... He drinks red water. The water rushes down the tubes and it ... It goes right down to the bottom of ... the ... sea ... '

The voice was murmuring so low, now, that it was hard to hear it.

'It's him ... Who makes the water red ... King Rat makes ... S'him ... He nev slps ... 'll th' tubes 'n th' wrld 're in is tummy 'n cross th' earth 'nside holes ... 'ttom 'f th' water ... He pnshes 'nyone who tries t' ... t' find out ... musn't ... talk ... 'th'wise he kills ... 'storpedo ... h'poons w'th hoo ... hooks th't sprng up ... whale ... squid ... inth ... water ... Dniel ... 'sgoin t'kill th'wha ... ale ...'

After that, the only sound to be heard was the scratching of the tape against the playback head, and a slow breathing in and out. Then the Narcoanalyst pressed the tape-recorder's stop button.

The small boy called Dumb Bogo did not like policemen. There were a lot of policemen round Hyperpolis, in the car park, in front of the entrance doors, and even inside. It was usually difficult to see them at first glance, because they went round in disguise. But Dumb Bogo could recognize them from a long way off. The policemen came in all shades: grey, green, black, blue. There were even some, along the edge of the road, who wore a kind of red phosphorescent jacket. These ones pretended to dig holes in the asphalt, with pneumatic drills, then fill them up again. But their eyes were slit at the sides, because what they were really doing was spying. There were others who looked just like ordinary people; they wore three-piece charcoal-grey suits, and pretended to be looking for their cars along the parking lanes. They carried parcels, led dogs on leashes, and were accompanied by women and children. But Dumb Bogo immediately recognized them by their gold-rimmed spectacles with lenses that glittered with cruelty. There were others, again, who pretended to light a cigarette with a metal lighter, in front of the cinema entrance, and then stood looking at the photographic display of scenes from the film. But Dumb Bogo knew that they were using the display cases' glass fronts as mirrors, to see backwards and spy on people. One had to take precautions. If one was not careful, the policemen would come running up, bar the way with outstretched arms, take him by the shoulder, and say, in a soft sinister policeman's voice:

'Now you're going to come along with us quietly, like a good boy, aren't you, Bogo, eh?'

223

And then they would take him away in a sort of small white van with iron grilles over the windows. One had to be very careful.

Dumb Bogo skirted the outer wall of the Hyper Super, trying to see where the policemen were hiding. Each time that he caught sight of one he made a detour, or hid behind a group of people pushing loaded trolleys towards their cars.

One had to keep a careful eye on the cars, too. Sometimes there were policemen hidden in what looked like limousines. At first sight these seemed to be ordinary cars like all the others. But if one looked closely one saw something frightening, and realized that they were police cars. For instance, a white car with tinted windows, that coasted slowly along the parking lanes. Dumb Bogo watched it carefully for a moment, then darted to one side and hid behind a pylon, just in time: he had suddenly noticed that a very long chromium-plated antenna was reaching into the sky from a rubber socket planted in the car's white roof. Or on another occasion, in front of the cinema, a long black saloon car, that was also edging along very slowly, stopped, then went on a little, then stopped again. And Dumb Bogo knew that it was dangerous to go near it: *the car had no chrome fittings*. Even the bumpers were black. Or again, an ancient grey van that was moving off, at the other end of the car park: Dumb Bogo had a narrow escape from being caught by that one. It was such a ramshackle old vehicle that he had hardly glanced at it. But just as it was moving off, at the other end of the car park, two big black cars near the filling station also started to draw away, and *they were moving at the same speed*.

The mobile guards were very cunning. They had lots of tricks with which to outwit Dumb Bogo; it needed just a moment of inattention on his part for them to come racing up.

Luckily, Dumb Bogo could see things from a long way off. For instance, there was this bus. It really did look like any other bus, with its high wheels, its sliding windows, its sheet-metal body painted green and yellow, and its great vertical windscreen against which the windscreen wipers' arms were folded. And yet the bus belonged to the mobile guards. Dumb Bogo had realized that, right away. To start with, there was this name shining just above the windscreen. Dumb Bogo had no idea what the name meant, but it was a very dangerous, tricky name, something like

TEUFENTHAL

and just above it was this design representing a white axe in the centre of a red shield. But that was not all. When the bus had come closer, Dumb Bogo had seen the driver's hand come through the window and make waving movements. Looking at this hand, Dumb Bogo had noticed that all the fingernails were trimmed, except for the one belonging to the little finger, and that nail was *very long*. When he had seen this nail, Dumb Bogo had frozen with terror. It was obviously a plot by the guards to immobilize him and capture him. Luckily, a group of women had passed by at that moment, and Dumb Bogo had been able to shake himself out of his stupor in time. He had run very fast towards Hyper City, and had managed to get inside by squeezing through a self-locking exit door that had just been opened from the inside by a woman and a little girl who were leaving. That had been a stroke of luck.

Inside the hall it was easier, because there were people about, and the light was not so bright. The guards could not catch him so easily in there. But it was more dangerous, too, because the guards might decide to close all the exits and make the people leave one by one. Then, as soon as Hyperpolis was deserted they would probably unleash their great fierce dogs which would race down the aisles, one after the other, sniffing at scents and barking 'Haw! haw! haw! haw!' and Dumb Bogo would be done for.

The small boy threaded his way through the crowd. He skirted the central aisle, keeping sometimes to the left, sometimes to the right; occasionally he even retraced his steps, so as to throw them off the scent. Or else he walked behind some stout woman pushing a trolley full of provisions, and made a great effort to place his feet exactly where the fat woman had placed hers, so that the footprints should blend completely. (And that was not at all easy.)

The guards were looking for him. They had been looking for him for days now, on the beach, in the courtyards of blocks of flats, in the public gardens, in the car parks, and now, for sure, inside Hyperpolis; they must have seen him as he was getting in through the exit door, or else the woman and little girl must have reported him to an inspector. The small boy scarcely knew where he was going, and looked over his shoulder so often, as he walked, that he began bumping into people. In fact, once, when he collided into a woman, she screamed abuse at him, and the small boy wished desperately that he could explain to her that if she went on yelling like that the guards would certainly be alerted.

Dumb Bogo entered the Self-Service Supermarket by ducking under the turnstile entrance. He started walking quickly between the stacks of tinned foods, then stopped to see if anyone was following him. But there were no guards around. Only people plodding gloomily onwards, pushing their trolleys in front of them.

There was another danger in the Supermarket. And that was the *voices*. In the hubbub of the hall, just previously, Dumb Bogo had not really noticed. There was so much noise and confusion over there that one could not really hear the voices. But here it was different. Everything was so white, so clean and white, that the voices reached you quite quickly. They echoed as though inside a church, and one could hear every syllable clearly inside one's ear. That was a new trick by the police. The guards were sending out their summonses in the clear gentle voices of women, in voices that were calm and tender. It was terrible, because they were irresistible. The soft vowels glided along the white plastic flooring, smoothly, like waves lapping a beach. They came nearer, smoothly, so smoothly, they glided, their clear gentle tongues wrapped themselves round your

226

legs and belly. There were consonants that were so beautiful and limpid that the small boy did not have the strength to shake them off. The sounds swirled round him: ll, kl, tl, gl and the others followed each other, collided, blended together like a woman's plaited tresses. The voices emerged from invisible loudspeakers, making their weird frightening music. They called out, went hunting along the corridors of the Supermarket. They slowly spread through all the lanes, one by one, through the mountains of tin cans, saying calm reassuring things that were hard to understand but which sent shivers along the skin.

They murmured:

'C ... come back ... Bogo, come, come, come, c ... come back ... lla-wo-tlalla ... Clam ... Chwunn ... Hidden ... Come come c ... come back ...'

'... Riall ... Dong ... Majdong ... Ajgallal lial abdull ...'

The voices were worse than looks, because one could not escape them. They found you easily, wherever you were, even behind the display shelves; they entered your ears and throat and penetrated deep inside your body.

Dumb Bogo was very frightened of the voices. He tried to stop his ears by pressing the tips of his forefingers very hard against them, but it was of no use. They were not really human voices; they were vibrations that sprang from everywhere simultaneously, that moved along the ground and through the air, and trembled in the light. There was no way of extinguishing them. Perhaps someone had slipped a tiny loudspeaker into Bogo's chest, while he slept, and the waves were rippling through his skin and nails and hair, talking and calling out.

To help him fight the voices, Dumb Bogo took from his trouser pocket all that remained of the Autorat: a short length of two-core electric flex with the red and black wires protruding from one end of the rubber sheath. He put the black wire into his right ear, and the red wire inside his mouth, clenched between his teeth. Then he looked quickly for a corner of the Supermarket where he could watch without being seen. He found a recess in the section where chocolates were on display, a fairly narrow space between two stands. The white plastic flooring gleamed brightly.

There were no loudspeakers or cameras in sight. The police were not on his trail, yet. He pressed his body flat against the back of the recess. Then, without moving his lips, simply by using thought-power, he began sending voices along the circuit of the black and red electric wires, to counteract the sound-waves.

The Guards were getting very close now. They were advancing across Hyperpolis, in a grid operation, moving methodically up the empty aisles that led to the sector where the chocolate bars were piled.

E. Raiga: Envy
F. Ravaisson-Mollien: De l'habitude
G. de Tarde: Les lois de l'imitation
University of Brussels: 'Analysis of the dominant motives orienting the activities of
 individuals in social life'
J. Urban: L'Epithymologie. La Désirologie
E. L. Manson: Handling of Personnel
Y. Tashy: L'Art d'influencer
Georges Bohn: Le grégarisme
G. Bohn and G. Hardy: La foule
Parker Tyler: Magic and Myth of the Movies
E. L. Bernays: Propaganda
W. B. Dygert: Advertising Media
E.T. Grunbach: Facts and Fetishes in Advertising
W.H. Jeabsby: Window Display for Profit
K. Koffa: Principles of Gestalt Psychology
Georges Bohn: La naissance de l'intelligence

PERCOLATE

WASH   WITH      AUTOMATIC
POWER
IRON

Ambition:
to make a massive offer:
the best

'Your massive Pontiac'
'No Lincoln has ever been so long, so desirable'
Chevrolet is using a team of seven psychologists to analyse the odours and sounds of new models.
Sound of the doors shutting.

The four portholes along the Buick's bonnet.

Ford Continental (1956) $10,000. More expensive than a Cadillac. It is rumoured that all 'candidates'
for this car will be submitted to an examination, and that their financial standing will be carefully
assessed. Ford refused to confirm this rumour, but suggested that Continental dealers in each
district would select those deemed worthy of buying this vehicle.

Jean Patou: 'The world's most expensive perfume' $45 an ounce.

Papermate: 'The $50 ballpoint pen'.

Triumph over consumer resistance.

absolute and total two-year guarantee

Continental Illinois National Bank and Trust Company of Chicago

231 S. LaSalle Street, Chicago, Ill. 60693

ACROSS
THE
FIELDS OF GRASS

G. Durandin: Propagande et publicité
Rosser Reeves: Reality in Advertising
Russell H. Colley: Defining Advertising Goals for measured advertising results
Robert Leduc: La publicité; une force au service de l'entreprise

The Masters of Thought. Yes, there are Masters of Thought. Nobody wanted to know about it. There was a time when people imagined that thinking was a simple process. They imagined that all that was needed was a little effort at concentration while gazing at the blue sea, or the sky, or a car. You just put on a slight frown, rested your chin on your hand, and ... hey presto, you were thinking! Or thought that you were thinking. Sometimes people thought without even the benefit of words; they simply felt a peculiar fluttering sensation in the stomach, a series of peculiar contractions of the throat, and a peculiar gyratory motion at the back of the head. People called these phenomena 'thoughts', and when other people asked them what they were doing there, they said: 'I'm thinking ... ' So then everybody else tiptoed away respectfully, and tried to be very quiet, and hissed at each other: 'Sh! Quiet! He's thinking ... '

But it was not true. There was nothing in the whole world that could really be called a thought. The earth was so silent and empty and powerful that it had no time to listen to what was being said by men, or birds, or crickets. It was completely indifferent. Even in places where there was nothing but chatter, places such as bars, theatres, buses, airports, shops, schools, and hairdressers' anterooms, the sounds that human beings made never succeeded in struggling free. So they did not get very far. They just produced a little puff of cloud round them, like a jeep bumping its way across a desert.

Perhaps if, instead of all this noise everywhere, there had

been some silence, then thought might indeed have put in an appearance. Thought might even have risen in the sky in the form of a golden disc thrusting the clouds aside, a vast bubble climbing gently above the horizon and into the black sky, roaring, and accompanied by the sound of war drums.

Perhaps ... Perhaps. But it is impossible even to imagine such a thing. It is not easy to travel backwards in time. There is no way of halting the precipice that has started plunging down and away, beneath your feet, swallowing you up. There is no way of stopping anything. Time meanders on its way, making, unmaking. And now thought no longer belongs truly to mankind; it is no longer men who fashion thought with their looks and voices and skin. Ideas are as vast as the ocean, and in that ocean men's bodies drift and sink. Sometimes, as though through Captain Nemo's porthole, a drowned body can be seen floating past, arms and legs splayed out, a pallid body sinking slowly into the depths.

No, men can have no concept of thought as a golden bubble in the sky. Mankind has always lived in the sea; not in the sky where the birds live, nor on the earth where the rocks and pebbles live. Some people talked as though they were surrounded by air and light and truth and so on. They said that they were standing where they were standing, and that they knew what they knew. And they said all this with words produced by their larynx, and with gestures made by their hands. They were constantly on the lookout for lights, and counted them one by one. But what they took to be stars or suns or beacons were merely the luminous warts that cluster round the mouths of fish in the ocean's lowest depths. They were the playthings of deep currents, the victims of uncontrollable happenings: clouds of mud, submarine landslides, eruptions from the ocean's bed. Men were without free will, prisoners of unfolding events. How could they imagine the air when they had lived their lives at the bottom of the sea? Human beings are unable to tolerate air: free air is too dry and lonely, it is a kind of scouring substance that is terrible to contemplate ... Impossible to endure. It would be necessary to come to the surface very cautiously, holding the breath. And, even then, fearing that the arteries or the brain may burst at any moment.

The Masters must surely be in the air. Masters, masters, where are you, my masters? Where are you hidden? Show yourselves at last, just once, show your faces, say your names, quickly, I beg! I am your humble performing dog, trotting to and fro behind the bars of its cage. I am your humble moray eel circling the waters of your fishponds.

But the Masters are not visible. If one could only see them, things would be simple. It would only be necessary to examine their eyes for a few seconds, their eyelids, eyelashes, eyebrows, the little wrinkles spreading out from the eyes' outer edges, the whiteish rim of the lachrymal gland: and they would no longer be the Masters' eyes.

Show yourselves! Appear on a cover of *Time*, or in the social columns of some Asian newspaper, or among the glossy photographs in some expensive magazine! Sometimes the rumour goes round that you are about to appear: photographs are suffused with a sort of fogging, there is a kind of ferment beneath the surface of the shots of bridges, buildings, factories, universities. Instinct insists that that is where you are, that that is where your power springs into being. But then the haloing is re-absorbed behind the surfaces, and you never appear.

There are no faces. There are no hands, no bodies, no names. You are always hidden behind the mob's high walls, on the far side of humanity's masses, invisible, unknown. You are the only phantoms, the sole mysteries, that the human race has ever created. How do you breathe? How do you live? Where are your parents, your wives and children? No one ever comes across them. The Masters inhabit another world, eat unknown foods, drink unknown liquids. Nothing about you is certain. It is as though mankind was eternally dreaming, as it sleeps in the prisons of its cities; whereas you never sleep, you alone maintain a constant vigil. And men's thoughts are your dreams.

Men, women, children all make great efforts to wake up.

They attempt to wrench their eyelids open, they move their lips as though to speak. In their deep slumber they toss around and laugh. Perhaps they are remembering the times when they were not asleep? A young woman with pale skin, and rather long brown hair, and freckled cheeks, is sleeping stretched out on her bed, in a darkened room, and the years pass by, one after the other. She moves a little in her sleep, her nostrils quiver, her lips tremble, the skin of her belly and breasts shivers. Her bosom rises and falls, gently, time after time, and the blood flows through her veins and makes her carotid arteries pulse. Then she is an old woman lying asleep on a yellowing pallet, with her yellowing hair and yellowing skin, and her yellowing lips stretched tight round her gums. Then she is no longer breathing. What has happened behind her façade? What is it that was born, and moved around, and ate the flesh of other living creatures; what is it that loved a few men, and a few children and a parrot? But all those things have taken place on the far side of sleep, in gigantic brains that cover the surface of the earth, in minds as big as volcanoes, as big as cities, registering the thoughts of lightning and the tides and the moon and the sun, thoughts that with a single thought-wave can scoop up millions of winged particles and make them pirouette. And all this has happened, not just once, and for a single woman, but thousands and thousands of times each second, opening and closing thousands of lips, making thousands of miles of skin shiver, travelling over the infinite pathways of the nerves, quickening life, making hearts beat, radiating a heat as great as that of the sun, lighting up the countless bulbs plugged into the endless ceiling, sweeping like a wind through a forest and making all the leaves rustle on all the trees, sound, unknowable repetitive sound of all the drops of water in the Pacific Ocean pattering on to each other, sound, light, heat, pain, shuddering, combining all that, *all that*.

Enough. The thinking of one person alone contains the seeds of madness. The thinking of one person alone is not thought. It says nothing. It is simply a tungsten filament, and when the lightning enters it through the brass orifice, no more than a single spark, one tiny crackling ball, falls to the ground. That is the danger of the kind of thought that thinks.

Who had the temerity to give language to mankind? It was an error to present to men something so big and terrible and weighty. They were not capable of sustaining the burden. If men had the dimensions of a whale, or even of a rhinoceros ... Perhaps things would have been easier. If they had been endowed with the strength of a tractor, or simply of the horse. If they had been as long-lived as the crow, as slow as the iguana, as relentlessly active as the ant, or as light as the bat. If they had had the intelligence of the squirrel, the skill of the racoon, the vitality of the earthworm. If their eyes had been as sharp as the jaguar's, if they had known how to run as fast as the hare, if they had known how to swim like the dolphin or dive like the kingfisher. If they had had the hide of an armadillo, or the teeth of a shark. If they had been as beautiful as the Quetzal bird, or as ugly as the vulture. If they had only had the courage of the rat. If their canine teeth had been filled with venom, like the cobra's, or if they had possessed a musk sac, or spines, or claws, or tusks, or stings, or anything else to use as a weapon or as a means of self-defence, something capable of killing or intimidating. If they **had** had masks, furry coats, tails, hooves, manes, scales, horns, beaks, or saw-tooth vertebrae. If only they had had *something*, I don't know what, knives sprouting from their wrists and elbows, or mouths and nostrils that belched flames ... But they had none of these qualities, none of these characteristics. They were simply men and women, who slept while the Masters' thinking led its life on their behalf.

Such puny heads for the immensity of thought, the enormity of language! Necks are not strong enough to support the weight of the brain. Necks bend like rubber tubes, and the head droops, bringing the body down with it in its fall.

Men's heads wanted to know so many things! They gulped up ceaselessly through all their openings, and as the concrete hardened it became heavy. Inside the head, images froze or congealed. The head was not an appropriate receptacle: a globe-map would have been better, or a star, or even something as vast and hollow as a planet. Men's heads should have been designed with an opening in the top of the skull, a permanently gaping fontanel. Food enters through the mouth, travels through the entrails, meanders round, gnaws away, liquefies, then exits. But heads are not equipped with an anus, and whatever enters their brain-pan is stuck there for ever. There was a kind of compressor that exerted increasing pressure, and steam accumulated in the generator, pressing with all its might against the walls, threatening to explode through the temples and the palate and the occiput. It pressed against the eyes and the eardrums and the nasal fossae. One day it will surely explode: language will have become too big for mouths to encompass, images will have become too brilliant for eyes to bear. There will be several flashes of lightning, several peals of thunder, and men's craniums will at last open up, releasing everything that they had been hoarding for centuries. One day the pale young woman will awaken, sit up abruptly in her bed, sweating profusely, her eyes will open slowly, and her lips will murmur something. Then suddenly she will emerge from her dream, and by plunging back into life she will break the bonds that linked her with the Masters of thought. And at that same instant the Masters will die, because — and this is the real secret — they lived in the dream of the young woman whom they had ceased to dream.

She will open her eyes, and what she sees will be so beautiful that it is hard to say what it will be like. Before her, nothing that existed had ever been truly beautiful. It will be as though she had suddenly been born, fully formed, from the belly of a mother as vast as a mountain. She will see the sky, the sun, the sea, the clouds, the stars, birds, trees, flies, plants, stones, flowers, streams, beaches, seaweeds, fish, sea-shells, fruits, hills, corals, horses, houses, fires, drawings and patterns, seeds, human beings, waves, colours, just like that, simply, without thoughts or images or words. She will no longer see these things as in dreams, but with her eyes open. She will no longer see them as though through hundreds of panes of glass super-imposed upon the skylight of her jail, but freely; and her hands will be able to touch what her eyes see. How to awaken her? How to halt the flow of the alien dream that possesses her? How to unseal her eyelids so as to allow the light to flood in? But the Masters cannot tolerate the idea that the young woman should awaken in this manner, and they keep watch over her sleep, day and night. The Masters have many watchdogs and many charms to ensure that her sleep shall endure.

It is necessary to go back inside the dream, even farther back, as far as it is possible to go. The Masters' thinking is im-measurable, a vast steppe where there is no North. The Masters' thinking thinks men's thoughts, snaps out orders, yells: 'To the left, to the right, upwards, downwards! Stand up! Sit down! *To heel!*' And men's thoughts grovel like lapdogs.

The Masters' thinking flashes orders. One thought says: 'Philosophize!' and the lapdogs philosophize. Another thought says: 'Pontificate about science!' and the lapdogs pontificate scientifically. Another says: 'Write poetry!' and the lapdogs write lapdog poems. Then: 'Fiction!' and the lapdogs write lapdog novels, and read lapdog novels. The Masters order: 'Metaphysicize! Dogmatize!' And the lapdogs talk about God and about progress in the world of lapdogs. And all this happens during their sleep, with just a few shivers, a few yelps, an occa-sional twitch of the paws, the jowls, the ears. Through the half-closed eyelids the eyes roll slightly, as though they had seen something.

When will it come to an end, this terrible sleep, this black oblivion that holds the whole earth in its grip?

One day, the Masters looked at the world through their sleep-inducing spectacles, and the whole world fell victim to narcosis. Then the Masters multiplied their infra-red rays, platinum discs, spirals, propellers, the ticking of clocks, the roar of water-falls, and it was really difficult to wake up. Even babies were born asleep. Even old folk died asleep. The Masters' thinking is sleep itself.

237

Perhaps if people did not sleep they would never have needed language? But it is impossible to know that, since the very act of formulating the question induces sleep. Words lure people into sleep, that is certain; they are like needles of ice that leave their poisoned crystals to melt inside the warm flesh they have stabbed. There are doubtless words that are not sleep's words. Surely there are some. But how to recognize them? There may be words that burn as fiercely as the sun, that cut as sharply as flints, that are as gentle as water. But the Masters keep all such words at bay. Perhaps there are words within words, like stones inside peaches.

The Masters' thinking is not gentle. It rejects gentleness. It has organized everything round it, and the sleepers glide along its channels. It dislikes chance, and love. It has built line upon line of walls. It has opened those doors whose bolts it has been able to draw. It has coloured the ceiling sky-blue, and the bathtubs sea-green. It has drawn up the plans of its labyrinth-gardens, and has imagined perspectives that are truly maddening. It has released its flights of birds: peacocks, pheasants, partridges, doves. It has covered the soft earth with its crust of varnish. It has placed mirrors everywhere.

Consciousness: self-awareness. In the dream that it has forced mankind to dream, the Masters' thinking has elaborated the most terrible of all its traps. Men and women see each other, but the looks they give return towards themselves, lull them to sleep, consume them. Sleep devours those who sleep. Consciousness is like a strongroom that sleepers construct round themselves, and so immure themselves. Who will knock down these cardboard ramparts? If only they knew that the Masters had pierced spyholes in the walls of these rooms. If only they knew that the Masters were lying in wait for them in the very centre of their consciousness, that the Masters were ceaselessly filming them in their ridiculous kingdom of solitude. If only they knew the nature of these crannies near the plinths of columns, these electric-light bulbs, these mirrors, these books, these pieces of furniture, these photographs, these water taps, these plugholes. Prisoners, ah, prisoners lying in the cells of sleep, wake up! Wake up and look at last at those who are looking at you.

The Masters' thinking is so powerful that it seems limitless. It works day and night, without rest, sending out its calls to sleeping brains. What is it saying? What does it want? It is difficult to understand its workings. To understand properly, one would first have to be free, to have succeeded in shaking off its steady gaze. Perhaps it needs nothing more than power, in order to exist. It invents everything. Everything derives from it, and moves in its direction. Passions, desires, pains, pleasures, likes and dislikes, images, words, emotions, obsessions: all these derive from the Masters' thinking, exist within it. The Masters draw up their plans, and wait. Then they measure reactions and study phenomena. They know all the things that are bound to happen sooner or later. They have anticipated each gesture. If a man kills a woman, it is merely an article of their law. If a man kills another man, or a man steals a car, or a man pours a can of petrol over the floor of a building, then puts a lighted match to it, these are merely acts in the collection of acts drawn up by the Masters. When a woman loves a man, or a woman looks at a woman, this is merely what the Masters themselves wanted, happening when they wanted it to happen. Freedom, happiness, enjoyment belong to them, always. Everywhere there are tiny mechanisms, photo-electric cells, barometers, dynamometers, speedometers, all gauging the phases of people's actions; and the impulses run along wires, across the universe, as far as the subsidiary brains that pick them up, condense them and send them off again to other brains, then through other wires, above the landscape of iron and cement, above the towns and deserts, across space, across the ocean, leaping from ganglion to ganglion, actuating the motors and calculating-machines that frantically pour out their streams of figures, their long poems of figures, names, figures, figures, figures, and names, storm clouds of figures, rain of names that drown men's thoughts, vibrate in the air, and lull to sleep.

Nabisco	2.20	41	49 1/4	48 3/4	48 7/8	—3/8
Nalco Ch	.80	13	51 3/8	51	51 1/4	+1/4
Narco	.60	3	23 3/4	23 3/4	23 3/4	....
Nashua Cp	.48	29	46 1/8	45 1/2	5 3/4	—1/4
Nat Airln	10p	24	21 1/4	20 3/4	20 7/8	—5/8
Nat Avia	.96g	21	21 7/8	21 1/2	21 7/8	+1/4
Nat Can	.45	7	27	26 3/4	26 3/4	—1/8
N. Can pf	150	10	48 1/2	48 1/2	48 1/2	....
Nat Cash R	72	520	46 3/8	45	46 3/8	+3/8
Nat Chem	30	88	46	44 3/8	45 1/4	+7/8
Nat City L	.90	24	25 1/2	25	25 1/8	—5/8
Nat Distil	.90	137	16 7/8	16 3/8	16 3/8	—1/4
Nat Fuel	1.68	20	24 1/2	24	24 1/8	+1/8
Nat Gnl	.20	106	24	23 1/2	23 7/8	—1/4
Nat Gyp	1.05	45	20 1/2	20 1/4	20 3/8	—1/8
Nat Homes		102	34 1/4	33	33 1/8	....
Nat Indust		36	6 7/8	6 5/8	6 5/8	—1/4
Nat Ind	pf. 60	1	12	12	12	—1/4
Nat Ind	pf. 125	12	13 5/8	13 3/8	13 3/8	—1/8
Nat Prest	1.10a	4	32 5/8	32 1/4	32 3/8	—1/8
Nat Svcln	.66	60	27 5/8	26 7/8	26 7/8	—3/4
Nat Stand	.75	4	40	40 1/4	40 1/4	—1/8
Nat Starch	.64	10	32 7/8	32 1/2	32 7/8	+3/8
Nat Steel	2.50	42	38 1/2	38 3/8	38 3/8	—3/8
Nat Tea	.80	64	14	15 5/8	14	+1/8
Nat Un Ei	.22d	87	20	19 1/8	20	+1 1/4
Natomas	.25	745	93 + 86 3/4	93 3/8	93 3/8	+5 5/8
Neptune	.40	12	17 5/8	17 1/4	17 1/4	—1/4
New Pow	1.24	25	39	38 1/2	39	+3/4
New Berry	1	7	19 1/2	19 1/4	19 1/4	—1/2

Alcoa, Alcan Aluminium Ltd, Siemens, Viscosa, Thomson-Brandt, Péchiney, Royal Dutch, AKZO, Massey, Merck, Hercules Inc., Firestone, Boeing, Texas Instruments, and you, Hoogovens, Hoffman-Laroche, Bayer, Nestlé, Philips, Courtauld's, Barclays, Shell, Great Universal Stores, Texaco, Unilever, Kodak, Burroughs Corp., Sears Roebuck, Olivetti, Montecatini, Air Liquide, Polaroid, R.C.A., Procter & Gamble, ... what are your thoughts? Where are you hidden? What is behind your beautiful and terrifying names? But you do not hear the voices of mankind, you are on the far side of life, on the side that holds knowledge to ransom. You are faceless, voiceless, without desire, and that is why all faces and voices and desires

ge of forms:
colour: tonality, bright
(Chevreul's chrom
field of colours lends

BOSCH

ness, saturation.
atic circle)
itself ideally to syner

Vifredo Pareto, *Mind and Society*, 'Non-logical conduct':

'Many men have tried to change people's behaviour through reasoning, but their efforts have often been singularly poor in results...People require to be directed through the manipulation of their instincts rather than the modification of their reasoning faculties. This is a reality that politicians have always appreciated, when they appeal to the electorate's feelings rather than attempt to use rational arguments that would have remained unheeded, or at least would never have proved effective in swaying the emotions of the masses.'

BOMBSHELLS OF WORDS EXPLODING

WITHIN THE WALLS

When Du Pont de Nemours, inventor of NYLON, discovered this fibre, round 1938-9, he needed to find a trade-name for it. With this in view, Du Pont de Nemours launched a competition among his employees for the suggestion of an appropriate name that would be easy to remember, euphonious, and pronounceable in the various major languages. From the mass of ideas that were submitted to the jury, it was the word NYLON that finally won approval. This word has absolutely no meaning at all: it simply incorporates the suffix -on, by analogy with 'cotton' and 'rayon'.

KODAK

SHATTER
TREE
TRUNKS

1971 KNOLL INTERNATIONAL

percutan

belong to you. And to you, McGraw Hill, Arthur Lipper, Lakeland. And to you, Metromedia. And to you, Bausch & Lomb. Are these, at last, the names of the Masters? Du Pont de Nemours, Wurlitzer, Woolworth, Zayre, Toledo, fabulous names of non-existent countries, Scovill, Rohr, Skyline Co., Signal, Pfizer, Tektronix, names of tyrants and jailers who do not exist, who never exist, names that fade away the moment one pronounces them, names of unknown craters on imaginary and unreachable moons, Digital, Interpace, MacDonalds, Chriscraft, Chrysler, Diam Sham, names of the future, perhaps, names of future dynasties that one pronounces within one's dream and that vanish in the dream's mist, De Soto, Bulova, Masonite, Maremont, Lockheed, Gulf, Iowa Beef, Mouldings, Eagle Cloth, Cook's, Batak, Behring Corp., Reeves, Tyco Labs, U.S. Radium, United Fruit, Voplex, sinister names of battles in which men die, Salem, Okonite, Plaza, Bata, Incomimbra, Cofonica, British Petroleum, Colocoton, Socophar, Thermonic, Westinghouse, Sobruma, Hohner, Dean, Minétain, B.A.T., Laminage à froid, Vanguard, Sequoyah Inc., Nytronics, Nuclear Data, Otis, PepsiCO, Gordon, Asamera Oil, your names constitute your thought, your names cover the earth, and dig and chop and devour, your names erode the base of mountains, drain deserts, scrape the ocean's bed, mark the sky with stripes, tirelessly, assiduously, while mankind sleeps. When your names are there, nothing else is able to appear. What is the point of talking about the sun, the rain, the dawn, the birds, when there are all these names around? How can anyone dare say 'I, me, my' when there are all these figures, all this external power at work, pushing inexorably forwards? I can no longer speak, I can no longer move, I can only sleep, and dream the dreams dictated by your names and figures. I can no longer think about thoughts. All that I can do is close my eyes, plug my ears and nostrils, and plunge into all the open wells. All that I can do is choose the Master of my thoughts, the one who will send waves coursing through my body from his mind's gigantic factory set up somewhere on the face of the earth to count and weigh and divide each second of my life. I know his name, a strange baleful name: it is inscribed above my head, and shines as brightly as an electric sign. Its name will be:

VARIOOM BROADCASTING PROPERTIES

Round my Master there is nothing but night.

Then one longed to think, think, think; one longed to launch the kite of one's thoughts into the sky. But my Master Varioom's thinking is opposed to kites; his thinking is like a tin lid covering the earth. Men's thoughts are blind bats beating their wings in the black air, flapping frenziedly between the incomprehensible partitions. The thinking of my Master Varioom is invincible, and his mechanical knowledge is so vast that it seems limitless. His wealth is so enormous that he himself cannot calculate it: each day it doubles or triples. Each time that a bat-man sends out a squeak as he glides round, the sound is picked up by Varioom's ears, and engraved on magnetic tape in fine serrations that can never be effaced. Each time that the bat recognizes an obstacle, the Master of the bats devours the information, then creates a fresh obstacle. The Masters' thinking consists in the multiplication of walls. Thinking is the art of setting traps.

Space is not free: networks of cobwebs, lattice-work, lakes, nets, trawls, screens of gas, smokescreens. Varioom is expert at digging wells into whose sparkling depths the greedy hordes will hurl themselves. Varioom knows how to project such beautiful gentle films on to the clouds that the glands immediately start secreting their juices and milks. Varioom is very fond of mankind's excretions, and nourishes himself exclusively on these, on the odour of sweat, and on the frissons produced by pleasure. Pain and pleasure are all the same to him: just nourishment. Inside the cities' hidden brains are great electrical machines transmitting impulses to the skin of men and women. When Varioom turns the button to the right, the men and women groan and quiver, and their eyes become glazed. Then Varioom turns the button to the left, and shrieks of terror, cries of pain and hatred, rise from all the closed rooms, as mouths start foaming.

Varioom, my Master, knows that, and knows many other things besides. He knows how to arouse love, jealousy, the taste for death, laughter, scowls, smiles. Its invisible machines are linked to all the points of the earth, to all the points of the body. It is he who wrote all the books, made all the films, sang all the songs, painted all the pictures, erected all the monuments. Perhaps he has always been there, perhaps he will never die. Men carry his name and live his story. He plays, all the time, remorselessly and grim-faced, and his game can never come to an end, since he is playing against himself. When one hand loses, the other wins.

Enough of all that. Man's thinking has proved incapable of liberating either words or desires. But there are so many walls everywhere, so many doors everywhere. There is so much knowledge: big mechanical brains devouring smaller brains ... It has to stop. Eyes are going to open, one day: they *must*. Already, eyelids are trembling, eyelashes are parting. In a few minutes, a few hours, a few days, the sleeping girl will awaken. That is clear from the way she is breathing, the way her breasts are rising and falling more quickly, more convulsively. The blood is beating very strongly in her neck, and her face is flushed. Her lips part, and soon words will enter her mouth and set her tongue moving. She is going to wake up despite all the electrodes sticking into her scalp and transmitting endless orders. Varioom, Alcoa, Viscosa, Gulf, Texas Instruments, B.A.T., Rank Xerox, Hüber-Bohner, Penn Central, I.C.I., B.A.S.F., the Rio Tinto Zinc Corporation are all speaking in their soundless voices, saying

SLEEP SLEEP YOU SHALL SLEEP

sending sweet dreams and fearful nightmares, and all their armies of monsters, and death's-heads named DANGER NO ENTRY and avalanches and desires, and caresses, and blinding red and green lights: yet the young woman will wake up.

All dreams have to come to an end sooner or later. The dreams fade away; the gentle lulling suddenly turns into fist-blows that pummel the ribs, and the sweet harmony suddenly bristles with thorns. Words themselves turn into explosive bullets that pierce agonizing holes. The Masters' minds have determined that sleep should continue for centuries on end. Yet the gaze is awakening, little by little, opening the pupils gradually wider, like two black suns rising above the horizon. What is it? It is not thought. All thought emanated from the Masters and served only their interests. This is more like a void, a summons from within the body, a strange disquiet that makes the muscles and the nerves vibrate. Perhaps it is the trees which have invented this new sensation. Perhaps it is the lapdogs. Perhaps real thought was even more powerful than that of the Masters, and perhaps one was steeped in freedom from the first stirring of life onwards, without knowing it.

Varioom desires intensely that the young woman should continue sleeping, but his power is fading in the coils and wires. Tear away the electrodes, cut the circuits! It was basically quite simple: all that was needed was to break the network of wires and lamps and condensers. It was just a matter of knowing how to locate the ganglions, and then inserting a long needle in exactly the right spot. After that, the electricity stops running along the wires, and no longer illuminates the spotlights trained hypnotically on victims' faces. A few seconds more, just a few seconds, and the light will go out. The dazzling dreams that have lasted an eternity come suddenly to a stop, curl up, and roll in the dust: three tiny balls of mercury. Is that all there was to it? The innumerable words, the beautiful images, the obsessions, the myths, the mannerisms and habits: all resolved into a few droplets that are rolling away, out of sight? The universe has not budged. Nothing has happened. Beneath the cities' crusts, the earth is still soft. Between the clouds, the star-filled sky is motionless, quite motionless.

Come over from the far side of time! Wake up: it is in eyes that the true light is to be found. The eyes open calmly, and their gaze sends the hypnotizers to sleep. In their turn, the eyes pour out floods of beauty and passion, two great stars that extinguish the Masters' lamps. When will that come about? The gaze is far greater than thought: it can scan the depths of space within a second. All the Masters' secrets were really small ones, mere flytraps. Just one young woman's gaze is a trap for the universe itself, and the Masters' minds are going to be swallowed by that trap. The eyelids will open, that is certain. They can no longer stay tightly closed. When the eyelids open, a terrible flash of lightning will dart forth, and the gaze will streak across the bounds of space, and the old dreams will turn round and dream those who created them.

What else do you see?

I see ... I see a big rectangular mirror secured to the room's right-hand wall. It is cold and smooth and flawless, and the light bounces off it without leaving any marks. When the room is dark, the big mirror glows dimly, with an enigmatic grey glow. In daytime, when the blind is raised, the big mirror is blank; and at night, when the neon tubes above the washbasin and on the ceiling are alight, the big mirror sparkles with all its might, like a slab of crystal.

It has been there, on that particular spot of the cell's wall, for a long time now. It has always been there. Perhaps, when they began building the great barracks complex of Hyperpolis, this mirror was the first thing to assume shape. It is cold and motionless. If one touches it with the back of one's hand, it feels like a block of ice. If one looks at it, it is as though one had been staring at the surface of a puddle for hours on end. But one cannot really look at it, because one is on this side of it, inside the eye, one's forehead pressed against the crystalline lens.

There were all sorts of things one could do, to help forget that the mirror was there. The young man called Machines tried to forget the mirror, but it was not easy. When one enters a particular room in the great barracks, some day or other, and notices the mirror standing stiffly there, on the wall to the right of the cell, it is as though one had always known it was there, as though one truly knew it. The young woman called Tranquillity (these are slaves' names, names of no importance) did not want people to pay any attention to the mirrors. She did not like them. But the moment that one entered one's cell, one saw the big mirror, and shivered, knowing what was going to happen.

There was no way of talking to the mirror: it did not like people to talk. For example, two people were sitting on the edge of the single bed, smoking. The young man called Machines was smoking small Italian cigars, and the young woman called Tranquillity was smoking American cigarettes with filters made of cotton, called Reynolds or Philip Morris or something like that. They watched the smoke coming out of their nostrils and rising placidly to the ceiling. The smoke from the Italian cigar rose more slowly than the smoke from the American cigarette. But the mirror paid no attention to all that. It was content to reflect the clouds of smoke; it did it coldly and without interest, because it was its job to reflect whatever went on in this cell of the barracks.

There is really no way of talking to the mirror. From time to time, there are sighs, sounds of heavy breathing, and stray phrases. For example:

'Like a cigarette?'

'In a little while ... '

'What are you thinking about?'

'Nothing.'

'My feet are a bit cold.'

'What's the time?'

'You've got a pimple there, does it hurt?'

and the stray phrases glide across the cold mirror, and the mirror does not think.

Sometimes, the young man called Machines becomes so frightened of the mirror that he begins to tremble, especially in the legs. He does not understand why he is trembling. The fact that the cell is tightly sealed may be the reason why he is trembling. Outside, there is the black night streaked by the lights of cars, and the dome of Hyperpolis glows like phosphorus. Maybe these are the reasons why he is trembling.

Playing games helps one to stop thinking about the mirror. A thought-guessing game, for instance. The young woman called Tranquillity thinks very hard about something, with her eyes tight shut.

'Is it big?'

'No ... '

'Round?'

'No.'

'Square?'

'Yes.'

'Is it beautiful?'

'No ... Yes, well, that depends.'

'Is it red?'

'No.'

'Blue?'

'No.'

'White?'

'No.'

'Green?'

'No.'

'So it's colourless?'

'Yes.'

'Does it breathe?'

'No.'

'Hmm ... Can you drink it?'

'No.'

'Is it visible?'

'Yes.'

'Is it something dead?'

'How do you mean?'

'Well, yes, is it alive or dead?'

'Hmm, that depends.'

'Is it useful?'

'Yes ... Yes.'

'Is it a machine?'

'No.'

'Is there one here?'

'Yes.'

'In the room?'

'Yes.'

'Can one see it from here?'

'Yes.'

'Does it give a light?'

'Yes.'

'The neon tube?'

'No.'

'Is it on the ceiling?'

'No.'

'On the ground?'

'No.'

'Is it on the wall?'

'Yes.'

'Is it the window?'

'No.'

'Is it made of glass?'

'Yes.'

'Can you see yourself in it?'

'Yes.'

Or else two people can play at thought transmission. It is easier than it sounds. All you have to do is lie down on a bed, bring your head very close to the other head, and look into the depths of the other eyes until both pairs of eyes melt into each other. The young man called Machines and the young woman called Tranquillity played at talking to each other like that.

'At my grandmother's, there was a flowerpot with a green fern in it,' she thought.

'Yes, and another thing that's very peculiar is the white streaks across fingernails,' thought Machines. 'And the moons are very peculiar, too.'

'I wonder how long a ballpoint pen lasts?' thought Tranquillity. And then she thought: 'The other day, walking by a restaurant, I saw a tank full of *live frogs*.

'It would be interesting, crossing the desert on foot,' thought Machines. 'One could set out from Mauritania and arrive in Egypt.'

'The most delicious fruit of all is pineapple,' thought Tranquillity.

'It would be nice, living on a beach,' thought Machines. 'I have a sister and I don't know her. Her name is Bolivia. Isn't that nice?'

'I like loving but I don't like others loving me,' mused Tranquillity.

The mirror paid no attention to any of that. It was of no particular interest. What *does* interest mirrors? Certainly not men. Perhaps basically they are a little fonder of women, but who can tell?

There are many cells, all similar to each other, in this barracks in West Hyperpolis. They are connected to each other by many pipes, drains, electric wires, telephones. One could go from one cell to another by travelling along the hot-water pipes: then one would gush out of the shower roses at intervals. It is difficult to share one single thought when there are so many shower roses.

Machines was very afraid of the mirror, and that is the truth of the matter. Each time that he turned his gaze away from Tranquillity's eyes he caught sight of the big empty mirror gleaming in its place on the wall. Even when he did not look at it he could feel it in his back, and it was a bit like an open window wafting cold air in. He would have liked very much to forget it and its counterparts. For there are many mirrors on the walls of many cells. One could voyage very far in their waters, floating from room to room. The mirrors wanted to devour men's backs, they inhaled with their openings, they sucked up thoughts from heads, they swallowed images, ideas, gestures. Each time that Machines thrust his loins against the young woman's loins he felt the mirror's cold breath on his back, and stopped moving. Or else he turned his head and looked at the mirror, but there was nothing to be seen except this shimmering surface of glass, or steel.

Mirrors do not concern themselves with the shivers that run along men's spines. They do not concern themselves with anything: they are glazed, icy. Men and women talk, eat, fondle each other in the cells of the barracks in West Hyperpolis. The mirrors are not looking at them: their gaze is fixed upon some distant horizon, and they cannot refocus their eyes onto a closer perspective.

It was dangerous to talk. Tranquillity made occasional attempts to talk. She caressed Machines's face, and murmured words in his ear. But Machines did not hear. He felt the words that had stuck fast in the back of his throat, and his legs trembled. He sat down on the edge of the narrow bed, and lit another Italian cigar. He looked at the lighter's flame, bringing it close to his eyes. These gestures of his were futile, though: mirrors cannot be forgotten just like that. They are stronger than human faces because they have a gaze but no eyes. Perhaps, in reality, everything had been built round the mirrors, some time in the past, and the cells were simply these animals' lairs.

The most dangerous thing of all was not the big mirror itself but what one saw in it. When Machines looked back from time to time, he saw a man lying on the bed beside a woman, their white naked skin, their shoulders, hair, folded arms, greyish legs, stretched out on the grey bedspread; and he saw the things round the bed, the metal-framed furniture, the lamps and books and newspapers, the glass ashtray full of cigarette stubs. It was all clear and distant, like something looked at through binoculars. Tranquillity also saw someone, a woman lying on her back, with legs drawn up, one arm behind the head, brown hair adrift, two white breasts with brown nipples, a white belly with a navel in the centre, and even the kind of tattoo on her thigh where she had been vaccinated against smallpox. It was really dangerous to see these people there in the room, motionless on the single bed, looking at you. It was worse than a photograph, because this was both a living image and a dead image.

The faces were particularly difficult to endure. The neon

light illuminated them harshly; they looked hollow-eyed and hollow-cheeked, and the outlines of their chins and skulls stood out sharply. Their hair was dry and lustreless, like a nylon wig. The eyes that stared into the mirror were more like little balls, two of them golden-brown, and two of them green, shining between eyelids. It was truly a fearful sight. The bodies were corpse-like, livid white, with peculiar grey shadows where the bones protruded, and peculiar pink patches where the blood ran close to the surface.

The mirror did not like to see life going on round it; it hated life. That is why it had been installed: to hang inconspicuously at the back of this lair in the barracks in West Hyperpolis, and devour those who entered the trap. It must have devoured many men and women, here in this cell, couples who had lain down together on the single bed, without suspecting anything. But each day the mirror had removed some element. It had destroyed all the words of human language, words of love, words of sorrow, words of pleasure. It had destroyed gestures and dreams. When people were sleeping in darkness, the glass glowed dimly, became phosphorescent, because it was drinking the light of human life. The mirror enjoyed drinking the warmth that emanated from a man and a woman after they had made love and their skin was glistening with sweat. Accursed mirror! Will it never be satiated? Must it always demand still more gestures, caresses, words, sweat, sperm? Machines tried not to think about the mirror: he tried talking, he tried smoking. Tranquillity tried to lose consciousness: they both tried, for hours on end. Sometimes it happened like this: they trembled feverishly, then flung themselves at each other, like two motor scooters colliding. They did that with such rage and desire that nothing else existed. The two bodies united at the loins and at the mouths felt the same wave surge up within them and rise and fill the whole of space. Tranquillity switched off the bedside lamp, and the room still blazed with light. The double wave surged up the channels of their bodies and towered so high that its crest was out of sight. Then suddenly it came crashing down in a thousand fragments, transformed into powder in a fraction of a second. Then the two bodies also fell apart, panting and sobbing loudly.

But at that moment the mirror shone with a really strange glow, giving it the appearance of eyes sparkling with desire and hatred.

Machines and Tranquillity watched the mirror glow with desire, and looked at the cell's walls, the unlit lamp, the pieces of furniture. In a way it was more terrible than being cooped up in the cabin of an ocean liner crossing the Atlantic. It was more frightening than soaring up to the one-hundred-and-thirty-third floor in a lift's steel closet. It was more pitiless than racing along a motorway in a car and hearing the wind roaring through the ventilators at 100 m.p.h. It was more dangerous than the cement huts where one can hear the singing of thousands of volts of electricity, it was more endless than a tunnel, more callous than a car park, more distressing than the façade of a high-school building, darker and more incomprehensible than the glass frontage of a bank at night.

Mirrors are like that. They let men and women embrace each other on a single bed, and afterwards the glass surfaces are impregnated with warmth and light.

Even so, there came a moment when Machines felt like saying something. He lit an Italian cigar and started saying something. He said:

'Listen, T, I ... '

But Tranquillity put her hand over his mouth, and made a sign to him to be quiet. Then she rummaged in her bag at the foot of the bed, and took out a notepad and a pencil. She wrote something on the pad and handed it to Machines, who read to himself:

Sh! We are being spied on

He wrote:

How do you know?

She wrote:

My girlfriend told me she once found a microphone in the lamp

254

Machines wanted to get up to examine the lamp, but Tranquillity stopped him. She scribbled hastily in the notepad and thrust it at him:

That would do no good. There are bound to be others

Then she took it back from him and added a line:

Tell me what you wanted to tell me earlier on

Machines shook his head. She wrote down:

Please!

He hesitated for a moment, then wrote down:

I want to go away with you

Tranquillity wrote:

Where?

Machines:

Anywhere — Kashmir, Mexico, New Guinea

Tranquillity:

I can't at present

Machines took the pad and printed in large letters:

THEN I'LL BURN DOWN HYPERPOLIS

When Tranquillity read that, she tore the page from the pad, screwed it up into a ball, and put it in the ashtray.

Now Machines lies down on the bed and closes his eyes. He feels Tranquillity's soft moist skin against his body, and feels her breath blowing air against his chest. He feels all these living sensations. But he cannot succeed in forgetting the mirror, or the wires connecting the microphones, or the hot-water pipes circulating through the barracks, or the shower nozzles. It is not so easy to forget such things. Everything, everywhere, is vibrating, running, tracing circles that shrink and shrink round you, although you always remain in their centre. Each heartbeat is like a drop of water falling into a basin and sending out its ripples. Each breath is like a tremor that spreads outwards, rebounds, returns, then starts out again. Impossible to sleep. Machines has closed his eyes; but other, lidless, eyes are keeping watch. Tranquillity does not speak, but the words leak out nevertheless: there is a haemorrhage of words in the throat and speech escapes with each puff of exhaled carbonic gas Perhaps they are going to be asphyxiated by the weight of words. There will be so many dead words in the cell, because of the mirror, that they will suffocate, like the man who goes into his garage at night, and shuts himself inside his car, and starts the engine after having fitted a rubber tube onto the exhaust pipe and connected the other end of the tube to the ventilator. The carbon monoxide gas rises gradually inside the car, rises like water in a bath, invisibly, and destroys the brain's nerve cells No one wants to die: it is the mirrors that desire people's death

In the mirror there are these two cold silent people stretches out side by side on a single bed. This other man and this other woman are pretending to sleep, but they are filled with hatred and feel no love for anyone on earth. They are empty images devoid of thought or desire or grief. They have never known enjoyment. Why are they there? What do they want, these people from the two-dimensional world? Machines half opens his eyes, and sees on the wall the reflection of the mirror's reflection. The look that the other couple give is hard and glazed. It takes away all warmth. It destroys life. They do not breathe. They do not eat, or perspire. They inhabit an aquarium. One sees them if one looks at them, but one cannot believe in what one sees. These over-familiar faces and bodies are merely shells. What is behind the masks? The cell is so filled with conscious-ness that the air is scarcely breathable. The consciousness is so thick and heavy that cast iron and marble resemble evaporating gases. It is as though, one day, someone had so hated the world — the whole world, with its trees, plants, grasses, animals, air, sun, rain, sea, rivers, lakes, pebbles, clouds — had given a look filled with such hatred that the lightning flashing from his eyes and imprisoned between the cell's walls was doomed to streak to and fro for at least a hundred thousand years.

The barracks and the dome of Hyperpolis are situated at the centre of the earth. And at the centre of this centre is the cell, the single bed, the mirror. But the mirror does not reflect the world, it simply reflects another mirror. Mirrors are like that: they only serve to create other mirrors. There they are, sprawled out in front of it, a naked man and woman interlaced so tightly that they resemble a double foetus. Then, little by little, they no longer know where they are. On the right of the mirror, or on the left of it?

If one is on the left, that means that the mirror is on the right. If one is on the right, it means that the mirror is on the opposite side. If one is on this side, it means that when one moves the hand like this, one is really moving it like that. If one turns the head, one is really turning it in the opposite direction. If only there was some kind of identification, a watch or a newspaper, or if one knew the location of the heart, the liver, the appendix, perhaps it would be possible to get one's bearings. If one did not dream, one might perhaps know what dreaming means. But acts are linked together, they spring apart in the same moment, they make and unmake. In the sun, in the streets, on the beaches, one knows exactly where one's shadow lies. But here in the barracks, one is caught in the trap. One is lost.

Mirrors are cruel. They shine with joy, they glow with pleasure, each time someone gets lost. Their gaze, the passionless gaze of a snake, is fixed on a distant point. But that is a deception, since the truth is that mirrors see everything, even the tiniest things. They examine your skin, your hair, your fingernails, with their magnifying glass, they notice the most fleeting shivers, the slightest aches and pains, they hear the lowest murmurs, they sense the least anxiety flitting across the moist surface of your eyes. Mirrors are in fact your eyes, your *eyes*. When they are there, they seize you by the tress of your glance and force you to cross over to the far side of the barrier of your pupils, inside the terrible vision-machines. Where do they come from? Who first conceived the idea of putting mirrors in cells? Who invented your eyes?

One should escape as far away as possible. One should take a boat for Carthage, or Byzantium, a train for Wangchow, a lorry for Samarkand, and begin a one-way voyage. But it would not be far enough. One should go so far away that one would never again see the barracks' flat roof, or the white dome of Hyperpolis. One should rip out all the tubes and wires and pipes that betray those whom they are ostensibly nurturing. Perhaps then one might find the spoken word again. Perhaps then one might love someone or something that was no longer one's own image.

Mirrors know science. They invented science in order to subjugate people, because they needed living warmth to animate their sombre aquariums and their cold rooms. They have turned men and women into foods for their nourishment.

The young man was trembling so hard, now, that he could hardly keep his balance any longer, at the head of the bed. The young woman was trembling, too, because she was afraid, and did not understand. With her mouth, she sought to breathe in from the man's mouth, and she dug her nails into the flesh of the man's shoulders. There were no sounds in the barracks, except for the sounds of their breathing and trembling. The mirror shone brighter and brighter on the wall, became phosphorescent with life. The water circulated in the pipes, the drains gurgle faintly, the wires were stretched to breaking-point by the energy of the electricity they carried. The young woman called Tranquillity gasped for breath: her mouth was dry, and the mirror's words were choking her. She tried to see into the eyes of the young man called Machines. But at this moment he was turned towards the mirror, staring at it steadily and unblinkingly. He had never looked at anything in that way. There had never been such a fiery star in the sky, there had never been such a dazzling flame upon the earth.

Suddenly, without understanding what he was doing — but perhaps it was not he who was doing it, perhaps it was the other man in the mirror who had got up and was walking on trembling legs, glass ashtray clutched in one hand — he moved towards the wall, filled with fear and hatred, and hurled the ashtray at the wall with all his might.

Tranquillity began to scream, because just as the mirror broke she glimpsed another room, and three men began to scurry out of the other room, then vanished. What is so terrible is not consciousness itself, but what lies behind it. It is not spectacles and mirrors themselves that frighten and wound, but what exists on the far side of them.

The slave-girl called Tranquillity entered beneath the dome of Hyperpolis. She found difficulty in walking, and the man in the dark-grey suit, beside her, held her arm as they went along the brightly lit corridor. She was very drowsy, because of all the sleepless nights she had just passed, and also because of the tranquillizer they had injected into her that morning. The slave-girl and the man in the dark-grey three-piece suit went slowly along the corridor side by side. Other men and women were passing in the opposite direction, walking quickly over the plastic flooring, and their footsteps detonated against the ground. They entered empty lifts that shot upwards in a single motion, then they walked along more corridors. The slave-girl had no idea of her whereabouts. After walking for a long time they reached a large room, decorated in black and white, and when they went in she saw that it was full of men wearing ties. These men were talking together in low tones; it was impossible to hear what they were saying. Perhaps they were speaking in a foreign language.

The man in the dark-grey suit led the slave-girl towards an armchair, and eased her into it. The armchair was new, and upholstered in black glazed artificial leather, swollen with seam-worked padding. It gave off a strange glow, like anthracite. The back had six vertical ridges, with one horizontal ridge on top at neck level. The chair's arms were broad, and the slave-girl's forearms stuck to the tacky surface. It was almost impossible to move. The seat was hard, and the padded ridge down its centre felt quite painful between the buttocks. The slave-girl was slumped in the armchair, feeling as heavy as though she was in a giant jet plane taking off. Her thoughts were entirely centred on the black armchair, and she made great efforts not to fall asleep.

In front of her was a long metal desk with just a few things dotted along its surface: a glass ashtray, a silver cigarette lighter, a packet of American cigarettes with Reyno or some such name written across the surface.

Sitting at the other side of the desk were six men, plus the man in the dark-grey suit who had escorted her. They were all wearing dark-grey suits and white shirts; only their ties differed, and these were, respectively, red with blue stripes, blue with red stripes, purplish red, maroon, red with black stripes, and black. The faces and hands differed slightly, too, but the slave-girl did not look at their faces or hands, only at their ties.

For a few moments everyone stayed like that: the slave-girl dozing in her armchair, and the six ties speaking some foreign language together in low tones. Two air-conditioning units hummed away, somewhere along the walls of the room. Occasionally there was a click and the units switched over automatically to the ventilator. Then, with another click, they began blowing cold air out once more.

The slave-girl shivered in the cold air. Even the electric light was cold and pallid, like frost. The room was at the very top of the dome, the highest point in Hyperpolis, so high that the clouds could not be very far away.

Then another man entered the room. His age was probably about forty, and he was wearing a navy-blue jacket with beige trousers, but no tie. He came up to the slave-girl and held out his hand to her. The slave-girl noticed that he was carrying a black suitcase in his other hand.

'My name's Hague,' he said.

The slave-girl tried to get up, but her back seemed stuck to the black imitation leather, so it was difficult. The man called Hague took her by one arm and helped her to stand up. He switched the suitcase to his other hand.

They left the room together, and started walking through a fresh maze of corridors. Sometimes, people crossed their path, and Hague flicked his hand at them in greeting. At the end of all the corridors there was an iron staircase, which they climbed, with Hague leading the way. At the top was yet another corridor, lined with green doors that had business cards pinned to them.

At the end of this corridor, Hague stopped in front of a door, fished in a pocket of his jacket and brought out a small gleaming key.

'Here we are,' he said.

Just as the door was swinging open, the slave-girl saw something really terrifying: it was a printed card, fixed to the door at eye level. There was a drawing of a red hand, in the centre of the card, the words HAGUE SYSTEM INC. printed across the top of the card, and below the hand, in big red letters:

SECURITY IN DEPTH

The man took the slave-girl's arm and ushered her firmly inside, saying in a calm soothing voice:

'Don't tremble so.'

The slave-girl looked round her and saw a narrow windowless office that contained nothing but two folding-chairs and a folding-table, and a naked light bulb hanging from the ceiling. On the right-hand wall there was a mirror on which were painted gaudy fish and seaweed.

Hague put the black suitcase down on the table and opened it with another key. He did not say a word, although from time to time he raised his head, and his grey eyes studied the slave-girl. There were deep creases at the sides of his mouth.

The man slowly removed the contents from the suitcase. First he took out six lengths of paired electric flex, and disentangled them. Then a heavy piece of apparatus that he put down on the table in place of the empty suitcase: it was something like a radio set or a record-player or a tape-recorder, with black plastic sides and a nickel-plated top. After positioning the apparatus, Hague plugged the six sets of wires into the appropriate sockets in its side, then unrolled a long black flex from the apparatus and plugged it into the socket at the base of the wall, under the mirror with its decorative fish.

He turned to the slave-girl.

'I'm going to begin now. Please don't smoke. Let me have your wrists.'

He fastened the end of a wire to each outstretched wrist, with strips of adhesive tape.

Then he took the slave-girl's hands and stuck two more wires to the palms with tape. After that, he pushed the tip of each middle finger into a sort of metal thimble that had a wire connected to it. He did all this quickly and skilfully. Then he murmured in his calm voice:

'Don't worry ... It's nothing.'

He unbuttoned the slave-girl's blouse and fastened another pair of wires to her skin, under the breasts, using a rather larger strip of adhesive tape.

'Breathe deeply,' he ordered.

He glanced at the apparatus on the table.

'Inhale.'

He walked up to the slave-girl, and shifted the wires below her breasts to a point nearer the stomach.

'Inhale.'

The slave-girl filled her lungs full of air.

'Good.'

He came back to her again, holding a small pair of scissors with which he snipped off a lock of hair close to the scalp, near the right temple. He fixed a wire to this bare spot, with a strip of tape.

'Close your eyes,' said Hague.

He fixed one final wire to the left eyelid, using a very thin strip of tape. Then he stood back a little.

'Look at my hand,' Hague ordered.

And he moved his hand to the right, then to the left, while

watching the dials on the face of the apparatus. The slave-girl followed his hand with her eyes.

The man sat down at the other side of the table, and took a notebook and a gold ballpoint pen out of the suitcase. He started to speak, rather slowly, in an odd solemn sort of voice. His face was expressionless. But the intense grey eyes shone brightly. The slave-girl looked at his eyes: the pupils were contracted, two black dots in the centre of ash-grey irises.

The man's voice echoed in the small room.

'I'm going to ask you a few questions,' said the voice. 'Try to answer without too much hesitation. That's very important. Even if a question seems difficult, even if you don't feel like answering a particular question, even if you find a question peculiar or absurd, I still want you to answer.' A pause.

'How old are you?' he started off.

'Twenty-two.'

'You were born in Romania, but your parents left the country when you were still a baby. Do you remember Romania?'

'No ... '

'You have one brother, I believe?'

'No.'

'Well, you had a brother, but he died before you were born.'

Hague glanced at the machine. At its centre, a roll of paper slowly moved past, horizontally, while six styluses traced lines of ink along it.

The man suddenly darted his hand towards the slave-girl's face. She jerked her head back, and the six stylus tips swung upwards in unison, tracing serrated lines along the paper.

'You hate your mother,' said the voice very quickly.

The stylus tips jumped even higher up the paper.

'No ... I don't think I do,' stammered the slave-girl. Her heart was beating fast, and her hands were sweating.

'Yes, you do hate her, but it's of no importance to me ... Why did you run away from home when you were fourteen?'

The slave-girl did not answer. But the styluses registering her breathing and her pulse had leapt.

265

'Do you go to the cinema a lot?'

'Yes.'

'How often? Twice a week? Three times? More?'

'It depends ... There are times ... Nearly ... nearly every evening.'

'What kind of films do you like?'

'Euh ... Cartoons.'

'Love-stories?'

'Not specially.'

'You go alone?'

'Yes, usually.'

'You don't have any friends?'

(Zigzags)

' ... No, it's not that, but — '

'Why don't you have any friends?'

'I don't know, I — '

'Don't you want friends?'

'Yes, but — '

'What about men?'

The six styluses jumped a little.

'You don't like talking about that?'

'No.'

'Have you ever made love to another woman?'

The slave-girl would have liked to hold the styluses in place, but they had already started sweeping up and down across the moving strip of paper.

'Answer me ... Have you ever had the desire to make love to another woman?'

' ... No, I ... I don't think so.'

The Galvanic Skin Reflex stylus traced a very sharp-angled serrated line.

'Do you sleep well?'

'Yes ... '

'Do you read books in bed at night?'

The styluses quivered slightly.

'Yes, sometimes.'

'What kind of books?'

'Oh ... Novels ... '

'What kind of novels?'

'Detective stories.'

'Do you buy your books, or steal them?'

The G.S.R. stylus and the one connected with the palms of the hands both jumped. Hague gave a slight twist to the control knobs of the stylus registering ocular movements.

'Do you often steal things?'

'N ... no, not very often.'

'Why do you steal?'

(Zigzags)

'You don't have any money?'

'Yes, but I — '

'Do you enjoy stealing?'

The six styluses inscribed two zigzags.

'Don't be scared,' said Hague. 'Like I said, it's not important.'

'I ... I take things occasionally, just for fun,' said the slave-girl.

'Money?'

'No!'

'You never have the urge to steal money?'

The styluses, except for the one registering the breathing, swung upwards together.

'I'd like to know what you dream about ... ' said the grave voice. 'Do you ever have frightening dreams?'

'Yes ... Sometimes, yes.'

'Would you like to tell me one of your dreams?'

'I don't remember them very well ... '

For a few seconds Hague said nothing. He simply looked at the roll of paper, with the six parallel serrated lines drawn by the styluses.

'Listen. I want you to tell me the truth, now, that's very important. Do you ever have the following dream: a woman who looks like your mother starts making advances to you, then seizes you and, after a struggle, being much stronger than you she pushes you down flat on your stomach, lifts your skirt, pulls down your knickers, and starts forcing a suppository into you. You scream and scream, but she goes on ramming the suppository into you quite brutally, and that hurts you terribly ... '

First, the G.S.R. stylus gave a great leap, then the other styluses followed suit: those registering ocular movement, perspiration of the palms, breathing, the heart, the brain. The slave-girl had gone very pale, and she was trembling so hard that she could scarcely murmur:

'I don't know, no, I don't know!'

' ... And then your father suddenly appears, and he ... '

'I don't know, I don't know!'

The slave-girl suddenly had the idea that all this was the electricity's fault, and that if she could destroy the electricity, maybe she would be free. She looked at the wall-plug on the skirting-board under the decorated mirror.

'You do have a girlfriend, don't you?' said the voice.

'Yes ... '

'Do you love her?'

'Yes ... '

'Have you ... have you ever thought of ... of caressing her? Answer me!'

The styluses jumped.

'You have nothing to be afraid of,' said the voice. There were moments, such as this one, when his tone changed, and became graver and more gentle. The grey eyes shone like electric-light bulbs.

'Are you frightened?'

'No ... ' said the slave-girl, in a very weak voice. She took a deep breath and repeated:

'No.'

'Do you ever feel like committing suicide?'

'No.'

(Zigzags)

'Are you thinking of killing ... someone?'

268

'No, absolutely not!'

'But you hate him, don't you?'

The styluses scribbled up and down along the strip of paper. Impossible to erase what they had just written.

'So you want to ruin ... someone, then go away.'

The styluses were trembling. The slave-girl's legs were trembling too.

'You know why I'm questioning you?'

'No, no, I don't know, I don't know,' the slave-girl began.

'Oh yes you — '

'No, I don't know!' she cried.

But the styluses had written: she knows.

In a moment, Hague had calmed down completely. He made a pretence of thinking hard, glancing at the notebook in which he had jotted down a few words.

'Now listen to me. The outcome of this ... euh ... conversation may well be that you will be transferred to another post. A very important post. But first we need to know the truth. This is a kind of test, you see, a series of tests to find out whether ... whether you merit the confidence of Hyperpolis. It may seem stupid to you, even hateful. But it's necessary. Are you afraid of the police?'

The G.S.R. stylus and the one registering perspiration from the palms both jumped.

'No ... Well, yes, like everyone else.'

'Have you ever committed acts that could get you into trouble with the police?'

The stylus remained calm.

'Have you done much shoplifting here?'

(Zigzags)

'No ... '

'Clothes?'

' ... Yes.'

'How often?'

'I don't know, how do you expect me to remember that sort of thing?'

'Gramophone records?'

'A few times, I don't remember any longer.'

'Jewellery?'

'Yes ... Yes, what difference does it make?'

'Do you know any malefactors?'

The styluses leapt upwards.

'Any what?'

'Malefactors. People who come into the stores with criminal intentions?'

' ... No.'

'Give me their names.'

The man leant over the machine to adjust the knob controlling the G.S.R. connection.

'You don't want to? Well, it doesn't matter. Let's change the subject. Have you ever had V.D.?'

'No.'

'Have you ever had an abortion?'

'No.'

'Do you know any doctors who perform illegal abortions?' The seven strips of adhesive tape and the two metal thimbles burnt her skin. She tried to move.

'Don't touch anything,' warned Hague. 'Do you drink alcohol? ... Answer me.'

'Not a lot.'

'Do you take drugs?'

'No.'

'You've never taken drugs?'

Hague glanced at the twitching styluses.

'How often?'

'Once or twice, just out of curiosity.'

'Hashish?'

' ... Yes.'

'Have you ever injected any kind of drug into yourself?'

'No.'

'Would you like to?'

'No, I hate injections.'

270

The stylus registering the breathing was over-reacting, and Hague adjusted the control knob.

'Let's talk about your girlfriend, she — '

'I'd rather she was kept out of this,' said the slave-girl.

'Why do you write love-letters to her?'

The styluses recording the G.S.R., brain, and palm perspiration made three zigzags.

'They are not love-letters, they are poems, you don't under — '

'Granted, granted,' interrupted the man. Then, in his solemn voice:

'Why are you angry?'

'I am not — '

'Yes you are. The G.S.R. and the encephalograph never make mistakes. So why are you angry?'

The slave-girl tried to think, but the effort was beyond her.

'You don't want us to talk about your girlfriend?'

'No.'

'And yet it was she who showed me your letters.'

'That's a lie!'

(Zigzags)

'It's true.'

He jotted something down in the notebook. The cramped room had become very warm by now. No doubt the electricity had sent the temperature up.

'Are you a communist?'

Hague noticed that the styluses were motionless, and re-adjusted the control knobs slightly.

'No.'

'Do you know any anarchists?'

'No.'

'You've never been back to Romania?'

The styluses moved slightly.

'No.'

'Have you ever thought of returning there?'

'Yes.'

'Have you ever read Karl Marx?'

'Just a little ... '

'Lenin?'

'No.'

'Is Che Guevara a hero of yours?'

'He used to be, yes. Now ... I don't know.'

The slave-girl began to feel drowsy again. She yawned.

'You have never taken part in any political demonstrations?'

'A few times, yes ... '

'At these demonstrations, did you ever see people who work here?'

'I don't know ... It's difficult to tell, in such a crowd.'

The styluses were quite motionless, now. Hague paused a while.

'Do you like the Arabs?'

The styluses stirred.

'Have you ever been to bed with a black man?'

The slave-girl did not answer.

'Are you an atheist?'

The G.S.R. and brain styluses answered.

'Do you like animals?'

'Yes.'

'Cats? Dogs?'

'Birds.'

'Why?'

'I don't know.'

'Do you ever stand naked in front of a mirror?'

(Zigzags)

'Do you masturbate?'

A pause. No answer.

'Often?'

No answer.

'Every night?'

The styluses traced hatch-lines across the paper.

'Have you ever taken money for sex, like a prostitute?'

The slave-girl suddenly felt like laughing, but her swollen lips prevented her doing so. Hague looked at her for a moment, with his sparkling grey eyes. Then he changed his tone of voice:

'I know these are ridiculous questions. But I have to ask them: they are an integral part of the programme. Would you like it if we had a brief pause now, just long enough to drink a cup of coffee and smoke a cigarette? You smoke quite a lot, I believe?'

'How much more of this is there?' asked the slave-girl.

'That depends on you,' replied Hague. 'But it shouldn't last much longer, now.'

'Am I really not allowed to smoke while this machine is switched on?' asked the slave-girl.

'When you are, so to speak, plugged into the apparatus, it's better to avoid smoking. It can distort all the results. You probably have no idea what an emotionally charged activity smoking is.'

He chuckled briefly. Then:

'You'd rather we finished right away?'

The slave-girl gave a slight nod.

'Perhaps we'll talk about someone else, now,' said the man.

'Who?' asked the slave-girl.

'You know who I mean,' said the voice, very slowly. But the voice was filled with menace.

'How should I know?' said the slave-girl.

The G.S.R., and the styluses recording perspiration and breathing were very jittery, but the stylus recording the heart-beats was quite normal.

'Well, let's play a guessing-game together,' said Hague.

He made a slight adjustment to the knob controlling the recording of her breathing.

'Someone you see often.'

'I see a lot of people.'

'Someone you like very much.'

'I don't know who you're talking about.'

'A man ... He has black hair ... He works here ... '

The slave-girl felt her breath quickening. It was the electricity's fault.

'You know very well who I mean.'

'No, I don't know, I keep on telling you I don't know.'

'No point in shouting. That won't alter what the machine is recording.' The voice had changed again. It had suddenly become harsh and metallic. The grey eyes glittered.

'He — he is responsible for the fact that you are here.'

'It's not true, it's — '

'Please don't shout. We already know quite a lot. But we need to fill in certain details, and your answers will provide me with those details.'

'I shan't answer any more. I have nothing more to say to you.'

'You have already said everything. Without knowing it, you have said everything. Listen, we need you, we need your collaboration.'

'I shan't say anything more to you.'

The slave-girl noticed that the pupils in the grey eyes had shrunk to pinpoints. The metallic voice pronounced these frightening words:

'Even if you don't speak, I shall still learn the truth! You cannot lie to this machine. With this, even when you say nothing at all you are still speaking.'

The slave-girl felt that all was lost. Her mind was a blank. Perhaps the electric wires fastened to her body, her left eyelid, her temple, had issued their orders and she had no choice but to obey them. Perhaps the electricity had consumed all her energies, and she was now no more than a piece of subsidiary apparatus belonging to the other apparatus on the table. She looked at the mirror with its floating fish.

'It's ... it's a two-way mirror ... ' she said in a low voice.

The man gave her a hard look.

'Yes.'

'Like ... like the other evening?'

'Yes.'

'And they are there, behind it?' Her voice was so weak that it was scarcely audible. But Hague heard.

'Yes.'

The slave-girl made a great effort not to fall asleep.

'So ... You know everything ... Why? ... '

'Why I've been asking you all these things?'

The man hesitated for a moment. Then he took out of his wallet a piece of crumpled paper. He showed it to the slave-girl.

'You've seen this piece of paper before?'

The six styluses made six columns of serrated lines.

'You know who wrote that?'

The slave-girl shook her head, but the G.S.R. stylus jerked frantically.

'Where is he?'

'I don't know ... I don't know.'

The styluses traced straight lines across the paper.

'You know, but you're protecting him.'

'No, no, I don't know! I don't know!'

'When is he going to set fire to Hyperpolis?'

'I don't know!'

'Tomorrow? During the night?'

The styluses quivered.

'This evening?'

The G.S.R. stylus and the one recording the breathing both leapt.

'All right, this evening. Does he really intend to do this? Is he capable of doing it?'

'No, no, it's just a joke!'

The G.S.R. stylus shot upwards across the paper, as high as it could go.

'You want to help him, don't you?'

'No, no, it's ... It was a joke.'

'Is he alone?'

The voice came straight out of the machine, and entered directly, by way of the fingertips, the palms of the hands, the temples, the wrists, the chest, the eyes.

'Is he — armed?'

The eyes rolled, under their lids.

'He's an agitator, isn't that correct?'

Her heart began to race. The sweat that poured out of her evaporated quickly in the hot atmosphere. Her breathing had become stertorous, her stomach muscles quivered. It was the electricity.

'He's going to start a fire ... He's really going to do that, eh? Why, the man's a dangerous lunatic!'

'No, no, he doesn't — '

The skin at the fingertips answered for her.

'So he'll come at night. Of course he knows his way round ... '

The brain sent out its waves to join the waves of electricity in all the electrocution wires.

'He will be there tonight ... You know that, don't you ... '

'No, no, it's not true! It's ... It's a joke ... '

'Where is he?'

Her heart was beating so fast, now, that it seemed it must surely burst. Her eyes were rolling wildly, as though they might turn up completely.

'Where is he now? Where is he? Where is he?'

'I don't know! I don't know!'

The slave-girl wanted to scream, but her voice was not working any longer. Electricity can break voices: it enters the throat and clogs the mucous membrane with blue sparks. Hague altered his tone once again. He assumed a calm slow voice, but the tone was as menacing as a high-tension cable. He said:

'Don't worry ... Don't be scared ... I'm not your enemy ... '

He watched the six styluses, which were gradually calming down. When they had almost stopped quivering, Hague looked at the slave-girl.

'Why don't you cut your hair short? It would suit you ... '

Despite herself, she turned her head to one side, and studied herself in the mirror. She saw her pale face swimming among red and green seaweed and parrot-fish.

'It will all be over in a few minutes,' the voice said. 'Then you are free to leave. You can go to your room and have a good sleep. Or go on the beach with your girlfriend.' After a slight pause the bored voice added: 'Do you enjoy going on the beach?'

The G.S.R. stylus and the one recording perspiration began to move up and down again.

'Yes ... I like going on the beach ... '

'By yourself?'

The six styluses all leapt in unison.

'With whom?'

'With ... With my friend ... It depends ... '

'Do you swim?'

'Yes ... '

'Do you take a rowing-boat out sometimes?'

'Yes, yes.'

'Your girlfriend too?'

'Yes.'

(Zigzags)

'Aren't you afraid?'

'Afraid of what?'

'Of dying?'

'No ... '

'Of drowning?'

'No, no ... '

The styluses were oscillating very strongly.

'You never think about such things?'

All the styluses rose together, then subsided again.

'You don't want to discuss that? All right, it's of no importance.'

The voice became more rapid. It was as though one knew in advance what it was going to say.

'Your friend ... Does she know?'

'Know what?'

'*I* want to know. Now answer me. I want to know the names of his accomplices!'

'What accomplices?'

'I want to know the whole truth about this criminal plot involving arson.'

(Zigzags)

'Is he acting alone?'

The slave-girl said nothing, but darted a glance at the wall-plug.

'There is no one else with him? Answer! Answer!'

'I ... I don't know ... what you're talking about ... '

Now the electricity was surging back. It was swelling the flexes with its power, flowing along the hidden wires. The slave-girl even heard the sound it made, a humming of bees that came from far away and gradually grew louder and louder.

'Where is he now? Where is he hiding? Answer!'

'I don't know! I don't know!'

'He is lying in wait, isn't he? He is hidden somewhere, not far away, just waiting for the night. And then, when night comes ... '

'It's not true!'

The styluses traced zigzags.

' ... When night comes, he will get inside Hyperpolis ... With his cans of petrol, and his matches ... '

'No, it's not true!'

'He'll find some way of getting in. People like that always do ... '

'It's not true! It's a joke!'

' ... He'll be able to get across the empty hall by skirting the walls. Because of course he knows where the cameras and photo-electric cells are positioned ... '

'You're lying!'

'He'll get right to the centre without setting off alarms ... '

'Untrue! Untrue!'

'He'll pour the petrol over the ground and light a match ... '

Electricity flooded the small room with zigzags and sparks. The voice continued inexorably:

'Then the searchlights surrounding the building will be switched on ... '

The six styluses spoke for her. But her voice protested:

'A joke, it's just a ... joke ... '

278

The styluses spat tiny flames like Saint Elmo's fire. Hague remained silent.

'You don't know anything! You're lying! Lying! ... '

The grey eyes, too, suddenly filled with electricity, taking on the appearance of spinning dynamos.

'No!' cried the harsh voice, 'it is you who are lying! The machine says that you are lying, and the machine is never mistaken! I know everything that has happened from the very beginning. We know all about you. Everything that happens here, is done by us. Your thoughts, your ideas, your adventures, your desires: all devised by us, all a part and parcel of Hyperpolis!'

The voice was an emission of ions, bombarding, spurting sparks. Perhaps if one could only succeed in cutting off the current, pulling some lever somewhere, this might all stop ...

'Listen!' commanded the voice.

At the top of the wall, above the mirror, there was a loud-speaker. Suddenly the slave-girl realized that music was coming out of it, and she recognized the music that the loudspeakers broadcast throughout Hyperpolis, day and night.

'Listen!' repeated the voice.

Now the slave-girl could distinguish another sound. Behind the music there was a very soft murmur, a whispering, like the humming of bees.

'You understand what that is, don't you? ... You can't hear it very well, but you understand it. Your encephalograph indicates that you understand ... For months now, you have all been hearing it, and you understand its meaning ... It is the Hyperpolis experiment ... Listen!'

Hague turned a knob, and the whisper grew louder.

'Listen! Now do you understand?'

'I don't understand anything at all!' is what the slave-girl tried vainly to cry out. But the styluses registering G.S.R. and perspiration and ocular movements swung into action, because suddenly the whispering had become quite clear. She could make out every word. It was just a single phrase, murmured, repeated behind the soft music, saying over and over again:

'HYPERPOLIS MUST BE BURNT DOWN
HYPERPOLIS MUST BE BURNT DOWN'

At the same moment, electricity exploded in the narrow office like a flash of ball lightning. It entered the slave-girl's body, making her glow from head to foot, it crackled from every hair in her head, it poured into her through every wire stuck to her skin with adhesive tape: from the tips of her middle fingers, from the palms of her open hands, from the arteries in her wrists, from the chest region between the left breast and the heart, from her left eyeball, from the tiny bare area of scalp at her left temple. A series of zigzag lightning-flashes could be seen running along the unrolling paper, and the reel of tape passing through the tape-recorder was covered with signs. Electricity plunged through the dark eye of the tachistoscope. Electricity sent the coils spinning inside the calculating-machine that devours encephalograms. Electricity sparkled in the narrow-pupilled grey eyes fixed on the slave-girl's own eyes. She made one more attempt to speak, stammered:

'The el-electric ch-ch-chair ... '

then ripped the taped wires off her skin and staggered towards the wall-plug at the foot of the wall under the mirror. Suddenly the mirror became transparent, revealing the six men in their variegated ties, watching the proceedings from behind the glass's garish decoration of seaweed and fish. A voice boomed harshly from the loudspeaker:

'The experiment terminates at this juncture, Mr Hague. Thank you.'

The clear light faded from the mirror. The slave-girl was still trying to reach the wall-plug when she found her arms gripped by two men wearing white tunics that had a red cross embroidered on the breast-pocket. They pulled her back, and walked her forcibly into the corridor, then into several lifts, then into a white cell somewhere not far from the centre of the spider's web.

The little boy nicknamed Dumb Bogo looked rather like a Tuscarora Indian contemplating the island of Manhattan. He was squatting on the beach, at the mouth of a little river called the Magnan or something like that. The only living creatures on the beach, besides himself, were a few gulls and pigeons. Dumb Bogo watched the mouth of the little river with cold clear eyes and impassive face. He had been coming onto the beach for several days, and the sun had burnt the skin of his face and hands, and bleached his hair. At night, Dumb Bogo slept in a kind of cave hollowed into the road's supporting wall; during the day, he hung round the Hyperpolis car park to earn a few tips. It was not very difficult to make money there. You could help guide motorists to a parking space, or open car doors for them. Or you could help women to carry their packages and to stow the things away in the boot of their car. Talking was not necessary on jobs like that, but whenever some woman did ask him a question he would give her an appealing look and make noises in his throat to show that he was dumb; then the woman would take out her purse and give him a coin. But he had to keep a careful lookout for guards and plain-clothes policemen. With the coins, Dumb Bogo bought sandwiches, chocolate, fizzy drinks and bubble-gum. Then he returned to the beach and concentrated his attention on the mouth of the little river called the Magnan or something like that.

It was a very beautiful river, emerging from under the road through a big pipe, and emptying itself into the beach. Perhaps it was really a sort of sewer, since the water was a peculiar blue chemical colour and smelt dreadful. The little river had formed a sort of deep basin in the pebble beach, and the gulls liked to splash around in it. After that the rivulet drained out through a narrow channel that led to the sea, and that was a particularly beautiful spot. It was beautiful because of the pebble dikes that flanked the stream all the way to the sea, like two parted lips. One of the dikes continued farther than the other one, and curled back a little, like an upper lip; while the other dike slid into the mouth, like a lower lip. The stream's current passed between the two lips and entered the sea after negotiating a series of rapids. A scene worth watching for hours on end: it was like being at the centre of the great Rif cliff formations, and sitting down and watching the place where the world is due to split in two. Or like flying for hours on end, high over the Orinoco delta. It was so beautiful that there seemed no point in thinking, or going away, or doing anything else. The most beautiful thing of all was the spot where the stream entered the sea. The chemical-blue water flowed out of the basin and hurried on down to the sea's grey mass, leaping over the intervening rapids.

Dumb Bogo spent his time watching that particular spot, where the torrent of fresh water penetrated the sea. He watched the eddies and the rapids and the continually breaking surf of salt water. He watched all this with his pale eyes, thinking of nothing. It was clear that the sea's ambition was to flow up the course of the little river, against the current. It made great efforts to do so with the waves that came thundering in from the horizon, and the salt water pushed the stream backwards, and the flat wave hurled itself between the estuary's two lips, rolling the pebbles along with all its strength, with the whole power of the sea behind it, but it grew tired, the stream's fresh water pushed against the sea's salt water, and the flat wave spread itself out, trying to inch its way farther up the channel, but it hesitated, became exhausted, the stream's fresh water covered it, and the wave retreated in a froth-flecked cataract, rushed down the estuary's slope, dragging the pebbles back along with it, towards the sea waiting to suck it in, to drink it up. Each new wave went through exactly the same process.

Sometimes a more powerful wave came roaring in from the other side of the horizon, riding the leaden sea, soaring above the other waves like a giant in the middle of a crowd, travelling slowly but with enormous power, topped by a line of foam. Dumb Bogo watched the wave approach him across the sea, and felt a little afraid; but his features remained impassive. His face was as cold and smooth as a pebble, and his pale eyes were like two broken-bottle ends worn smooth by the sea. The great wave arrived, and one could hear the sound it made as it rolled the pebbles round with its undertow. For a moment it hovered above the estuary, seemingly motionless. Dumb Bogo was motionless, too, squatting on the pile of pebbles, below the wave. Now the wave began to break, first on either side of the estuary, and then against the little river itself. The wave crashed down upon the stream, slapped against the rapids, submerged the estuary's two lips, quickly angrily greedily thrust forward its sheet of foam-flecked salt water, rushed up the channel making sounds like a forge and a steam-boiler combined, hissed, thrashed, repulsed the fresh water, climbed up the beach, creating wild whirlpools on its way, flowed up against the river's current, swelled between the pebble banks, then reached the chemical-blue-coloured basin and filled it like a bath so that the water came pouring out on all sides, reached the small boy's feet, tried to whisk away his feet and legs so as to melt them in its boiling liquid, but at that very moment the level of the blue basin subsided suddenly and the sea retreated, emptying itself into the surf at the mouth of the estuary, so that almost the whole breadth of the beach was exposed, revealing for a few seconds an expanse of big black pebbles that seemed filled with a strange menacing identity.

That was the most beautiful part of the scene: the little river, the sea, the rising and falling waves. There were many other sights as well: the wind, the sun, the wispy clouds, aeroplanes, capes and peninsulas, the horizon like a razor blade.

But the efforts that the sea made to push back the little river were particularly beautiful. The estuary with its two lips, the rapids, the petrol-blue water, the steel-blue sea, salt water, fresh water, the froth, the waves, the frightening noises: that was all truly beautiful and moving and unforgettable. So it was easy to just remain there, squatting on a heap of pebbles, with an impassive face, watching it all, with no thought of doing anything else.

Dumb Bogo was not alone on the beach. Lots of gulls and pigeons were standing and sitting round on the pebbles near the estuary. Dumb Bogo did not much care for pigeons, but he was very fond of gulls. The gulls were big and white and fierce, with little black eyes and long tapering red beaks: they flew across the little river's estuary, screeching shrilly, or else floated on the sea, beyond the surf, letting the waves carry them along. Occasionally they all took off together, without apparent reason, alighted in the basin full of chemical-blue water, bathed, then flew back to sit on the beach once more. When they glided through the sky, above the small boy's head, they looked very much like vultures hovering above Death Valley. They were very hungry all the time, and that is why they screeched so loudly.

Dumb Bogo knew the gulls very well. Every day, since he had run away from home, he had come to this spot to watch them. Sometimes he was very fond of them, but sometimes he did not like them at all. He usually brought something to give to the gulls: a hunk of bread, a slice of ham, an orange. When they saw that he had things to eat, they worked themselves up into a passion. They began flying to and fro above his head, giving out peculiar sharp cries that ended on a plaintive note. They were very wild and almost never came up close to him. Dumb Bogo threw bits of bread, and the gulls swooped down onto the pebbles, screeching. From time to time an especially furious gull would circle above him, screeching and flapping its wings. Dumb Bogo held out a big chunk of bread and the gull flew towards him, swerved aside and away, then finally darted towards his hand and snatched the chunk of bread. It was so hungry that some saliva dribbled from its beak and spattered the small boy's hand. It was really terrible to think that so much hunger and rage and fear could exist.

The gulls would eat anything. When the bread was all gone, Dumb Bogo would throw them bits of ham or cheese, or even the skin and pips of a tangerine, and the gulls gobbled it up in an instant. They even accepted used bubble-gum, hurling themselves furiously at the discarded blob and screaming as they clamped it between their beaks.

Sometimes Dumb Bogo pretended that he had stopped, but the gulls knew that he still had things to eat, and they waited on the beach, a few yards from him, hopping round on their long legs, fluttering into the air, then flopping down on to the pebbles again. They squabbled with each other. Occasionally a gull opened its beak and made a whimpering noise, then arched its back and strutted towards another gull, clacking its beak like a pair of scissors.

Dumb Bogo watched the gulls, and listened to their cries and complaints, and everything whirled round him dizzily. The pebble beach, the estuary disgorging its chemical effluvient, the waves, the horizon as sharp as a razor blade, the sky, the sun, the clouds, the aeroplanes, all began to pivot round the axis of his body, like numerous spheres moving at different speeds, overtaking each other, star-like entities encircling the earth, gliding silently through space. Perhaps the effect was really produced by the gulls that wheeled round and round, white vultures making increasingly wide circles above a dead cow. Or by the endless ebb and flow of the waves that never quite succeeded in penetrating the estuary of the little river.

The most important thing was to keep the face impassive, to betray no signs of fear. There were Guards, too, wheeling in the sky's white space, in search of prey; and there were words fluttering hungrily, so hungrily, in the air. Hunger was the cause of all this dizziness, HUNGER FOR ANYTHING AT ALL. Hunger gnawed away at the belly, dug its bottomless well inside the body, sucked out a hollow space within the cranium. The gulls' black eyes were bradawls trying to pierce space and tap more supplies of bread and meat and orange pips. Their eyes were ravenous, cruel, intent upon eating. Their sharp-edged beaks gaped, saliva dripped down the white feathers and fell, drop by drop, on to the grey pebbles. Their wings beat furiously, and Dumb Bogo felt their wind on his face, a frightening wind that made him shiver, like the wings of bats in pitch-dark caves. The cries they gave were terrifying: shrill cackles that emerged from gaping gullets and whirled through the beach's silence, calling, calling, calling anything at all. Sometimes the furious cries all spurted out in unison, hurtled into the air like clouds of arrows, and fell back on to Dumb Bogo in a shower of sharp points, cries, words. The gulls were attempting to speak. They wanted to say things, say anything at all. They needed to express all this hunger and suffering and fear and rage. But their efforts were in vain. Animal-like, all that they could cry was 'Kyow-kyo-keeyoh kheeyooook!' with their red beaks stretched wide apart. If fear had not been present, they would have hurled themselves at the small boy in a single mass, and devoured him in a few seconds. Their long tapering beaks would have torn out his eyes, slashed his cheeks, eaten his tongue. Their long bloody beaks would have torn his clothes into ribbons, then his skin, his intestines, his heart, his liver.

At this point, Dumb Bogo grew so scared that he picked up a handful of pebbles and threw them at the gulls. But they were so hungry that the stones did not frighten them. They simply hopped to one side, then rushed at the thrown pebble to see if it was something to eat.

When they realized that there really was nothing left to eat, the gulls flew down to the edge of the sea, and stood like a line of soldiers along the beach.

The gulls were not all of the same kind. Even closer to the sea, behind the line of ordinary gulls, stood some huge brown-plumaged gulls that were even fiercer and wilder. Those were the ones that Dumb Bogo liked best of all. He tried to persuade them to come up close to him, by proffering them some titbit, but they were too distrustful. As soon as Dumb Bogo made the slightest movement they flew seawards, beating their great savage wings, and making raucous yelping sounds. Because of their wild cries and their size and their fierce appearance they were known as sea-hyenas.

These sea-hyenas had no love for human beings. They inhabited the ocean's deserted valleys, and they were always hungry. When their hunger grew unbearable the sea-hyenas killed one of the gulls from the flock, and devoured it in some isolated spot. That is why they came here, to this beach, when Dumb Bogo distributed his pieces of bread and cheese. The sea-hyenas prowled slowly, on their long legs, round the white gulls, looking for any bird that was too old, or too young, to defend itself. They were not interested in the bits of bread, but in the birds.

That was the kind of thing one got to know about, on this beach, near the estuary of the little river called the Magnan or something like that. The small boy called Dumb Bogo had learnt a lot of things since he ran away from the Education Centre and started living on the beach. He had learnt to stay squatting for hours on end on the heap of pebbles, with impassive face and cold eyes. He had learnt to tell the time from the sun. He had learnt to recognize the really big waves, the ones that came from the end of the horizon and thundered onto the beach and swirled up the estuary's channel as far as the chemical-blue basin.

He had seen all sorts of things since he had come to live here. He had seen the fishermen's boats creeping silently through the night, dropping their nets behind them. He had seen a jet plane with an engine that had caught fire, making a great smoky circle high in the sky before returning to the airport. He had seen a car accident on the road, not very far from Hyperpolis. He had even witnessed the attempt, one night, to start a fire inside the Supermarket. All the building's exits had been blocked by police cars, searchlights had been trained onto the roof of Hyperpolis, and they had captured the man who had started the blaze. Dumb Bogo had been too far away to see what the man looked like, but he had heard very clearly when the commander of the Guards had shouted into a loudspeaker:

'Hullo! Hullo! You have exactly five minutes to give yourself up! We are about to use tear-gas! Hullo! Hullo!'

And then:

'Hullo! Hullo! I repeat! All resistance is useless!'

Meanwhile, the firemen extinguished the blaze with CO_2 powder. Then Dumb Bogo had heard the sound of grenades exploding. Hyperpolis had been surrounded by crowds of people, all watching and talking.

One learnt really a lot of things, just staying on the beach, beside the little river's estuary.

Here, there was no need to talk. Here, there were no days or hours or anything like that. It was enough just to be there. That was all there was: grey pebbles, sea, sun, clouds, as well as the mouth of the little river, the waves, the gulls and sea-hyenas, and the unlovable pigeons. If one wanted to look at cars, it was not far to walk to the highway, the Gulf petrol station, and, at the end of the bay, the dome that looked rather like a fat white cheese.

Dumb Bogo looked at all these things without thinking. He broke pebbles in half, to make axe-heads out of them. Or he stared at the horizon's sharp blade. Here he was surrounded by sounds that had no desire to be charming, and by voices that said nothing: the rattle of the pebbles beneath the waves' impact, the gulls' cries of hunger, the roaring of four-engined jet planes taking off. The Guards might arrive at any moment. They must be searching everywhere, with their keen eyes, but perhaps they had not yet thought of investigating this particular spot.

Now the small boy sits down on a heap of pebbles and looks at the sea with all its different-shaped waves. He watches the waves that try to flow up between the estuary's lips. Not a ripple disturbs the flat surface of the chemical-blue water in the basin.

The bottom of the basin harbours two rotting tyres, the framework of a motorcycle, and a few old oil-cans. The seaweed is streaked with peculiar black stains of unknown origin.

There is no one on the beach. The sun is blazing down, and Dumb Bogo has to screw up his eyes to look at things. Suddenly he sees some people: it is two girls walking along the beach. They are talking as they stroll along, but it is too far away to hear what they are saying. From time to time they stop and look in the direction of the sea. The small boy does not move. He stays squatting on his heap of pebbles, his face as hard as a pebble. Through his screwed-up eyes he sees the two girls continue along the beach, stumbling occasionally over the slippery pebbles. They are both beautiful. They are tall, long-haired. The one on the left has blonde hair, the one on the right has brown hair. They are dressed alike, both wearing white slacks and a white blouse. The one on the left has a beach-bag slung over her shoulder. They are walking barefoot over the pebbles, and since they are not used to walking barefoot they occasionally stumble. They are talking a lot, and from time to time they laugh. But their voices are indistinct, and all that can be heard through the sounds of the wind and the sea are bursts of laughter, and sounds such as:

'Aaah-oo'

'Aaah-wa-ah-di'

They pass in front of Dumb Bogo without seeing him, because he is as motionless as a stone. Then they continue towards the end of the beach, where there is a cement jetty with a boat moored to it.

The gulls have all abandoned the estuary of the little river that, if it had a name, might be called the Magnan. When the girls reach the boat they untie it. It is a small boat made from some yellow plastic material. They are still laughing, and call out something to each other, but the wind blows the words away:

'Ha-hi! Oh-ho!'

Dumb Bogo watches them steadily, like a Mescalero Indian.

He sees the two girls in the boat. With their backs to the horizon, they row, each wielding an oar. They laugh, and talk to each other. The yellow plastic boat makes slowly for the open sea, pitching as the waves grow higher. The light bounces off the water. When the wind blows, the sun's heat dies down. The boat skirts the jetty, then leaves it behind. By now Dumb Bogo can no longer make out the two shapes in the boat. It is a sort of black-and-yellow blob moving out over the sea, something like an old rusty petrol-can. But Dumb Bogo keeps his eyes fixed on it. The boat is so far away, now, that it vanishes between the crests of two waves. At that moment a shot rings out: it is the brown-haired girl firing a bullet into the boat's hull. Then, a few seconds later, another shot can be heard, louder than the first, and it produces an odd echo: the fair-haired girl has just pressed the trigger of the 22 L.R. pistol that she is aiming at her companion, and the bullet has passed through the heart of the brown-haired girl.

SLUAGH-GHAIRM

What do you see now? What do you see?

I see so many things that it is difficult to speak of them; there are so many things that the only way to speak of them at all would be to find words to express them simultaneously, several words, words that divide like protozoa, or that fuse like molecules. One would need one's own personal words, not those sounds that human beings produce with their mouths, nor the sounds made by typewriters as they deposit their rows of larvae on sheets of paper.

But perhaps that will come about. When one desires something very intensely, it can happen. And there is so much desire! It swells up over the earth like a storm, hovers over the flat plains of cities with their thousands of neatly patterned cubes, over the railway networks, airports, hangars, factories, wastelands, arenas, fields, tunnels: one can sense the presence of a strange menace that is gradually distending its thorax, one can already see the lightning-flashes darting between the clouds' globes, one can feel the power of the rain that is poised to erode the roofs of houses.

If only one knew how to read the lightning, how to interpret all these signs, then perhaps one might feel a little more secure. The small boy called Dumb Bogo longed to be able to read what was written in the sky: that is why he spent his time sitting on the beach, not far from the little river's estuary.

One way of guessing what the sky desired would have been to take the small boy as a focal point, as though he was the centre of the world, and to circle round him, faster and faster, like the whirling flights of hungry gulls, one's body expanding as it turns in an ever widening, ever faster circle, scooping up floating debris on the way and attracting it all towards the centre of the vortex. It was a dream, no doubt, one of the world's most ancient dreams, half horrible, half pleasurable: the body's white mass spinning round on its own axis, adding an extra layer of skin at each completed turn, growing huger and huger. The belly, back, arms, legs, skin of the face accumulating more fat at each revolution, swelling, exuding water and lymph. What did the body want? What do dreams want? From the first moment of life, in the belly's secret darkness, growing, growing, growing, expanding in space.

The slaves desire to speak. But soon there will be no words left, soon all words will have exhausted their strength, and will simply fade away suddenly, soundlessly, like stars, leaving the sky black. And that means that there is nothing to understand. Desires build up their dark globes above the city, pressing tightly against each other.

There are so many voices that it is difficult to speak. The voices make their sounds in unison, and these sounds mingle with the sound of the sea, the noise of cars, the noise of aeroplanes. There are so many sounds competing within a single head that the cranium might well explode like a bomb. Craniums are dangerous. When one sees them balanced on top of bodies, like that, row after row of them, one can feel a kind of tremor pass through them, and one knows that at any moment they might explode. Eyes, hands, hearts are dangerous. Even the pebbles on beaches, even blades of grass, even old rusty petrol-cans and old rags are dangerous. There is too much thought, everywhere, too much consciousness.

Perhaps things are as they are because the giant is on the point of awakening. Perhaps ... Or perhaps this is nothing more than a twitch in his heavy sleep. He moves his hands and legs slightly, he breathes a little faster, his eyes roll under the closed lids, his tight throat begins to snore and whimper. How can one tell? How can one tell *who* the giant really is? Occasionally one can see a small boy sitting silently on a heap of stones, on a beach, not far from the estuary of a little river, and one says to oneself: supposing *he* is the giant? Or, in a white department store, there is a girl who looks at one with eyes that are ringed with fatigue, and one says to oneself: supposing *she* is the giant? And then one sees a man wearing white overalls, pushing a convoy of metal trolleys, and one thinks: could *he* be the giant?

But these are not really desires that swell up and utter their menacing sounds. It is perhaps something simpler than desire, something terrible and beautiful that exists within life and cannot be halted. It is something that needed no words in order to appear, something as vast as the ocean, as hard as pebbles, as cold as the sky, as scorching as the sun. There is nothing apart from that. All the rest belongs to the Masters. All the sentences in all the books, all the films and songs and theorems and chemical formulas belong to the rulers. But this force and passion belong to nobody. They are real and tangible, they are alive. How can one name this force? Might it be possible to give it a simple name, something like

HUNGER,

without the Masters' gaping mouths immediately swallowing it up? Better to say nothing about it. Better to transform it into a cold stone and hide it deep inside oneself. Better to give it its real name,

ONYX,

and set it in a gold band to be worn round the second finger of the left hand. Then one stares hard at the stone, and the black light flowing from it burns one down to one's very roots; the look it gives is like a squirrel's, a gleam that is gentle and matt and hard, so hard that there is no other kind of look that compares with it. This pitiless look surveys the whole world, sees through walls and masks and clothes and armour. It is a steel needle capable of piercing all secrets, able to reach out to any distance. Will it conquer? Useless to veil the eyes with tinted glass, or tears, or clouds of cigarette smoke, or sleep, useless to set up a screen of pleasure or pain: there is no way of halting this black point that transfixes. A curse upon those who invented arrows, a curse upon those who desired that arrows should be invented.

I wanted to say FREE YOURSELVES, just that, in a voice like the look that the onyx gives, an unfaltering voice. The flights of gulls, the air, the sun, the wind, the trees, the waves, the stones, and even the white-domed buildings are saying the same thing. But before saying it, one must have seen it and heard it, one must have got to know it.

There are so many desires everywhere that hunger itself is no longer perceptible: it resembles all the other sounds. There are so many desires that the lips become numb and stiff, anaesthetized by the cold. There are so many raging desires pouring from all the mouths, crying out, groaning, crying out, sexes gorged with blood, lips taut, eyes dilated, heart thumping, lungs gasping, sweat oozing from every pore in the skin of the back, the thighs, the chest, the brow, the armpits, there are so many desires emanating from things and from living creatures that one is left speechless, helpless. The body spins round on its own axis like a planet, growing larger at each revolution. The body becomes enormous, a fat larva with swollen rings, a tuber, a bursting fruit. It is because of these desires that people are not free. Or else it is because people's desire for freedom is too strong, and when one desires something too strongly it is as though one suddenly did not desire it any longer.

There are tremendously powerful needs that we do not even know about. A young woman lies asleep in her bed, in the locked darkened room. Then she feels a strange menace inside her body, and suddenly she wakes up screaming, because something terrible has just happened: her back has exploded. As

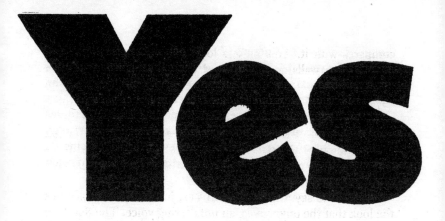

Emotional security: refrigerators, air conditioners
Self-satisfaction: medicines should appeal to the physician too
The creative instinct: producing a cake is like producing a child
      General Mills: Bisquick means better cakes
The feeling of power: McCann Erikson, in a motivational study for Esso:
the word POWER is endowed with a magical power

ABSOLUTE POWER

Evinrude motors: 3 hp—25 hp—40 hp, one for each age group
Roots: Mogen David: survey on wine: family life: the good old days — that
fine home-distilled wine that granny used to make
Immortality: life insurance denies death by prolonging the influence of the
father

THE HERO

TEARING OUT THE ROOTS

H, Piéron: Principles of Experimental Psychology: Thought and the Brain
B. de Plas & H. Verdier: La Publicité

'I dreamt I went walking in my Maidenform bra' (Norman, Craig &
Kummel)

Robert N. McMurry: Handling Personality Adjustment in Industry

you are already a Mercedes man.

though her internal organs, her backbone, her loins were charges of dynamite, like a booby-trap camouflaged as a dolphin, and the explosion shatters her back, and she hears the flames crackling. Then she wakes up screaming.

People want to know more, always more. They want to devour everything they see, everything they hear, they want to go on talking, talking interminably. But everything contains its own hidden abyss. There are truly deep wells within such things as:

> bottles of water
> paper
> walls
> television aerials   steel-blue eyes
> the number 293
> strelitzia blossoms

There are moments when one is calm, so calm and slow that it is as though the world was encased in ice. Then there are moments when one is transformed into a cloud of midges, dancing in the air, darting towards all the lights, detecting fissures everywhere. Then there are yet other moments when one seems to be brushing up against the bellies of giant spiders.

Men and women are all alike, and also completely dissimilar. Go on, find out why, if you can!

That is how language was born, that primal language that is still developing. It comes and goes, like a magnetic storm, with zones of silence, mute points, areas brimming with rage, unleashed passion: divided, reunited, divided. As soon as one person learns to speak it, the other becomes tongue-tied. The true battle is within words themselves, and from the tops of their watchtowers and high hills the kings of the rival armies watch the internecine slaughter. Battles that are never fought among the mountains, but only in the valleys (and the ricefields).

But one day language will break out of all these feuding camps, smashing through doors and windows and walls. Impossible to know exactly how or when it will happen: but language *will* be free. Perhaps language will achieve freedom by

298

slaying the other language, that of slavish desires. Words will inflict wounds on words, and streams of blood will flow. There will be words like stilettos that will open up other words and disembowel them with a single thrust of their hatred. Words like cobras' fangs, that will strike and pierce the flesh, and the uttering of these words will constitute their poison. There will be great whirlwinds of language, fearful sounds that will echo in men's heads and exterminate all other sounds. There will be a corrosive rain that will strip flesh down to the bone, and a light so white and intense that water will turn into powder. Then language will take its revenge: an event so long awaited, so long hoped for.

When that moment arrives, no one any longer can have the name Dumb Bogo. The small boy who knows how to talk is walking along some street, or perhaps strolling up to the great white dome called Hyperpolis, or something like that, and works wonders:

He says: 'La ... La luz ...', and immediately all the electric-light bulbs shatter.

He says: 'Autorat ... Autorat', glancing from side to side through slit eyes, and immediately the black roadways are covered with great black rodents fleeing the light of the sun, travelling at great speed, losing blood through mouth and anus.

Then he says: 'Palace! Palace! Palace!' and the immaculate buildings become phosphorescent, their windows shrink into tiny pore-like holes, and the outside walls are bathed in such dazzling light that the concrete melts into little grains and flows on to the beaches.

Or else he looks calmly at a bald-headed man whose eyes are hidden by glasses, and whose face is a cardboard mask: the glasses' lenses stick to the man's eyes, the hairs sprouting from his nose are white with frost, his hand grasps a large syringe and injects into the veins of his own arms the substance that drives men mad.

The small boy who knows how to talk, no longer needs to

rely on anyone else. He tears out the wires that are protruding from his ears, pulverizes the microphone between his teeth, and with simply a few words smashes aside the circle of Guards. The Guards totter and fall, grow transparent. All that the small boy does is shout at them a few times:

'Poo! Ghosts! Ghosts!'

and the Guards break and scatter, melt into the circle of trees, stones, electric pylons.

And this other man with a fat round face, wearing large plastic-framed glasses with blank lenses that dart out death-rays: all that the small boy has to do is look at him and slowly pronounce the Master's name,

'EGGS!'

and immediately the face becomes as flat as some anonymous photo-portrait.

Those are the kind of things one can do when one has learnt to speak.

It is not a question of learning, or volition: such things have to happen of their own accord, gently, effortlessly, without having been consciously sought for. One's mind is elsewhere, one's gaze is fixed on something else, one *is* something else. For example, one says:

'Does a dog have the Buddha nature?'

and the answer comes:

'*Wu!*'

Or else one says:

'Miajiru, miajiru ... Bankwa kiruta, todolodia chi ekarra toëdda kurasanümua'

and one hears the answer:

'Hampa!'

Sometimes it is not violence that liberates language, but gentleness, absolute gentleness.

The man who is still called Machines looks up above the service station at the word Gulf swaying in the wind, at the centre of its circle. It is a very tall wide word, swaying in the wind. It soars above the white building, above the cement platform and the petrol pumps. The man looks at it, and the evil realms fade and vanish, with all their fangs, claws, death-ray eyes, crunching jaws, groping hands. Not very far from the sea, the word Gulf. The great bay of Mexico with its beaches, islands, peninsulas. Corpus Christi's vast esplanade stretching along the coast. The sun is hot, the wind is blowing hard. In the centre of the circular frame, the word shines like a star, but a star that one can look at without being struck blind. The word speaks, in a calm voice that says simply:

'Gulf ... Gulf ... Gulf ...'

And because of it, one is no longer afraid of suffering, or dying, or being alone.

There are many words like that one. It is just a matter of reading them. If one looks for them one will never find them, but if one has eyes that do not seek, and a head that does not think, they appear on every side:

Montego
Union Textile des Vosges et du Nord
La Ponche
Xalpatlahuac
Stratochief
Kurile
Kiwi
Malaparte
Tome
Iriomotejima

These few words alone can overthrow the Masters, capsize them gently and effortlessly like a wave. Perhaps one day the only words left will be of that sort, and then one will be free. Only, one will never know it, because words like 'freedom' will no longer exist.

Sometimes, too, it is simply a matter of beauty, or love. The young woman who is no longer called Tranquillity writes poems to her girlfriend, and each word that she inscribes on the sheet of paper erases a terrible sound. She is writing solely for her friend, and there is no way of knowing what she is writing. But the mere knowledge that she is writing a poem is enough to renew one's strength, and one can see the frightening phrases gradually dissolving. This is how she writes:

Management of salesmen. Checking by result.
Offensive and defensive publicity in mixed-marketing schemes.
Merchandise promoters.
Work out strategies.
Market testing. Display potential.

Informational Simulated Programming.
Direct publicity: put over on massive scale. Habituate.
Respect the eleven criteria of effectiveness.
Define the *target*.
Permanent merchandising:
comprehensive, sample assortment, emphasis on new ranges.
Gondolas, small islands, projecting counters.
The Rule of the 3 Cs.

There are many things to say, or do, with words. Fear, death: these things happen when words remain exterior, when they seek to enter or conquer. But when words come from within, suddenly the Masters of language seem petty, and their ruses ridiculous.

One can tell many stories, to help those stories free themselves. One can tell the story of the grey face with eyes like searchlights, of the man who was called Motul. One can tell the story of the Rio Tinto, or the story of Puerto Armuelles where huge distrustful insects fly overhead. One can tell the story of the conquest of the moon, and its transformation into a military

302

base. One can tell the story of the white race plunging its own sting into itself, like some fat scorpion. One can tell the story of the Rojas brothers who seized control of a whole prison, armed only with a knife, a rifle, and a stick of dynamite. One can tell the story of Nele Kantule, or the story of Réal Choquette, or the story of Louis Riel, or the story of Condorcanqui. There are really many stories worth telling.

Brazil Nut Story

Once upon a time, in Puerto Maldonado on the Rio Madre de Dios, there was a factory belonging to a German. Work, heat. For twelve hours the day-shift is in the factory. Then it returns to the encampment. For twelve hours the night-shift is in the factory. Their work is identical: take a chestnut and place it between the jaws of the shelling machine, then press the lever. Or take an almond, and throw it on one of two piles: on the right for the confectioners, and on the left, when the nut is rotten, for the manufacturers of sweet-almond soap.

Sweating napes, skinny torsos, bulging veins, foreheads without thoughts behind them, men and women obeying orders, dim and motionless amid the uproar of the generating unit, endless toil, odour of smoke and urine and sweat, flesh-less hands, skeletal bodies. In the distance, rising pyramids of money, food, luxury articles: but from here one cannot see those things, one can see only pyramids of discarded shells.

Many stories: Pessicart Story, Spada Story, Texaco Story, Naucalpan Story, Bull Machines Story. There are many places that have a curse on them! Stretches of scorched earth fanned by the heedless wind, an iron wind sweeping across man's misfortunes. One inhales cold air, and awaits the sun. But nothing comes. What is terrible is the hunger, *the hunger for anything at all*. Gaping wounds of manganese and coal, mining villages, clouds of gas, excavations, ploughed land, boulders, drought, and those great hexagonal ruins that emit smoke but never burn.

303

The masks will fall from words. Yes, but that is only the beginning, for other masks will take shape, and doubtless the process will never end. There are so many prisons everywhere, prisons made of air, water, the horizon. There is the prison whose wall is the sea. There is the prison created by knowledge, the kind of knowledge that is incapable of reconsidering itself. And the solar prison, from which there is no escape.

Prisons formed by cement buildings with narrow, barred windows. Locked lifts. Glass doors with flanges pressed tightly together. In the streets, the face of every woman going by is like a vulva. The face of every man going by is like a penis. Hatred, hatred, abominable, abomination, loathe. The red veils shroud, the red liquid falls. Falls. Falls. The sky is a cloud of blood. Blood. Blood. Veils: eyes: bleed. The vast colour stretches from one end of the sky to the other. Raising one's eyes, one sees the sky's plasma between the buildings' towers. There is no time left. Hatred, so much hatred! Want to ... Want to ... ... the hands. The fingers are twisted, nails dig into the flesh and carve half-moons of blood out of the palms. Lights flash like silver foil, and the projectors turn, pivot, swing. Forwards, backwards. Bleeding skin and hands, rapids, rapids and water-falls of blood thrusting aside two snowy blocks, river forcing the two white knees apart and emptying itself. Panting noises. The breath catches, sticks in the throat, becomes a rasping stone column. Skin tears off in strips. Feet trample. The ground is covered with fused gravel, with tiny triangular points that gash the toes. One may run as fast as one likes, but *where*? One scratches one's ankles furiously with one's nails, drawing blood. *Rash.* The skin is suffused with red. Colour penetrates pores, inserts needles. Stinging hairs of nettles. Water is needed, and oil, to anoint and soothe. But the taps are sealed shut. Everything is dry. No oil, no ointments. The breath ignites, at each exhalation, the overheated air, the world is, embers ablaze, eternally, a locomotive.

Red passion, haze ... Should ... Want to ... But to no avail. The red cloud swoops down, screeching like a lammergeyer,

its two great outspread wings thrashing the air. It caps your
head, envelops you in its folding membranes, tightens them
and chokes you, then tries to reach you with its beak. Sound the
alert! There was a time when one was alert, expectant, but no
longer. The flame travels so fast that it has already entered the
other colours, cold white, the cold blues and greys. Black. They
are what they are and, at the same time, they are already red.
Sheets of scarlet flow forward along the sloping ground, flow
down staircases, flow along gutters. Liberty ... Freedom.
Where has consciousness gone? Thoughts have fled. The red-
purple-scarlet-crimson flow oozes from between cracks in walls
and spreads over the roadway. No one laughs any longer. No
one has any great desire to remain alone, any longer. No, indeed. But where can so much blood be coming from? From what
wounds is it flowing? It is not real blood. At least, not to start
with. It is colour, merely colour. Wherever it passes, things
become rigid. It is made of ice. One would like ... to run, but
one cannot. One wants. But. The colour enters through the
eyes, nose, throat, filters through the skin, floods up through
the anus and along the intestines. Red mucus. It is neither life
nor death that is the real problem: it is coldness. Coldness burns
red, it ignites the heads of matches, it points its frozen flame up
into the air like a carrot.

There are so many reds, blacks, whites, silences, murmurs,
noises. One day, the streets of towns suddenly fill up with bands
of naked men whose skin is painted in colours that break and
kill and burn. Their cheeks are scored with vertical red lines,
their plaited hair is tied with a black ribbon. They carry a fragment of mirror dangling from the chest by a cord, and they
carry in their hands cans filled with petrol that they empty inside glass-lined department stores. Then they casually strike a
match. They smash loudspeakers, rip out electric wires, blow
up transformers. They dig up pipes and block drains. They
burn dictionaries and directories and school primers. They
throw cameras into the sea, as well as tape-recorders and telephones and television sets. Car engines explode as soon as the

ignition is switched on, and the tyres burn with a thick black smoke. The sun illuminates the colours with which the men have daubed themselves: blood-red, green, ochre, night-blue, black. The light makes the mirrors glitter; and flames, swollen by the wind, mount high into the sky. It is all over in a few seconds: the world was nothing more than a hotchpotch of celluloid and plastic, and such things burn quickly. The naked paint-striped men swarm through the city: not thinking, just yelling and destroying.

Like the man called Machines, for example. He walks along the beach in the direction of Hyperpolis. It is evening, and the sun is just above the horizon. The man squats on the beach. He takes a piece of broken mirror from his trouser pocket, and with the mirror's edge he slowly gashes his cheeks from below the eyes. Blood trickles down his chin and on to the pebbles, but the sun is still hot and the blood soon dries. Later, when night has fallen, he heads for Hyperpolis, carrying a big can of petrol in each hand. He makes slow progress, because the cans are very heavy. When he reaches Hyperpolis he stops for a moment, searching for something with his eyes. Then he skirts the white wall as far as a ventilator-shaft grille that he manages to open. He squeezes through, dragging the two cans after him. The great hall of Hyperpolis is empty. He goes to the centre of the hall and empties one can over the floor, round one of the pillars. He strikes a match and the yellow flame shoots up very high. A little farther on, he empties the second can. The scream of sirens can already be heard. He tosses a second lighted match, and the flame roars up towards the ceiling. Then he retreats a few steps, and sits down with his back against a pillar. He watches the great waves of flame shooting straight up towards the ceiling, he hears the sirens screaming and whistles blowing. But he does not care. He simply sits and waits.

What to do now? Cry out, surely. But no: the cry, too, has formed a fiery whirlwind deep in the throat, and it emerges as a red knife-blade. Terrible. Relentlessness. Desperate relentlessness. Books are coloured red, so are letters, and the stamps

306

on envelopes. One turns the pages of a magazine in a dentist's waiting room, slowly, painfully, as though they were paving-stones thudding noisily against each other, and from time to time one sees this vast untouched expanse with hardened reflections, which sticks to the eyes, and fuses with the fingertips like a tube frozen to a temperature of — 180° C. — the accursed colour! Colour that gives no peace and never allows itself to be forgotten. The eyelids remain half open, metal shutters ajar on either side of the black pupil: kept open by the force of the blood. Why should such a colour exist? Everything could have been so pure, so simple. One might have ... One would have remained at peace, together with sun, sea, engines, birds, eyes, stones, clocks. Blood! Blood! Adoration overthrown, words overthrown, thought overthrown. The current gulps up from the very depths, devours, pumps up, swallows, swallows. The syringe spurts blood as its plunger is pressed home: blood for the Masters to drink. They have a fearful need of human blood, to maintain a kind of life within themselves.

Hatred of colour, when it arrives. Colour is the ruling force over mankind, hurling itself upon people, paralysing them, covering them with poisonous spittle. It enters the body, goes straight to the nerve centres. When will this process end? Speak! Cry out, speak, or remain silent, but do not let the language of the Masters hold sway! The Masters' light has spread its glare over women's skin, over the sea and sky, so that nothing remains. The Masters' light tightens its jaws around human necks, and the vice-like grip of the light's teeth will never be relaxed.

Blackness, black velvet that halts the light, terrible powerful blackness of space. If only one could ... If only ... On the pages of books there appear expanses of black, negative plates that stretch to the mind's farthest reaches.

There is nothing to be heard. Just silence. The knobs are turned all the way to the left. The electricity is weak, tenuous, a sweating liquid.

silent

whiteness   of vast blanks

If only one could free oneself from this blank-
ness, say something so forcefully that it would
echo like a gong for years on end.

Words: so weak, low, aphonic.

Speak speak.

Engulfing slippery corridors, tiny
drawings, and, crosses, and, angles, broken
circles, corridors, strokes, dots, no
limits, doors opening onto mirrors;

Who invented this silence and why?
Impassive mask of a disdainful Buddha
contemplating mankind, smiling
saying nothing.

Gulf is Oil

                    Folly of buying, the years pass
                 so very quickly when hooked on to
                    objects Forget cease to be there
                  Hide emptiness Intoxication's nourish-
                 ment, love Empty orifices absorb,
                    drink up life's years Chasms of emotions
                 connected directly to the entrails
                 by the cord that plunges into the black
              caverns where sweet music writhes

Gulf is Oil
Gulf is Oil
Gulf is Oil   When lost in depression
                      NOVERIL
                       Wander

SPEAK

You mute mouths say something anything make any kind of sounds that you know so that the sound of silence can no longer be heard so as to tear out the cudgel that has been thrust down the throat so that the ears and tongue may bring freedom say say what you are say whose you are

SPEAK

Gulf is Oil
Gulf is Oil
Gulf is Oil
Gulf is Oil
Gulf is Oil
Gulf is Oil
Gulf is Oil
Gulf is Oil
Gulf is Oil
Gulf is Oil
Gulf is Oil
Gulf is Oil
Gulf is Oil
Gulf is Oil
Gulf is Oil
Gulf is Oil
Gulf is Oil
Gulf is Oil
Gulf is Oil
Gulf is Oil
Gulf is Oil
Gulf is Oil
Gulf is Oil
Gulf is Oil
Gulf is Oil
Gulf is Oil
Gulf is Oil
Gulf is Oil
Gulf is Oil
Gulf is Oil
Gulf is Oil
Gulf is Oil
Gulf is Oil
Gulf is Oil

FALCONBRIDGE
Pitiless eye of the bird of prey
scrutinizing the Dominican Republic

— Exit —

ANALIBRETEROS

Enough blank silence
we have waited too long
we are exhausted with waiting
The Masters are terrible, distant, invisible,
they say:
       '   ,

But now one can hear something, vaguely
something, a gentle fluttering of the tongue, a
slight rattle in the glottis,
     ffrtlss spd
   frntwhl drv mks fr bttr hndlng
th llgrs lctrc clng-fn s thrmsttcll cntrlld
cls th ngn vn whn ts dlng ... nq sspnsn sstm rds n gs
bsrbs dp nd dv nd vns t th shcks nd bmps
rdnmc dsgn by Ggr th stblzd strng dgnl dl brk crct
Teeth emit whistling sounds, lips lisp,
truly a strange language
       Speak louder we need to hear
       your words why disguise your voice like that?
       What have you got to hide?
       From now on there are no more secrets

KEYTAPES

Gulf is Oil 144,000,000 lines of type
Gulf is Oil There cannot be several languages that is
Gulf is Oil impossible. If there were several of them it
Gulf is Oil would mean that we would never learn how to
Gulf is Oil talk. Why these whisperings and murmurings?
Gulf is Oil Switch off the black light, erase the micro-
Gulf is Oil images! We want to see and hear everything.
Gulf is Oil We are eager for noise and light.
Gulf is Oil
Gulf is Oil Animals do not talk.
Gulf is Oil
Gulf is Oil fffschwtt fffschwtt fffschwtt fffschwtt
Gulf is Oil fffschwtt words hide other words, words open
Gulf is Oil up and their gaping jaws frame the glow
Gulf is Oil of rapid unknown lightning-flashes so rapid
Gulf is Oil that it is as though one had dreamt them
Gulf is Oil
Gulf is Oil WE ARE BREWING MORE THAN COFFEE
Gulf is Oil IN COLOMBIA
Gulf is Oil
Gulf is Oil
Gulf is Oil   Black detonates
Gulf is Oil   Red detonates
Gulf is Oil   White detonates
Gulf is Oil
Gulf is Oil Words are coming now
Gulf is Oil jostling each other
Gulf is Oil about to spurt out
Gulf is Oil
Gulf is Oil   OSPAAAL
Gulf is Oil
Gulf is Oil Words add themselves to each other
Gulf is Oil constructing their violent pyramid
Gulf is Oil
Gulf is Oil   A
Gulf is Oil   LA
Gulf is Oil   PLAZA
Gulf is Oil
Gulf is Oil The Masters send their whirlwinds

310

Gulf is Oil
Gulf is Oil
Gulf is Oil
Gulf is Oil
Gulf is Oil
Gulf is Oil
Gulf is Oil
Gulf is Oil
Gulf is Oil
Gulf is Oil

they would like — would love to see people
swept away

Speak, speak
Defecate or something.

Perhaps everything started the moment one
entered this bar. The War Machine. It was
called SECA MISSILE. First there was this
screen, which showed a weird desert landscape,
a sort of violet-coloured plain with dunes, and
on the horizon a line of dark-green mountains.
The sky was pale-blue. The violet plain was
covered with tanks and black aircraft. One
scrutinized all these things. The dashboard was
inscribed with the legend:

Missile Launcher Control   Firing   Flight Control
Then three rectangular windows overprinted
with black figures,

1000

1200

1400

1600

1800

and red ones,   2000

2200

2400

2600

2800

3000

In the centre, an imitation radar screen.
Three red lights winking on and off alternately,
in this order:

1.2.3

2.3.1

3.2.1

1.2.3

Then one studied carefully what was written,
Gulf is Oil   to the right of the Machine:

Gulf is Oil
Gulf is Oil
Gulf is Oil
Gulf is Oil
Gulf is Oil
Gulf is Oil
Gulf is Oil
Gulf is Oil
Gulf is Oil
Gulf is Oil
Gulf is Oil
Gulf is Oil
Gulf is Oil
Gulf is Oil

As we say — Gulf is Oil

INSTRUCTIONS

1. After a coin has been inserted, the bombers will fly overhead. Adjust your aim by pressing the left-hand or right-hand button.

2. Sight the bombers in flight and press the firing-button.

3. The Missile's course can be corrected by moving the flight-control lever.

4. When a bomber is hit, the Missile explodes and the window indicates your score.

5. The game lasts until the second-hand has completed one circuit of the dial.

Score above 2000: ONE FREE PLAY

Perhaps it was better not to talk too much about all that. Perhaps it was better to talk about dreams, or hopfields, or the heaped mass of pebbles along the seashore, where a small boy is sitting as though on the edge of a planet, gazing out into empty space. But one can cross to the far side of his fears, if there is another side, in order to be free.

One must write and think and act in riddles;

HERE
THE WOLVES FROM OLE TOWN
THERE SHEPERD HAS ALREDDY PASSED 50
MADE COWARDS OF THE SHEEP
THE LONG RED STANE

Tapisift in Silquipan

Zip! Zip! Zip!
Wit! Wit!

Tapisift in Silquipan
Tapisift in Silquipan
Tapisift in Silquipan
Tapisift in Silquipan
Tapisift in Silquipan
apisift in Silquipan
'apisift in Silquipan
apisift in Silquipan
:pisift in Silquipan

.e *pseudo*-rational

IANT WORDS
.it men
·main dwarfs

EYSTONE

0-14 av. Rio Branco Rio de Janeiro
Central Post Office Box 1115 Montreal
2 via della Mercede Roma
·iersstrasse 11 München
2 rue des Comédiens Bruxelles
.lfonso XX no. 48 Madrid
eilergraben 43 Zurich
Central P.O. Box 204 Tokyo
ienerale Hanrisa 23 P.O. Box 566 Belgrade
Santiago del Estero 556 Santiago

the tachistoscope
the eye camera

Kodak

PLU

Haughty letters
Haughty names looking
down from on top of your
tall downstrokes Perched
on the inaccessible
summits of your golden
peaks heedless of your golden
peaks heedless of man-
kind's misty valleys,
DO I NOT
HATE YOU?

Men: cars
Women: domestic appliances

THE MOST TERRIBLE WORD IN ANY LANGUAGE IS
ROHR

Diesel Power:

'Whereas miraculous progress has been made in the technical field, the science of human
motivation has been lamentably neglected. This science consists in the moulding and
adaptation of the behaviour of personnel in industry. By making use of these techniques,
a worker's skill and resourcefulness can be matched by a new capacity on his part to
show a co-operative attitude towards his job, his boss, and his fellow workers. It may
really be possible to witness the creation of the made-to-order man who is ready to
devote himself entirely to the elaboration of a great industrial future.

DIVERT THE RIVERS

Hyperpolis must be burnt down

PPZ

The Guards wear these harsh insignia
on their chests

silver - copper - stainless steel

D. Sington & A. Weidenfeld: The Goebbels Experiment

Intercontinental Markets Advertising
Edipress
Giorgi
Foote Cone & Belding
Multilith Offset
La Déesse
Psycho
Icita
AGPP
Havas
Synergie
Interplans
Publigyr
Sodipa
Publi Rexor
Publicitas
Publistip
Publichoc
Promoplan
Propart
Propublic

YOU

WHISPERING CAMPAIG

The Sign of lightning,

Tractability through suggesti
Automatic suggestion
Automatic imitation

Rorschach Tes
Woodworth Tes
Bernreuter Tes

terrible, rapid

I look at this sign
and I am afraid

NAMES NAMES NAMES OF POWER

Polygraph, Keeler Polygraph, Deceptograph, Reid
Polygraph
Lee Psychograph, Stoelting Cardio-Pneumo Polygraph,
Detectograph, Reactograph, B. & W. Electric Psychomotor,
Darrow Behavior Research Photopolygraph

Words that soar flies bees bats aeroplanes helicopters
words throbbing in search of men hidden between the trees
words whose propellors whirl round and slash slash slash

BUILDERS OF DESERTS

$$S = \frac{83D}{K + 0.027D} + 0.29D$$

Giant letters crushing beneath their concrete pillars
Tiny letters infiltrating through the pores of the ski
Letters. Letters. Animals.

THE HISTORY OF VINTAGE

The famous American publisher Alfred A. Knopf (1892–1984) founded Vintage Books in the United States in 1954 as a paperback home for the authors published by his company. Vintage was launched in the United Kingdom in 1990 and works independently from the American imprint although both are part of the international publishing group, Random House.

Vintage in the United Kingdom was initially created to publish paperback editions of books acquired by the prestigious hardback imprints in the Random House Group such as Jonathan Cape, Chatto & Windus, Hutchinson and later William Heinemann, Secker & Warburg and The Harvill Press. There are many Booker and Nobel Prize-winning authors on the Vintage list and the imprint publishes a huge variety of fiction and non-fiction. Over the years Vintage has expanded and the list now includes great authors of the past – who are published under the Vintage Classics imprint – as well as many of the most influential authors of the present.

For a full list of the books Vintage publishes, please visit our website
www.vintage-books.co.uk

For book details and other information about the classic authors we publish, please visit the Vintage Classics website
www.vintage-classics.info

www.vintage-classics.info